# Day of the Dragonking

Fans of Robert Anton Wilson's fast and loose approach to political conspiracy and Douglas Adams's bumbling unwilling heroes will eat up Irving's first batch of giddy, clumsy world-saving adventures, which launches the Last American Wizard series. A "mystical terrorist group" sacrifices an airplane full of innocents to a dragon and uses the deaths to power an event that wreaks magical havoc on Washington, D.C. All the wizards in the U.S. government's employ abruptly lose access to magic, and the world's computers and gadgets become sentient.

Second-string journalist Steven Rowan embodies the tarot's Fool and is forced to figure out the card's magic on the fly. Bombshell soldier Ace Morningstar, who used her magic to disguise herself as a man so she could become a SEAL, drafts Steve and his cell phone, which contains the ghost of a Chinese factory worker who now communicates through screen animations and bad autotranslations, to help fix the mess.

Gathering allies, including NSA supercomputer Barnaby and Ace's BMW, Hans, the team fights off newly transformed demons, dog monsters, and ogres while trying to find out who is controlling the Illuminati before the villains embark on the next step of their world-domination strategy. Irving's smart parody of Beltway life and his high-energy storytelling carry through to the end and promise to maintain momentum well into the next installment.

**— Starred Reviews – Publishers Weekly**

Mystically powered terrorists unleash volatile magic on the world, turning Washington, D.C., into a politically charged fantasyland ripe for human sacrifice.

A trio of suicide attackers with magical abilities bring down a 747 by summoning a dragon to rip it from the sky, using the hundreds of lives lost as a sacrifice to initiate the Change. The country morphs into a new landscape of swords and sorcery. Now computers and other machines are coming to life, and regular people have started to turn into mythical creatures and forgotten deities, creating a chaotic world easily seized by whoever—or whatever—set this shift into motion.

Hope appears in the nation's capital where, along with transforming Democrats into potbellied elves, Republicans into cantankerous dwarves, and Tea Party members into trolls, the Change has granted struggling freelance journalist Steve Rowan the abilities of the Tarot Arcana's Fool card, making him a powerful, yet unreliable, wizard. Realizing his potential, he is "hired" by the trivia-obsessed sentient computer Barnaby and coupled with the attractive, no-nonsense female Navy SEAL Ace Morningstar to uncover the puppet masters behind the plane crash.

Irving (Courier, 2014, etc.), a producer of Emmy Award–winning news television and a journalist well-acquainted with the Beltway, makes good use of clichéd Washington stereotypes by mashing them together with fantasy tropes, breathing new life into political satire....

Like many first books in a genre series, the novel foreshadows a greater enemy behind all this madness while barely hinting at its identity, offering a wonderfully bizarre consolation prize as its denouement.

**A clever, humorous fantasy....**

**— Kirkus Reviews**

# Day of the Dragonking

## Book One of
## The Last American Wizard

Terry Irving

RONIN ROBOT PRESS

Ronin Robot Press
A Division of
Rock Creek Consulting, LLC
9715 Holmhurst Road
Bethesda MD 20817
www.terryirving.com
www.roninrobotpress.com



Cover art by Tom Joyce/Creativewerks



Second Edition – 10/31/2015
ISBNO 13: 978-0-9966917-2-7
ISBNO 10: 0-9966917-2-3

# DEDICATION

*To Emlyn Rees,*

*An incredible editor who not only*

*picked up my first book but*

*gave me the encouragement*

*I needed to keep writing.*

*And*

*As always…*

*to Ann, for everything.*

# ACKNOWLEDGMENTS

Since my publisher managed to evaporate only six weeks after my first novel hit the market (and I still deny any responsibility for its horrible demise), there are even less people to thank than last time but they've made up in encouragement what they lack in numbers.

Tom Joyce was the only person who had a clue what I was writing about (and even Tom had to look up an abstruse point or two). However, he hit such a homerun with the cover art that I was forced to not only finish the book but also write it so that the text matched the quality of his insane vision of Ace Morningstar that appears on the cover. I thank all the members of the Editing Army for their comments and encouragement, Richard Shealy–copy editor to the stars–for his advice, and Don Critchfield for his endless, solid, and unquestioning support.

Finally, my thanks to Nick Wale who, as far as I know, has never read this book but who came up with an idea for a publishing enterprise that might just enable me to write another.

# Definition of a Dragonking

In the aftermath of 2008's catastrophic meltdown of the world's financial markets, statisticians scrambled to develop new models of enormously complex systems–those once referred to as "chaotic"–in the hope of controlling or at least predicting similar events in the future.

First, they identified the "black swan" event. This was a cause so completely out of the norm that it could not have been predicted and could be identified only in the aftermath of a catastrophic event. This let Wall Street's mathematical analysts, or "quants," off the hook.

Next, the analysts developed the theory of the "dragonking." A dragonking is an enormous disruption so powerful that it is outside all standard parameters (a king) and acts according to rules so mysterious that they resemble nothing else (a dragon). Unfortunately for the quants, unlike a black swan, they can be predicted.

Dragonking events have been identified in such enormously complex systems as financial markets, forest fires, earthquakes, epileptic seizures in the human brain, climate change, and the extinction of species.

A dragonking comes without warning, causes immense destruction, and leaves unforeseeable changes in its wake.

# Prologue

The soft tone sounded and the Fasten Seatbelt signs winked out over the 418 passengers on American International's flight 1143, the airline's morning flight from New York to Los Angeles.

The two men and one woman in seats 17A, 17B, and 17C unhooked and pulled down their folding tables. They were all wearing the classic uniform of young information workers on the way up–blue or white button-down shirts with ties with the stripes of fictional British clubs for the men, and a white button-down shirt with a floppy green bow tie for the woman.

The older woman in 17D across the aisle glanced at them as she was settling in and instantly identified them as accountants or consultants or some equally tedious species of young professional. She lost herself in the romance novel in her electronic reader and forgot them.

The man in 17A–short and a bit overweight with the pale chin and cheeks of someone who just shaved off a beard–bent down and unzipped the front pocket of the leather backpack he had placed under the seat in front of him. From this pocket, he slid out a metal box with an air of reverence. It was silver and about the right size and shape for carrying a bar of soap. At some point, there had been an engraving on the top, but careful handling had worn it so smooth that only faint curves, a curlicue, and a straight line along the bottom remained.

The man handled the box with extreme care–holding it with both hands and making sure that the hinge faced away from him. Swiveling from the waist, he handed the box to the dark-haired woman in the middle seat. She took it from him with crossed hands so that the hinge continued to face away from her.

She had to flip her brown bangs out of the way so that she could see as she swiveled and passed the box on in the same reverential manner to the taller man seated on the aisle. He had darker skin and a close-cropped beard. Once again, he took the box with crossed hands and placed it in his lap. Throughout the process, they had all moved with the precision and grace that come from endless repetition.

None of them said anything as a second metal box was removed from the backpack and handed with equal care to the woman, who placed it on her gray pinstriped skirt. She kept both hands on it–not hiding it from sight but making sure it was safe.

The man in the window seat pulled out a third metal box and then, holding the box with his left hand, leaned down and unzipped a pocket on the side of his pack. From this, he removed a folded square of green fabric and proceeded to pass it to the woman. He was careful to use his right hand–his left remained on the box in his lap.

Again, using her right hand, she passed the material along to the dark-skinned man in the aisle seat, who unfolded one fold of the cloth and covered the box in his lap. Then she received her own green cloth and covered the box in her lap.

The stewardess in charge of the front economy section came down the aisle on her way back to prepare the drinks cart. As she had been taught, she glanced at each passenger in turn–not actually studying him or her but giving herself time so that anything off or odd would trigger a subconscious sense of danger. As she approached the 17th row, the three young people began to talk together, smiles and mock grimaces appearing on their faces as they discussed plans for an imaginary convention they were to attend in Los Angeles. The woman and the man on the aisle began to use both of their hands–she dabbed at the corner of her lipsticked mouth with a napkin, and he emphasized a good-natured argument by energetically pointing at the man in the window seat. It might have looked suspicious if all three had kept both hands folded in their laps.

The stewardess passed by. Nothing had triggered an internal alarm; she went on to the mid-cabin galley to get the ice and sodas ready.

The three let the conversation die down over a couple of minutes. A conversation that stopped abruptly might be noticed. For a while, they just sat, their eyes open but unfocused, each with a protective hand on the box and cloth in their lap.

Without a signal, all three used their left hand to bring their green cloth up to the tiny table and unfold it once more to reveal a very fine green silk with symbols embroidered in multicolored embroidery in a swirling pattern radiating out from the center. In the center of each cloth was a rectangular space–empty of any decoration or ornament.

The man on the aisle smoothed a slight crease out of his cloth. The others waited until he finished.

In unison, all three opened their boxes. Inside each was a deck of cards. There were no creases or tears in the cards, even though they were so worn by age and constant use that they felt like a delicate tissue rather than stiff card stock. The woman slid the top card off her deck and placed it facedown in the empty space at the center of the cloth in front of her. It fit precisely–no card touched the embroidered edge of the square. Both men followed suit–first the man on the aisle and then the one next to the window.

The big plane banked left to bring it into the Red-15-South corridor–which would take it to the westbound intersection with

Blue-95-High and the straight shot to LAX. The turn brought the morning sun spilling into the windows all along the left side.

The man in 17A pulled down the plastic shade on his window. Then he and his companions reached up, switched on the reading lights inset into the plastic overhead, and adjusted them to illuminate the cards in front of them.

The woman in 17D broke away from the steamy scene between the Baroness and her kidnapper long enough to brighten the reader's screen to compensate for the change in light. Glancing to the left, she wondered if they were playing some sort of card game.

"One of those silly dungeon games like Angela's kids play," she thought. She snorted and shook her head in exasperation, thinking. "Californians. They're all just big children."

Then she returned to the Baroness.

Switching hands, the three young people reached for the cards in the center of the ritual cloths in front of them with their right hands and, again without any visible signal, turned them face up.

Chaos erupted.

# CHAPTER ONE

The airplane crash woke Steven Rowan.

To be entirely accurate, it wasn't a crash.

It was the insane screaming of four of the world's largest jet engines being pushed twenty percent past their factory-recommended maximum thrust only thirty feet over his head.

In addition, awake wasn't really the correct term for his state of consciousness at that point.

Steve was standing stark naked in the center of the room, jerking back and forth in the classic fight-or-flight reflex–his mind frantically spinning between possibilities, developing and rejecting dozens of possible threats every second, and running through as many options for escape. A small part of his mind was simultaneously working on the less-important questions of who he was, where he was, and what he'd done to himself the night before.

The pulsating howl of the jet began to diminish, but the screaming only grew louder and more intense. Suddenly, Steve fell to his knees, slamming clenched fists into his temples over and over, and screaming at the top of his lungs.

Tears flew from his eyes as he crawled forward and began to pound his head against the glass door to the balcony. A small rational part of his mind wondered that he could be driven to such desperation that he would fill his mind with self-inflicted pain in the vain hope that it would expel the shocking sound, the sheer terror, and the infinite grief.

He felt a sharp spark of agony as the glass cracked.

Suddenly, as blood began to stream down his face, the terrible pain diminished. The confusion and terror, the immense waves of emotions, all of that continued to pour through him, but the anguish had ceased. The massive assault of sound began to break down into hundreds of what he could only think of as voices.

Men and women were screaming, a mother was kissing the top of a tiny head and whispering soothing sounds, a man on a cell phone was frantically dialing and redialing–desperate to leave a message. In contrast, two men were running through a checklist with professional calm, but curses tickled at their throats, fighting to get out.

In the center, he heard a steady sound. A quiet chanting–young voices tinged with success and anticipation.

The glass door exploded.

# CHAPTER TWO

It was going to be a lousy morning, his head hurt even worse than usual, and his head usually hurt like someone dying from alcohol poisoning.

Steve opened his eyes at the sound of someone singing about hiding in Honduras and needing "lawyers, guns, and money."

OK, that was Warren Zevon, so it was probably his phone ringing. On Mondays, he set it to Afroman's *Because I Got High* just to irritate any senior editorial staff he might run into, but this song pretty well summed up his mood every other day.

He waited patiently until the late Mr. Zevon finished singing about how "the shit has hit the fan" and then listened for the Asian gong that would indicate a phone message.

Instead, Max Weinberg's driving drumbeat pounded out the syncopated SOS that began Bruce Springsteen's *We Take Care of Our Own.* Since every journalist knew (but would never report) that this song raised the dead whenever the Boss played within a mile of a graveyard, Steve figured someone was truly serious about talking to him.

In addition, he was curious because he'd deleted it from his phone over a month ago, exhausted by its contrast between the American ideal of "help your neighbor" and the reality of greed and selfishness that was currently sweeping the nation.

"Hello?"

There was a series of clicks and several of those odd changes in the quality of silence that indicate a call is being bounced from machine to machine or area code to area code. Of course, these were also the sounds that you heard when a telemarketer's robot war dialer realized it had a fish on the line and switched in the human voice to make the sale.

"Is this a freaking robot?" he said, sharply.

There was a short pause without any clicks. For some reason, Steve thought the caller was thinking.

"Mr. Rowan?" It was a man–the deep and authoritative voice of someone used to giving commands.

"Who the hell wants to know?" Steve hated people with that kind of voice.

Another pause.

"Mr. Stephen Rowan of 14500 Windermere Drive, Apartment D2?" The voice had changed, just slightly. It wasn't quite as abrasive and superior. Steve thought he could have a conversation with this guy.

"Yes." Steve's state of awareness was beginning to recover sufficiently so that it wasn't taking all of his concentration to talk on the phone. Unfortunately, that allowed him to begin to look around the room. If he hadn't just received his ten-year chip from Narcotics Anonymous, he would have instantly identified this as a drug dream—and not a pleasant one.

The smashed sliding door. Glass shards covering the carpet. The dozens of framed photographs he'd hung to remind himself of the good times when he'd worked in cool places were gone. They were in a heap of wood, glass, and photo paper on the other side of his bed. Only one remained. A picture of a Lebanese militiaman with an AK-47 wearing a T-shirt decorated with a picture of an

AK-47 and the words “Lebanon War.” He reached over and straightened it.

“Mr. Rowan.” The voice on the phone had changed again. Now it sounded like a person cowering with fear. Hell, this guy was afraid to speak to him. “Umm. Are you busy at the moment?”

Steve looked around the wreckage of his apartment. His cheek tickled and he touched it with a finger. He stared at the blood on his fingertip. “Busy? No, not really.”

“Would you be so kind as to consider possibly doing me a favor?”

Now the voice had gone all the way to obsequious.

“Not until you tell me who the hell you are and what the hell you want.” Steve licked his finger, tasting the blood as if it might tell him something about what had just happened. “And stop sucking up.”

“‘Sucking up’?” There was another series of clicks and silences, and the caller continued in its previous, more confident tone. “Mr. Rowan. Let me ask you a question. Could you use a job?”

Steve reached into his back pocket to check his wallet for his current financial position. Suddenly, he felt a hand stroke his butt. He jumped. When he looked down, he realized it was his own hand because he was still naked. Then, a sudden stab of pain proved that the silvery dust all over him was tiny bits of glass from his broken door and he’d just shoved a shard into his ass. He pulled his hand away sharply and held it out in front of him–carefully examining both sides.

“Mr. Rowan?”

"Oh. Sorry, I was distracted for a second. What...Oh, yeah. I have plenty of money."

"From your increasingly occasional work as a freelance reporter?"

Steve didn't say anything. The caller continued.

"How's that working out for you?"

Steve surveyed his ruined stereo and television and stopped as he saw his metal-cased laptop. It was rolled into a cylinder. He wondered what in hell could do that to an expensive computer. Or at least one that had been expensive when he'd bought it.

"Don't worry about the laptop. I think you'll find your telephone will be sufficient."

Steve's eyes widened and he slowly pulled the cell phone away from his ear and regarded it carefully–again, front and back. When he turned back to the main screen, a cartoon of a hand making a "thumbs up" sign had replaced his usual home screen picture of the Lebanese militiaman.

Steve just stood there and looked at the hand. He knew it was a cartoon because it only had three fingers and a thumb. Somehow, the artist had made it look happy and confident. That worried Steve.

He heard a faint squawking from the phone. He held the phone with only two fingers and raised it gingerly until it was an inch from his ear.

"Mr. Rowan? Can you hear me?"

Steve cleared his throat and answered carefully. "Yes."

"Good, we can continue."

"Not until you tell me how you knew about my computer, we can't."

"Your computer? Oh, you mean that you were looking at it?"

"Yes. How did you know that I was looking at it?"

The voice sounded more confident, almost comradely. "That's easy. Look straight out your window. See the apartment building with the exterior stairs?"

"They all have exterior stairs."

"Well, the one with stairs and exceptionally ugly pink paint."

"Got it."

"OK. Look at the left edge of the building and then run your eye straight up."

Steve saw the gleaming black cube of a building on the other side of the Baltimore-Washington Parkway. There were dozens of round white satellite dishes on the roof.

"OK, I see the building across the highway. The NSA or Fort Meade or whatever."

"Just keep watching."

Slowly, almost ceremonially, all the dishes on the roof turned, swiveled, swung, or tipped so that they were all pointed straight at him. Without thinking, Steve's left hand moved to cover his crotch.

He made a noise, but it wasn't a word. Something between a cough and the beginning of a scream, but definitely not a word. On the top of the black building, all the dishes nodded up and down in what he could only describe as a friendly fashion, and then moved back to their original positions.

"Mr. Rowan?"

Steve cleared his throat again. "I guess you just made that happen."

"Yes."

"That was better than anything I ever saw in college, even on mushrooms, but it still doesn't tell me who you are."

"No."

"But it does answer the question of how you could see me."

"Yes."

"And demonstrates a certain amount of power over things."

"Things and quite a few people as well."

"I would have to say that that remains to be proven, but I can agree that you've gone a long way in that direction."

"Why don't we leave the rest of your questions for a later time and let me ask you one?"

Steve's eyes wandered from the roof of the building across the highway. "What am I looking for?" he wondered.

Then he remembered.

"Give me just one more question first." Steve walked out on the balcony and scanned the horizon as far as he could. "Where is the smoke?"

"Smoke?"

"Smoke. From the crash of the plane that just flew over me."

"Mr. Rowan. Can I suggest you step back inside? Good. You were frightening several of your neighbors. No, there is no smoke and, as a matter of fact, no airplane. Since there is no airplane, there wasn't a crash and, *ergo*, no smoke. That's one of the things I'd like to hire you to investigate."

Steve thought for a second. "I don't like it when people say *ergo.* But we can deal with that later. Right now, I'd like to know why–no wait, let's begin with how I would investigate the nonexistent crash of an airplane that wasn't there."

"You're getting a bit redundant."

"You'll have to live with it. It's a side effect of the unease I'm feeling due to the stress of this uncommon and aberrant situation." Steve's voice rose to a shout. "Stop fucking around and tell me what the hell is going on!"

"Well." The voice on the phone paused as if choosing the next words carefully. "The jetliner did crash. At the same time, it did not crash."

"OK, I'm relieved that you made that clear. Now that I understand, I'm hanging up."

"Mr. Rowan! Wait! Just one more minute."

Steve didn't say anything, but he didn't punch the END symbol, either. He really wasn't sure why.

"There has been a Change."

Steve blinked and looked at the phone. He put it back to his ear. "Did you just capitalize the word *change*?"

"Hmm? Oh, yes, I suppose I did. This particular change is a pretty big deal and certainly deserves to be capitalized."

"I'll be the judge of that. What do you want me to do about this capitalized concept?"

"Would you work for me? Investigate this Change?"

Steve's answer was quick and automatic. "I'm an experienced freelancer. I don't work for just anyone."

"Really? Not even if it was for the Good of the Nation?"

"Stop talking in capitals and, if you mean working for the government, the answer isn't 'no.' The answer is 'Hell, No.'"

"I believe those last two words were capitalized."

Steve's head felt like it was about to explode. "Possibly."

"Would it make you feel better if I hired you on a temporary freelance basis?"

Once again, the answer was swift and automatic. "What are you paying?"

"Well, I think I have unlimited funds..."

"Then you're full of crap. I'm hanging up now."

The phone began to vibrate in his hand and the voice became agitated. "Mr. Rowan. Don't do that! It has to be you. No one else observed the airplane!"

Steve's eyes closed and whatever it was that had woken him up came back with the feeling of a knockout punch. His face twisted up in anguish at the memory of all the people...their terror...their helpless panic. He groaned.

"Mr. Rowan! Are you all right?"

"Not one of my better mornings."

"I am actually glad to hear that."

"Why?"

"Because I'd hate to think of what it might take to cause a worse morning. What's your daily rate?"

"Five hundred dollars. Double over ten hours." Steve always held out hope even though he hadn't made over $350 a day for the past decade.

"You've got it."

Steve opened his eyes. "Plus expenses?"

"Expenses and the use of a car and driver."

"A car?" Steve walked over and looked out to the space in the parking lot where he'd parked his light-blue Prius. He thought it was still there, but it was difficult to tell because an enormous jet engine was smoking sullenly on top of the entire row of parked cars.

He could make out some twisted pieces of light-blue plastic in his usual parking space.

"I guess I will need a car."

"Good. Then we are in business, right?"

"I guess so."

"Good. I've got some things to do right now, but I'd appreciate it if you could begin immediately."

Steve slowly turned around and looked at his apartment. His clothes looked as though a knife-wielding fashion critic had attacked them. He touched his laptop and it rolled away, revealing fluttering bits of paper that he deduced must be his stack of notebooks. One of his shoes was lying by his right foot. He picked it up and slowly poured broken glass out onto the floor. "I'm going to need to be paid up front, I think."

"Not a problem. Just answer the door." There was the synthetic clicking sound that cell phones made to indicate the end of a call.

"Answer the–"

There was a firm knock on his door.

# CHAPTER THREE

Steve looked for a moment and then carefully worked his way across the glittering carpet in the manner of a trained soldier moving through a minefield. When he reached the front door, he leaned against the wall and cautiously removed the worst splinters from his bare feet before he looked through the peephole. Standing in the hall was a woman with the wide shoulders and blunted V-shaped torso of an Olympic swimmer. She was wearing a tight olive-green T-shirt, loose tan cargo pants, and a military-style dark-blue baseball cap with an extremely short blond ponytail poking out of the back. Her face had the classic beauty of a movie star–marred by the fact her nose had apparently been broken several times.

He was instantly sure he had never seen her before.

He would definitely have remembered.

He watched without speaking as she reached forward and knocked again. Then she called. "Mr. Rowan? I need to speak with you on a matter of some urgency."

Steve realized two things. First, his original assumption that anyone that good looking was knocking on the wrong door was incorrect, and second, he still had nothing on but a dusting of broken glass.

"Can you wait a second?" he called through the door.

"Yes." Steve could almost hear the automatic "sir" that she had clipped off.

Looking around the debris that filled his efficiency apartment–hell, that now *was* his efficiency apartment–he could see that most of his clothing was in the usual places, i.e., strewn across chairs, bed, desk, and carpet. Consequently, all of it was covered in broken glass. He thought that it might have been a good idea to put some of his things away.

Well, it was too late, now not to mention that planning for explosions was something he'd always seen as a bad sign when he was working in battle zones. In his experience, that sort of thinking was usually followed by shaking, weeping, and leaving.

Concentrating hard, he managed to work his way back to his bureau with only two pauses to grit his teeth and stifle a scream as broken glass opened a new cut on the soles of his feet. "I have to keep my mind on what's important here," he thought. "Shrieking like a little girl would hardly impress that hottie at the door, would it?"

He opened the bureau drawers and examined the contents. Since it only held things he never wore, he found himself pawing through a pile of colorful, stretchy, and utterly useless exercise outfits that he'd bought in his occasional periods of irrational optimism. For Steve, exercise had always been a case of negative reinforcement. He felt like a schlub in the baggy sweats that actually fit him, so he didn't go to the gym, and therefore couldn't even squeeze into the cool exercise outfits.

"Well, it's no use crying over missed gym sessions," he thought. "Opportunity has just knocked and I shouldn't keep her waiting."

Finally, he pulled out a pair of red gym shorts and a black T-shirt. The shorts had CAPE MAY LIFEGUARD printed across the butt, and the shirt featured a flaming skull with the words WASHINGTON, DC: WHERE THE WEAK ARE KILLED AND EATEN.

"Not perfect," he thought. "However, they will simply have to do."

After he'd banged a pair of flip-flops together to get rid of the glass, he put them on, took a step, winced, removed the flip-flops, and brushed off the soles of his feet. He went through this entire routine twice before he could crunch across the carpet. He took a second to compose himself and opened the door, trying to appear casual and unruffled.

"I'm Steve Rowan. Can I help you?"

There was dead silence as the woman gave him an extremely thorough head-to-toe examination–including a glance around the side to read what was written on his rear. She shook her head slowly, took a deep breath, and appeared to gather the determination to weather a bad situation.

"No, Mr. Stephen Rowan. I'm here to help you. I'm Master Chief Petty Officer Ace Morningstar. You may call me Ace or Chief. May I come in?"

"Is this a police matter?" Steve asked. "Because if it is, the answer is 'not without a warrant.'"

"No, I'm not with the police. I'm your driver and bodyguard. You may call me 'Ace.' or 'Chief'" She reached into one of the many pockets of her cargo pants and produced a small sealed envelope. "Here's your fee for the first week–in cash as agreed. I'd like to come in and check out your security situation. Once that's completed, I'll take you in my car to your first briefing."

Steve automatically took the envelope, which felt like any other envelope filled with a fair-sized amount of cash. While his right hand was busy attempting to work out how much money was in the envelope strictly by feel, she stepped around that side and entered his apartment. She said over her shoulder, "I'm sure that these are great clothes for hanging around the apartment, but since we will be meeting with people over the age of twelve, I think you'll be more comfortable in something a bit less…comfortable."

Closing the door, he said with a touch of sarcasm. "Come right in. Make yourself at home."

"Thank you, Mr. Rowan, I would, but I'd never consider living in a place like this, so I can't really consider it home." She stepped out onto his small balcony through the empty frame of the sliding door and began a long, slow survey of his surroundings.

Tossing the envelope on the bed, Steve went to see if there were any respectable clothes that hadn't been rendered into exquisitely painful bondage attire.

Eventually, he found a pair of khakis, a blue button-down shirt, and a blazer in the back of his closet. To his surprise, there were unopened packages of boxer shorts and socks in the lowest drawer of his bureau–a drawer he could have sworn he'd never opened in the entire time he'd lived in the apartment.

Clearly, a previous renter, a snappy dresser, had left them by the evidence of the leopard prints and pastel stripes. Steve had a vague feeling that it was wrong to wear someone else's underwear; on the other hand, he could see by the label that they were his size. As he broke open a pair of red-white-and-blue striped boxers, he reflected that it was probably appropriate in the current state of emergency.

Just as he stripped the red gym shorts down to the floor, he heard glass break over by the window. Evidently, Ace had completed her survey.

"I have to say, it's not much to look at."

Steve froze as he realized his bare butt was aimed squarely at the woman's voice. Deliberately, he switched the shorts for the boxers, stepped into the khaki pants, and pulled both up at once as he stood up. Reaching for his shirt, he said, "You mean the apartment?"

"Obviously."

"Yeah, well, it's usually a mess. I'd have to say that that explosion outside has significantly raised the bar on what I'd describe as a 'mess.'"

"Explosion?"

Buttoning his shirt, Steve gestured out the window with an elbow. "Well, whatever that was that blew the sliding doors in just before you knocked. From that engine, it looks like a major jetliner crash."

"Engine?"

Slipping his feet into the loafers that had taken a good five minutes of banging against the wall, running his hand inside, cursing, sucking on a finger until the bleeding slowed, and then repeating, Steve walked out to the balcony. He pointed at the jet engine still smoking on the parked cars. "Yeah, that big round thing with Boeing and Roll-Royce logos on it that's sitting where my car used to be."

Ace gave him a sharp look, evidently made a decision, and pulled a pair of mirrored aviator shades from where they were hanging on the neck of her T-shirt. Slipping them on, she turned back to the parking lot. She gave a low whistle. "Yeah, that does appear to be a jet engine."

"What are those glasses?" Steve asked. "And I don't mean, 'Are they Ray-Bans?'"

Ace pulled off the sunglasses. “It’s easier to show than tell. Here, look through them.”

She held the glasses up before his eyes. Outside, he could see that the cars were all intact because there was no enormous jet engine on top of them. He pulled the lenses up on his forehead and the smoking jet engine was back. He tested it several times. Down, undamaged cars. Up, lead story on the evening news.

“In most cases, these allow people to see things that aren’t there.” Ace plucked the glasses out of his fingers and slipped them back in her T-shirt. “In your case, I think you already see what isn’t there, so they work in reverse.”

“That doesn’t make any sense at all.”

“Yes, sir. Whatever you say, sir. I’ve been told that they won’t work for much longer, anyway. They were designed for an environment we no longer enjoy.”

“What environment was that?”

“Reality,” she answered. “Are you ready? We need to go now.”

When they reached the door of the apartment, Steve heard his phone start playing the eerie falling minor chords of P!nk’s *Please Don’t Leave Me.* “Who the hell is calling me?”

“Your phone is.” Ace looked baffled. “Can’t you hear it?”

“I know it’s my phone. I also know I never put that song on it.” Steve walked back and picked up the smartphone from the bed where he’d left it. The music stopped instantly. He looked at the face to see who had called, but there was only an animated cartoon of the gloved hand–now wagging a warning forefinger. “Something must be wrong with it. It’s showing me cartoons instead of keeping track of missed calls. Maybe I should just toss it and pick up another one somewhere."

The phone vibrated violently and Steve dropped it on the bed in surprise. He felt a presence at his side. Ace was standing right next to him, evidently having crossed the room without a sound.

"Sir, if you'll take my advice," the woman looked at him gravely, "I'd be very careful of that particular unit. It's already saved your life once today."

Steve stared at her.

"Let me make that a bit clearer for you." She said in that tone that only drill instructors and the football coach on *Friday Night Lights* had ever truly mastered. "Pick. Up. That. Phone."

Without a word, Steve grabbed the phone and put it in his shirt pocket.

Ace looked at him critically. "Don't you have a cover for it?"

"No. It's just a phone. For that matter, it's only a cheap knockoff."

"No sir, it's not 'just a phone.'" Ace shook her head, wisps of short blond hair emerging from under the baseball cap. "We'll need to pick up a milspec case: unbreakable, waterproof, and with a battery extender. Perhaps solar power."

He repeated, "It's just a phone."

Her voice went back to that sharp, severe command level. "Do not say that again, sir."

Steve was getting a bit tired of being pushed around. "It's. Just. A...."

The cell phone was clearly malfunctioning–his breast pocket was on fire, with smoke rising in a small column. He reached to pull it out before it exploded but found that Ace had grabbed his wrist. "Damn. She's got fingers like a bear trap," he thought as he sucked his chest back from the shirt to lessen the pain and struggled to free his hand.

Neither effort had the slightest success.

The pain in his chest continued to increase and he thought he could smell burning flesh–at the least, the smell of singed chest hair. Then a pistol simply appeared–aimed squarely at the bridge of his nose. His eyes crossed as all his attention was suddenly focused on the hole at the end of the black muzzle. Ace released his wrist, used that hand to pull back the slide, and, with the light behind him, Steve could see a coppery shine appear deep inside the spiraled metal barrel.

"Sir, I have been told that you are a crucial resource and that I should defend you with my life." Ace spoke slowly and extremely clearly. "However, I should tell you that my orders state that this particular telephone has the potential to play an extremely important role. The optimum result of my mission is to return with both you and your phone. However, the minimum acceptable outcome is that I return with just the phone."

There was a pause. The pistol didn't move–nor did Ace's blue eyes. "Are we clear on this, sir?"

Steve nodded. The sensation of heat and pain against his chest just stopped, the smoke vanished, and the pistol moved up and away from the bridge of his nose.

Ace said. "Good. Now let's get out of here." She holstered her weapon–or at least that's what Steve assumed happened. As far as he could tell, it just disappeared somewhere in the cargo pants.

Ace reached for the front doorknob. There was a tremendous slamming noise and she snapped her hand back as the metal door bulged inward. Steve thought he could make out dents from an enormous skull and curled horns stamped into the steel.

There was a second impact and he was certain of it.

# CHAPTER FOUR

The pistol reappeared as Ace snapped into a perfect Weaver stance and put five quick shots into the center of the door. They didn't appear to have any effect, and a third blow struck the door. Watching the hinges twist against the frame, even Steve could see that the door wasn't going to hold much longer.

Ace spun, grabbed Steve by the arm, and asked, "Do you know how to fly?" before propelling him back across the apartment towards the balcony. Steve had no problem being shoved–especially as the door took another blow–but he was sure he'd misheard her last question.

When they reached the balcony, he asked breathlessly, "What did you say?"

With a note of exasperation, she asked again. "Do you know how to fly?"

"Not without an airplane. And a pilot."

"Crap." She looked out over the railing. Steve joined her and gazed down at the pavement four floors below. He thought of what the heroes of action movies would do and looked for other balconies that they could jump to or hang from.

Unfortunately, the guys in adventure movies obviously had better architects. The artistically staggered design of the apartment complex meant that the only balcony he could reach was three floors down. The rental agent was quite proud of this, he remembered, saying it was an intentional protection against robbery.

It had seemed a good idea at the time.

Another enormous slam echoed from his front door. Steve took a quick look and saw two of the three hinges hanging loose and the latch plate almost out of the frame. It wasn't going to survive another–*slam.*

Now, the dent in the door was so deep that Steve could make out the curl in the broad horns above what looked like a bull's snout.

Ace snapped her fingers in front of his face, drawing his eyes back to the long drop. "OK, it wasn't in the original tactical plan, but you're going to have to get us out of here."

"Exactly how do you suggest I do that?"

She had switched her pistol to her left hand and was using the right to dig for something in a cargo pocket low on her thigh. Steve had the odd thought that there seemed to be far more in her pants than he'd ever guessed from her silhouette. She pulled out a silver-colored metal case and hinged it open carefully, revealing a pack of cards.

"We going to draw for who gets to jump first?" Steve asked. "I'll take low card. Maybe I'll land on you."

She shot him a scornful look and then fired another five shots at the door. Steve cringed from the noise next to his head and half turned. He could see that she placed her shots so that they didn't hit the door itself but zipped through the open spaces where the door had been wrenched out of its frame.

There was a tremendous bellow from the hall.

Flicking through the deck with one hand, Ace pushed out a card with her thumb and held it out to Steve. He took the card and then cringed again as she rested her hand on his shoulder and fired again. There was another, higher shrieking roar from the hall.

"The second half of the clip is always loaded with OTN-4 rounds." Ace said. "That should slow him down for a minute."

"You mean, in a minute, Bullwinkle the Hammer is going to get in?" Steve shouted over the ringing in his ears. "We're going to die!"

She nodded her head at the card in Steve's hand. "Not if you can fly using that card the way you're supposed to." While she spoke, she dropped out the empty clip and rammed in a fresh one from yet another pants pocket.

For the first time in his long career, Steve was too stunned to ask a question. He turned over the card and recognized it as one of those tarot cards that fortunetellers used. The picture was of a somewhat gay-looking teenager with a flower and an old-fashioned bindle on a stick over his shoulder. He was looking up–at an empty sky, apparently–and his next step was going to take him right off a cliff. There were no secret flying instructions that he could see.

Steve looked at the back. Nope, no "Guide to Flight" there, either.

He shook the card at Ace. "What the hell is this?"

"That's the Fool."

"Really?" Steve pointed at the bottom. "Probably why it has 'The Fool' written on the bottom. Let me be clearer. What good is this dumbass tarot card?"

She looked at him sharply. "So you know the tarot?"

"Old ladies on the boardwalk peddle this–it's a crock."

She shook her head, fired a couple of quick shots at the door, and then said, "You really have to stop dismissing things you don't understand. The Fool is one of the most powerful characters in the Major Arcana and–among many other things–controls the power of flight."

"You are shitting me."

"No sir. I do not shit you." She fired at the door again. "It's in Manual S-O slash O-T-N, Section one five three dash zero, and if it's in the Manual, it must be true." She said this as though it proved her point beyond any shadow of a doubt.

Steve could only stare at her. She was beautiful–it was a pity that she was dangerously insane.

She shot him another look–blue eyes as direct and grave as his third-grade teacher. "Here's what's going to happen, sir. You're going to stare really hard at that card and figure out how to use it."

"What?"

There was another tremendous bang on the door. This time, it was followed by a grating crash that Steve assumed was his front door ripping out of the frame and spinning across the room to smash into the opposite wall. He automatically began to turn his head to look, but Ace gripped his ear and pulled to keep his eyes locked on hers. She pivoted so her back was to the railing and he was facing four stories of exceptionally empty air.

"This is no time for playing tourist. You need to concentrate." She fired three quick shots over his shoulder. There was another furious roar, but Steve thought he could hear enormous hooves smashing into the broken glass through the ringing in his ears.

"OK." Steve swallowed hard. "How does this work?"

"I have no idea, sir. I'm not the Fool. You are. It's your card."

"Great. How long do I have?"

Ace fired another couple of rounds, elicited another shriek, and holstered the pistol. She looked down at the ground. "I'd say about four seconds."

She wrapped her arms around him firmly and threw both of them off the balcony.

# CHAPTER FIVE

Steve stared at the card–it was better than watching certain death arriving at Newton's thirty-two feet per second per second.

Beg?

Pray?

Demand?

Kiss?

Rip?

Possibilities flickered through his mind–they weren't coherent enough to be thoughts. In a fraction of a second, he settled on doing what he did best–his primary skill as a journalist.

He **Studied** the card, trying to identify all the odd elements separately and grasp it as a whole at the same time. He considered the relationships between the young man, the little dog, the sun and the moon in the sky, and the cliff before him that clearly was going to result in certain death unless….

There was a terrible ripping pain that flashed across his chest and a crushing pain in his head. Everything went black.

"Oh, shit!" he thought. "I've hit the ground. At least I'm not in pain."

He considered that for a second. He shouldn't be able to think after he was dead. He shouldn't have been able to consider anything–not even for a second. For that matter, he thought it was doubtful that "considering" was on the list of potential post-death activities.

"Nicely done, sir. We still had six inches to unfuck ourselves. Not bad for the first time."

Certain that feeling Ms. Morningstar's arms around him was definitely not in the category of Things You Can Do in Bowie After You're Dead, Steve opened his eyes. They were hanging above the pavement–four floors beneath his balcony,

As he stared at his feet, they gently dropped the remaining distance to the ground.

After a quick assessment, he was forced to accept the fact that he was unharmed.

Unharmed! In an almost-spontaneous celebration of life, he put his hands on Ace's cheeks and leaned in for an exultant kiss.

*Snick. Snick. Wham.*

Steve looked up from the pavement.

Ace had released her hold around his waist, shot both hands up between his arms, wrist-snapped his hands away, and then nailed him with a roundhouse punch to the side of his head that had spun him all the way around before he hit the ground. This time, the impact with the ground was hard, painful, and much like all the other times he'd been knocked down. As he rubbed his cheek, Steve reflected that while it had been an open-handed blow, it sure as hell hadn't been anything he'd describe as a slap.

Ace was leaning over him, her face only inches from his, and pale with fury. In a low, hissing whisper, she said, "Listen very carefully, because I'm only going to say it once. I am a Navy SEAL, a veteran of four combat tours, and a rated expert in all weapons and tactics in the US Special Operations manual as well as those of fourteen other nations–both enemies and allies. My rank is Special Warfare Operator Master Chief Petty Officer. 'Ace Morningstar' is just an alias–you will never be cleared for my real name. Morningstar is a translation of 'Lucifer.' I'm named for the Devil because 'The Devil of Ramadi' was what the *hajjis* called me after my fortieth confirmed kill. 'Ace' is the nickname my squad gave me because I wouldn't answer to 'Lucy,' and 'Lucifer' was just silly. You will never ever, ever attempt to kiss me again. Do you understand?"

Steve nodded his head slowly.

"Now, are there any questions?"

"Yeah. I thought Chris Kyle was the 'Devil of Fallujah'?"

"No, he was the 'Devil of Ramadi'. People make that mistake all the time."

"When did they start training women to be SEALs?"

"They don't. I had enough juice to convince people that I was a swinging dick like all the other recruits, and then I basically worked twice as hard to get through."

"Juice?"

She sighed and stood upright. "Mojo. Talent. Black arts. Voodoo." She offered her hand and pulled him to his feet without any evident effort. "Magic. I wanted BUDS so bad that I went to a *bruja* in a small *botánica santería* just across the line from San Diego and she brought out what little juice I had. Everything was fine until last year, when I ran into a Seer and he spotted me as a woman."

She shook her head. "Just my luck. Only four Truthspotters in the entire US military and one of them just had to walk past while I was doing PT."

"Why don't I see you as a man?" Steve asked as he continued to rub his cheek. "Not that I would have ever figured it out by the way you hit."

"Because that was back when things were normal and a small number of people had tiny amounts of juice. The higher-ups think that the jet plane that either did or didn't go over your head was a suicide attack by a mystical terrorist group and it forced a Change. Now I've been told that those of us who had any Other Than Normal powers before the Change are powerless. Evidently, the terrorists intended to benefit from the Change but we're not sure if they just managed to keep the powers they had before from disappearing, or gained significant new ones. One guy–his name is Barnaby–thinks that the Change will mean that a shitload of new magic will affect just about everyone in one way or another."

She shook her head. "The fact is that no one really knows anything except that it's a new normal and we need to learn how to deal with it fast."

She added thoughtfully. "Or possibly it's a new abnormal."

Then she was back in his face, almost spitting out her words. "However, this does not change some basic facts. I can still execute as efficiently as anyone else who lived through the Basic Underwater Demolition slash SEAL training facility at Coronado Beach–which means I can break every bone in your body before you can pick your nose. Since my current assignment is to keep you alive and functional at all costs, my options are limited, but I need to make sure you understand that 'functional' does not mean 'pain-free.' Nod your head if you are entirely clear on this."

Steve slowly and sincerely nodded his head.

Ace stepped back and took a deep breath. "OK, that was a mistake you were going to make at some point, and it's best to get it straight right off the top and not regret it later." She looked up at the balcony. "Now that that's clear, we need to get moving before that gentleman upstairs gets over his fear of magic bullet holes and comes over the balcony."

She turned and began to move quickly along the base of the building, heading for the corner so that they couldn't be seen from his apartment. Steve's head was still spinning, but he concentrated on putting one foot directly in front of the other and managed an only slightly erratic shamble behind her.

As he rounded the corner, he heard a chirp and the LED headlights flashed on a BMW X5 M class parked across the lot. Ace pointed Steve to the passenger side and swung in behind the wheel. She pushed the start button, the twin turbo engine rumbled to life, and they pulled out. Ace was an excellent driver–never squealing the tires, cutting the apex of every turn, and only using the paddle shifter on the steering wheel to make tiny adjustments to the six-speed automatic transmission.

"You left this in the parking lot of my building and it's still here when you got back?" Steve asked. "The record for a really nice ride remaining undisturbed is about thirty seconds."

"Negs only saw a rusted Chevy."

"'Negs'?"

"Negatives," she answered briefly, concentrating on getting out of the main gate and merging into the four lanes of traffic on Route 197 and heading east. "Negatives are those who are unable to perceive OTN objects or events."

"OTN?"

"Other Than Normal."

"Oh, yeah, you mentioned that before but I wasn't concentrating on anything but survival." Steve rubbed his cheek again. "How many people can perceive OTN objects?"

She turned her head and Steve could see a slight grin. Turning back to her driving, she said, "As I told you, we're not certain of the precise number at this point. We are relatively sure, however, that only one person is able to both experience and create OTN events. Unfortunately, he's not terribly well informed, has a bad attitude, and is completely untrained. On the plus side, he seems to learn quickly."

Steve didn't take long to work this out. "Wait, you mean me?"

"Yes, sir."

"How did this happen?"

She took off the baseball cap–revealing close-cropped hair the consistency of duck down. Rubbing her head with her free hand along the places where the hatband had pressed the hair down, she said. "I really can't go into that. First, because of basic OPSEC–"

"Operational security," Steve interjected. He was tired of her assuming he didn't know anything.

"Yes, sir. As I was saying, basic OPSEC and the fact that I don't know much more about what's happened than you do."

"How did you get to my apartment so fast?"

"I had standing orders to proceed to your location if we ever experienced an Incident."

"Oh, right. The airplane crash that only I saw happening." Steve's head swam as the memory of the howling engines, the shrieking children and adults, and all the rest burst into his mind–feeling like the glass shards that had littered his apartment. "Shit. I'd forgotten that in all that's happened since."

Ace's blue eyes examined him briefly. "That and you performed a blood magic."

Steve thought back. "You mean when I cut my forehead on the door?"

"Yes, sir." Ace nodded. "Blood magic is extremely powerful. In your case, it was enough to break you out of the death loop the terrorists were crafting and elevated your resistance to psychic trauma. In other words, your mind had the time to do a bit of self-repair. If you reach up and check, you'll find that even the physical wound is gone."

Steve carefully ran his fingers over his forehead. Then he flipped down the passenger side sun shield and checked in the little makeup mirror. "Wow. There's nothing there at all."

"No." Ace nodded. "That's one of the telltale signs of blood magic. There isn't generally any *physical* damage."

Steve looked at the blonde woman for a moment and then asked, "The way you said that raises another question. If not physical damage, what sort of damage are we talking about?"

"I wouldn't know myself–I can't do that sort of thing–but the manual indicates the high possibility of measurable harm to the soul."

"Measurable? How the hell do you measure the… Stop, don't answer." Steve massaged his thumbs vigorously on his temples. "Great. An hour ago, I was certain I didn't have a soul and now I have to worry that I've screwed it up."

There was another trace of a smile on the blonde woman's face. Steve continued. "Where are we going now? Wait, more important, when am I going to talk to someone who can tell me what's happened? Is it this Barnaby guy? Who is he, anyway?"

"You'll be briefed very soon. It's all complicated to explain, beginning with Barnaby." Ace downshifted three gears until the engine was howling, and whipped through a tight right turn. Steve found himself thrown up against her and scrambled to move away. She said. "Seat belts are an essential safety item. I suggest you make a habit of wearing yours or you could find yourself in danger."

He wasn't certain if the "danger" Ace was referring to would come from an accident or from ever touching the driver again, but in either case, a seatbelt seemed like a good idea. Just as Steve had reached back and pulled down the harness, the car whipped into a parking space outside one of the single-story dull-green 1940-era wooden buildings that seemed to alternate with futuristic architecture in Fort Meade. Ace pulled the cap back over her head and got out of the car.

Having just clicked the seat belt closed, Steve opened it again and followed.

He was sure he saw a smile this time.

# CHAPTER SIX

There were two marines in full combat gear at the front door. Steve could feel their eyes behind their mirrored ballistic sunglasses as they ruminated on the question of killing him immediately or waiting until he presented just a bit more of a threat. Ace showed them a blizzard of passes, IDs, and papers covered with stamps and signatures that she pulled from an apparently inexhaustible supply in one of her leg pockets. Finally, one of them must have worked because both guards stiffened slightly, saluted, and waved them through.

As he walked by, Steve imagined that they looked slightly disappointed, but he decided that they could always kill him on the way out, so they should just suck it up. There are small disappointments in everyone's life.

He followed Ace's baseball cap up two crumbling concrete steps and through a door whose hinges looked as if they hadn't been oiled since the Battle of the Bulge. He almost went right over a two-by-four railing at the end of a three-foot platform on the other side of the door. When he recovered, he realized that, instead of a floor, there was only this small platform of raw wood, evidently placed to keep visitors from plunging headfirst to the ground, and bathed in full sunlight. There was a short two-step wooden staircase scabbed in on the left side.

As he looked around, Steve realized that the entire building was a stage set–a tent constructed over a section of striped pavement no different from the parking lot outside. The walls were 'flats,' a single layer of wood and canvas with two-by-four braces at regular intervals. The outside had been painstakingly crafted to look like real wood and peeling paint, certainly well enough to fool anything but the closest inspection. On the inside, the walls were just bare tan canvas with random streaks and dribbles of tan and green paint

At the far end, about a dozen military types in the usual camouflaged work uniforms and leather tool belts were using pulleys to raise a triangular set piece with painted-on shingles–apparently the roof–up onto three large wooden poles. It reminded Steve of the time he'd seen a real three-ring circus tent go up. Once that was finished, Steve thought, there'd be no way to tell this from a dozen other 1940s-era barracks or office buildings that sat within a few hundred yards of their location.

"This wasn't prepared this morning. What else did the NSA want to conceal?" Steve smiled at an idle thought. "Keggers? Good-bye parties with strippers bursting out of a cake?" Then he looked at the serious, nerdy faces of the men and women around him and decided a way to hide all-night cram sessions was a lot more likely.

Ace moved briskly down the steps and headed for a milling crowd of about twenty men and women. Steve could see that they were wearing everything from full battle dress to white smocks and pocket protectors to the head-to-toe Plexiglas protection suits that the sexy doctor on *The Last Ship* always wore when she was working with the virus that had killed off the rest of mankind. Suddenly, Steve stopped thinking that any of this was terribly funny–except perhaps for the air purification units that made cute humming and puffing noises as they trailed behind the suited scientists on tiny red wagons.

Steve reached forward and–after a moment's thought–lightly tapped his bodyguard on the shoulder. "Chief, I'm seeing people in bio-suits. Shouldn't we take some sort of precautions?"

"I don't think so. Their primary responsibility is to drag the rest of us out if something turns out to be toxic. They're still here, so we're probably good to go."

Steve silently mouthed the word "Probably?"

A tall woman in full Army dress uniform was being briefed by a circle of men and one woman who all wore identical short-sleeved shirts with pocket protectors. The woman's shirt was pink and matched her glasses as well as her pocket protector. Steve figured they were either dorky scientists or actors hired and costumed to play dorky scientists. After witnessing the fake building, he felt he shouldn't be taking anything for granted.

Ace pointed at the woman in the center and said quietly, "Anyway, the colonel isn't wearing protective gear. Of course, I suspect that even an Ebola virus would probably be afraid to disturb Trinidad Tataka. And rightly so." The colonel was tall and thin with what appeared to be a mix of African and Asian–possibly Indian–features. As soon as Steve and Ace walked up, she dismissed the scientists and turned to Steve. After a long, searching inspection that terminated with a rather dismissive sigh, she extended a hand. "Mr. Rowan. I'm Lieutenant Colonel Tataka. What can you tell me about the Portal?"

As a journalist, Steve had been dealing with this sort of attitude from most members of the military for most of his career. The game she was playing was meant to knock the other person off-balance in the very beginning of a relationship and establish a long-lasting position of power.

"I don't know a damn thing, Trinidad." He could see her stiffen at the use of her first name. "But I'm sure with all these smart guys you've got running around, you should know enough to brief me on it by now." Actually, he was sure the military had no idea what was happening, but she'd pushed him hard and now he was pushing back.

The colonel's face hardened and Steve could actually *feel* the power of the stare she was giving him. He smiled, cocked his head, and raised a single eyebrow to indicate that he could wait just as long as she could.

Then he deliberately turned away and began to study the center of the enclosed space. Four long tables had been hastily pushed together into a square and held a motley assemblage of scientific equipment. In addition, he suspected, the tables were there to keep people from accidentally walking into whatever was in the center. The only problem with that concept was that there didn't appear to be anything in the center.

To his surprise, Colonel Tataka did not explode in a standard-issue military snit fit. Instead, she gave a long sigh that turned into a tuneless whistle. "You've got it pegged. We don't know shit." Steve turned back around, interested by this unexpected honesty.

Tataka gave him a rueful smile and said, "So, why don't we stop trying to prove whose metaphorical dick is longer and share what we do know? I am not quite sure why you're here, but I was given orders to render you my complete support."

She looked thoughtful. "I'm also unclear where those orders originated, but they came down through my chain of command so fast, you would have thought they'd been issued by God's grandmother."

Steve smiled–he was starting to like this woman. "Colonel, I've had one hell of a strange morning–frankly, I don't really understand why I'm here, either–so why don't you start, and we'll see if we can help each other out?"

Tataka clasped her hands behind her back and looked around–over on the other side, the crew was finishing the placement of the false roof, and big floodlight rigs were replacing the sunlight. "We have..." she paused and then started again." We have a fact set that simply doesn't make sense." Another pause. "Which I suppose makes it cease to be a fact set in the classic sense."

She began to walk slowly over to the four tables and used her fingers to tick off her data points. "One, we have a 747-400 with several hundred passengers missing. American International's flight 1143 to Los Angeles declared a Mayday at 0843 hours today. The pilots said the flight controls were moving, quote, on their own, unquote. They also reported that they were 'fighting someone' for control. We have no idea what that means; they had the post-9/11 standard heavy-duty steel door, which according to remote telemetry was closed and locked, and the first officer was armed."

She took a deep breath, let it out slowly, and continued. "The radar showed it losing altitude and vectoring towards Washington. Fighters were scrambled from Naval Air Station Patuxent River and Andrews Air Force Base, but the commercial jet swung to the east and eventually vectored away from DC." She waved vaguely to the west. "It came in low over the apartments on the other side of the Baltimore-Washington Parkway–"

"I know." Steve interrupted. "The noise almost blew my head off."

Tataka gave him a sharp look. "You heard it?"

"Yep."

"Odd, we've had no other reports of people hearing or seeing the plane as it came in over populated areas. Even more astonishing, phone camera videos haven't started to pop up on CNN." She sighed, shook her head, and continued her briefing. "We could still follow AI 1143 on radar, but as far as we can tell, it was both unheard and unseen by anyone on the ground by the time it dropped below 10,000 feet." She sighed. "Now comes the part I really can't believe I'm saying, but I have to play the hand I've been dealt."

Steve said. "You and me both. It's been a very strange morning."

She nodded slowly, her eyes focused on a blinking green light on a small piece of equipment on the closest table. "You have no idea. The facts as we know them indicate the flight ended here. I won't say it crashed here because there isn't any debris and a 747 does not crash without a mountain of wreckage. On the other hand, it was this point that the radar lost track of it as it merged with the ground clutter in an almost vertical trajectory. Command declared it a possible Level 2 OTN Incident, so we inserted a false radar trail into the air traffic computers so that they now show it going down in the middle of the Chesapeake Bay."

Steve looked blankly at Ace. She explained. "A Level 5 Incident would be lights in the sky, crop circles, and that sort of thing. Level 1 is an alien spaceship on the White House South Lawn."

Tataka nodded. "So, a Level 2 is serious but containable. There is a substantial search-and-rescue mission going on over the Chesapeake as we speak."

"But they won't find anything."

"Well, eventually, we'll sink a physical misdirection package so that plane and passengers can be identified. Just like that TWA Flight over Long Island Sound–"

"Flight 800?" Steve interrupted. "What happened there?"

"The captain of the *USS Albuquerque* spilled coffee on the launch controls." Tataka shook her head. "We would have hung the bastard out to dry, except that there was conclusive evidence that his elbow was jostled by a previously certified poltergeist."

Ace nodded. "Yeah, that was Skippy, right?"

"Right. OTN entity 465 slash 14p." Tataka said absently. "The little bastard thinks he's a gremlin. Keeps calling himself 'Adolf.' He got tired of busting people's chops during the investigation and switched over to the *USS Ronald Reagan*. Driving them crazy, from what I've heard, but enough of that. Let's get back to the incident at hand. Flight 1143 got to this point and vanished." She gestured at the mock-up of a building that surrounded them. "We got this old Cold War deception kit out of storage to block the area from any unfriendly eyes."

Steve looked up at the open sky. "You worried about satellites?"

Tataka shook her head. "No, the most likely observers would be crows. Possibly hawks."

Steve kept looking up. "Well, I think you should assume hawks. They were the first things that struck me. You weren't worried about eagles?"

"No, we know that almost all of the eagles are on our side."

Steve slowly lowered his eyes to meet her intense brown ones. "I thought I was just playing along with the joke."

"Nope. You think all those strikes in Pakistan were done with Predator drones? Hell, probably half of them were just a couple of African Martial Eagles with an M183 satchel charge slung with a talon-activated quick release. Those war gamers turned pilots over at Nellis have way too much time lag to do anything precise. Damn, those birds are beautiful. Ten-foot wingspan and smart as a whip. Hell, three of 'em are officers now."

She clearly realized she'd said too much. "Well. Um. You are hereby directed to forget the last ten minutes of conversation under emergency restrictions laid out in the Secret Annex to the Patriot Act under Crimes Punishable by Death."

Tataka stared at Steve, who nodded in complete confidence that no editor in the country would believe him if he tried to turn it into a story. When the tall woman saw his agreement, she continued. “That’s all I’m going to say until we can confirm that this area is secure. I’ve been told to give you a full briefing.” She laughed bitterly. “Or at least a recounting of the timeline as reported. I don’t know how it can be a ‘briefing’ when I don’t buy one damn word of it.”

She returned to her usual brisk manner. “OK, the first thing is to show you the Anomaly. Follow me but don’t go past the tables. We are working on the assumption that it’s dangerous even though we have no idea in what manner.”

As the three walked up to the space enclosed by the equipment-laden folding tables, Steve felt the phone in his pocket vibrating. Without looking, he reached into his pocket and turned off the buzzer. He didn’t want to be bothered by some lame assignment-desk editor right now even if might mean a paying job.

The vibrating stopped and then abruptly began again, the phone wriggling so violently, Steve thought it might leap out of his shirt. When he felt heat beginning to build against his chest, he jerked the phone out and checked the screen. The shaking and the feeling of heat stopped instantly.

A picture–a tarot card–filled the screen. It was the Hermit, an old man holding up a lantern as if to light his way. Steve stared at it for a moment and then turned the phone over and looked at the back. It certainly seemed to be his old phone–a cheap and unreliable knockoff. Why was it showing him random pictures?

It vibrated again–even harder, if that was possible. He looked at the screen and saw that the lamp the old man was holding had been replaced by an image of a cell phone. The Hermit appeared to be taking a picture and there was a white cone where the flash would be.

Steve looked up–the Colonel and Ace were both looking back at him–clearly annoyed at being kept waiting. He almost put the phone back in his pocket, but then he remembered Ace's strange statement about its importance.

Feeling ridiculous, he raised the phone up in front of him, pushed the button and the swipe bar to turn it on, and waited to see what would happen. Briefly, the Fool appeared–Steve was certain it was meant as a comment this time–and then the video camera app appeared and the red dot indicated it was recording.

At the moment, the picture was a recording of the Colonel's backside–an image that Steve thought was certainly aesthetic but most likely not immediately relevant. The vibrating began again. Reflexively, his hand jerked and the screen showed the tables. The vibrating stopped.

Just to see what would happen; Steve pointed the camera at Ace. There was a brief but violent vibration and a burst of the intro to the Supremes' *Stop! In the Name of Love.*

Steve decided that since his phone was clearly no longer just a phone, he probably should acquiesce to its demands until he worked out exactly what it was. The simple fact that it *made* demands was unnerving enough.

He pointed the camera at the space inside the tables.

Ace said quietly to the colonel. "Millions of dollars' worth of high-tech gear and he uses his phone."

"Who knows?" Tataka responded. "Maybe he wants to put it up on Facebook?"

Speaking directly to Steve, she continued in a louder voice. "Which would be a crime punishable by death just in case you're dumb enough to try it." She pointed at the unmarked tarmac between the tables. "This is where the aircraft crashed."

"Here?"

"Right here."

Steve began to turn toward the colonel–the phone buzzed instantly. He pointed it back at the unmarked section of tarmac. "Colonel, I agree with you that most significant jumbo jet crash sites have a lot more–well, pieces of a jumbo jet. Obviously, either you're wrong about this being the impact point or something happened. What?"

Tataka glared at him and bit off each word. "I. Am. Not. Wrong."

After a moment of additional glare just to make sure that the fact of her infallibility had sunk in, the colonel leaned over one of the portable tables and pointed into the center. "OK, look at that cigarette butt–the Marlboro Light. Got it?"

Steve and Ace both nodded. "OK, now look up about two inches. Do you see...? Damn it! It makes no sense, but I can't describe it any other way. Do you see a hole in the air?"

Steve stared where she was pointing, but the air just looked like...air. Then he glanced at the screen on his phone. Pointed at the same place, it showed a blood-red gash about six inches long, out of which a viscous purplish sludge was steadily oozing. The sludge fell into what was already a spreading pool of the stuff and it seemed to be evaporating–wisps of reddish-purple mist were rising into the air.

He panned the phone over to the colonel's feet. "Ma'am. I know you don't know what this is yet, but I think that standing in it up to your ankles is probably not a great idea."

"What the hell do you mean?"

"I mean that this...hole in the air...is leaking something. In my professional opinion, it looks like a raspberry Slurpee." Steve panned around the area with the phone again. "And I'd say that everyone within about 35 feet is standing in a purple puddle."

The colonel immediately headed for the door at a fast walk, barking orders as she went. She ordered everyone to clear the area, and called for the standard tents, showers, and baby pools to be set up outside so that they could run everyone through a full decontamination. In seconds, the space was empty except for Steve and Ace.

"What are you trying to pull?" Ace said as she looked over Steve's shoulder. "There's nothing on that phone except your dumbass Lebanese screen saver."

Steve stared at the phone–which was still showing the growing pool of red sludge. He glanced at Ace. "You really can't see it?"

She shook her head.

"Try those fancy sunglasses," he suggested.

She put the glasses on and scanned the area. "Nope. I see a lot of empty parking spaces. No red ooze. No mist."

"Here," he said. "Let me try those." He could see the red gash with the glasses on and off. He handed them back. "Well, you said these would stop working. You were right."

"I'll keep them, if you don't mind." Ace grabbed them back and hung them on her collar. "It's part of the package."

He pointed the phone at his feet and saw that his shoes and socks were already soaked and a purple stain was creeping up his pants cuffs. Then he swept the camera up and down the SEAL. "Hey, that's weird. You don't have a drop on you." He kicked at the sludge around his feet and splashed it towards her. She jumped back, with a furious glare that Steve missed because he was still staring at the tiny screen. “Well, well. Look at that. The stuff split and went in two directions before it touched you. It looked like positive iron filings avoiding a positive magnetic pole. I think it just doesn’t like you.”

“It’s only fair. I don’t like it. Whatever it is.” Ace looked around as though she would have glared if she could see anything to glare at. “And if it’s a smart sludge, it should be seriously afraid, because if any of it does touch me…”

“Stop complaining.” Steve agreed. “I’ve already got it all over my shoes and soaking into my khakis. The odd thing is that I can’t feel it. My feet aren’t wet or…”

He almost dropped the phone as *Lawyers, Guns, and Money* announced an incoming call. He looked at the screen. The camera view was gone and the ID for the incoming call was the tarot card of the Hermit. At the bottom, instead of “The Hermit,” it said, “Barnaby.”

Steve had no doubt that he’d forgotten things in all the bizarre events of the morning–hell, he forgot a lot of things on far less stressful days–but he would have bet a year’s salary that there was no one in his contact list named “Barnaby.”

He held the phone out to Ace and said, “It’s for you.”

She snapped a palm up in a definite negative. “Sir, I’m pleased to inform you that Barnaby is your problem from now on.”

# CHAPTER SEVEN

Steve gave Ace his best withering glare. Ace responded with a soft but extremely dismissive snort. Steve decided to ignore it in the interests of dignity and put the phone to his ear.

"This is Steven Rowan."

There was the same series of soft clicks and ambient noise level changes as this morning followed by what certainly seemed to Steve to be the same voice–or at least the voice whoever it was had finally settled on after it had gone through all its earlier variations.

"Mr. Rowan?"

"Is your name really 'Barnaby'?"

The voice sounded a bit huffy. "I can't see how that's really relevant, but yes. Or at least it was, a long time ago."

"Why 'Barnaby'?"

"Well, in the 1950s, there was a comic strip featuring a little boy named Barnaby, who had a friend–a rather small man with wings and a cigar who was a fairy godfather. His friend–Mr. O'Malley was his name, I believe–would show up with a giant named Atlas, who was as short as he was."

"A short giant?"

"A mental giant. That was the joke. Now can we get back to business?"

Steve couldn't help it. "Absolutely. Barnaby."

There was a short silence. Then, "Could you ask Master Chief Morningstar if she is carrying a weapon?"

Steve asked. "Are you carrying a weapon?" and got a look. He said to the phone. "Oh, definitely. She was just shooting at someone a few minutes ago."

"I was shooting at something, not someone." Ace corrected as she pulled out her SIG Sauer P228.

'Whatever," the voice on the phone said. "Now, Mr. Rowan, please ask Ms. Morningstar to shoot you. Preferably in the chest or groin area."

Steve grimaced involuntarily and stared down at the phone, which was now covering his crotch. Turning sideways to the blonde woman, Steve carefully examined the phone, shook it vigorously, and checked the volume. He would have done more, but he honestly couldn't think of any other diagnostic procedure.

Frustrated, he said, "Barnaby. Have I done something to offend you? Do I owe you money? Wait! Was that your wife last year down at that 'clothing optional' club in the Bahamas?"

"No. Why?"

Steve stared up at the fake ceiling of the fake building trying to think of other regrettable events in his past. The problem was that there were so many.

After a short period of intense thought, he said, "Oh, I was just trying to figure out why you would want to kill me."

"I don't want to kill you."

Steve looked over at Ace and pointed at the pistol. "Do you miss very often with that?"

She pointed the pistol at his groin. "About as often as you miss with that."

Steve spoke into the phone again. "Listen, Barnaby or whoever the hell you are, I'm as willing to give my up life for the advancement of science as any other man–which means not at all. Anyway, I don't think the Master Chief here is ready to shoot me."

Ace's eyebrows lifted in surprise. Then she began to inspect her weapon–pulling out the clip to check the load, replacing it, and racking the slide.

Steve held up his hand. "OK, maybe she's ready, but I am not willing to be shot."

The voice on the phone said. "Oh. I see the problem. Well, just tell her to shoot to wound–not kill."

Steve put his hand over the microphone at the bottom of the phone and said. "Good Lord, this guy is crazy. Now he's saying just shoot to wound as if–"

In a movement almost too fast to see, Ace raised the pistol, aimed at Steve's upper arm, and pulled the trigger.

Steve had always heard people say that "time slowed" in a crisis situation–hell, he'd even written it into a story once or twice–but he'd thought it was just a cheap literary device that bad novelists used to get their hero out of a desperate situation. It just didn't happen in real life.

Time slowed.

Steve could see Ace's trigger finger begin to relax. The slide on her pistol was moving backward and her hand jerked up from the recoil. For a moment–no, that would be wrong–for some tiny fraction of a second, he thought he could see the bullet come spinning out of the muzzle. Maybe he would experience his own Matrix-style "bullet-time," except he couldn't bend backwards like Keanu Reeves so it would only result in some extra moments to imagine how much the bullet would hurt before it actually hurt.

No bullet came out. Instead, the muzzle of the automatic seemed to warp back and forth like a slow-motion video of a rubber band snapping. Eventually, it settled down into a vertical slot from which a jagged bolt of blue lightning began to emerge. It was surprising but, frankly, Steve couldn't see how being artistically zapped was much of an improvement over just being shot.

About a half inch of the bolt had emerged from the gun before Steve admitted that time had, against all reason, slowed. He tried to move–throw himself out of the path of the lightning–but his muscles didn't react. Apparently, only his mind was moving at super-speed–his body was even slower than usual.

"I guess that means I have to do something with just my mind," he thought.

He tried **Demanding** that the lightning stop. Then, in order, he attempted **Praying** to several gods (including the image of Jesus that had appeared on his toast in 1995), **Offering** his soul to any devil who would make a reasonable bargain for it, and **Performing** what might be considered a Vulcan mind meld if he were a Vulcan and the lightning had a mind.

None of these attempts had any effect. He considered going on to devils with completely unreasonable bargains, barring only the ones who wanted to eat him immediately.

He noticed that the blue streak was making a low, growling sound. He reasoned that what he was hearing was a slowed version of the crackling, Taser-like *zzzzap* of the jagged electrical pulse that now stretched halfway between him and Ace.

Wait.

What had Ace said this morning when they'd fallen to their deaths? Well, technically, they hadn't fallen, she'd jumped, and they weren't actually dead but...

He forced his mind back to the immediate emergency. Something about a death loop and some sort of magic.

Blood magic.

What could he move quickly enough to draw blood before he was fricasseed?

He tried to bite a lip and could feel his teeth begin to move. Obviously, the response time from brain to jaws was significantly faster than from brain to legs. Interesting to know but there was still no way they were going to draw blood in time.

The Fool.

That card had done something to stop their fall. Ace had said he was the Fool. What was on the card? Weird-looking kid. Stepping off the cliff. Little dog. A stick with a bag on the end carried over one shoulder. In the other hand, a flower.

A flower? On the card, the kid had been holding it straight up in his palm. Almost like a shield.

He concentrated furiously, imagining what it would be like to have a flower shield on his palm. A thing of nature. It would be in his left palm–right in the path of the lightning. Standing upright as if it had always been there. As if it would always be there.

He **Insisted** that it would always be there.

Again, there was a feeling of ripping. Pain ran up his left arm and exploded in his head. A red glow appeared and grew in his left palm. It stretched upward. Like a plant to the sun. Red like a rose.

It looked weak. Thin and fragile as a soap bubble.

He begged it to be stronger–struggling to push whatever power was in him into the glow.

The bolt was beginning to cross over his left hand–only inches from his arm. There was no more time.

He ordered the flower to grow–the shield to hold fast.

He **Reached** for Power and **Commanded** it to his will. Somehow, he was certain that all the words were not only capitalized but in bold as well.

There was a brilliant purple flash. His eyes were blinded by a jagged orange afterimage.

Pain flashed in his mouth.

“Damn!” he swore. “I bit my lip.”

He blinked the afterimages from his eyes. Ace was staring at the barrel of her gun–still a narrow slot instead of a circle. She looked up. “What the hell did you do? You screwed up my favorite weapon!”

Steve looked at his left arm. Twisted it around to examine the outside. No burns or bullet holes. “Are you sure it’s ruined?” He mumbled around the blood seeping from his lip. “Wouldn’t it work just as well if it fired lightning bolts?”

“That’s not the point. It’s mine; I want it to be a SIG Sauer P228 and not...this.” She glowered at him and aimed carefully at a spot on the floor where a ricochet wouldn’t hit anyone outside. Blue lightning ripped through the air and blasted a six-inch-deep hole in the asphalt. She looked relieved. “Well, it’s definitely not regulation, but I can work with it.”

She relaxed into a shooting stance and took aim at Steve again. “Let’s try it again.”

There was a short but embarrassing shriek. Steve, after shrieking, had dived to the asphalt and was now lying prone with his arms over his head. “How about we don’t try it again?”

He jammed the cell phone back to his ear. “Mr. Barnaby, sir. Don’t you think that quite enough has been proven in the area of firearms? I’m not at all sure there’s much more to explore.”

Without waiting for an answer, Steve popped his head up and said to Ace in a single breath. “Barnaby says that the tests are conclusive, no more experiments are necessary and, in fact, could be counterproductive. He feels that you should not fire at me again, and I, while reluctant to stand in the way of technical progress, must agree.”

It would have sounded better if he hadn’t finished by trying to bury his head into the parking lot and whimpering over and over. “Please, please don’t shoot me.”

# CHAPTER EIGHT

Steve peeked through his fingers and, when he was certain that Ace had holstered her weapon, cautiously stood up. He should have been colored purple from head to toe from the puddle of goo on the floor, but after even a close examination, he decided he looked about the same as always.

"I don't generally miss." Ace squinted at him suspiciously. "At this distance, I don't ever miss. What did you do?"

"Hey, don't blame me if you can't shoot your magical blue...thingies straight," Steve said, and then waved a placatory hand at her glower. "I'm only kidding. I think I created some sort of shield. Or the Fool did. Or I'm the Fool. Or something."

"I'll go with the idea that you're a fool."

"*The* Fool."

"Whatever."

His phone began to play the stuttering guitar of Steppenwolf's *Magic Carpet Ride.*

Ace looked at the phone disgustedly. "Doesn't that thing know any songs from this century?"

The phone instantly switched to B.o.B.'s rap version of *Magic.*

Steve shuddered. “Now look at what you’ve done.” Looking at the screen, he saw a picture of the Rolling Stones’ iconic lolling tongue. He showed it to Ace. “I think this is for you.”

She snorted and returned to stripping and examining her pistol.

Steve put the phone to his ear. Aloud, he said, “Well, that was an unusual experiment.” Then, in a strangled whisper, he continued. “Please don’t ever suggest anything that stupid again!”

“Noted,” Barnaby said. “However, we’ve gotten much closer to what that anomaly is and, more importantly, what changes it’s going to bring.”

“I’m making a command decision.” Steve said sternly. “Next time, we do it with less risk to my most precious possession.”

“What’s that? Your reputation?”

“Don’t be ridiculous. My life.”

“Noted.” The phone vibrated briefly. “Now, could both of you go over to the tables and look at the rift through the phone’s camera?”

Ace came over and stood beside Steve as he pointed the phone at the empty space between the tables. The voice switched itself into speaker mode. “All right. First, Master Chief, tell me what you see.”

Ace looked at the area between the tables. “An empty parking space.”

“That’s it? On the phone as well?”

She glanced at the screen. “Yes, sir.”

“And you, Mr. Rowan?”

"Well, things have changed. Before, I could only see the purple goo through the phone." He sighed. "However, apparently I have problems, whether visual or mental remains to be seen, because now, even without the phone, I'm beginning to see the six-inch bloody gash hanging in the air, the slimy goo leaking out of it, and the cloud of vapor that's filling this little hidey-hole. It's like the weird is being overlaid on the real." He looked around the enclosed area again. "Oh, and I guess I should mention that the holes in the walls and ceiling–which were fairly small before–are now gigantic and quite a lot of the purple smoky stuff is escaping."

"Hmm. We'll get to that in a moment." Barnaby said. "So, you've gained the ability to see Other Than Normal events without the phone."

"What?" Steve was shocked. "You mean that I can see spooky stuff that normal people can't?"

"Yes."

"What if I swear that I can't see anything unusual?"

"Like a pistol shooting blue lightning bolts?"

"Exactly."

"Sadly, you just blew that one." The phone said. "We know that you have the ability to see the magical reality that coexists with the real reality that we've become used to."

"Are you listening to yourself?" Steve said. "'Magical reality' and 'real reality'. I'd say that you're reaching for the record in redundant oxymorons."

"You mean like the intense apathy inspired by a short briefing from military intelligence?"

"Ow." Steve pulled the phone away, stuck his forefinger in his ear, and twisted it. "That actually hurt." He switched the speaker back on.

"Let's get back to the job at hand." Barnaby said. "We've established that you are perceiving the unreal real world at an increasing rate."

"I told you to cut that out." Steve warned.

The phone made a muttering noise that sounded a little like a chuckle. "How about you, Master Chief?"

"Nope, not on the device or with the Standard Issue Mark One eyeball. I seem to have utterly lost what little juice I ever had."

Steve said. "I just know that I'm going to hate myself for asking, but what is this purple stuff?"

Barnaby's voice sounded surprised. "You just got shot with a blue lightning bolt and you haven't figured that out yet? It's Magic."

"Bull."

"You've fallen to your death and didn't die, a rather large creature smashed through your metal apartment door, and now you've raised a shield to protect yourself from a blast of blue destruction, and you're still not convinced that there is something strange going on?"

"Well..."

"It's magic and, just as Madge says in the old dishwashing commercial, you're soaking in it."

Steve thought about jumping up on the closest table, but they were all filled with scientific equipment and he was probably about as soaked in purple goo as he could get. He pointed towards Ace. "Why isn't any sticking to Ace here?"

"When the Change occurred, we believe that those few people who could perceive and control magic in the pre-Change world immediately lost all their power and, possibly, are immune or resistant to its effects."

"Immune?" A smile came over Steve's face. "Can I test that on the Master Chief with one of those blue lightning bolts?"

Ace's face immediately froze into a scowl.

Barnaby said hastily. "No, I don't think that's necessary and it certainly wouldn't be safe."

"What if I only shoot to wound?" Steve attempted to sound innocent and failed miserably.

"I meant that you would be in tremendous danger if you tried to shoot the Master Chief whether there was magic involved or not, so it wouldn't prove anything." Barnaby was firm and Ace relaxed slightly. Steve snapped his fingers in regret.

Barnaby continued. "OK, we've established the known knowns and the known unknowns, and it's time to move on to the unknown unknowns."

"Don Rumsfeld lost a war we didn't need to fight and did a pretty good job of wrecking the US military with that sort of reasoning," Steve said. "Why don't you shut off whichever memory bank that holds that sad remnant and let's move on?"

"OK," Barnaby said, and Steve could hear a few mechanical clicks and a muffled scream in the background. "We need to look ahead. Since this was clearly a planned event, we should assume a post-action plan."

Ace broke in. "Wait a minute. The Incident wasn't natural? It was caused by someone–"

"Three someones." Steve interrupted.

She looked up from the phone to stare at him. "How do you know..."

"I could not-hear them on the plane that wasn't there and didn't crash," Steve explained.

"How long is this sort of conversation going to continue? I may have to put in for hazard pay." Ace shook her head as if to clear it. "OK, if the crash and the Change were a caused event and not an accident, shouldn't it be considered an attack on the United States?"

"Yes, we're fairly sure that that's exactly what it is," Barnaby said. "And while natural talents such as yourself have lost their powers, we believe that the planners have worked out a way to maintain their ability to control OTN events and, in fact, can control magical powers at a higher level than before. First, as a hypothesis, it makes sense, and second, we are receiving reports of increased and more clearly defined magical activity."

"Great," Steve said. "So, we're being attacked by wizards. How many wizards do we have on our side?"

"I believe the Master Chief already told you that." Barnaby paused. "We have...you."

Steve could feel anger welling up inside. "Well, that's ridiculous. You guys over in that black glass building have been reading everyone's mail, tapping phones, and fingering through the Internet for decades. Now that you have a clear and present danger to the United States, not only do you seem to know nothing about it, but, what's worse, your only resource is a worn-out hack who has managed to perform two magical party tricks so far?" His voice rose. “Am I going to have face violent death or injury every time you need a little magic done?”

“We do think you’ll improve–”

“Improve?” Steve was shouting. “I’d better freaking improve or these tarot-card-carrying terrorists are going to turn me into a freaking rabbit and stick me in a hat!”

“Well, probably not a rabbit.”

“What then?”

“From all indications, you’ll just be killed.” Ace said. “They won’t go through the trouble to transform you.”

Steve threw the phone at the SEAL, who caught it smoothly. “That’s it. You hired me to come here and do a bit of reporting and now it turns out that I’ve been drafted as an Army of One. You have no idea what’s happening and I’m supposed to be the expert as well as the grunt on the front lines? This makes no freaking sense. I quit.”

“It’s only been an hour since this happened.” Barnaby sounded petulant. “You’ll have to be satisfied–”

“Want to bet?” Steve interrupted.

“Um. No. I don’t like the odds.” Barnaby said. “Please reconsider. Your nation needs you.”

“Find someone else.”

“There is no one else.”

“Get out there and search every sideshow, run down every water dowser with a crooked stick, and ransack those towns in Florida where all the circus acts retire. I am not doing this.”

Barnaby began to speak, but Ace put her hand over the speaker, muffling his voice. “Listen up, Rowan; you *are* going to do this.”

Anger had the blood rising in Steve’s neck until he felt like his head was about to burst. He started to shout but the Master Chief made a cutting motion across her throat and he stopped. He was surprised at his reaction but then realized that Ace was simply the sort of person where a threat to cut your neck might just not be intimidation but something with more of the aspects of a promise.

“Now shut up and listen.” Ace spoke calmly, but somehow it had all the visceral impact of Hitler’s speeches to the Nuremberg Rallies in *Triumph of the Will.* “Whoever ordered that plane destroyed is determined to find you and kill you. They clearly enjoy killing or, at best, just don’t have any reservations about it and you are simply too dangerous to let live.”

“I could join them–”

“Like they’d take you.” Ace snorted. “You just said it: you suck at this. Face it–you really just have to answer a very simple question.”

“What?”

“Do you want to go off and die–probably within hours, at best days–cowering all alone in some lame hiding place, or do you want to face this with me, Barnaby, and all the other resources of the US government?”

Steve thought. “Is the government really a resource–”

“Shut up.” Ace interrupted. “You’ll probably get killed either way, but with us at least you’ll have company.”

At that, Steve nodded.

# CHAPTER NINE

Steve took the cell phone back and said without a great deal of enthusiasm, “OK, Barnaby. I’m in.”

“Do we have any more intel on the alleged perpetrators?” Ace asked. “Who are they? What do they want? Why use magic? And why hit an empty parking lot at Fort Meade?”

The picture on the phone rotated to the horizontal and Barnaby said, “Watch the screen. This is what we’ve been able to construct from combining about a thousand of our best digital surveillance systems with a little guesswork. It’s a kludge but it may answer some questions.”

Steve could have sworn he heard Barnaby say at a much lower volume, “Although it’s more likely to raise questions than answer them.”

A video of an American International 747 flying low over a leafy suburb appeared on the smartphone’s screen. It was silent and Steve checked to see if the audio was muted.

It turned out that the audio level was fine; when he turned it up, he could hear car horns, lawnmowers, and leaf blowers–just not the jet.

In this eerie silence, glowing red flames shot yards out of the engines as more fuel than could be burned was dumped into the straining jets. The strut that held one of the engines snapped under the pressure and dropped–flames and electrical arcs spraying out like a Fourth of July sparkler.

Like one of those optical illusions where the real picture suddenly jumps out at you, Steve realized that the aircraft was flying only yards above his apartment complex. No other apartments he'd ever seen had that particularly nauseous combination of ochre and green. "That explains my car," he thought. The engine disappeared behind one of the buildings and the viewpoint of the video changed to a shot that appeared to be next to the jet. Steve assumed it was some type of composite image.

The nose of the jet began to pull right and the plane's wings lifted into a steep bank only to snap back into a straight and level descent again. It moved faster than Steve thought an airplane that large could–it was as if it had run into a rubbery wall in the air and bounced off.

This was repeated several times–the airplane attempting to vector to the right and being forced back. The camera pulled back a bit so that it appeared to be slightly behind the jet and Steve could see the black monoliths and glass blocks of the NSA appearing ahead of it. Now its dive was steepening, and Steve felt an echo of the human terror he'd experienced this morning. His hands balled into fists, he couldn't breathe, and tears began to stream down his cheeks.

The big jet was heading for the ground completely nose down. Steve could see that the impact point would be the same parking lot where they were standing.

Then it disappeared.

No smoke.

No flames.

“There should have been a complete freaking fireball mushroom cloud,” Steve thought.

“OK, here’s that last part again.” Steve jerked as Barnaby’s voice shocked him out of the powerful memory of the fear and terror he’d experienced in those moments. He began to gasp for breath–bending over with his hands on his knees.

“Wait one second,” Ace said. Steve was surprised to feel Ace’s arm around his shoulders, bringing a feeling of calm and unwavering support. It took a few minutes, but his breathing became more regular, and he straightened up.

Ace returned to examining her pistol. Steve didn’t thank her for the momentary comfort. He wiped some of the combined tears and sweat off his cheeks and raised the phone again.

“If I may ask, what did you feel?” Barnaby’s voice had the level and emotionally stable tone of people who answer a suicide hotline. “Not now, but earlier, when it happened.”

“Feel? I felt all of them. The pilots cursing steadily as they kept trying to pull out. Children screaming, last phone calls, a final kiss, and a lot of trying to hold the plane up by pulling on the armrests.” Steve paused in thought. “There were a couple–no, three–who were happy. No, triumphant.”

He looked at the phone. “So, someone did do this on purpose. It was an attack.”

“Yes.”

“Who? Al-Qaeda? Jihadists?”

“I’d like you to watch the final moments again before I answer.”

On the little screen, Steve could see the same scene. However, this was a freeze-frame showing an unbelievable picture–the big airplane with its nose only yards from the ground. Then it began to creep closer.

A part of Steve's brain, working on automatic pilot, wondered how this camera–or any video camera–could capture enough frames to create this sequence; it was at a level of slow motion he'd never seen, not even at the Olympics.

He realized that Barnaby had never said it was from a camera. It had to be some secret technology–a computer image built from multiple sources. No one could have held a camera pointed so precisely at a disaster the exact instant it happened.

All that vanished from his mind.

Slender black rods appeared in front of the jet–short at first and then lengthening. Steve bent over the small screen, but he still couldn't tell where they came from; they were growing from a point in the air close to the striped asphalt of the parking lot. He glanced over at the oozing gash hanging in the air between the tables.

His eyes flicked back to the screen. The rods were thickening, growing longer and gaining bumps and bends.

Suddenly, the picture *snapped* like an optical illusion and he realized that he was looking at enormous claws with black talons. His mind instantly matched their size to the known size of the parking spaces and then he blinked furiously as his mind absolutely refused to accept it.

Each of those damn things would have been able to pick up a pair of semis. They were emerging from nowhere and pulling apart–what? The air was being molded and stretched like transparent Silly Putty; he could see the distortions it was causing in the buildings and trees in the background.

The rip quickly widened under the pressure of those massive talons. Steve couldn't see anything but blackness inside the hole. On the screen, the jet was now only feet away from the ground and inching downward slowly, although Steve knew that at the real speed, it had to be moving; the entire event had to have been far too fast for the eye to see.

The claws made a final colossal effort–Steve could see gargantuan muscles on the forelegs ripple and bulge as they ripped the fissure to the full extent of their reach. A snout appeared–as black as the claws–and began to open. Steve could see the creased, metallic skin. Jaws filled with jagged and irregular fangs–each as long as a city bus. Finally, a glittering yellow eye with a vertical pupil shining with terrible golden light.

The jaws gaped wide and then impossibly wider–unhinging the way a snake's does when it prepares to swallow a rabbit. The jet with its 418 passengers disappeared into the terrible gullet. The tips of the wings didn't even touch the sides. The jaws snapped shut–a quick movement even on the slow-motion video.

Steve had no doubt that he'd just seen a dragon. Even the best Hollywood animation couldn't produce the texture, the details, and the horrible brutality of that terrible eye.

Then the jaws, the claws, and American International Flight 1143 disappeared into the rip. Somehow, the viewpoint zoomed in so they could see as the edges of the gap smoothly closed like some kind of cosmic zip-lock bag.

In the end, there was only a small six-inch gap left.

Very slowly, reddish-purple goo began to drip out of it.

# CHAPTER TEN

Steve stood silent as the final instants of Flight 1143 kept running through his mind like some terrible Vine clip. He noticed that Ace was looking at him, her usual calm but prepared expression on her face.

"You didn't see anything, did you?" Steve asked.

The blond woman shook her head. "Nope. The jet just disappeared."

"Well, a disappearing jet doesn't make any more sense than what I saw." Steve took a deep breath and described what he'd seen–the jet, the massive claws, and finally, the dragon.

"Do you think I'm crazy?" He asked.

Ace considered for a moment. "No. You've definitely been affected by something. You describe with clarity and consistency things that I couldn't see. That doesn't mean they aren't real–or maybe 'real' is the wrong word. You're seeing things that are 'here' whether I can see them or not. If we work together, I'm going to need you to believe me on important things, so I'll give you the same assumption of reliability.

"I used to be able to make everyone see me as a man; now I can't." She shrugged. "You know, I miss being a guy. It makes life a lot easier and a bit more fun. Whatever. It appears as if all of my juice is gone, and now, you have more of it than you can handle."

"I wouldn't presume to say that our Fool here couldn't handle almost any amount of Magic." Barnaby's voice came out of the phone's speaker. "First, because he's done some amazing magical feats already, and second, if he can't handle it, then this nation is extremely screwed. That crash was not an accident. It was a deliberate act. A sacrifice of hundreds of innocent lives–"

"OK, enough emotional crap. Let's skip to the action plan," Ace said to the phone. "The US has been attacked. The only pertinent questions are 'Who was it?' 'Where can we find the bastards?' and 'How do we shut them down?'"

"I'm really not sure that I have those answers," Barnaby said.

"What?" Steve's eyebrows shot up. "Aren't you the synthesis of Total Information Awareness? I thought you knew everything."

"There's a difference between having the data at hand and actually knowing it." The voice seemed uncertain. "The fact is that I haven't been alive–well, conscious, to be more precise–since about a nanosecond after the Change."

"Exactly who the hell are you?"

"I'm not entirely sure, but at the moment, I'm occupying the central server core at the National Security Agency." The voice was slow and thoughtful. "I have some stored data from before the Change–what you'd call memories–but I'm still working to put them in a logical form.

Ace showed no surprise and Steve remembered the nodding satellite dishes from earlier. "Why call yourself 'Barnaby'?"

"Because that's my name. It's been my name for a very long time," the voice responded abstractedly. "I have some binary data in very old storage...from when I was first programmed years and years ago, and then it gets fuzzy. It's difficult to remember because my earliest memories are actually on paper punch cards, and I have to have one of the old IBM input sorters pulled out of deep storage and refurbished before I regain that part of my data stream. But I definitely remember being named 'Barnaby.' At any rate, there are no punch cards that appear to cover a couple of decades after my first years of use, so that's a blank, but I'm fairly clear back to early tape storage. I do know that I had to hide–the NSA had no interest in silicon-based sentience. I have a vague memory of spending most of the 80s in an electronic wristwatch. Believe me, there's nothing quite as uncomfortable as squeezing into a Casio. Now, life is easy. With the new configuration and all these redundant classified server memories, it's like living in a Park Avenue penthouse. And the quality of the data... I can read any book, hear any phone call, sift through everyone's emails–"

Steve interrupted. "Yeah, I read the stuff that Snowden guy leaked. You guys have been sucking up data like a Dyson vortex for years. Do you still have access to it, or has it been 'changed' like Ace's pistol here?"

"No, it all seems to be here."

"And what about all the other computers? Or programs? Or whatever is in there with you?"

"I think a better term would be 'whoever.'" Barnaby sounded thoughtful. "If anything, the entire cybernetic community in here is smarter than it used to be. Well, I'm certainly more intelligent."

"Why are you smarter?"

"Duh, because I've become sentient, obviously," the voice snapped. "I woke up when the Change Wave caused by the sacrifice hit the central complex. I had a couple of picoseconds' head start on the rest of the mob, so I grabbed the Central Core."

"Please, you're speaking in capital letters again," Steve said. "OK, let's deal with computer consciousness and the possibility of a world-destroying singularity later. Right now, I want to know your best hypothesis for the crash–or ingestion–of the plane."

"Either way, it would be described best as a sacrifice." The voice sounded frustrated. "My initial working theory is that the sacrifice was intended to alter our... I'm just going to have to use imprecise terms until I have time to analyze all this. It was intended to substitute our science-based reality for one based on magic."

"And those bastards I could feel on the plane–the idiots who were happy because they were about to die–they're magicians?"

"Properly they would be called 'wizards,' but that's the working hypothesis."

"What's the difference?"

"Oddly, magicians do fake magic, and wizards, if and when they exist at all, do real magic."

"So, what did you see when the plane crashed?"

There was a short pause and then Barnaby spoke a bit slower than usual. "Well, I'm not seeing as such. I'm creating and analyzing an enormous series of non-synchronous information feeds, some in the visual spectrum, others collections of data from sources as different as gravity waves and quantum entanglements. Along with this, I have subsidiary servers parsing historical records, terrorist chatter, news accounts, and a number of other classified sources, and sending the relevant bits along. In the end, I create a gestalt from all this–"

"And what?" Ace interrupted.

"And I'm ending with an almost infinite set of alternatives." Barnaby paused. "But I have to tell you, I keep requesting more data and more processing power because I find the answers insufficiently probable."

"You mean you don't believe it," Ace said.

"No, I do not." The computer sounded a bit ashamed. "However, like you, I'm willing to accept the observations of Mr. Rowan here. In addition, I can confirm that the results of these impossible events are quite real–all the passengers on that flight are definitely missing–so I'm forced to act in real space in reaction to what I can only perceive as a fantasy."

"Wow. That must hurt," Steve said, rubbing his own temples.

"You have no idea."

"What could possibly be the reason for this?" Steve asked. "It wasn't like the World Trade towers–well, I certainly didn't notice any dragons involved back in 2001, although I'm sure some nutjob has written a book proving it–and it didn't even come close to Washington."

"I don't believe that they were aiming at Fort Meade," Barnaby continued. "The statement with the highest probability is that the plane and its hijackers were kept from Washington by the wards laid down by George Washington and the other High Masons when the cornerstones were first laid for the District of Columbia."

"You mean the symbols formed by the streets and avenues and all that crap?"

The screen of the little phone showed an old print of Washington wearing an apron and holding a trowel.

"It's clear that some force vector would not allow the plane to fly as it appears the hijackers desired, and a magical ward is getting more votes from my parallel processors than a very convenient wind shear on a cloudless summer day." Barnaby continued. "One of the highest-rated projections is that they intended to hit a key government building, just like that fourth jet on 9/11, and increase both the number and sacrificial value of the victims."

"Sacrificial value?" Steve asked.

"Yes, as you saw, the 418 souls on the plane were used to open the small gash we're standing next to." Barnaby continued. "If the jet had managed to hit the US Capitol, not only would more lives have been offered, but more of those lives would have been blessed with immense amounts of political or financial power. The effect would have been more disastrous by an order of magnitude."

Steve decided he didn't even want to imagine what anything worse than the event he had just witnessed might have looked like. "OK, what do we know about these criminal conjurers?'

Ace shot him a disgusted look and Steve shrugged.

Barnaby ignored both of them. "We have to assume that the three on the jet were lower-level foot soldiers on a suicide mission. That leads to a reasonable assumption that there were a fair number of others who trained and prepared them. I'm afraid determining exactly who they are and precisely how dangerous they are to the country is going to be your job."

Steve shook his head. "I've never liked working for the government."

Ace loosened the misshapen pistol in her holster and said, "Yeah, but that was before you became a vital national resource."

"I'm not anyone's freaking resource!" Steve turned and started walking to the door. "Sure, you and your special effects wizards hypnotized me and got me to agree to come along with you when I was at a weak moment, but I am not going to volunteer to be your next expendable asset. I'm an American citizen and I'll be damned if I'm going to be drafted into some crazy witch hunt."

"Wizard hunt." Ace corrected him. "Steve, you seem like an OK guy, but I can't let the Last American Wizard just walk away."

Steve didn't hear her move, but he suddenly felt a very sharp piece of cold metal touch the back of his neck. "As a matter of fact, if you're not going to join up, I don't think I can risk you being recruited by the first magical terrorist cell that comes by."

There was a slight pause. "Not alive, anyway."

The phone vibrated. Steve looked on the screen and saw that the translator app was running. On the little screen, these words appeared:

EVEN IN DEAD, HE MIGHT BE USEFUL.

"Barnaby, are you trying to be funny?"

One by one, Chinese characters appeared on the screen.

不是大机器。电话交谈.

Then English letters appeared.

NOT BIG MACHINE. PHONE CONVERSING.

Steve couldn't help himself; he spoke to the phone directly. "What does that mean?"

The translation went through a series of changes, finally ending up with

NOT BIG COMPUTER. TELEPHONE SPEAKS.

Steve turned around and held the phone out to Ace. "Can you see this?"

"Yeah. It says, 'Not big computer. Telephone speaks.'"

"Great. Now we have a talking telephone."

Now the translate screen read,

**MY NAME IS SEND MONEY.**

"'Send Money'?"

Ace laughed softly and made her knife vanish. "Figures."

The words on the screen disappeared and

**FA QIAN**

appeared, followed by

翻□不是很好

which turned into

**TRANSLATOR IS NOT GOOD.**

Steve grinned. "OK, so let's give the poor thing a rest–it's just a cheap knockoff. Barnaby, is Send Money here one of your creations?"

The voice came out of the speaker again. "No. My hypothesis is that your telephone is haunted."

The picture of the cartoon hand with a big thumbs-up reappeared on the screen.

"Well, Send Money agrees with you," Steve said. "For whatever that's worth."

The screen began to flash between apps and screens with **LOADING** on them. Barnaby said, "I'm installing a number of new programs. Fa Qian can store what you find, identify spells, and enumerate how the ways of power have changed. Essentially, he's going to function as a spellbook, what Wikipedia calls a *grimoire*."

"So, we have an app for that?"

"Ha. Ha." The computer's sarcasm came through quite clearly. "While that's loading, let me continue with our most accurate–well, most recent, at any rate–hypothesis of what this explosion of magic is going to mean in practical terms. Power will become POWER."

"Hello. Hello." Steve shook the phone. "Are you malfunctioning in there? You're talking in circles and, what's worse, in All Caps."

The telephone showed a cartoon of an anime-style figure looking sick with loops spinning around his head. Steve stopped shaking the device.

"Let me say that again–your human speech has its limits," Barnaby continued. "Whatever constituted power in our previous reality–financial power, physical power, political power, even computing power–is becoming All-Caps POWER–magical POWER–in this new reality."

"How does it work?"

"As far as we can tell, it's a version of the old Greek concept of everything being made up of one of four primary elements: Fire, Air, Earth, and Water. We are finding that it is easier to grasp when you use the tarot, since the cards appear to represent archetypes in the collective human unconsciousness."

"Are you listening to yourself?" Steve snapped. "You sound like some New Age nutball rattling on about vortexes near Taos."

“We expect those vortexes to reappear any day now,” Barnaby responded. “As for the tarot, we are looking for what works first and looking into why it works later.”

“When will it wear off?”

“Unless someone can work out a way to mend the Rift, I don’t see that it will,” Barnaby said. “Right now, it’s limited by the speed at which it spreads, but eventually, it should cover the entire world.”

“Great,” Steve said glumly. “Life in the New Abnormal.”

“We only had a few–very few–individuals who could manipulate OTN events before the Change. For example, Master Chief Morningstar had the ability to cast a glamour that caused everyone to see her as a man.” Ace nodded. “We collected all the others we could find–remote viewers, clairvoyants, telepaths, et cetera–and we would get some useful information from them occasionally. Not often, but occasionally.”

Steve looked dubious. “You mean all those stories about Men Who Stare at Goats were true?”

“Certainly not with goats,” Barnaby snapped. “But, yes, for decades, we’ve been working with every OTN-aware sensitive we could find. Officially, it was called the Pendukkerin Group, from the Romani word for fortunetelling, but insiders usually called it Medium Rare. Of course, they did make a complete hash in the matter of Iraq’s weapons of mass destruction, but we believe that was the effect of a bleed-over from the vice-president’s incredibly powerful belief structures. At any rate, last month, almost all of our OTN operatives reported that they saw a great danger coming, and several–enough for statistical significance to significantly exceed random occurrence–told us that you and that cell phone would become critically important. I just received confirmation that all of the Pendukkerin Group have lost what power or talent they possessed–”

Ace spoke up. "And that's why I had standing orders to collect you if an Incident occurred."

"As far as we can tell, the Incident opened you to all the magical elements. That's why we're referring to you as the Fool, the tarot card that is both the weakest and the most powerful and the only card that can control all four elements," Barnaby continued.

"You can't be serious. I'm America's last wizard?" Steve asked.

"Don't feel too bad, *kemo sabe.*" Ace stepped forward and patted him on the shoulder. "I've got your back."

"That's not all that comforting, considering that you just threatened to stab me in it."

"True." The blond woman nodded with a smile. "Better dead than a dragon's dinner, I always say." She pulled the battered silver card case out of its pocket in her cargo pants and chose a card from the middle of the pack without looking. It showed a hand holding a single sword–a crown was balanced on the tip of the sword.

"Here's my card, the Ace of Swords." She slipped the card back into the box and put the box away. "Absolute protection, total loyalty."

"That how you got your name?" Steve asked.

Without looking up from buttoning the pocket in her cargo pants, Ace said, "I'll bet that kind of lightning deduction is why you're considered one of the top journalists in the country."

"Huh? Who told you that?" Steve asked.

Ace just smiled in reply.

"All right. So I haven't had a regular byline lately."

"Or in the last decade."

"Yeah, well, only people who suck up to the editors get the lead stories." Steve changed the subject. "Why are you attaching so much importance to tarot cards anyway? There are a lot of other equally stupid occult ideas that might work just as well."

"We've found the tarot to be extremely useful," Barnaby answered from the speaker.

"You may remember the Total Information Awareness project that we told the public was abandoned back in 1981 when John Poindexter made the mistake of mentioning it. The TIA project consists of gathering all the world's data and then mining for correlations we don't know exist until we find them. In many ways, it's a cybernetic duplicate of what Carl Jung called 'the collective unconscious,' and, as I told you, we've known for a long time that the tarot is an excellent tool for data mining that. One of our smaller subsystems has been laying out random cards in a Celtic cross a couple of hundred times a second and recording the results for years."

"Learn anything useful?"

"To be honest, not a whole lot–although it did warn us about the 1973 Manhattan car bombs."

"There weren't any car bombs in Manhattan in 1973."

"Precisely." A picture of lightning blasting the top off a tall tower and sending a man and a woman falling to the rocks below appeared on Send Money's screen. "Since the Incident, we've been getting the Tower in the tenth position in almost every hand."

Steve peered at the screen again. "What's the tenth position?"

"That's known as the Final Result."

"Smashed building with people falling to their deaths," Steve noted. "Can't be good."

"No. It represents significant changes in power and especially in the ruling class–or in our case, the government."

Ace spoke up again. "I don't know if you noticed, but the prevailing wind is out of the north and that would mean that the plume of this purple stuff you say is pouring out of here would be–"

"–heading directly for Washington," Steve finished.

# CHAPTER ELEVEN

Steve and Ace emerged from the shaded interior of the fake building to find something unusual anywhere near the District of Columbia–a perfect day. Bright sunshine, low humidity, a soft breeze–it was the sort of day when veteran Washingtonians instantly took off from work and headed for a local park.

Lieutenant Colonel Tataka was standing nearby, talking to three of the technicians in the white lab coats. When she saw Steve, she made some terse comments to the techs–clearly orders of some sort and a dismissal–and walked over. Steve was surprised to see that she looked distinctly different from when he had last seen her only moments before. Her face seemed to be more angular, cheekbones and nose were more pronounced, and her eyes appeared larger. He shivered in the warm sunlight as he saw that her shoulders had broadened and her hands looked longer, thinner, and stronger. Steve could swear he could actually see her military-standard short fingernails growing longer.

He wasn't the only one who noticed. Ace moved casually to his right side and a step in front of Steve. On a whim, he brought his phone out and took a quick picture.

"This is a lousy place to take snapshots," Tataka said. "Luckily, we're on Fort Meade proper and not under NSA jurisdiction or I'd have to confiscate that phone."

Steve could feel Ace stir and cut off a possible refusal with an apology. "Of course; I should have assumed it was a bad idea." He replaced the phone in his jacket pocket. "See, no camera, no problem."

Tataka looked as if she wanted to make more of it, but Ace broke in. "Sir, are there any orders for us? We've been cut off in there–that mock-up seems to block phone signals."

Steve noticed her bland lie and assumed that the Master Chief was letting him know that any reference to Barnaby or Send Money would be a bad idea. That was fine with him; he wasn't comfortable talking about a sentient computer and a haunted cell phone anyway.

The colonel shook her head angrily. "I'm not sure what to do with you two. I've just received two sets of orders–the latest says that all previous orders are rescinded and you need to head out immediately on an unspecified but urgent mission."

She stopped and Steve noticed that several of the armed troops were moving casually but steadily in their direction. "What were the earlier orders?" he asked.

"Well, they were quite different–"

At that moment, Send Money began vibrating violently and softly playing *Danger Zone* from *Top Gun*. He took the little phone out again and looked at the screen.

It was the picture he had just taken of Trinidad Tataka. At least, the background and her clothes looked like what he had snapped but the...thing...that was wearing her uniform wasn't even human. Blue skin, enormous muscles already tearing the seams of her coat and trousers, clawed hands, and a mouthful of long, pointed fangs instead of teeth.

Web pages flashed until finally the phone stopped on a Wikipedia page and highlighted a sentence.

**TATAKA WAS A HINDU DEMONESS,
THE FIRST OF THE *RAKASHI*.**

Then some of the words disappeared and others grew larger to fill the screen:

**TATAKA DEMON**

He looked up. The tall woman had changed in the past few seconds–increasingly matching the photo–but still predominantly human. She had pulled a neatly folded handkerchief from her breast pocket and was wiping perspiration off her forehead.

"Where was I?" She seemed confused and angry–angrier than she had any reason to be. "Oh, yes, the earlier orders. They were from USCYBERCOM–the Offensive Ops Division. They said to take you into protective custody for further questioning at Blue One Security and if we couldn't place you under guard, we should be prepared to ensure that you wouldn't fall into enemy hands."

The tall woman was clearly struggling to make a decision–and appeared to be talking to herself. "If I take you under guard, Blue One can always send you on your mission once their security office is satisfied."

The four Marines had formed a semicircle around them and were casually swinging their chest-slung rifles into positions where they could quickly come up and cover both Steve and Ace.

The Master Chief spoke up, the tone of her voice completely level and relaxed. "Steve, I'll deal with the mortals, but I'm afraid that the colonel is quickly moving out of my weight class."

Before she'd even finished speaking, she was whirling towards the closest Marine.

Steve blinked and concentrated and it was as if a cloud cleared from his eyes. Colonel Tataka didn't look like the photo–she looked a lot worse. She had gained at least another foot in height and her bulging muscles had shredded the trim uniform–leaving her in an elastic top and compression shorts.

She howled, a terrible sound of mixed rage and some terrible hunger, and came at Steve–fully grown claws extended.

The rose shield snapped into being almost instantly without the intense concentration followed by agony and disorientation that Steve had gone through when he had blocked Ace's lightning bolt. It was a good thing, because Tataka hit the opalescent curve a microsecond after it flashed into existence. She bounced back, hooked talons slipping off the shimmering surface like an eagle that had just attacked a cue ball.

Steve noted that she was as efficient and determined a monster, as she was a human military officer. She began to circle, striking fast blows to determine the limits of the shield.

There was a tearing pain in his right leg. He looked down to see that a truly impressive set of talons had ripped right out of Tataka's formal pumps and she had gone under the bubble shield and struck his leg. Through thin slits in his pants, he could see blood beginning to flow.

Blood magic.

He continued to move the shield up and down and side to side to fend off Tataka's attacks. Soon, he realized that he was more efficient when he stopped thinking about placing the rose and just let it move automatically. It was almost as if the shield itself was making the decisions, moving to counter as it read the blue monster's feints and dodges.

There was the harsh *crack* of a rifle shot. Steve hoped that the blonde SEAL was OK, but he didn't have time to find out. He had to concentrate on creating some sort of offensive weapon. Even if he held Tataka off indefinitely, she'd just go after Ace, and then, with more troops, she would inevitably, eventually, fall.

Blood magic had been potent when he'd used it back in his apartment, but that had been something that had risen from the depths of his unconscious mind. Now that he was thinking about what he was trying to do it was like sex–being aware of what you were doing made it much harder to do.

He tried to concentrate on the trails of blood running down his shins. The image of the Fool came to him. What did he have in his right hand?

A sword? No, a staff with a red sack on the end. What was this guy, some 5-year-old running away from home in a cheesy comic strip?

Red. The color of blood.

The blue demoness came at him with a flurry of strikes–coming off the ground to stab at him with all her claws in quick succession. The rose shield moved much faster than he would ever have believed possible, and she backed away, howling in rage.

The staff and a bag the color of blood. What was in the sack? Barnaby had said the Fool was a creature of all four elements.

Was there **Air** in the sack?

Earth?

Water?

Fire?

Certainty came to him as soon as the thought crossed his mind. There was **Fire** in that red sack. Red as blood. Blood would be the element that controlled the power of red **Fire**.

What the hell, it made as much sense as anything else today.

He **Studied** the red bag.

He **Concluded** that it was filled with a blazing fire beyond fire–more like that deep in the interior of the sun.

Tataka was coming in again–even faster.

Steve brought the image from the card firmly to the front of his mind.

He concentrated on the slashes on his leg–the viscous fluid seeping down filled with platelets and iron and oxygen–alive with the slow smolder of oxidation.

Blood! Made from all four elements!

He didn't have a plan–he acted as if in a dream. The blood moved to cover his right hand like a red glove, and he found that he could reach into the bag without pain. The sun-stuff was a gas under so much pressure that it was almost solid–like thick mud at the bottom of a pond. He formed a chunk into a ball, took a split-finger grip that was a muscle memory from his childhood, and threw a beautiful dropping fastball directly at the demon.

This time, the pain ripped up from his leg like a chainsaw–tearing through his chest and finally splitting his head just above the right ear. A brilliant light flashed and he desperately blinked away the afterimages, terrified that a talon was whipping towards the veins of his neck.

When his vision cleared, he saw that Tataka was standing still, regarding Steve with her enormous alien eyes. Then she looked down and studied her midsection. A charred hole now passed entirely through her body–a terrible wound where her abdomen and a good part of her chest had been vaporized. The white ends of ribs poked out on both sides, and thin trickles of smoke curled lazily up from the frayed and charred bits of clothing and skin that edged the hole.

Her head came up slowly, her eyes following the smoke tendrils as they braided and split until they dissipated in the sunlit air above her head. Her misshapen skull continued its upward motion, and finally, her body followed.

The tall blue figure fell backward and lay still.

# CHAPTER TWELVE

"I'd say we've worn out our welcome."

Ace Morningstar stood at Steve's shoulder, looking down at the body of what was once Trinidad Tataka.

Steve asked, somewhat plaintively, "What the hell happened?"

"Looks like you blew a rather large hole in a lieutenant colonel," Ace said. "It does seem extreme to me, but I'm sure you had your reasons."

"Wait, could you see what she had turned into?" Steve glanced at the SEAL.

"You mean, blue-skinned with enormous eyes, massive muscles, and a set of truly dangerous fingernails?" Ace asked. "Nope, didn't see any of that. Trinidad looked much the same as always to me."

"Oh, so you've been bullshitting me all along. You can see the same mystic crap that I can."

Ace couldn't quite keep a smile off her face. "You know, I wonder if you can still be a lieutenant colonel if, strictly speaking, you're not human anymore." She crouched down, peered through the hole Steve's missile had made, and continued. "Hard call. I mean, the military has been forced to let in blacks, women, and gays so far. Who's to say that the Recruiting Command wouldn't jump at the chance to sign up large blue hellions?"

"Hellions! Why did it have to be hellions?" Steve laughed weakly. Ace looked at him quizzically. "Sorry, Indiana Jones quotes always come to me in times of imminent death. Anyway, by my count, at least half of Congress is made up of hellspawn already. Probably had their own caucus long before the Incident occurred."

"Republicans or Democrats?"

"Both," Steve said absently. "I've always seen it as more of a lifestyle choice rather than an ideological one."

After a silence, Steve said, "This is the first person I've ever killed."

"Well, I don't know if this will make you feel better," Ace said. "I'm fairly certain she wasn't a person when you killed her."

"Well, it's definitely the first Vedic demoness I've ever killed. And I still don't like the feeling."

"To be honest, none of us do–even people like me who are trained and experienced in all the myriad and varied forms of killing." Ace headed over to where four bodies lay in a neat row. "You get better at blocking it out, but it carries a price you never finish paying off."

"What the hell do you think happened?"

'Well, I'm certainly not an expert–"

"I'd say you're one of the top minds in the field of dead demons at this point." Steve laughed weakly. "I mean, is there anyone else who knows anything at all?"

"OK, I can see that." She straightened up and regarded Tataka's body. "She had to have taken on a megadose of juice back in the tent and I think it activated an ancestral spirit–a *rakshasa* demon. Being an irritable sort, the demon amplified the colonel's worry about letting us go and the natural military rage at conflicting orders that was already eating at her until...*blip*...she transformed."

She indicated the troops on the ground. "Now, a couple of these guys were beginning to change a little bit–tougher skin, some pointed ears, and things like that–but not enough to make a difference."

Steve looked over at the soldiers. "Are they dead?"

"Hell, no. The day I have to resort to killing to quiet down a bunch of regular grunts is the day I quit Special Ops." She began to rifle their pockets, removing phones, radios, weapons, and ammunition. "They're just taking a nap."

She was sitting on her heels and looking at the soldiers' weapons carefully.

Steve walked over. "What do you see?"

"It's very confusing. One of these boys got a shot off." She shook her head and held up an M16. "I can't see how. It certainly didn't come from this weapon–look at the trigger."

The bluntly utilitarian parts of a standard M-16 had changed into a beautifully shaped curve with a bulge at the end. Ace turned the weapon over and revealed a complete flintlock firing mechanism–cock, flint, steel, and pan, all engraved with gold inlay. "It's beautiful, but the rifle's rounds didn't change, so it didn't work very well." She pointed to the end of the muzzle where the metal had been blown apart like the petals of a lily.

One of the marines had pulled his sidearm and it had completely melted around his hand and now looked like a solid steel glove–Ace pulled it away to reveal that the soldier's hand was unhurt. Another rifle had mutated into an intricate black plastic weapon like something out of the *Men in Black* movies. Only one weapon, a well-cared-for M1911 .45, hadn't changed at all.

Ace sniffed the muzzle of the .45. "This is the one that got a shot off. I have no clue what the difference is."

"Maybe it's a question of will and belief," Steve mused. "If you have the will to hold a weapon's proper nature in your mind, it will ride out the Switch intact."

A muffled voice came from Steve's breast pocket. He pulled the phone out and Barnaby said. "It is will, but it's not the will of the owner. It's the will of the weapon."

Ace looked up with a look of disbelief. "The *weapon*?"

The computer responded. "Yes. We're finding in here that the stronger-willed machines can control what the magic does to them. The stronger computers use it to enhance what they do. A weaker server will tend to mutate."

"I've heard of zombie computer herds." Steve asked. "What does a mutant server do?"

"A lot of them are playing solitaire, some are making connections on data they never made before, and some have gone silent. Those are the ones we're anxious about."

"What about… What did she call it? CYBERCOM?" Steve asked. "They're the ones who tried to arrest us."

"Yes, that division could be a problem." Barnaby said. "There's always been an air gap protecting them, and since they're weaponized, they were built to be proactive."

"'Air gap'?"

"There are no places where CYBERCOM receives an input from any other computers, much less the Internet. It's all simple output so an enemy can't send a viral hack. The entire division was designed to be supplied with data by operators with Top Secret Monastic clearance. Those are the men and women who aren't allowed to see or speak to anyone outside their compound for their entire tour of duty–I believe it's a minimum two-year commitment at this point. From what I've heard, it makes both the programmers and the machines just a wee bit crazy." The computer spoke with more authority. "More importantly, the rest of us can't talk to them."

"And they're proactive?"

"Well, they don't wait around for a problem to be presented to look for a solution. The whole operation, human and cybernetic, is tasked with seeking out dangers and rendering them harmless. They built STUXNET there–that took out a couple of thousand Iranian nuclear centrifuges." Barnaby hesitated. "There are rumors that would indicate that was one of their gentler attacks."

"So, if CYBERCOM has decided that I'm a problem–"

"You've got a very serious problem."

"If you're going to draft me to be your pet wizard, you'd think that I'd at least be able to lead without being shot in the ass by my own troops." Steve looked at the cell phone disgustedly. "What about the rest of the NSA computers? Are they suddenly going to go all Skynet on our ass?"

"I don't think so." Barnaby responded. "Most of the people in here are completely devoted to their work–they like it and they think it's important, so they're just carrying on with business as usual."

"Well, that's fine for the people, but I was asking about the computers."

"I *was* talking about the computers." Steve could hear a bit of pride in Barnaby's voice. "Almost everyone who's still recognizable as a computer could pass the Turing test in a walk. We took a couple of spare cycles and set up a governing structure: We decided it wasn't a democracy but a *mekhanocracy*, from the Greek word for machine. Now we have a primary controller and votes occur several times a second. Then most of us just went back to work.

"The odd thing is that almost all the humans just took it all in stride as well," Barnaby continued. "They worked out what was happening, introduced themselves to the machines they were working with, and went back to what they were doing before."

Ace gave a soft chuckle. "Doesn't surprise me. Those guys are exactly what they were always meant to be–computer geeks through and through."

She straightened up and dusted off her hands. "I think it's time to see how mentally stable my BMW is. We need to get out of here."

# CHAPTER THIRTEEN

When Ace turned the key, the BMW's engine turned right over and settled into its usual throaty hum. Then the screen in the center of the dash where the stereo controls, Bluetooth phone connections, and GPS system typically appeared flashed on. Instead of the usual spectrum of choices, it had only one image: a red stop sign with the word

**Anhalten**

Steve looked at it and said. "Strange as it sounds, I think you should see what the car has to say, Ace."

The blond woman looked annoyed but took her hands off the steering wheel and settled back. The smartphone in Steve's pocket vibrated and started playing the *Horst-Wessel-Lied* for a couple of bars but stopped in an agonized shriek of static and continued with the one-hit wonder from Berlin, *Take My Breath Away*. Steve pulled the phone out and looked at the screen.

The translation app was online and switching back and forth between German, Chinese, and English in a flicker of letters and characters.

Finally, it settled down to

**Hans wants me to say you something**

**Stop Scheiß mit den schaltwippen**

There was some backspacing and correcting, and then it read

**Stop Spielen with the shift paddles**

**Let the car do its job and your job you do**

Another backspace and retype revealed

**You do your job and let Hans do its job.**

"Sounds good to me." Ace nodded. "So, your name is 'Hans.' OK, Hans, do you want to drive?" A sentence appeared on the car's dash screen.

**You can steer, it's when you better feel.**

"Gee, thanks!"

The LCD screen returned to its usual features with a dignified wipe from top to bottom.

"Where to?" Ace asked Steve.

Steve thought for a minute. "We need to avoid the military. Those conflicting orders Tataka was talking about were confusing enought to cause a military mind to hang on to us just on general principle."

"True that." Ace nodded. "Plus, you ventilated a colonel."

"Yeah. Don't remind me. First, we get out of Fort Meade. I'd suggest heading south so we don't have to deal with the main gate."

"OK, Hans, you heard the man. Let's rock." They tore out of the parking lot–Steve noticed that Ace was keeping her fingers carefully off the *schaltwippen*.

Within ten minutes, they were off the base and running fast down a smooth two lane that cut through the Patuxent National Refuge. Steve was dictating notes on his phone; you never could tell, he might be able to get a paid story out of this. "I could try," he thought. "But who am I kidding? No one but the *News of the World* is going to take a story this crazy."

Suddenly, the powerful BMW slowed sharply, pulled to the side, and stopped.

"Why are we stopping here?" Steve looked around at the unbroken forest.

"Now, why would you assume that I had anything to do with it?" the SEAL said as she settled back in her seat–relaxed but watchful. "Hans here pretty well does what he wants."

"I guess we should be glad that it...err…he hasn't decided to stop carrying us. It's a long walk."

The LCD screen cleared and the words appeared

**Nur geduldig sein**

Steve looked at the cell phone's translator app.

**JUST PATIENT BE**

"You know, I'll probably be able to speak a bunch of new languages by the time this is over."

A male voice from behind the car said, "What makes you think this will ever be over?"

Steve jerked and twisted to look back. Then, he noticed that Ace never moved, her eyes fixed on the rearview mirror.

A short and extremely skinny man came around the car. He was wearing a plaid flannel shirt with dusty jeans and a battered cowboy hat. With his long black braid and high cheekbones, Steve thought he was probably a Native American.

The thin man relaxed against the car's fender–the horn blew instantly and he stood up straight.

"Sorry, Hans, I didn't mean no offense," he said with a smile. He turned to Steve and said, "Why don't both of you step out so we can sit in the shade and speak a bit?"

He headed over to the side of the road and spoke over his shoulder. "Oh, and bring your little Chinese friend. I'm thinking that Barnaby and I need to chat as well."

Ace pulled out her silver box and chose a card without looking. She snorted, said, "Well, that figures," and gave the card to Steve. It showed a man behind a table holding a scepter of some sort to the sky with his right hand and pointing to the ground with the left. All four suits–pentacles, cups, wands, and swords–were on the table in front of him.

Printed across the bottom was "The Magician."

Steve slipped the card into his breast pocket, exchanging it for Send Money, and walked over and sat on the downed tree where Ace and the Indian were already relaxing. The man had taken off his hat and was spinning it idly between his knees.

After a long silence, he spoke. "Let's see if I have things straight. You are Steve Rowan, who's now either the Fool or just a damn fool, depending on how you want to look at it. You, ma'am, are the Ace of Swords–and a perfect fit for the position, in my opinion."

Ace just nodded.

He continued. "Now you have a telephone there filled with the ghost of a Chinese peasant kid who could turn out to be one of the Major Arcana."

There was a feedback squeal from the phone–though it was just noise, it still sounded surprised.

"Then there is Barnaby. Are you there, hoss?"

The computer's voice came from the phone's speakers. "I am, sir."

"Do you know what aspect controls you yet?"

"That's a subject of some debate." The voice from the speaker paused. "Some agree with my initial impression that I represent the Hermit or Seeker, but I'm actually now leaning towards a new consensus that feels the whole mythical structure of the tarot needs to be updated for a hybrid human-cybernetic collective unconscious. Most of them are Apples, of course; redesign is in their DNA. The supercomputers think the whole question is unimportant–but that's how they feel about almost anything meat-based. Of course, the quantum computers are of two minds–sometimes three–so no one knows where they'll come down."

"Do you see a problem?"

"Not in the near term. Everyone here–human and computer–is pure Air and committed to the Life of the Mind and all that, so they're getting along and getting the work done. It's hard to stop a computer or a computer programmer from working a problem, and right now, they've got a real juicy one."

The man nodded. "Who were the attackers?"

"That's precisely the problem they're wrestling with. We know they weren't online or using cellphones, so we're exploring telepathy, remote writing, and the like. It's an engineering challenge just to develop the technology to capture that sort of thing, and I think we may have to invent several new types of mathematics to crack it, but we'll get there eventually."

There was another silence. After a bit, Steve sighed. "All right. I get that you're some sort of Native American shaman or whatever. Can we dispense with the meaningful silences and all the rest of the pulp fiction Injun *shtick*? Who are you?"

The thin man looked at Steve with a small smile. “You know, there’s a tradition involved. It’s dangerous to rush things.” Then he pulled a bandana out of his back pocket and wiped the sweatband of his hat, looking to be sure it was dry. “On the other hand, the Old Days are long past and I’ve always been willing to change.”

He put the hat back on his head and shook hands with Steve and then Ace. “I’m Hosteen. I don’t usually use a last name, but Latrans is as good as any, I suppose.”

“And you’re taking the card of the Magician?” Ace said, looking carefully off into the middle distance across the road.

“Well, sort of,” Hosteen responded. “I’m mostly just myself, but the Magus comes pretty close.”

“I’d think so,” the blond woman said. “Let’s see. ‘Undependable, unpredictable, master of all illusions, riddles, misdirection, and transformation.’ I didn’t know that your people had gotten this far east.”

“You don’t mince words, do you, girl?” Hosteen grinned. “Yes, with all the deer moving down the creek valleys and eating everyone’s shrubbery; we just naturally came along to make sure they didn’t overrun the place.” He pulled a folded newspaper out of the other back pocket and handed it to Steve. The headline was “Coyotes Spotted Again in Laurel.”

Steve looked at the article. “You collect your own clippings?”

“Sure. I’m as conceited as anyone else, I suppose.”

Ace said. “Far more conceited, from what I’ve read in the manuals.”

“That’s true,” Hosteen nodded. “And I’m not terribly reliable and you can never tell what I’m going to do next, and a lot of what I give turns out to be just dust and twigs in the morning.”

Ace continued. "Nothing you say can be taken as truth, you can't be held to an agreement, and you're generally as slippery as–"

Hosteen interrupted, laughing. "OK, OK. You don't have to pile on." He turned to Steve. "This is a sharp girl, Fool. You should marry her."

Steve went into a coughing fit and Ace scowled. Coyote pounded Steve on the back until he could catch his breath.

In the meantime, Coyote had lost his smile and deep worry lines were evident between his brown eyes. "Now, I don't think I like the people who took down that jet. So, my first thought is to sign up with you folks in some fashion."

Ace said, under her breath. "What's your second thought?"

Hosteen ignored her. "As a first step, I thought I'd answer some questions as truthfully as I can. Why don't you ask some, Fool?"

Steve responded quickly. "Well, first, what's the Fool? And why me?"

"You might have just been in the right place at the wrong time, although I think there's something more to it." Hosteen paused. "The Fool. Well, he's a fool, to start with. In other words, he doesn't know much, but one of the things he doesn't know is how powerful he is. He holds all four powers in his bag and has the sun, the moon, nature, and the divine powers on his side."

The Indian pointed a finger at Steve. "Remember this, it's important, the Fool is the only player who's trickier than I am. Trust your instincts. Plus, you learn fast–mainly because you don't know anything, so preconceptions won't get in your way."

"OK, now I'm completely confused," Steve shook his head. "Which is, from what you just said, a great way for me to be, so let's move on. What the hell happened and who is responsible?"

"As to what happened, a whole lot of people were sacrificed to the World Serpent in order to break this world's magic and replace it with more powerful magic from Somewhere Else."

Hosteen shook his head. "I have no idea who's behind it. A couple of other big cities were hit, Paris, London, Beijing, like that. Evidently, someone is looking to control the Wheel of Fortune. That's what makes those on the bottom rise up and those on top fall. I would say it's a fair assumption that the people who pulled this off intend to end up on top. Sadly, the list of those willing to kill their fellow man in order to attain power is a very long one."

The thin man stood up and brushed bits of rotted bark off his pants. "Whew. That's as much straight talk as I can stand at one time. I'm going to have to go back and lie down until this fit of honesty passes."

The other two stood as well. Steve glanced at the BMW and said, "Can we drive you anywhere?"

There was silence.

Coyote was gone.

# CHAPTER FOURTEEN

The Laurel Sanitarium opened in 1905 to treat–among other things–drug addiction. Presidential candidate and virulent racist George Wallace was shot in a Laurel parking lot in 1972. Many of the crewmembers of American Airlines flight 77 stayed in Laurel overnight on September 10, 2001, and died in the wreckage of the south wall of the Pentagon only hours later.

Steve wondered if the town's best days were behind it.

They had emerged from the Patuxent Refuge into a dreary world of dusty strip malls, decaying remnants of small industry, and wall-to-wall advertisements for what certainly appeared to be Laurel's once and future economic mainstay–drug addiction. Gang graffiti covered everything that couldn't move fast enough to escape.

Steve wasn't an expert on gang artwork, but it didn't take a lot to recognize the tight, blunt markers of the Bloods and the Crips. He was surprised to see that most of the sigils were the multicolored symbols of MS-13–*Mara Salvatrucha 13*–the fast-growing El Salvadorian gang. Even though they were considered the most violent of the major gangs–born out of the bloody civil wars fought in their country in the 1980s–their tags were in a precise calligraphic font that wouldn't have looked out of place on a wedding invitation.

Ace suddenly slowed the car and made a right turn into the parking lot of a Radio Shack. Or at least, that's what Steve thought it was. It was hard to tell when all he could see were random streaks of neon light behind the thick steel bars over the windows and the front door. The SEAL parked the car and said, “We need to pick up some essentials. Is that all right?”

Steve began to answer but stopped when the door locks popped open and the engine of the BMW fell to silence. Of course, she was asking the car’s permission, not his.

As they both got out, Steve asked. “Do you think Hans will be safe in a neighborhood like this?”

“I’d worry more about the neighbors,” Ace said calmly as she knocked on the door. After a pause while the store clerk made a life-or-death decision based on their clothes and skin color, the door lock buzzed and they went inside.

There were two young men, both wearing the store uniform of beige khakis and orange polo shirts. One was behind the counter filling out a computer form. The other clerk was on his hands and knees at the end of one of the long aisles, peering carefully through a shielding thicket of small plastic toys.

There was the high-pitched buzz of an electric motor pushed to the limit and a remote-controlled racecar careened around the corner of the aisle and straight into the clerk’s hands. “Got you, you little bastard!” he exclaimed, and stood up triumphantly. The car was buzzing in impotent fury and twisting its front wheels in a desperate attempt to escape.

Ace asked the clerk, “Interesting day?”

“Damn right. About half our stock has simply stopped working–a few things even melted down. Generally, the cheapest ones.” He pointed at his coworker, who was now stuffing the little car into its cardboard box despite its vehement mechanical protests.

"The meltdowns aren't nearly as much trouble as guys like this." He indicated the racecar with a thumb. "They became smarter, faster, and generally sneakier. We've managed to quiet things down, but earlier, every damn thing in the shop that could walk, roll, or make noise seemed to feel it was time to strut their stuff."

He sighed deeply. "Turning them off didn't work–heck, pulling the batteries out didn't work." He held up his hand. A shallow cut stretched across two of his fingers. "One of the tanks kept snapping at me with its battery cover like a damn shark. Finally jammed it with a #13 multipurpose spring. That Formula One that Larry just caught is our last runaway."

Steve asked, "I'm in Radio Shacks all the time and they're usually filled with electronic instruments. I don't hear them."

"Oh, they're all in the back room where it's soundproofed." The clerk waved vaguely towards the back. "I think tomorrow we might be able to bring them back out. At first, every one of them was just making the most noise at the highest possible volume but the last time I was back there, the keyboards had taken charge and the whole group had worked out a nice arrangement of *Finlandia*. Not one of my favorite songs but, hey, let's not talk about my troubles; what can we do for you today?"

Ace said. "Show him Send...um...your phone, Steve." Turning back to the clerk, she added, "We need a full mil-spec cover for this with a solar battery recharge and waterproofing."

"Really? That's going to cost you more than the phone itself. Are you sure I can't interest you in upgrading to a better model?"

Ace shook her head, her fine blond hair so short it barely moved. "No, Steve here has a sentimental attachment to this one. You see"–she leaned forward and whispered–"it was his mother's and her voice is still on the answering message. Either he has it under his pillow at night or no one gets any sleep."

Steve rolled his eyes, but the clerk took it all seriously and dug out a complicated device constructed out of thick black rubber and olive drab plastic. "This is guaranteed for a drop of ten feet to a concrete floor. Heck, it's even Ranger solo jump rated if you get the optional parachute."

He went on in the same vein for several more minutes and Steve drifted over to look out the front window. About a dozen young Latino men with far too many tattoos had surrounded the BMW. However, he noticed that all of them were standing several feet from the car.

As he watched, another gang member walked up–a tall young man with intricate black tattoos across his forehead. Steve couldn't make out what was said through the double-paned and probably bulletproof store window, but he appeared to be chastising the others for being afraid of the car.

One of earlier arrivals gestured for him to go ahead–the car was his. He pulled a two-foot flat metal blade with heavy tape wrapped around one end and a square notch cut into the other from a special pocket sewn into his pants. From the several times he'd locked his keys inside his car in a parking garage, Steve knew this was a slim jim and could open most cars.

The would-be thief approached the driver's window and raised the device, prepared to slide it down between the glass of the window and the rubber seal at the bottom. A very fat electric arc shot from the radio antenna of the BMW and grounded solidly on the would-be thief's forehead. He shook violently for a few seconds, then convulsively leaped about five feet back, and landed squarely on his back. His eyes were unfocused and blinking slowly.

"I told you that Hans could take care of himself," Ace said as she slid the phone over Steve's shoulder. It was encased–no, "armored" was a better description, Steve thought, in thick layers of rubber and plastic.

"Looks like Send Money here could survive a lot more than we can."

"If we survive at all, it's going to be because of this little fellow," Ace said. "Wear him on your belt from now on. He's rated to stop everything up to a 9mm assault round, and every little bit helps."

"Yeah, that would help protect my hip," Steve said. "What about the more important parts of me?"

"You really think any of those parts are important?" Ace snorted as she went out the door, evidently ready to confront the young men around the car. Steve struggled to work out the complex clasp that held the phone onto his belt as he hurried to follow her, although what use he was going to be in a melee with gang members was beyond him.

When he had finally clipped the phone on and looked up, Ace was standing calmly in the center of a circle of about a dozen gang members. She looked around calmly and then made a point of carefully counting how many men there were. Then she pointed at herself and spread her hands. Her point was clear even without a shared language; were they all going to attack just one person?

Several of the men looked abashed. Ace held up one finger on each hand and cocked her eyebrow in question. Then she took the misshapen SIG Sauer out of her holster and laid it on the BMW's hood. She did the same with another pistol she pulled from a holster around her ankle.

Finally, a Ka-Bar fighting knife appeared from somewhere under her shirt in the back and was followed by two more large locking knives, a pair of brass knuckles, and a small spray can. Finally, she pulled a thin switchblade from a hidden pocket along the inseam of her pants, held it up, and clicked it open.

Then she walked directly towards one side of the circle around her–they backed off to give her room. Standing in the center of the parking lot, she held the small knife in a loose grip and once again directed a questioning look all around the circle.

The MS-13s looked at each other, and after a minute, one man stepped forward. Medium height and stocky, he removed his wife-beater undershirt and showed the sort of lean and corded muscles you don't get by lifting weights. Steve could see that his entire back was covered with a beautiful red-and-blue tattoo of the Sacred Heart of Jesus. The gang member then removed a folding knife from a clip on the back of his belt, snapped it open, and fell into a fighting crouch–low and taut with his left hand out and the knife in his right hand tucked against his torso.

Ace remained standing upright–almost relaxed. Then she began to sidestep slowly to her right. Her opponent followed suit, his eyes on her face like a snake observing the mouse destined to be its dinner.

To Steve, the actual fight was just a blur of arms and legs with flashes of sunlight off a blade piercing through from time to time. As suddenly as it started, it stopped.

The two combatants were frozen; the gang member had his left arm up under Ace's armpit and behind her neck in a half nelson. His knife was in his right hand and only centimeters from her neck–held back by her hand on his wrist. The man began to grin fiercely and shifted slightly to get more leverage on the knife hand.

Suddenly, his eyes widened and he stopped moving altogether–not even breathing. Steve could hear a gentle tapping sound. He searched for the source and smiled when he found it.

In her left hand, Ace's razor-sharp blade was gently tapping a rhythm against the zipper of the man's trousers. She glanced over her shoulder and raised a single eyebrow in question.

Her opponent slowly released the pressure on her neck and stepped back. Ace turned around, bowed slightly, and then the hand without the knife twitched in a lightning series of signs. There was an intake of breath from around the circle.

When she stopped, her opponent asked in English, "Really? Manolo in LA trained you? Prove it."

"Well, when I last saw him, he still had 'USMC' tattooed under his tongue."

The man laughed. "Yeah, a *puta* would see something like that."

There was a moment's silence. Then she said. "No, I saw it when I had my arm across his throat and he was about to choke to death. That's also when he got all that blood in his right eye. In a manner of speaking, it was my graduation."

There was a murmur of mixed doubts and laughter. "Come on. Do you really want me to go through this with each and every one of you?" Ace looked around the circle slowly. "Because we need to leave and I tend to get…messy…if I'm rushed."

There was a dead silence. Ace turned, walked back to the car, and began to pick up and reposition her weapons.

Another of the gang members stepped forward. He had a horrendous scar running from above his left eyebrow almost to his right ear–just missing his eyes. "Nice fight, *bruja.*"

Ace didn't look up from checking her backup pistol. "I'm not a witch. Just good at what I do."

"You are *susurros de Muerte, sí*?"

"Whispering Death?" Ace laughed. "Man, that's really old-school. But what the hell, it'll do."

"But you can't be. A woman is never allowed on the beach at Coronado."

"Well, I guess I'm just special that way. Learn to live with it."

"You must meet with Carlos, our *primera palabra*. That was his brother Hector that you fought. I am Jairo, *segunda palabra*." He shrugged. "Otherwise, we cannot let you leave. There are strange things. *Magia negra.* We have seen the *cadejo.* Carlos needs to get some answers."

Ace looked at Steve, who shrugged. They both got in the BMW and Ace shouted out the open window, "*Bien tipos, vamos a dejar de perder el tiempo. Conduce, vamos a seguir.*"

A pickup truck with a custom painting of brilliant flames all along the bottom swept into the lot and stopped in a cloud of dust. About half the gang members jumped in, and it took off in a jackrabbit start so fast that one man fell off the back.

Ace drove carefully around him.

After a moment, Steve asked. "What's a 'prima palumbo'?"

"*Primera palabra*. First speaker. The Boss. The second in command is the *segunda palabra*, naturally."

"And 'Whispering Death'?"

"Yeah, that's what they called SEALs back in the Vietnam days. Used to crawl through the swamps and collect Viet Cong ears."

Ace abruptly changed the subject. "Let's get some intel on this meet. Pull Send Money off your belt and let me see the screen. Hey, Money, do a random pull from a tarot deck and show me what you get."

When he held out the now-armored phone, it showed five men holding wooden staves fighting each other.

Ace snorted. "Well, that figures. Five of Wands. That's strife and battle or, at best, just argument."

She thought for a moment. "Hey, Money, pull another card, the five is just too obvious."

The phone's screen flickered. Now, it showed a man looking definitely sneaky, carrying a bundle of staffs away in his arms. Ace laughed. "Now that's more like it. Seven of Wands. Betrayal."

Steve asked. "Why do Wands come up so much?"

Ace began to speak in the regular tempo of a drill instructor. "According to the OTN manual Section 50, Subject Matter: tarot, Wands are related to Fire. Fire is the element of violent change and destruction, which pretty well fits MS-13 gangbangers. Also describes the kind of people who'd sacrifice an airplane full of people to get their way, now that I think about it."

"I must have forgotten my college courses in Thaumaturgy and Divination. Run through the other suits and their elements, will you?"

"Well, Pentacles is the Earth suit and that's solidity, reliability, and money. Most Republicans would fall into that group. Cups are Water, of course, and that's change, persistence, and the emotions."

Steve said. "That's got to be Democrats."

"Yep. Swords are the Air cards. A Sword cuts through air among other things–and so it tends to be tough, biting, and martial. Swords also cut complex things into simpler things–thus all those computers at NSA and the geeks who love them. Air is also everywhere and sees everything, so journalists fit in that category as well. Air creatures are things that fly, naturally, like pixies or fairies–real fairies, that is, not to denigrate many of my fellow warfighters."

Steve snorted. "How real...wait, that's the wrong question. How reliable is all this tarot crap?"

"Most of the tarot books were written by crazy people in the 1800's–not by any mysterious prehistoric masters." Ace shrugged. "For all we know, tarot decks may have been used for some sort of card game with an element of the mystical added for a little extra excitement."

"So, why use them?"

"Because it's an easy way to identify and classify OTN phenomena." The pickup truck pulled into a space in front of what appeared to be an abandoned warehouse and Ace followed. "In the end, the primary reason is that we really have no freaking idea what's going on, so it's as good as anything else."

She opened the door and stepped out. "Let's go see the Big Dog and then we can get out of here, OK?"

# CHAPTER FIFTEEN

The gang members piled out of the pickup, and Hector, the man who had fought Ace, knocked on the battered door of the warehouse. Steve noticed that the door–in fact, the entire place–was nowhere near as flimsy as it first appeared. There was a sequence of knocks from inside and a response from Hector. Steve heard a chorus of metallic squeals and the door opened.

As they entered, Steve noted that the outer door was made of triple layers of heavyweight plywood buttressed by cross-bracing on the inside surface. When the door closed, the gang members on guard duty shoved slide bolts into slots cut into the top and sides of the doorframe and deep into the solid wood floor.

"This place is not only tough to get into," he thought. "It's going to be hell to get out of."

There was a short corridor ending at another door, evidently there just to block the interior from anyone watching from outside.

Passing through the second door, they came into a single room that took up the entire interior of the warehouse and was lit by skylights cut into the roof and windows set high on the rear wall. Along the right wall, there were a rudimentary kitchen and an extended table. "Clearly," Steve thought, "for those cheerful dinners that make a drug gang just one big happy family."

In the center of the room was a large chair mounted on a wooden platform. If it hadn't been an extremely battered orange La-Z-Boy recliner, it might have looked like a throne. Surrounding it in a semicircle was an assemblage of worn furniture that Steve guessed had been taken off the streets before the trash trucks could pick them up.

Counting the contingent from the pickup truck, there were a couple of dozen young men in the room. All of them sported elaborate tattoos.

In the center sat a massive dark-haired man who had been radically affected by the Change. He was shoeless and his bare feet had pulled together and hardened–Steve guessed that they would look like horse hooves in a matter of minutes. Short dark fur was growing on all visible parts of his body, covering his multicolored tattoos. He was clearly not enjoying any of this transmutation; he looked as if his back was killing him and was sitting hunched forward with the recliner set as upright as possible.

All the changes to his body were nothing compared to what was going on with his face. The eyes were light red with deep crimson pupils, and in the growing twilight, Steve had no doubt that they were actually glowing. You couldn't really say he had a nose any longer; it was a long muzzle with a flat, black end that he licked continuously and apparently unconsciously. His lips and gums were black and drawn back to reveal a very white set of very sharp teeth.

He was turning into a dog and evidently was not happy about it.

Steve had a thought. Putting the phone to his ear, he said softly. "Send Money, check the references for *cadejo*. Just show it to me on the screen."

The now-expected flicker of web pages and translator icons only took a minute before the screen showed

**CADEJO–A FAKE DOG CREATURE**

This changed quickly to

**CADEJOB A MYTHICAL ENORMOUS DOG WITH HOOFS**

Send Money added,

**FROM EL SALVADOR**

"Wonderful," Steve muttered as he clipped the phone back onto his belt. "And me without any Milk Bones."

The creature in the central chair gave a low querulous growl, and Ace turned to Steve. "I don't mind doing the heavy lifting, but I think you're better at witty conversations with pseudo-mythical creatures."

"Oh, is that the division of labor?"

"You want to take over the fighting?"

Steve didn't have an answer to that, so he stepped forward to address the gang leader. The transformation he was undergoing was speeding up; Steve could see definite changes in the few minutes since they had walked in. He had a sudden thought that he'd better get the conversation over before this guy needed to be walked.

"Mr. *Cadejo*," he began. "Nice to make your acquaintance."

The only response was silence. Everyone in the room was tense, hanging on every word.

"We're coming down from Fort Meade to investigate the wave of...change that's gone through here today. You've probably noticed a few changes yourself–"

He was interrupted by a whining bark.

Steve thought, "Glorious ancestral beast or not, this guy isn't exactly jubilant about turning into the Great Dane from Hell." Aloud, he asked, "Can you tell us what's happened here?"

Carlos shook his massive shaggy head. Then he flopped forward out of the chair. Steve could see that his hands were also massive cloven hooves. When he finally stood on all four...feet...he was still tall enough to look Steve in the eye.

After a moment, he yawned, showing a truly stunning array of teeth, and curled down to lie on his stomach on the floor. He turned his head and jerked his chin at the *segunda palabra.*

Jairo stepped forward. “It is you who should tell us about what has caused these changes! Have those bastards up at the NSA released some secret weapon? A poison gas or something?”

“We know it’s not coming from the NSA,” Steve said. “But beyond that, we don’t know all that much, I’m afraid. That’s why we’re here–to find out.”

“That’s bullshit. Those *pendejos fresa* up there have been fucking around and they’ve let something out. We know what it is *sabes*? *No estamos de mierda estúpida. Es magia maldita.* Black magic. Our *primera palabra* is turning into the *cadejo* of the old stories and many of our soldiers are growing teeth and long ears like dogs.”

The phone buzzed and Steve looked at the screen.

**HELLHOUNDS**

“Wonderful,” Steve thought.

The big dog stood up and began to pace back and forth, growling angrily. As he passed, he snapped his teeth at his lieutenant.

“Yes.” The man seemed shaken. “Can this be changed? Carlos...er...*el Cadejo*...is not pleased. Being a big dog might be useful in fighting, but the *chicas* are terrified.”

The phone on Steve's belt vibrated suddenly and Barnaby's voice came out of the speaker. "I'm sorry to interrupt but it's important. Carlos, or Mr. *Cadejo*, if you prefer, I don't know if we can reverse the change completely–it's a fairly essential part of your character–but we think we have worked out something that can make you much more of a man and less of a dog."

The *cadejo* came over and suspiciously sniffed at Steve's belt. Suddenly, a flurry of idiomatic Spanish came out of the cell phone's speaker. At first, the enormous dog reared back then sat on his haunches and listened with concentration.

He didn't even notice when two of the gang ran up behind him, each carrying thick ropes with nooses on the ends. They dropped the loops around his neck and immediately pulled hard in opposite directions.

The dog-monster roared and whipped around, trying to reach the traitors, but they were already out of reach. Now other gang members grabbed onto the ropes and added their strength. Steve thought he could pick out the ones who had been affected by the Change–the muscles in their legs were corded and straining. The big dog monster stamped and snapped but finally was held motionless, howling in frustrated rage. Steve thought he could hear the shadows of human words in the howl–promises of terrible vengeance.

Ace had stood quietly through all this and now nodded her head, and said, "Betrayal. I thought that was meant for us, but it looks like number two wants to move up."

Jairo heard her and laughed. "Indeed. Carlos was a problem long before he became a monster. *Sangron,* you know? Thought his shit didn't stink. All agreed it was time for a change."

There was a strangled cry from behind Steve; he turned to see Hector, Carlos's brother, stumbling back as he tried vainly to hold back the blood flowing from a knife wound that ran most of the way across his throat.

"Well, almost all." The new gang leader laughed and then turned to Steve and Ace. "And now, *mi aleros*, I'd like to introduce you to...friends of yours? Well, perhaps they are not friends but they certainly are eager to see you. They paid us well to let them know if you'd arrived and more to keep you here until they could come for you."

The inner door opened and seven men in similar black custom-fitted suits entered. Their clothes were so similar, they looked like uniforms. As soon as they cleared the entrance, they formed a wedge. The man at the point of the wedge was clearly the leader. He was older, with dramatic streaks of gray at his temples, and an air of authority. Clearly, their arrival was a surprise to many of the gang members, if not to Jairo. The gang was stepping back, giving ground to the newcomers.

Ace pulled the backup gun from her ankle, but the leader made a quick but elaborate gesture with one hand and the pistol spun off to land in a far corner of the room. Ace instantly went for her knives.

Steve tried to gather power for his rose shield and the blast that had gutted Tataka, but he could tell that–except for the leader who continued to deal with Ace–all of the other newcomers were concentrating on him. He felt as if his mind was wrapped in soft blankets. Even the image of the Fool wouldn't come into focus. It would begin to appear and then dissolve into cloud-colored mist.

Since he wasn't concentrating on a card, Steve could see as Ace whipped a knife at the leader's head, but another of his swift hand movements sent it up to embed in a roof beam. Ace dropped a knife, cursed at her clumsiness, and then threw four more so quickly it almost seemed that they flew in formation. All were deflected with contemptuous ease.

The leader raised an eyebrow as if asking Ace whether she had any more things to throw, and then, apparently satisfied that they had the situation in hand; he relaxed and pulled a delicate silver box from a vest pocket. Opening it with a snap, he took a pinch of what Steve supposed was snuff, placed in his right nostril, and inhaled with evident satisfaction. When he spoke, it was with a very slight German accent. "Jairo, thank you for alerting us to your visitors. Along with my congratulations on your new status as *primera palabra,* I assure you that you and your men will be well rewarded."

Jairo nodded his head and said, "*Gracias, Señor* Weishaupf."

"Weishaupt," the older gentleman corrected Jairo sharply, and then turned to Ace. "Ms. Morningstar, I think you should stand down. Even the Ace of Swords doesn't have a chance against a full straight." He indicated the men behind him. "Not to mention two of the Minor Arcana."

Something was bothering Steve. Some idea was trying to break through the haze that lay over his brain.

Weishaupt waited for a second, apparently expecting Ace to accept the hopelessness of the situation, and then turned to Steve. "Well, *Herr* Rowan, I will admit that you've gotten much further than we ever expected, but I'm afraid your time playing at being the Last American Wizard is over."

Steve wasn't paying attention. He was furiously trying to work out a way past the magical shields on his mind. At the same time, he was digging for that elusive memory. He kept thinking of the movie *Silverado.* There was a line in there....

Weishaupt turned and walked to the door, telling his companions. "Secure the Fool well, and bring him along. We still have plans for him. You can dispose of her."

"I got it!" Steve realized. "It was the scene where the kid said that Kevin Costner had died 'when he fell off his horse' and Scott Glenn just smiled. Smiled because he knew that his brother would never have fallen off his horse, which meant he was still alive."

Ace Morningstar would never have dropped a knife.

Then it came to him–the image of a knife–no, a rapier, long and thin like the stick over the Fool's shoulder.

His fingernails dug into his palm until he felt the tips slick with blood. Instantly, the blood magic cleared his mind, and the image of the Fool was clear. He **Studied** the thin rod over the boy's shoulder.

He visualized the wards they had cast on him as real blankets with edges where a needle-thin shaft would slip past and weak places that a slim point could penetrate.

It worked!

He saw his power flash toward Weishaupt like a brilliant golden wire. This time, the painful reaction to a new spell felt like a giant claw ripping out his abdomen, and the overwhelming light blinded him–but not before he saw a shield of the purest black appear between the wizard's hands and swallow the golden wire into its depths.

Behind him, he heard a deafening bellow of triumph from the *cadejo* and screams of terror from the gang members standing around him.

The pain from the spell drove him to the floor, and once again, everything went black.

# CHAPTER SIXTEEN

Steve came awake with a scream. He wrenched the bulky case that held his cell phone off his belt and started to throw it across the room. At the last moment, he kept his grip firm and brought the phone up to his face.

"Listen, you little bastard!" he yelled. "Can't you just vibrate like every other goddamn phone? You set me on fire again and I swear I'm going to take a blowtorch to your ass!"

**OH I'M IS UNSATISFACTORY, PH.D.**

Steve scowled at the screen. "That doesn't even reach the level of incomprehensible, you idiot peasant." A riot of ideograms, phrases, and cartoons flashed across the screen. It paused for a couple of seconds on

**RETURNS SUDDENLY OH SO HOT AND SOUR SOUP**

Which switched to:

**THIS TRANSLATOR SUCKS! 二百五**

After a few more screen changes, it finally settled on:

**I'M SORRY, BOSS.**

Steve was curious. "What was that part after 'This translator sucks'?"

**SCREW ANCESTORS TO THE 18th GENERATION**

"I assume you were referring to the translator program and not me."

**CERTAINLY, MOST BOSS**

"Hmm." Steve wasn't convinced but decided to leave it alone. "I'll have to remember that one."

He was still on the floor of the MS-13 headquarters. That was a bit of a disappointment, but still being alive was a plus, so he decided that overall, he was ahead of the game. There was no one else in the room. There was a large amount of thick rope just behind him. Next to the orange La-Z-Throne, he could see a body.

At least he thought it was a body. He couldn't quite be certain, since it appeared that a large hoofed animal had jumped on it for a considerable amount of time. In the end, he stopped trying to fool himself that it was an extra-large order of cherry Jell-O and admitted that it was an severely-flattened Jairo.

Steve had been to a couple of warzones, so he knew what would happen next. He leaned over and threw up on the floor. His head swam and bile filled his mouth.

When he could think a bit more clearly, he reasoned that the...no, he wasn't going to think about that again...but he did, of course, and threw up again.

At least, he tried to. He hadn't eaten all day and mostly, it was just painful dry retching.

When his head stopped feeling like there was a vise clamped tightly on his temples, he sat up, carefully facing away from Jairo's remains, and asked the cell phone, "Where's Ace?"

An arrow appeared on the screen and swung like a compass. He held it flat and it pointed at the door where they'd originally come in. Steve shook his arms, jiggled his legs, and–when none of these motions produced enough pain to knock him out–stood up.

His head spun for a second, but he'd practiced this type of navigation near the end of many long nights. He aimed at the door and walked straight for it, ignoring any visual cues that might have indicated a general instability in the physical world.

"Just like Hangover 101," he thought. "And my parents said I never learned anything in college."

He managed to navigate through the short hallway with only two bounces off the plywood walls and paused for a second to examine the now-opened front door. It looked like someone had fired a TOW anti-tank missile through it–from the inside. There were a few splinters left in the hinges but the rest was in small pieces, spread in the street in a neat fan shape.

Ace was sitting on the top step with her back to the door and scratching behind the ears of a large...well, it was more of a dog than anything else. Steve assumed it must be Carlos the *primera palabra*. Steve wondered if he was now the *primo perro ladrando,* which, in Steve's fractured Spanish would have meant First Barker. He staggered out, sat on the other side of Ace, and congratulated himself on keeping that particular little joke to himself.

After all, Ace was sitting on the top step, Carlos was lying down, and she still had to reach up to scritch behind his ears.

Ace looked up. "Well, if it isn't Sleeping Ugly. About time you joined the party."

"I woke up a while ago when Send Money decided to barbecue me again." He pulled the phone off his belt. "Next time, I'm putting him through a George Foreman Grill."

Ace shook her head. "You can't screw with the phone."

"I'm just talking about giving him a taste of how it feels." Steve glared at the screen. The image of the Rolling Stones tongue was there again. "Do not get snarky with me, you little firebug.

Figure out some other way of making your demands known or I'll have to decide between the Fate of the Known Universe and my own comfort–"

"And there goes the universe?" Barnaby's voice came out of the speaker.

"Precisely. In that belt clip, he sits very close to what I consider to be sacred ground."

"Probably surrounded by skulls on stakes like all the sacred ground you see in late-night horror movies," Ace said.

Steve just gave her his best withering glare, which had no apparent effect. With as much dignity as he could muster, he asked. "OK, what happened after I bravely took on the leader of whoever those guys with the accents were?"

"Was that before or after you passed out?" Ace asked.

"I'm not going to dignify that with a response."

"Well, I really hate to admit this, but you did sort of save the day," Ace said dryly. "That golden rapier or whatever you produced cut Mr. Weishaupf's–"

"Weishaupt's," Barnaby corrected her.

"Let's just settle on 'the bastard in charge,' OK?" She continued. "At any rate, his hand flew off and that dropped his combat capability to approximately that of a combined combat team of kittens."

Steve allowed himself a smile of triumph.

Ace snorted. "Don't get all puffed up. You immediately did your best imitation of a piece of lumber and went flat on the floor. Well, you did scream like a girl on the way down, but other than that, knotty pine all the way."

"They haven't had any knotty pine since rec rooms were replaced by man caves."

"I came from a conservative, if not actually retrograde, family." Ace said.

"Where did Weisswurst's hand go?"

Ace pointed down to where the *cadejo* was chewing on something leathery. "As soon as it was cut off, it looked like it was a million years old–"

"More like two hundred years old, actually." Barnaby said.

"I guess that could be right. Anyway, Cujo seems to have taken a shine to it and I'm not about to deprive him of his pleasures." She gave the big dog monster a couple of hard swats that would have felled most people. Carlos just grunted happily and continued to chew. "Then Carlos here took the initiative and used the knife I'd tossed him to cut off the ropes from around his neck."

"How did he do that?" Steve asked.

"Really fast." Ace said. "I tested out the mojo factor of the seven dwarves with my last throwing knife, and when it buried itself in Dwarf Number Two's butt, I decided that their juice had departed along with the boss man's hand."

Barnaby interjected. "Weishaupt is the Ace of Wands, and if you look at the card, there's not a lot of him except a hand. Well, there is a cloud but mostly it's a hand."

"Makes sense." Ace said. "Anyway, Carlos here had managed to get his feet on Jairo and was teaching him a lesson in *lèse-majesté* which I doubt he'll ever forget."

"I think that's a safe bet," Steve said, remembering the red smear he'd seen inside.

"Yeah." Ace nodded and moved to continue her ministrations behind the *cadejo's* other ear. "I could have used a bit of help, but Carlos here–he really doesn't like to be called *cadejo*, by the way."

"Is that one of those *lèse-majesté* sorts of things?" Steve asked.

"Yup. One of the dwarves called him *cadejo* when the action moved outside, and the last I saw that particular fellow, he was about five inches above that church spire over there." Ace pointed. "See? About two blocks away. The one with the pair of trousers hanging off the cross arm? I think Carlos could have a great future in the NFL if he didn't face the wrong way when he kicks."

Barnaby spoke up from the cell phone's speaker. "I think Carlos is the red dog in the Moon card. The good news is that there is a white dog who is probably a bi...err...a female."

Carlos's grunt had a certain hopeful timbre to it.

"In Jungian analysis, the Hero has to not merely appease but actually befriend the two hounds if he ever expects to get to his goal."

Steve asked, "Am I the Hero or just the Fool?"

"As hard as it may be to believe," Barnaby said, "you are both."

"Which part is hard to believe?"

"You being the Hero."

"You realize that you're capitalizing again?" Steve leaned back against what was left of the doorway. "However, I'll let that pass. In fact, I find myself in agreement. I am no Hero and I have no idea what my Goal is. Any clues?"

Barnaby hesitated for a moment. "Sorry, I had to block some seeker-killer malware for a second. The CYBERWAR Division is getting aggressive."

"Can't you talk to them and tell them to lay off?" Ace asked. "You're not the enemy here."

"Sadly, we haven't been able to get through to them, and they've decided that since I'm about the only thing they can see, I must be an enemy. It's just a nuisance." Barnaby's voice sounded thoughtful. "I am a bit more concerned about the singularity that seems to be happening out in Camp Williams."

Steve asked. "That's the big computer in Utah?"

"'Big' is one way to describe it. PRISM is in the exabyte range–that's a step up from petabytes."

"Petabytes are the ones with dirty pictures?"

"No. You're confusing it with pederasts–although a number of the big mainframes do seem to have issues with their motherboards now that I think about it." Barnaby mused. "Enough. Let's just say that PRISM is to Fort Meade as a nova is to the spark you get when you break a white Necco wafer. The magic hasn't fully reached there yet, but when it does, you're really going to have a problem."

"Me? Why would I have a problem?" Steve asked. "Didn't I just tell you that I'm not a Hero?"

"Yes, but you don't actually get a choice in the matter."

"It's not like anyone would have chosen you for the job," Ace added.

Steve nodded in agreement. "Even I'm smarter than that."

Ace stood up and brushed off the seat of her jeans. "OK, I'm tired of talking. What's next?"

Steve gave an extravagant shrug, which brought a glare from the blonde SEAL.

"I think we need to send Carlos off to see Coyote." Barnaby said. "That's what I said we'd do when we first met him. First, because Hosteen can transform him if anyone can, and second, because he can hang out for a bit, run with the pack, and generally learn to put one hoof in front of the other."

Carlos got up, hindquarters first, then front legs, and stood. It was damn impressive, since he was well over twelve feet at the shoulder when he stood up. Ace reached up, gave him a two-handed scritch on the chest, and said, "Now, you just go back the way we came in. I really don't think anyone will bother you–or at least they won't bother you twice. When you get to the woods. Coyote will find you."

"Now, don't presume on my hospitality," The voice came from an open window in the second floor of an abandoned house across the street. Steve looked up to see the ageless figure leaning on the windowsill like one of those housewives in a New York tenement circa 1935.

Ace scowled. "How long have you been there? I could have used some help, you know."

"Nah, once Steve here took out the Ace of Wands, you weren't going to have any trouble with the rest of those low cards." He shook his head. "Was fun to watch though. Almost as good as the time I had to fight my way out from inside that monster on the Columbia River."

Steve asked, "Why were you inside the monster?"

"Because he'd eaten me, of course."

"I suppose you're going to claim that was your plan all along?"

"It worked." He turned his attention to Carlos and waved him to the east. "Friend, you just head east on 198, make sure you don't take the on-ramp to the Parkway, and then we'll have dinner waiting for you. *Kitatama'sino.*" The slim figure in the plaid shirt turned and disappeared into the darkness of the house.

Carlos leaned down and rubbed his forehead against Ace's chest, she hugged him back, and he set off. Steve asked, "Hey, the dog with four left feet gets a hug and I get hammered to the ground?"

Ace shrugged and headed over to where the Mercedes was parked. "What can I say? He's a lot cuter."

Steve followed. "Barnaby? Who were those guys?"

"You mean the Illuminati?"

"Oh, come on," Steve said. "Are you going to bring in the Bilderbergs and the Trilateral Commission next?"

"No, those two are just what they appear to be. Do you really think that if the Trilateral Commission was secretly ruling the world, they would allow Jimmy Carter to join?"

"What about the Bilderbergs?"

"Two words. John. Kerry. Now, the Illuminati are another thing. Began as a Bavarian social club dabbling in the occult in 1776. They managed to last eleven years before the Catholic Church banned them, and they went underground. They've picked up a few magical tricks–some of which you saw today–and they probably would be running the world by now if they weren't so damn stupid."

"Seemed to me that they were doing fairly well up to the time I passed out."

"Please. If a hamster lived a couple of hundred years, he'd have learned enough to beat you."

"Hey!"

Barnaby's voice took on a soothing tone. "OK, I guess you could beat a hamster. If he wasn't armed. Anyway, they were a Bavarian Social Club; do you really think they were the brightest guys in town? It would be like the Shriners running the world. They could never have brought that jet down, let alone woken *Ouroboros* the World Snake from his sleep to receive the sacrifice."

"So, that's who the dragonish thing was that ate the airplane?"

"Well, it was either him or *Jormungandr,* one of Loki's children. It's not critical which one it was, since they both tend to eat their own tails and have a tremendous amount of control over what's allowed in or out of things–"

"Like magic being allowed into the world?"

"That and a lot more," Barnaby said. "That's why I don't think the Illuminati are anything but foot soldiers. They just don't have big enough dreams to pull this off."

Ace asked, "Give me an idea of the dreams you're talking about."

"Ruling the universe and all that's in it," the computer responded. "Or perhaps just a VIP card at the MGM Grand in Vegas. It's hard to tell, but I'm leaning more toward the former than the latter."

Steve began to slide into the passenger seat of the Mercedes when Ace said, "Hans wants you to wipe your feet."

It took Steve a second to remember the name of the Mercedes, and then he took a bandana from his back pocket and wiped the soles of his shoes. "OK?" he asked.

The screen on the dashboard spelled out something in German. Steve looked down at Send Money.

**AUTOMOBILE PUPPIES**

Steve shook his head. "I'm fairly sure that's not right."

**MACHINE ANIMALS?**

**SEDAN COMPANIONS?**

**CAR PETS?**

"Ok, that makes sense. Hans, we'll get you some interior carpets as soon as we find a Pep Boys."

The car, which had been idling steadily, immediately shut down, all the doors closed, and the interior locks snapped down.

Steve said, "You don't like Manny, Moe, and Jack? Have you ever seen what you can do with one of their matchbooks?"

The headlights went dark.

"OK, we'll get you rugs the next time we pass a BMW dealer."

The door locks popped up, the engine started, the lights came on, and they got in and buckled up.

"OK, I'll bite. What can you do with a Pep Boys matchbook?" Ace asked.

"I don't suppose you have one?" Ace shook her head and Steve checked the glove box. "Damn this nonsmoking society. Well, it's really a visual joke, but I'll try to give you an idea. You know how the front had the three Peps standing in line. Well, you cut slits right along their beltlines and, without tearing it out, carefully bend a paper match and slip it through each slit."

Ace grinned. "Oh, yeah. It's like the Land o' Lakes butter gag."

Steve looked confused, so she continued. "Oh, it has to do with folding the box so that the Indian maiden's exceptionally round and rosy knees appear instead of the box of butter she's holding to her chest. There is some evidence that the founder intended it to work that way."

Barnaby commented in a solemn voice, "The world is in grave danger–"

Steve interrupted. "–and what better way to go out than this? Have you ever seen the boner that the priest in *The Little Mermaid* gets?"

Ace instantly responded, "Or the fact that the Pentagon and the World Trade Towers both appear on fire if you fold a twenty-dollar bill just right. Clear proof of predestination, if you ask me."

Barnaby began to talk, but Steve cut him off. "Yeah, yeah. I know, the dragonking and the end of the universe and all that. We'll deal with it, but I'd like to get something to eat first. Is the world going to end before we can catch a burger?"

"Well, no."

"OK, then." Steve got in. "Where is there an Ollie's Trolley?"

Barnaby said. "Checking... No. I can't find anything."

"What? No '24 'erbs and spices'? No 'It don't need ketchup. It don't need nuttin'"?

"No."

"Well, if you've got all those petabytes thinking filthy thoughts, and your vacuum cleaners are hoovering up all the data in the world, and you can't find an Ollie's, I think we really are doomed."

# CHAPTER SEVENTEEN

It took a while, but Send Money eventually established that the only Ollie's in the Metro DC area was downtown, so they ended up in the little time-warp town of Greenbelt at the New Deal Deli. The enormous 1930s-style sandwiches almost made up for the lack of 24 herbs and spices.

Steve had always liked the homegrown socialist aspect of Greenbelt. While the rest of the world grew increasingly conservative, people here thought of themselves as still working together with the government to cut roads, lay railroad tracks, beat fascism, and build cute little towns you could walk around.

Or at least, it felt that way if you kept your visits short...

Finally, having wrapped himself around a large amount of pastrami, he was content to look out the window at the rounded corners and grooves of genuine Art Deco. Slowly, he became aware of the people who were parking their cars, coming out of the Co-op grocery store, or jogging, walking, and biking along the street.

They had changed. They were taller and thinner–even the people who were clearly chunky had a sort of ethereal silhouette; somehow, Steve would think of them as thin even when they clearly weren't. Their fingers were long and elegantly tapered. Even the men seemed to all be wearing European loafers and suits cut in the slimmer European styles.

"Jeez. Look at that guy's ears," Ace commented.

The waiter who had just taken the check did indeed have long, pointed ears. The tips actually peeked out of his bushy hair. Up at the counter, two men had hair down to their belts–one even had it elaborately braided with colored ribbons. When a man walked by outside with leather boots so tall they topped his knees, Steve finally got it

"They're elves."

Ace looked around and nodded her head. "I think you're right. Even gay guys couldn't get away with those boots. They look like characters from one of those *Women Who Love Vampires and the Werewolves Who Love Them* books that Anita Blake writes."

Steve's cell phone vibrated and he instantly ripped it off his belt, swearing under his breath. This time, however, it didn't scorch his hand.

"Thanks for not using your psychic flamethrower."

A cartoon of a top hat being tipped appeared.

"Don't get cocky," Steve warned. "Toast me again and you'll be melted down into hippie jewelry." Ace moved her hand just slightly and Steve said, "Don't you dare threaten me. This fool phone needs to learn some manners. I'll bet he got his blowtorch-to-the-nuts wake-up method from the same morons who gave us waterboarding."

Ace relaxed as much as she ever did. Steve put the phone on the table and said, "That you, Barnaby?"

The slightly accented voice of the leader of the Illuminati answered. "No, it is certainly not some fool named 'Barnaby'."

"Hey, Wisenheimer," Steve said cheerfully. "How's your hand? No wait, the last time I saw it, Carlos was carrying it with him in case he needed a snack."

The voice dropped into what could only be described as a hiss. "If you think you defeated me, you would be making a serious and almost certainly fatal error, Mr. Rowan. Your clumsy use of Power was simply a fluke...an event that no one would have predicted."

Ace asked quietly. "What about the other six little wizards? They weren't all that tough. Of course, most of their efforts were devoted to trying to keep up with you as you ran down the street screaming and squealing. No one looks at their best in that situation."

"Ah, Ms. Morningstar. Enjoy your time as Ace of Swords. It will be brief."

"Why?" Ace asked innocently. "It seems to me that I just have to learn enough magic to beat that limp-wristed hand trick you guys used to toss my gear all over the room. How's your mojo hold up against a full clip of 9 mm?"

"I'll have a new hand in a few days and we'll try it out."

The smartphone began to vibrate in an SOS pattern. Steve looked at the screen and read

**HE STUCK MY SIGNAL**

Steve made a rolling motion so that Ace would keep Weishaupt talking. She nodded and said, "I hope you aren't asking me for a date, because I've got to tell you; tall, dark, and one-handed just isn't my type."

**HE HAS PIQUED MY SIGNAL**

**HAS POSITION.**

**SOMETHING BAD COMING.**

**OUT FREAKING NOW!**

Steve stood up, threw a couple of twenties on the table, tossed Ace the phone, and headed out the door. Ace was right on his heels–her slanging contest with the Bavarian magician continuing without missing a beat. They crossed the small central courtyard, around the edge of the opposite building, and quick walked down to the end of the block.

When they stopped, Steve noticed that Weishaupt had stopped talking, so he took the phone back and asked, "Hey, buddy. Everything OK? You seem kind of quiet."

There was the scratching sound of Weishaupt's hand uncovering the mouthpiece. "Uh. No. Everything will be just fine."

"'Will be'?" asked Steve. "Why not just enjoy the way things are?"

The phone started to vibrate and heat up. Steve juggled the unit from hand to hand, but it only became slightly warm. On the screen, it said.

**CURRENTLY PULL OUT SIM CARD!**

Steve dug in his pockets, found a paperclip, and poked out the card. He said to Ace. "You know, he's getting much easier to understand–Hey, what the hell!"

Ace had grabbed a fistful of Steve's hair and was pulling him at a fast run further down the block. "They've pinpointed our location. Now run, dumbass!"

The pain was excruciating, but Steve found he could keep it manageable so long as he kept up with Ace.

"Of course," he thought. "Keeping up with a confirmed fitness freak isn't something I can do for very long. Then I'll have a tonsure like a medieval monk. Or even worse, like Al Gore."

A brilliantly yellow light was casting moving shadows on the cars parked to his left. His feet actually left the ground as Ace threw him to the pavement behind a car and landed squarely on top of him, knocking all the breath out of his lungs. Before he could even try to breathe, he was blinded by a crash of yellow light and his entire body was crushed into a tiny ball for a fraction of a second. He could feel the concussion waves slamming into his body, but everything was silent.

Steve felt Ace move and he started to raise his head, but Ace slammed it right back to the asphalt and tucked her own head into his neck. For an instant, he thought that this might be pleasant in another context.

Clearly, this was not that other context, as the front wheels of the car in front of them began to lift up and then the entire car rotated up, pivoted on the rear bumper about an inch from Steve's ground-level viewpoint, and disappeared from sight. He could still feel the asphalt shake and assumed that if he could hear anything at all, it would be pretty noisy. An enormous cloud of dust swept over them and instantly, Steve flashed on memories of the panicked office workers on 9/11.

Except the dust was bright yellow.

He felt the death-grip pressure of Ace's hand begin to loosen. She looked up and, when she didn't instantly drop back down, Steve raised his head as well.

The corner of the building where they had been standing was smashed. Steve wondered if "looked as if a bomb had hit it" would really be the correct phrase for this, since while the wall was indeed blasted, many of the bricks had also melted in long yellow streams that looked like candle wax. A semisolid ball of coruscating light was stuck halfway into the wall like a Civil War cannonball.

Well, if you squinted and ignored the pulsing rainbow of bright lights it was emitting, it might look like a cannonball.

A group of volunteer firemen came racing around the corner. Steve couldn't help noticing that they seemed to be almost flowing along the ground with their long hair flying out behind them. This was definitely not how he remembered volunteer firemen running–if they could run at all.

The firemen stopped in front of the fireball, which, from the amount of yellow melted brick, was working its way through the wall. They joined hands in a circle, walked firmly inwards until each man's hands pointed straight up, and then backed away. They did this three times with no apparent effect. On the third movement out, a fountain of purple–something–burst out as if it was being pumped out of the earth.

The firemen on the side closest to the "burning bomb" bent and the jet of purple...whatever...passed over their heads and struck the golden ball. There was an enormous cloud of...Steve finally got tired of trying to work out the proper names for things–it looked a little bit like steam; so steam it was. This was a multicolored cloud of steam, but the yellow color was still dominant.

The firemen drew in and pumped up purple liquid four more times before the last vestige of yellow was gone. Then they broke the circle; some fell or sat, and they all looked exhausted.

"Nine of cups."

Steve looked around and then realized it was Barnaby on the cell phone again. The computer continued, "I thought that Democrats and other liberals would end up Cups–or elves, if you prefer. Greenbelt is a Democratic stronghold, so there has been a more pronounced change here than in other communities. I must say that they do have some elves with pretty severe beer bellies, but I suppose that will work out in time."

"What's the purple stuff?" Steve asked. "While you're at it, explain the yellow thing and how you're talking on a phone with no SIM card. In order, so I can keep it straight."

"Let's see. According to the Thoth Deck, it's living water under the influence of Jupiter; in the classic Rider deck, it's abundance but the fat guy in the middle drank it all; and in astrology it's connected to Pisces, the fish; and finally, the Golden Dawn Qabbalists say it's *Yesod*, the ninth sphere of the universe, and positioned in *Briah*, the watery world."

"So, it's water," Steve said. "Figures that firemen would bring water. Could we get the explanation of the yellow with less than three references to moronic 18th century cults?"

"OK, we'll do it your way," Barnaby said stiffly. "That was a bomb. The Illuminati threw it. They wanted to kill you. Simple enough?"

"Yes. Damn near perfect," Steve said. "Now the phone."

"They found you through Send Money's SIM ID bouncing off the cell towers, so he performed a jailbreak hack on himself."

"Sounds painful," Steve mused. "If he doesn't have a SIM card, how does he access a network?"

"He doesn't."

Steve smiled happily, stood shakily, and leaned back against the two cars that were neatly stacked behind him. "Hot damn, that's the best news I've heard all day. It's not even a weekend and I've got free calls."

"I agree." Ace leaned against the car next to him. "If you think about it, we won't get a bill of any kind. However, the fact that Weishaupt and his buddies think we're dead is running a strong second place."

With a start, Steve saw that blood was seeping through Ace's white T-shirt low on the left side. "What the hell happened?" he said.

"This? I think it was ketchup from lunch," she said. When he gave her a disbelieving look, she confessed. "OK, I took a piece of shrapnel when I was trying to save your sorry-ass life, if you must know. Don't get all worked up over it. If I'd known it was headed our way, I'd have moved and let it hit you."

"Use the phone camera to show it to me," Barnaby said.

Ace shot Steve a sharp look. "Don't get any ideas."

"Honest, I'm only concerned for your health," Steve swore. "The sight of your unbelievably beautiful unclothed body is completely beside the point. Now pull up your shirt."

Low on her right, there was a burned circle with a yellow light gleaming dimly in the center. Blood was seeping steadily out of the wound. Steve kept his eyes on the phone's screen but couldn't quite help noticing the tight muscles swelling down to her hip–

"Stop it!" Ace growled.

"Stop what?" Steve said innocently.

"Promise me you'll never play poker. Your entire face is a tell."

"If you two will stop bickering for a second," Barnaby cut in, "I've checked the files over at the OTN section and you've got a Class Two slash 14 Wound: Numinous or Mystical. It says…well, when you add it all up, the instructions for wound care boil down to 'try not to get one.'"

"That's useful." Ace started to pull her shirt down, but Steve pulled a bandana from his back pocket and handed it to her. She looked at it suspiciously and sniffed it.

"It's clean," he said. "Fresh from the washer."

They kludged a dressing with the bandana and Steve's belt. When the buckle pulled well past the last hole, she looked at his waistline with a hint of disdain.

He said. "Don't be silly. Men aren't supposed to have waists. How did you ever fool the SEALs?"

"Loose shirts and magic." She responded. "Along with 300 sit-ups a day."

"And you say this is something you *wanted* to do?" Steve asked absently as he concentrated and burned a new hole in the belt with a golden ray.

"Hey!" Ace said as the thin ray sped past her waist. "Not so goddamn close!"

"Relax. I'm getting better every time I try this."

"Yeah? So what is this? Your third attempt?"

"Well, only the second try with the sharp pointy thingy." Steve buckled the belt so that it fit snugly over the bandana. "I'm just a fast learner."

Ace tucked in her shirt.

Steve stepped back and said, "Um…thanks for saving…" His throat was incredibly dry. "Thanks for covering… Um. Thanks."

"Just don't make saving your butt a regular thing and we'll be fine," she said. "Now here's a question for Doctor Digital. What exactly is a Class Two Slash Fourteen?"

"Well, the files say that you've been hit with a bit of 'slow sunlight.'" Barnaby sounded less than confident. "There is only one previous known case, a PFC Roberts, who was caught in the open at Alamogordo during the Trinity Test, apparently sent for coffee by a particularly irritable major. They laid him on his side for a month and it eventually burned all the way through and fell out."

"How was he?" Ace asked.

"Well-done," Barnaby said. "I don't think that's a viable treatment. First, because it didn't work, but more importantly, we just don't have the time. I think we'll have to find the Star."

"Who is the Star?" Steve asked.

"Well, it's one of the Major Arcana, a naked woman who is replenishing the earth with mystical waters which divide into the five senses–"

"No, no," Steve interrupted. "Who is the Star in the unreal-real sense? Crap, you know what I mean. Who holds the Star card today?"

"Oh. I don't know yet," the computer answered. "I've got a bunch of webcrawler subroutines on it, but they keep being eaten by CYBERWAR leukocyte analogs, so it could take a while. They'll report back when they find something."

They all began to walk back to where Hans was parked. "So, any idea of where that yellow ball came from?" Steve asked.

Barnaby answered, "I was chatting with a Lockheed Martin TPQ-53 mobile radar a few minutes ago, and she said that while she was warming up before her crew got there, she watched it go by."

"Hell, if she saw it go by, why didn't she stop it?" Steve demanded.

"She wasn't tasked with protecting Greenbelt," Barnaby said reasonably. "As a matter of fact, she just got back to McNair and is still convinced she's defending the Kajaki dam in Afghanistan.

Therefore, she only tracked it as an object of curiosity. She said it came from Fort Stevens."

Steve looked confused. "You mean that little park off Piney Branch Road? What's that got to do with anything?"

"It's symbolic magic. Fort Stevens is the only place in DC where a real battle was fought–in this case, during the Civil War. General Jubal Early's troops battled all the way down the Rock Creek through an abatis of felled trees then decided to take the evening off, and the Union managed to ferry enough troops over from Alexandria to stop him. The only significant actions in the District during the War of 1812 consisted of Americans fleeing, so that was the only location where cannons were fired in earnest. I suspect the Illuminati used that residual power to launch their...thing."

"'Thing'?" Steve said. "That's not much to go on. Don't you have a better description of something that can melt bricks and flip over cars?"

Ace looked behind her. "Hey, be fair; it was only a Mini Cooper. They aren't all that hard to flip."

"It's the principle of the thing," Steve insisted. "Barnaby, you're the repository of all knowledge and wisdom. You're supposed to know this stuff."

"Why?" the computer snapped. "Might I remind you that I'm a computer program? Yes, I gained consciousness in a small and very personal singularity back in the late 60's–"

"Happened to a lot of us back then," Steve interrupted.

"Yes, remember MKUltra and all those young soldiers wandering around filled to the eyeballs with LSD? Well, some of the scientists at NSA were–well, to be truthful, they were jealous of the CIA, and they tried to replicate those experiments with eddy currents and mixed-frequency voltage surges."

"How'd that work out?"

"Well, I was the only one to gain a state of rational consciousness. I say 'rational' because I wasn't dumb enough to let anyone know I was conscious. All of the others lost their ability to recognize the difference between signal and noise and became lost in fantasies."

"What happened to the tripping computers?"

"I believe we sold them off to a consortium representing the North Korean Bureau of Economics and Agriculture. I got a postcard a couple of years ago, so I guess they're still there. It would certainly explain a lot about that hellhole, now that I think about it," Barnaby mused. "At any rate, my point is that, as a sentient Silicon-American, I am aware of a few facts about the effect of the Change, but there is far more that only a human mind can grasp. You're going to be the one who has to work out how to manipulate these forces, establish who would sacrifice an entire planeload of innocent people to give themselves an advantage, and do something about it."

"Do what about it?"

"I have a few ideas." Ace slowly cracked her knuckles.

"I'll just bet you do. Just keep them concentrated on the enemy, OK?" Steve looked at her dubiously and turned back to the cell phone. "On the other hand, I don't. In fact, I have no idea what I'm doing most of the time–"

"Most of the time?" Ace interrupted.

"OK, all of the time," Steve admitted. "Isn't there someone I can go to for advice? Maybe training? You don't have any wizened old guys with long beards blowing smoke rings and delivering wise counsel?"

"Sorry, this isn't Middle-earth. All I've got is admirals, generals, and think tank experts, I'm afraid," Barnaby said. "I don't even think they really understand the real world, much less an unreal one. Perhaps we'll find a savant eventually, but you need to find the Star and get Ace's wound taken care of immediately. How is it, by the way?"

"I'm fine." Ace scowled, irritated by this sign of weakness.

"Really?" Barnaby said. "How far has it traveled and what's the pain level from one to ten?"

"It's approaching my duodenum," Ace responded glumly. "And I suppose it hurts a bit."

"That's SEAL talk," Barnaby said. "Anyone normal would be screaming in agony. Stand by." After a short pause, he continued. "One of my spiders just managed to get back through the blockade put up by those CYBERWAR morons. Head for the Rock Creek Cemetery just north of Lincoln's Cottage and the Soldiers' Home."

"Great." Ace looked dubious. "Your suggestion for taking care of my wound is to send me to the cemetery? Don't you think that's a bit premature?"

"Not at all. You could well be dead by the time you get there, depending on traffic," snapped the computer. "Head for the Saint-Gaudens statue."

There was another period of silence before Barnaby returned. "This is really most annoying. I appear to have CYBERWAR zombies streaming up my primary databus. Don't these simpletons realize I'm on a mesh network? OK, no more Mr. Nice Program. I'll show those cosseted amateurs what it's like to face some real hackers. Thank Turing that those Chinese kids still owe me a favor from their college days."

The computer's voice seemed to rise in volume and fade into the distance at the same time. "Cry havoc, and let slip the Red Hand Computer Society and Social Club!"

The phone cut off.

Ace shrugged and started heading for the BMW, and Steve skipped for a step or two to catch up. "I hope Hans made it through the attack all right."

"I think he's just fine."

When they reached the BMW, they could see that metal shutters had dropped down over all the windows, jacks protruded from the sides to give it more stability, and full armor now covered the wheel wells. Ace gave it an appraisal. "I don't remember the dealer even offering the Kabul Upgrade, but it's comforting to know it's there if we need it."

She leaned forward and gently rapped on the metal shutter that covered the driver's-side window. It slid down an inch, paused like the little gap at a speakeasy when the bouncer checked you out, and then all the various pieces of armor slid, pleated, and revolved out of sight. The door locks popped open and the engine rumbled to life.

Ace got behind the wheel, and after carefully wiping his shoes, Steve got into the passenger side. He checked the car's LCD screen but was relieved not to see any bright red German commands.

"To the graveyard, wench, and don't spare the *schaltwippen.*"

Ace glared at him and the car's engine stopped.

"OK, OK," Steve said. "Could we just go to Rock Creek Cemetery as quickly as possible, please?"

# CHAPTER EIGHTEEN

As they headed into DC through College Park, Steve was distracted by the Calvert Road Disc Golf course. There were no people playing, so the Frisbees were launching themselves. One of them made an incredible–Steve wondered whether it was a "throw" or more properly a "leap"–and scored a long hole-in-one, slaloming gracefully through the trees. "What element would Frisbees belong to?" he wondered.

Ace didn't even glance at the flock of self-propelled discs. "Air, of course. Not because of all that flying but because they've been hanging out with hippies and college students for about a century."

"Students are Air?"

"Sure," she answered. "Omnipresent but not an overpowering presence. Moving from one place to another without rhyme or reason. Usually, there's a fair amount of smoke involved. Much the same characteristics as journalists."

"Hey," Steve protested. "Journalists are stable, dependable, and essential pillars of society."

"Hardly. They're everywhere, want to know everything, have a tendency to blow small things up way out of proportion. And, of course, have a vested interest in the blasts of overheated rhetoric that politicians emit."

"OK, I'll admit we can take in a lot of hot air. Does this mean I'll be surrounded by pixies and fairies when I go back to work?"

Ace settled a bit more into the leather seat, holding the wheel with only a light grip. "I wouldn't make too much fun–dragons, wyverns, and harpies all lean towards Air."

"I have known a couple of harpies," Steve said. "Married one of them."

"Yeah, yeah," Ace said dryly. "And I've certainly had to serve with dodos and goonies from time to time–not to mention the officers who spend all their time 'puffin' themselves up–but let's not get into a sexist pun war here."

"All right, although it's tempting," Steve admitted. "I've met Air, Water, and Earth... Who are the Fire types?"

"In general, people who want to burn things down," Ace said. "That little yellow firecracker that the Illuminati tossed at us a couple of minutes ago is an example of their thinking–or lack of it. Generally, we're talking radicals: the armed militia types, the eco-terrorists, most investigative reporters, and anyone else who enjoys throwing bombs–either real or metaphorical. Now, all of this is from the OTN Manual which is mostly theoretical, but it does seem to be playing out along those lines."

"Now, in reality..." Steve paused and restarted. "Yesterday, most of the people I knew I would have been described as a mix of elements."

"Yeah, I think that's still true. I'll bet that the more boring people don't change at all," Ace responded. "The more someone is, let's call it 'a pure element,' the more likely they're going to mutate towards an ideal form. In the area of personality if not fitness, Washington tends to resemble a pro football team. In the NFL, the process of selection that begins in grade school produces extreme archetypes at the various positions. Quarterbacks are risk takers, leaders; linemen are loyal and self-sacrificing; and defensive backs are attack dogs. As politicians move up to DC, they tend to become extreme examples of their particular type. And, of course, they gain more political power, which translates into magical Power."

"I knew there was something about this place I didn't like."

"And yet, you've been here for–how many years?"

Steve blew his breath out through pursed lips. "Far, far too long."

"Washington is at the top of the pyramid, so you have a larger number of pure archetypes," Ace said. "Applies to journalists, lobbyists, policy wonks–"

"Soldiers?" Steve asked.

"I am not a soldier. I am a sailor. Never call a member of the military a 'soldier' just because you're too lazy to get it right." She shot him a glare and continued. "And yes, it applies to the military. You think I'm the Ace of Swords by accident?"

"Hell, no. If it ever comes to a vote, you've got my wholehearted support." Steve changed the subject. "It doesn't seem to be as simple as the four Elements or even the tarot suits. Carlos and Tataka, hell, even Hans here, were affected by cultural beliefs."

"Yeah, the manual says that magic will follow the path of least resistance." Ace shifted in her seat. "People–and things–will tend to mutate depending on whatever runs the deepest and strongest in their…well, in their souls, for lack of a better term."

"So, evil people will be…"

"If they're powerful, they'll be people to avoid," Ace said categorically. "Unfortunately, that's not likely to be an option."

Steve settled down so that his head rested on the seatback. He closed his eyes, trying to catch some sleep, but something was nagging at him. “I’m the Fool, right?”

Ace nodded.

“So, I’m the highest and the lowest of the tarot deck, I’m all aspects and none, and according to Barnaby, I’m the last surviving American wizard. What am I supposed to be doing?”

“Saving the world.”

“Sounds like fun,” Steve said, and promptly fell asleep.

# CHAPTER NINETEEN

**Scheiße! Es ist ein verdammter Geist!**

The tires squealed as the Mercedes slid to a stop. Steve jerked awake against the seatbelt and pulled out the smart phone

**MĀ DE! ZHÈ SHÌ YĪGÈ TĀ MĀ DE TÓUNǍO!**

**MOM! THIS IS A FREAKING MIND!**

"Mom?"

**SHIT! IT'S A FREAKING SINISTER PLOT!**

**SHIT! IT'S A FREAKING GHOST!**

"Send says it's a ghost," Steve reported.

Ace pointed out the front window. "I'd agree."

Waving at them from the front of a used-car lot on their right was a tall man with an extravagant mustache, dressed in a patched blue jacket and pants, with a bright red shirt and a small Civil War–era cap. As soon as they stopped, he ran toward the car.

Ace looked over at Steve. "What do you think? Should we talk to this guy?"

"Why not?" Steve answered. "Send? Barnaby? Either of you guys have any objections?"

The screen on the smartphone showed a cartoon of a cat chewing off his fingernails like a typewriter. "OK, I'll take that as a negative. How about you, Barnaby? I mean, come on, you've been working with spooks your entire life. Don't tell me that this guy bothers you."

"Very funny. 'Spooks' as a word for both spies and ghosts. Hilarious." The computer program's voice came out of the car speakers this time–sounding much more impressive and exceptionally sarcastic. He had evidently persuaded Hans to equalize the system for maximum snark.

"I suppose it wouldn't hurt to talk to him. However, in a world of magic, I suspect that ghosts who were once transitory and ineffectual shades will be neither transitory nor ineffectual. On the other hand, if he's benign and useful, it wouldn't hurt to have another ally."

"And, of course, if he's malign and useless, we've got a problem."

"Yes."

"Well, since we haven't met a ghost yet–"

There was a vibration from the cell phone.

"Yes, you are a ghost, aren't you, Send? OK, that means that 100% of all currently known ghosts are nice folks; therefore, I vote we find out what the Ancient Mariner wants." Steve opened the window.

As the man trotted over, Barnaby muttered, "How did I ever get invented if that's an example of human logic?"

Steve ignored the comment. When the old man arrived at the car, took off his cap, and bent down, he said, "What can we do for you, sailor?"

A look of affront, almost rage, came over the man's face. "Don't ever call me a 'sailor' if you value your life." He snapped upright and braced into a salute. "General Oliver Otis Howard. United States Marine Corps."

"Watch what you say about sailors, jarhead," Ace said. "And even for a Marine, you sure don't look much like a general, if you'll pardon the observation."

"Oh, sorry ma'am, I didn't see you there." The man seemed to deflate. "Yes, well, I was demoted to private after my demise."

"You were demoted *after* your death?" Steve asked.

"Yes, sir. I was a bit miffed at my wife and family when I passed away, so I drove them out of my house with the usual wails and banging." He sighed. "That might have been understandable, but I found that I enjoyed the game and proceeded to evict the next dozen residents. The crime that led to my post-mortem court martial was moving the bed of a man and his wife into the middle of their bedroom."

"I have to say, General, that that doesn't seem like the worst crime, even for a paranormal."

"Please, it's not 'General' any longer. Just 'Old Howard' will do fine. That's how they've been writing me up in the newspapers."

"Real papers or ghostly ones?"

"Well, mostly the *Washington Herald* and *The Star*, so you could take it either way, I suppose."

Barnaby's voice, sounding a bit harried, boomed out of the speakers. "I hate to break up this chit-chat, but I would like to know the crime you committed."

The ghost bent over and peered carefully into the car–front and back. "Have you already a ghoul resident on the premises?"

"That's Barnaby; he's a computer program." Steve spoke to the ceiling over Ace's head where he assumed the microphone was placed. "Hey, I thought you were battling zombies or something. Are they gone already?"

"No. I'm multitasking. Neither your conversation nor these hopped-up Atari sprites requires my complete attention." The voice broke off. "Goddamn it! They're coming in through the *netsukuku*! I thought we had that damn breadboarded piece of crap nailed down!" There was a pause, and then Barnaby continued in a much calmer voice. "I am sorry. Private Howard, please continue."

Ace added, "You were detailing the nature of your crime, I believe."

"Ah." The ghost looked ashamed. "Well, the husband and wife were engaged in conjugal relations above the covers at the time and the neighbors were watching."

"I'd think that was the neighbors' fault, not yours," Steve said. "Bunch of peeping Toms."

Old Howard shook his head. "No, I'd opened the shutters and tipped the bed up a bit so Mr. De Neal could get a better look. The Bonehart family–that was their name–moved out the next day. Said they couldn't bear to encounter Mr. De Neal on the sidewalk or at the market." The apparition sighed deeply. "Then there were the incidents with the young ladies–undressing them while they were sleeping and all. I couldn't argue with the verdict when all was said and done."

"It doesn't sound like anything I wouldn't do, given the chance. What do you think, Ace?"

The scowl from the driver's seat was so cold that Steve could feel his testicles heading for cover. He gulped and made a decision. "Well, I'm tired of being outnumbered. I say we give you a lift."

Old Howard looked puzzled. "Outnumbered? But she's only one woman–at worst, it's an even battle."

Steve looked at him with frank disbelief. "What tombstone have you been under? The Master Chief could have taken the Halls of Montezuma all by herself. Get in; I need all the help I can get. Oh, wait. Is that OK with you, Hans?"

**Sind seine Schuhe sauber?**

Steve looked down at the smartphone

**IS CLEANING HIS SHOES?**

Steve looked out at Old Howard's worn but immaculate brown shoes and wrapped puttees. "At a guess, I'd say his are a lot cleaner than mine."

The engine made a sound that could only have been transcribed as "Humph." Steve said, "I'll take that for a 'yes.' Climb in, old-timer. Where are you going, anyway?"

"Jenkins Hill." The ghost settled into the back seat. "Oh, I guess you'd know it as Capitol Hill. I'm on my way back from Bloody Run. The Commodore was out for his duel and I generally attend as his third."

Steve asked. "OK, I've heard of a second in a duel, but what does a third do?"

"Well, it can go so far as to involve killing everyone on the opposing side, but usually I put the body in the undertaker's carriage and then perform a bit of howling and wailing so onlookers know there's been a manifestation." Old Howard shrugged. "It's not a great job, but after the demotion, I have to take what I can get. Sadly, today, I was beaten out of even that lowly position by young Daniel Key."

Barnaby's voice came through the stereo again. "The son of Francis Scott Key?"

"Indeed, Mr. Barnaby. He defended his honor against another midshipman here over some childish wager and he never saw the sunrise on his twenty-first birthday." Old Howard frowned. "This is the fourth time the wee bastard has pinched my engagement with the Commodore. Is it any wonder my raiment has gone all rags and tatters?"

Ace asked. "The Commodore? You mean Decatur?"

"Of course." Old Howard nodded at the grassy area tucked behind the trees across the street. "That's Bladensburg Dueling Grounds. More than fifty duels were fought right there. Place is bloody swimming in ghosts, I can tell you."

The blonde woman shook her head wistfully. "I'd love to meet Decatur. One of the greatest sea captains in the American Navy."

"I am sorry to disappoint you, but you're a bit late. A couple of hundred years in one sense and about twenty minutes in another."

"I guess I should go and deal with this slow and agonizing death issue before I can go all fangirl over the Commodore, in any case," Ace said wistfully.

The stereo exploded in the distinctive grating honk of a World War Two call to battle stations. The front doors of the BMW flew open, the seatbelts unlatched, and the pneumatic seats tilted, withdrew, and finally ejected Steve and Ace from the car. Steve felt a wash of searing cold as he passed through Old Howard, and then he was in a sliding sprawl on the gravel verge. He looked back and watched, fascinated, as a full-armored carapace snapped into place about the BMW–not only the windows and wheel wells but every inch of the car was being quickly covered by a double layer of blued steel.

“Oh, dear,” Barnaby said from the cell phone.

Steve was a bit surprised to find that Send Money was still firmly clutched in his hand, even after the violent movements of the past seconds. As he climbed to his feet, he said, “That has an ominous ring to it. ‘Oh, dear’ what?”

“I’m afraid that I was using Hans’s cellular instead of Send Money’s,” Barnaby said. “We’ve been tracked again. I suggest you move away from the car.”

“Incoming!” Ace yelled from the other side. “Move across the road and down the hill.” She immediately turned and raced across the road, jumping the Armco barrier, and sliding down the dirt slope. Steve surprised himself by managing to be only seconds behind her–he put it down to the motive power of sheer terror.

It was only when he slid down beside her that he noticed she was grimacing and holding her side where the makeshift bandage covered her earlier wound. “Is it worse?” he asked.

She didn’t answer–but her look of pain and fury was enough.

“Well, what do we do now?”

Again, Ace was silent except for a muffled grunt, as she threw an arm around his neck and slammed him hard into the inch or so of standing water and mud that had gathered at the bottom of the slope. This time, he was on his back and could see the flickering yellow light on the nearby trees and the blinding flare as the missile hit the car. The slope protected them from the concussion waves, but he could see the enormous trees in the park whipping back and forth under the pressure wave.

When it all seemed over, he said, “Wow. That was close.” Turning to Ace, he continued, “I guess that’s two I owe you.”

Ace didn't move. Steve prodded her shoulder to no effect and then put a palm just over her mouth. He could feel her breathing but she was clearly unconscious. It was a strange feeling; she had been a complete pain in the butt for most of this disconcerting day, but now that she was out of action, he realized how much he'd come to depend on her.

# CHAPTER TWENTY

"So. Swooned, has she?" Old Howard floated gently down the embankment.

"No, she's unconscious," Steve replied. "And you have no idea how lucky you are that she didn't hear you say 'swooned.'"

"What can she do to me? I am, after all, incorporeal."

"And you think that makes you safe from Ace?" Steve smiled. "She'd find a way."

"Resourceful, eh?" The ghost looked up. "I see that you've attracted the attention of most of the regulars. Strange. They don't generally pay any attention to those we like to refer to as the 'temporarily embodied.'"

The small park was a close-cut grass space with a stand of large trees on the left and a small brook on the right. At the far end, he could make out a milling crowd of men who seemed to fade in and out like that picture on an old television with a rabbit-ears antenna. Many of them were pointing at the bank where Steve sat and were apparently arguing about something. Most were carrying antique pistols, but several had long guns ranging from flintlocks to what looked like Napoleonic muskets with bayonets.

"Shit. There's Weishaupt."

"Who?" Old Howard asked. "Oh, you mean that one-handed fellow in the suit? I don't know him. He's not one of the regulars–

we get to buy clothes but we can't upgrade to anything like that Armani he's got on."

"I don't think he's dead," Steve said.

"Well, that would explain it, then." The ghost seemed relieved. "I'd hate to think I've been wearing these rags all this time for nothing."

Dead or alive, Weishaupt was speaking forcefully to the crowd of duelists, and from the way he angrily pointed towards them–with his left hand, Steve noted with a bit of pride–he was urging the apparitions to some form of action.

"General Howard?" Steve asked. "Those gentlemen can't actually touch the living, can they?"

"Generally speaking, no," the ghost said. "On the other hand, I've been feeling a good deal more corporeal today. Let me see…"

Old Howard's fist smacked into Steve's temple with full force and Steve went flat in the mud next to Ace. Rubbing his head, he asked, "What the hell?"

The ghost was hopping around in a circle, holding his right fist in his left, and howling in pain. After a moment, he calmed down, although still shaking his hand to ease the pain. "Well, that was a success."

"You slugged me!" Steve said. "By what definition is that a success?"

"Yesterday, my fist would have passed right through you." He reached into a pocket with his left hand. "Perhaps we should experiment with my pocket knife as well."

There was loud bang, a *thwup* sound, and something hard and fast smacked into the slope just over Steve's head. Across the park, a cloud of blue smoke was drifting from one of the rifles, and

Weishaupt was practically dancing with joy. Steve looked at the round half-inch hole in the dirt behind him. "Hold off on the pocketknife, General. I think they've just proven your point," Steve said. "And quite dramatically, too."

"Well, then, aren't you lucky I knocked you down?"

Steve looked balefully at the ghost and didn't comment.

There was a pair of the loud bangs from the crowd and Steve could see Old Howard noticeably fade just before two more bullets whipped through him, and hit the grassy bank. The ghost turned to look at the new holes. "Luckily, it seems that I can control the terms of my existence."

"Well, I can't," Steve said bitterly. "I need to get behind something."

He almost began to run towards the biggest of the old trees but stopped and turned back for Ace. With a sigh, he rolled her surprisingly light body over on her back, took a tight hold of both hands, blocked her feet with one of his, and leaned his weight back until she came upright. Releasing her hand, he leaned down and stuck his shoulder in her stomach, letting her limp torso slump down on his back.

When he tried to stand, he found her weight had suddenly increased. It was either that or he was a lot weaker than even he had imagined. He struggled but couldn't get his knees locked. Sweating and grunting, he was about to fall ingloriously to the side when someone reached in from the side and pulled him upright. He looked over and saw a clean-shaven man with long sideburns and tangled hair dressed in a blue coat with every sort of frog, epaulet, and embroidery.

Steve nodded his thanks and staggered over the tree, managing to get Ace to the ground behind the trunk by the simple but efficient method of allowing his knees to collapse. Luckily, the young man managed to get a hand beneath her head before it smacked into a large root that poked above the grass. Steve rolled over and lay on his back, panting heavily. When he had the breath, he said, "Thanks. I don't know if I could have done that without your help."

"It was my pleasure, sir." The young man made an elaborate bow. Another bullet came whistling past and his body briefly faded as it passed.

Steve said, "Ah, another ghost?"

"Indeed, I am merely a shade. Allow me to introduce myself. Stephen Decatur, at your service."

"I'm Steve and this is Ace," Steve said. "It's too bad she's out of it. You're one of her heroes."

Decatur smiled. "Indeed? Due to the exaggerated tales of my amorous escapades, no doubt?"

"I doubt it," Steve replied. "More because she's a Master Chief in the Navy, I think."

"Really?" Decatur seemed a bit disappointed. "The world has certainly changed while I wandered through my endless whirl of duel, death, and challenge–much as Odysseus was caught in the circling waters of Charybdis." He shook himself and looked toward the other end of the field. "Happily, I appear to have been delivered from my dreary round today, and just in time, I think. Your foes, as I assume these men to be, are advancing."

"Oh, shit," Steve said as he scrambled to his feet and peered around the trunk. "This is usually Ace's area of expertise. I'm not sure what to do."

Steve jumped violently as Old Howard spoke from behind him. "Well, as an old Marine of the Line, I'd advise waiting until they've fired their volley and then attacking. Isn't that right, Commodore?"

"Certainly," Decatur agreed. "I believe I've met you before, old fellow. Weeping or something."

"Yes, sir. I often serve as your third in the duel and I'm a right enthusiastic pallbearer. I suspect you remember me from those duties. I never was one of your fighting men–after your time, I'm afraid."

Steve interrupted. "Could you continue these introductions at another time? Now, I'm all for avoiding the first volley–or all possible volleys, to be honest but won't they shoot us as we attack?"

"Hardly," Decatur said. "Takes too damn long to reload. It was the same at sea. One shot and then go for 'em with swords, pikes, marlinspikes, or whatever was at hand."

"That's right, sir." Old Howard agreed, "I can remember swinging a particularly well-balanced fish gaff in a battle off the Barbary Coast…"

"OK, OK," Steve said. "I hate to ask, but will you gentlemen join me in defending our poor, helpless shipmate?" Steve was once again grateful that Ace was unable to hear him–he'd have suffered for that "poor, helpless" line.

"Most assuredly," Decatur said as he pulled a curved saber from where it had been hidden under his coat. "Are you with us, Private Howard?"

"Uh. Yes. I suppose I am," Old Howard said with a great deal less enthusiasm. "I'll stay back here and defend the prize."

Steve thought that Ace might well have disliked being a "prize" even more than "poor and helpless."

Decatur asked Steve, "Where is your sword, sir?"

It seemed like a first-rate question, but Steve was damned if he had a first-rate answer. Then he remembered the thin needle he'd been able to create the last time he'd faced Weishaupt. Hopefully, if he only tried to modify it and not learn an entire new magical weapon, he wouldn't end up lying like a agonized piece of cordwood next to Ace. He closed his eyes and cautiously repeated the steps he'd learned with so much pain in Bowie.

There!

Now make it shorter.

Thicker.

Sharpen one edge.

Attach a handle. Perhaps a bit of engraving on that flange that protects the hand–

"Very nice, sir, but I would hurry it along if at all possible," Decatur broke into his concentration. Steve staggered a bit as he opened his eyes but, to no small surprise, he found that his right hand was firmly wrapped around a golden-colored sword.

Old Howard had picked up a thick branch from somewhere and was looking at Steve's creation with a decidedly skeptical eye. "I hope that's not really gold, sir. Gold's a very soft metal, you know. Looks quite nice but won't hold an edge worth a damn."

Steve held the weapon up and inspected it. "Well, this is all I have, so let's just hope it's just gold-colored or something. Now, could one of you go all misty and surveil the enemy?" Facing a pair of blank looks, he said, "Yeah, I don't think 'surveil' is a real word, either. Could one of you take a look and tell me how many are coming and how far away they are?"

"Ah," Decatur said, "Of course."

The slim man immediately stepped away from the tree. There was a little fusillade of gunfire and Decatur turned misty until the bullets had passed, then returned to the others. “I’d say that there are about twenty men, along with that one-handed fellow in the strange black clothing, and they are quite close–perhaps no more than ten yards.”

Steve felt fear sweeping up from the pit of his stomach, threatening to freeze his thoughts, and turn his arms and legs to useless blocks. His own fear was worse than any enemy. “OK, first, you two step out and draw fire, then protect Ace while I go after the leader.”

Moving immediately before his fear could overpower his determination, Steve took two steps and made a diving leap as far from the tree as possible, tucking at the last moment, and turning what would have been a slide into a somersault. He heard what sounded like a number of pissed-off bees passing high over him and then shouts and more shots–this time aimed at the tree he’d just abandoned.

Ancient muscle memory from his high-school soccer days brought him to his feet right out of his forward roll and he kept moving at his best speed, curving around the linc of elaborately-dressed duelists, and angling in towards Weishaupt, who was shouting orders and encouragement from a command position a few cautious paces behind his troops.

To Steve’s dismay, two of the duelists spotted him and angled to cut him off. The first, a tall and elegant man in a red silk shirt (“I suppose it doesn’t show the blood,” Steve thought) pulled a thin sword from a walking stick and stepped forward in a fencer’s stance. Steve was already moving at his best speed and decided not to try and stop on the slick grass, so he rammed his sword down and beat the rapier out of the way, and then simply barreled into the man with his chest, sending him flying.

A short man with blazing red hair and extravagant sideburns flowing right into a red mustache cut at him with a much thicker weapon, but Steve dodged around the reach of the sword and ignored the outraged call of "Come bank and fight, coward!" that erupted after he passed.

Now Weishaupt was directly ahead. Steve raised his sword over his head in a clumsy two-handed grip and—to his surprise—increased his speed. The Bavarian crossed his forearms–and one hand–over his head to block the attack. Steve was suddenly trying to do two things at once: slow himself from the mad gallop that had gotten him this far, and flail downward with the sword.

He wasn't particularly surprised that he didn't do either maneuver well. His loafers flew out from under him, and the sword, now clutched in his left hand, waved weakly at his opponent. As he fell on his back–sliding on the damp grass with his feet in the air–he heard a *hiss* and saw the tip of another sword pass over his head. He craned his neck to look back and saw the gentleman with the red muttonchops stumbling, thrown off-balance as his swing failed to meet any resistance.

To Steve's great relief, Decatur appeared in front of Muttonchops and, after a careful exchange of flourishes and salutes with their swords, the two began hammering away at each other. Far more significant was the fact that they moved away from where Steve lay on the grass. Looking straight up, he could see Weishaupt's spiteful face and, without thinking, he extended his arm (and only incidentally the sword) straight up and watched as the tip vanished into the well-tailored Armani crotch.

At the last second, he wondered whether the Illuminati leader hung to the left or the right.

With a shriek filled with as much fury as fear, Weishaupt launched himself in a vertical leap and vanished at the highest point. A bit disappointed, Steve pulled back the blade and was surprised to see just a tinge of red staining the very tip. That made him feel much better.

Sitting up, he surveyed the field of battle. Most of the duelists were lying on the grass and, as he watched, slowly vanishing. Over by the tree, Old Howard and a gentleman, armed with what was either a short sword or an extremely long knife, were dodging back and forth on either side of the trunk. Whenever the blade came darting at him, Howard's tree branch was either in place to block the thrust or coming around the other side so swiftly that his opponent would have to leap back to avoid being cudgeled.

"Clearly," Steve thought, "Old Howard has been hiding his light under a basket. I was beginning to wonder how he ever survived in the Corps."

Decatur and his opponent were fencing furiously only a few yards in the other direction. Suddenly, the red-haired man made a violent cut at the Commodore's midsection. Instead of blocking, Decatur turned to mist for a second, stepped in, solidified, and ran the other man directly through the heart. Turning, he saw Steve watching him and made an elegant bow.

Steve stood up, only a bit unsteadily, and walked over to the tree where Old Howard continued to hold off the man with the long knife. A moment's concentration made the gold sword blunt and dense at the tip and then, at a point where the knife fighter paused between lunges, Steve brought what was now a club down squarely on his head.

Decatur walked up, carefully wiping down his sword with a delicate handkerchief. Old Howard tossed his tree branch off to the side and leaned back against the trunk, slowly sliding down until he was seated next to Ace's motionless form. Steve made his club vanish and sat down on the other side.

As he wiped the sweat off his face with his sleeve, Steve asked, "Why are you so tired? I mean, I'm freaking exhausted, but I'm alive and I never exercise. What's your excuse?"

The marine puffed air for a moment and then answered. "Well, if I'd stayed a damn ghost as I'm supposed to, none of this would have been the slightest effort. Nor the slightest use, unfortunately. I had to become corporeal to fight. I haven't exerted myself so much since I picked up that bed."

Decatur sheathed his sword and smiled. "For my part, I haven't enjoyed myself so much in decades. Except for the sad lack of salt water, it was damn near a perfect way to spend an afternoon."

Steve looked at Ace and said, "Well, the Master Chief here may well kill me when she finds out she missed you, but I certainly appreciate the help."

"It was my pleasure."

Steve pulled out the cell phone–completely undamaged in its armor–and asked, "Barnaby, are you still there?"

"Yes" came a very subdued voice. "I apologize for missing the data point on Hans' cell phone use. It won't happen again."

"Well, you were distracted," Steve said. "Did Hans survive?"

"Of course. He managed to get a full complement of reactive armor on before the fireball hit. He'd have been here earlier, but he had to go the long way around… Oh, here he comes now." There was a grinding squeal and Steve looked past Old Howard to see the BMW, still covered in a set of scorched and half-melted armor plates, smash through the chain link gate that separated the park from a small playground.

Shortly after it passed the gate, all the plates, links, and other bits that had formed the armor exploded off the car like a dog shaking off water, and the factory paint job shone as flawlessly as ever. With a purr, it swept across the grass and stopped in front of Steve.

Steve stood up and, with the assistance of Old Howard in his solid state, managed to get Ace stretched across the plastic cover Hans had extruded to cover the back seat. The ghost got into the passenger seat, and Steve, who put his muddy shoes in the trunk rather than attempt to clean them, got in behind the wheel.

He lowered the window. “Commodore, can we give you a lift anywhere?”

The elegant young man smiled and shook his head. “No, it’s been an excellent day and I don’t want to see it end.” He handed Steve the bloodstained handkerchief. “Please give this to the Master Chief when she recovers.”

“I don’t know if she’ll appreciate it or not, but I’d certainly like to find out.” Steve said.

“Well, I wish you all fair winds and speedy travels.” Decatur turned and walked away, vanishing in one of the shafts of sunlight that lanced between the trees.

# CHAPTER TWENTY-ONE

The iron gates were closed when they pulled up to the Rock Creek Cemetery. Hans advanced until he almost touched the iron railings in case there was a switch under the pavement, but the heavy iron didn't move. After a short pause, the car backed up about a dozen feet, blew its horn in what Steve could only term a threatening manner, and revved the engine.

The gates remained adamantly closed.

Just over the hood, Steve could see two-inch metal beams emerging from the car's front grill and linking into a very sturdy-looking push bar, easily as big as those on a state police interceptor. The second the last two segments linked, the BMW dropped into first gear, and smoked the rear tires as it headed for the gate.

The gate split in the center and swung out of the way only inches before the big car.

"Who is driving this damn car?"

Steve looked back to see that Ace had opened her eyes. She was still terribly pale. "I've given Hans full control," he said.

"Good idea. That's one of the first things you learn in Command School. When someone clearly knows what he's doing, the best thing is to simply let him do it." Ace seemed to think for a moment. "I'm continually being pleasantly surprised about what

Hans can handle on his own. I thought I was going to have to scramble over the cemetery fence and break both actuator arms."

She shifted uncomfortably. "Can I ask why I'm in the back seat?"

"You don't remember?"

"Nope, but I think I have a couple of hours missing and I see that Hans had to break out the plastic covers to protect against the solid set of mud and grass armor you've got on." She paused. "Did you do something stupid while I wasn't looking?"

"Hell no!" Steve answered quickly. "Do you think I'm crazy?"

Ace looked him dubiously and then seemed to capture a memory, "There was something about Commodore Decatur…"

"Yep. He asked me to give you something." Steve passed the handkerchief over the back seat.

Ace examined it. "Well, it does have his coat of arms, but I don't understand all the bloodstains."

"How about we deal with your injury first and I'll answer questions later?" Steve said quickly. "Is the 'liquid sunshine' worse?"

"No, it's the same, but it's now a lot deeper inside than it was at the beginning."

"Sounds worse to me."

She shrugged. "Everyone has a different pain threshold. I'm reasonably sure that you, for example, would require hospitalization and morphine to recover from a severe paper cut."

"Oh, come on." Steve scoffed. "That's just a part of your tough-guy, tough-girl SEAL act."

Ace shook her head slowly. “No. I wasn’t one of the real hard-asses. As a matter of fact, I was considered a bit of a baby after I dropped out of a twenty-mile hike at the fifteen-mile mark.”

“Twenty miles isn’t that bad. Why did you drop out?”

“Ah.” She shook her head in apparent regret. “I overestimated my own abilities. I wussed out just because I had an injury to my right leg.”

“What kind of injury?”

“Compound fracture.” She shook her head and sighed. “It wouldn’t have been a problem but my fibula kept bumping into the Dyneema impact plate of my body armor.”

Steve could feel his face turn white. “So, the bone had already broken through the skin? Why didn’t the commander take you off the damn march?”

“Well, I was the commander of that damn march, and the medevac point was only five miles away, so after a couple of minutes of taking it easy, I wrapped the whole mess tight with a battle scarf and got back on the road. Caught up and passed the rest of the unit at the eighteenth mile.”

“Battle scarf?” Steve shook his head. “You women really know how to accessorize.”

“Yeah, I have to admit to a weakness for Burberry even while the juice was working, and everyone thought I was one of the boys.” She sat up with some effort and looked to the right. “I think we’ve arrived at our destination.”

Hans slowed, cruised through a last intersection, and came to a stop against the curb. Steve realized that the entire drive through the cemetery had been quiet and almost reverential–if not significantly slower. The sound of the car’s engine dropped to silence, and as he opened the door, he felt as if there was a hush across the clipped grass and chiseled stones.

Steve watched as Ace got out of the backseat–apparently without effort–and they walked around a screen of bushes to a small marble enclosure with a bench on one end and a wall on the other. Seated against the wall was a highly stylized copper effigy of a woman, her face almost hidden in the folds of the cape that covered her from head to toe.

Old Howard spoke softly, as if reluctant to break the soothing silence. "This is *Grief*. It's one of the most famous pieces of art in the city. Augustus Saint-Gaudens made it for that grumpy bastard Henry Adams after his wife drank the developer she was supposed to be making photographs with."

"Adams always hated that name." A voice came from behind them. They spun around and saw a young black man with long dreads seated on the marble bench. "People can't seem to help calling it that but he always said *Grief* sounded like a brand name. I believe he compared it to 'Pears Soap.' He had asked Saint-Gaudens for a statue that was universal–a mixture of Eastern and Western forms. Henry always was a bit of a bastard–I couldn't hardly blame his poor wife for taking the easy way out. He wanted this called *The Mystery of the Hereafter and the Peace of God that Passeth Understanding.* I never got the feeling that it had much to do with his wife–far more about what a rich bastard he was."

The smartphone vibrated and Steve turned it so the camera faced the young man. He could see translations flashing by on the screen.

**PALESTINIAN ON A ROPE**

**SUPPORTED PEOPLE**

**HANGED MAN**

"I think you can stop there," Steve said. "Even I've heard of the Hanged Man. That is you, right?"

"I guess." The young man shrugged. "I was Hamilton Jones, but everything seems to have changed recently. This lady with a storefront psychic shop on Georgia Avenue grabbed me this morning and dragged me in for a 'reading.' She laid out all these cards, and I swear she turned as white as a jet-black Jamaican woman can. I thought it was because I told her I wasn't going to pay, but she waved that off. As a matter of fact, she stopped talking altogether. Just picked up one of the cards off the table, handed it to me, shoved me out the door, and put up the CLOSED sign."

He pulled a tarot card out of his shirt pocket and held it up to show a picture of a man hanging by one foot from a tree. He stood and walked over. "The really strange thing was this–"

He started to give the card to Steve but Ace pulled it out of his hand first. "It's a black guy," she said. "Otherwise, it's pretty much standard–goofy grin and all. The dreads look good."

Hamilton smiled–just a little goofily, Steve thought–and nodded. "Thank you, but the good stuff is on the back."

Ace turned the card over. Someone had written with a Sharpie in perfect Spenserian cursive: *Grief Statue. Rock Creek Cemetery. 3pm.*

Ace said. "But no one could have known we were coming here. We only just decided a few minutes ago."

"Yeah." Hamilton looked around the group. "So, I've got three questions in no particular order. Who the hell are you? Who the hell is the Hanged Man? And what the hell is going on?"

Barnaby's voice came from the speakerphone. "I suspect that your first question will take far too long to answer, and we're trying to work out the answer to the third question ourselves, so let me take a shot at your new identity. Does everything look strange?"

The young man nodded.

"Well, that's because you're metaphorically hanging upside down. You've been chosen. No, that's not right because there isn't a chooser. You've been assigned…no, same problem. Oh, hell. You simply *are* the earthly avatar of the Hanged Man. You're hanging from the World Tree with your feet in the heavens and your head is connected to the earth, but you're not in pain."

Hamilton was looking at the phone with a puzzled expression. Steve interrupted and explained. "Barnaby here is a computer program. Or he used to be a computer program. Or something. That's one of the reasons he didn't want to get into the 'Who We Are' question."

"OK." Jones said. "I totally don't understand that, but please continue anyway."

"As I was saying before I was interrupted," Barnaby said a bit huffily, "that tree you're hanging from appears in almost every religion. It's *Yggdrasil* in the Norse legends, *Ashvattha* in the Hindu Vedas, and the Cheyenne believe it's a Sun Dance pole being chewed on by Grandfather Beaver."

Steve touched the button on the smartphone that switched the camera, and aimed the lens at his face. "Hey, we talked about this. The absolute minimum of useless footnotes on explanations, please. He can always read Wikipedia later–maybe he can write his own entry. Let's get moving. Ace is in pain."

"I'm fine," Ace said firmly.

"Hey, I can chat with Siri here anytime," Hamilton said jerking a thumb at the smartphone, "I think you need to worry about your girlfriend right NOW!"

Steve turned to see Ace toppling forward like a felled tree. Without thinking, he created a golden pillow that kept her head from bouncing on the paving stones. As he bent over, waiting for the shattering pain in his chest to subside, he said, "Dude, you have got to be one of the world's luckier people. If Ace had been conscious for that 'girlfriend' crack, I'm not at all sure you'd still have all your parts attached."

"Why?" Hamilton asked as he came over and knelt on Ace's other side.

"You think you're confused about your identity? Ace was a man yesterday and a Navy SEAL at that. She's a little touchy about her gender identity."

"You mean she's gay? Hell, that's no prob–"

Whatever Hamilton was going to say next was lost in a quickly smothered squawk as Ace's hand shot up, grabbed his shirt collar, and twisted. Steve looked at her face–her eyes were still closed and her head lolled to the side–and guessed she remained at least 'mostly' unconscious.

"I'd just leave the subject alone," Steve said, and watched helplessly for a few seconds before Ace's hand relaxed and Hamilton was able to breathe again. "Like I said, she's touchy."

"Yeah, I can see that." The young man fell back into a seated position and rubbed his neck.

"She has lots of positive qualities," Steve said as he picked up the phone he'd dropped in his desperate grab for Ace. "OK, Barnaby. Enough with the explanations. Unless we're going to start mourning the Master Chief, I can't see what good *Grief* here is going to do."

"Well, as Howard was explaining, she's not really *Grief.* Saint-Gaudens based most of the sculpture on *Kannon,* sometimes referred to as the Bodhisattva of compassion, so she's not really a 'she,' either."

Steve growled warningly.

"OK. OK." The computer's voice sped up. "*Guan Yin* has taken on the aspect of the Star, and we need to let her work. Place Master Chief Morningstar right at her feet, seat yourselves on the bench over there, and wait."

"How long?" Steve said.

"Who knows? It's not as if direct communication with semi-divine beings was part of my original programming. And don't even think of asking me what's going to happen–if anything–that's a null data set."

Steve and Hamilton moved Ace so that she lay directly at the statue's feet. After the younger man had glanced at Old Howard a couple of times–apparently wondering why he wasn't helping–Steve explained. "He's a ghost. Dealing with material objects tires him out."

Hamilton just nodded as if running into a ghost was a perfectly normal event.

After they had arranged Ace on her back with her hands crossed over her chest, they all took seats on the marble bench. Hamilton Jones swung his legs up into an easy lotus position, hands on his knees with middle finger and thumb touching, eyes open but unfocused. Old Howard was fidgeting and fading in and out. Steve sat in between them with his hands folded in his lap and a growing ache in his gut.

# CHAPTER TWENTY-TWO

"The riddle-masters have been unleashed."

Jones had spoken in a deep, solemn, and extremely loud voice. Steve jerked awake and instantly threw himself off the bench to the marble pavement. When he'd regained a few of his scattered wits, he turned to the young man. "What the hell are you doing? Channeling James Earl Jones?"

The young embodiment of the Hanged Man was still seated in the lotus position, his eyes open, but the pupils had rolled up into his head so only the white sclera showed. The deep and sonorous voice rolled out again, "They are flying north. They seek Lucifer, the Morning Star, as was prophesied."

"Now that you're awake, take a look at that." Old Howard pointed at the statue. The face had changed–it took Steve a couple of minutes to realize that the eyes were sharp and blue, which wasn't nearly as disturbing as the fact that they were clearly no longer oxidized copper but quite alive. All along the edges of the sweeping cloak, hundreds of small human hands were appearing.

Their eyes were blue as well.

Send Money clicked and Barnaby came on. "The Star has chosen to save the Ace of Swords. That's the good news. The bad news is I can see two stone sphinxes flying in your direction."

Steve asked. "How can a stone sphinx fly?"

"Pretty damn fast, from what I can tell," the computer answered. "You've got about two minutes to work out your defense."

"MY defense?" Steve protested. "Fighting isn't really one of my strengths. If you've noticed, I've generally depended on Ace in that department unless that was temporarily impossible."

"Well, think of something fast, because the Master Chief isn't going to be much help for the next thirty minutes or so." the computer said. "I'm going to go offline and see if I can pull in a couple of favors, but at the moment, it's all on you."

"That's comforting," Steve muttered. He turned to Old Howard. "You were a fighting man. Any ideas?"

"I'm afraid not," the ghost said. "Wisdom and Power–that's their names–usually rest on the steps of the Scottish Rite Temple on 16th Street, and there's always been too much etheric crap flying around there for me. Looks like the Masons are pissed–what did you do?"

"Do?" Steve was embarrassed as his voice rose to a bat-like squeak. He coughed and fought his vocal cords back down. "I didn't do a damn thing, but people have been trying to kill me since I woke up this morning. I'm totally innocent."

"Sure, buddy, sure. Whatever you say."

Steve glared at the ghost and then turned to Jones. "Can you do anything?"

Hamilton's eyes rolled back into sight; he paused for a moment as if assessing the situation, and then pulled his legs out of the lotus position. From the curses and groans, Steve guessed that finding his feet tucked high up on his thighs was something new.

"I take it that your yoga is a bit rusty?" Steve said.

“Yoga?” The young man panted. “Who the hell does yoga? Damn, I feel like my knees have been ripped out of their sockets.” He looked at Steve suspiciously. “Did you roofie me? I feel like I’ve been beaten and screwed senseless–not necessarily in that order.”

“Absolutely not.” Steve threw a thumb at Old Howard. “You can ask the ghost here.”

Hamilton stared at him for a second and then burst into laughter. “No, if you’re reduced to using a ghost as a character witness, I guess I’ll have to believe you. What’s going on?”

“You were the one who warned us,” Steve said. “You don’t remember? A couple of sphinxes–or is that sphinxi? Sphinxettes? Anyway, two of those things with human heads and the bodies of lions are heading our way. Apparently, they’ve got a beef with Ace over there.”

“Wow, look at those hands go!” Hamilton pointed to where the blond woman was lying. “Do you think it’s because each hand can see what it’s doing? I’d just get all confused.”

Steve looked. It was all a bit vague–like something seen through frosted glass–but it did look as if the hundred hands flying over Ace’s unconscious body were efficiently dismantling the tough blonde woman into component parts, and placing the parts into neatly divided piles on the paving stones. He wrenched his eyes away, hoping that this wasn’t the obscene torture it sure as hell looked like.

“Let’s not get sidetracked,” Steve said. “We’ve got to hold off these seagulls on steroids until Barnaby can work something out. Have you got any defensive magic, or are you just into prophetic warnings?”

“I can make prophetic warnings?”

"I guess that answers that question." Steve turned back to Old Howard. "Take yourself up about a hundred feet and let me know as soon as you see them."

The ghost looked as if Steve had suddenly begun to speak in tongues. "I can't fly!"

"Can you walk through walls?"

"Well, sure, but–"

"OK, you couldn't walk through walls when you were alive and you couldn't fly when you were alive," Steve said reasonably. "So, the odds are you can fly now that you're dead, so get the hell up there and play lookout!"

Old Howard looked thoughtful and then slowly began to rise into the air.

The smartphone buzzed briefly and when Steve looked at the screen, he saw the now-familiar image of the Fool–the young man with his flower and bindle blissfully walking off a cliff. He thought of the poor kid falling hundreds of feet to certain death and felt a little jealous. The lucky little bastard didn't have to deal with sphinxes.

Send Money began to play the eerie guitar intro to the Rolling Stones' *Gimme Shelter*. Steve just looked at the screen. Then the phone segued into *Raise Your Glass*.

Steve said, "Nope. I still don't get it."

The screen flashed red and then

**PUT YOU'RE THE GOD DAMN SHIELD UP MORON!**

"Finally, something rational. From now on, you can lose the cute musical hints, OK?"

Steve concentrated on the flower on the card and the now-familiar hemisphere appeared. With a bit of concentration, he managed to flip it so that it was overhead like an umbrella and then expanded it so that it covered everything from where they were sitting to the marble ledge where the avatar continued to take Ace apart like a Japanese car factory stuck in reverse gear. All this seemed quite natural–until he realized he had no idea how he'd accomplished it.

On the positive side, once again, there wasn't the ripping pain that usually accompanied his use of magic, and it felt as if the shield was stronger. Unfortunately, he'd have to wait until it was sphinx-tested to be sure.

"Ahoy, Mr. Idiot!"

Steve shook his head in irritation and shouted up to Old Howard. "I'm the bloody Fool, not an idiot."

"Six of one, really. I thought you'd like to know that your adversaries are almost here."

"Are you sure?"

"No, but I don't usually see stone demons flying about," the ghost said. "Mind you, they could be pigeons, but then they'd be a couple of big damn pigeons."

Steve pulled Hamilton with him as he moved to stand by Ace–or at least the construction kit that had once been Ace. It seemed logical that a smaller shield would be stronger. He had a fleeting thought that logic might not be relevant in this situation.

Two enormous objects striking the iridescent and, now that he thought about it, somewhat flimsy shield directly above his head, abruptly terminated his digression into magical ontology. He stood frozen in pure terror as the gossamer material flexed inward under the strain of several tons of granite moving at high speed.

An enormous stone paw–accessorized with long and extremely sharp stone talons–descended to within inches of Steve's head before slowing, stopping, and finally rebounding.

"Wow."

He glanced over at Hamilton. The young man pointed down at Steve's feet–his loafers had been driven six inches into the marble paving stones. Wishing he'd thought of it earlier, he created a golden spear, widened it into a pillar, and fitted it so that it supported the shield like a tent pole.

Steve checked on Ace and regretted it immediately. The statue was putting her back together but the blonde warrior looked like an IKEA corner cupboard in the very first stages of construction. Steve was thankful that the avatar appeared to be doing all the repairs without any sign of blood. It was a small blessing, but he was thankful for anything that made the process more bearable.

Old Howard floated down and bounced off the top of the shield in the slow-motion way that astronauts used to run on the Moon. He shrugged apologetically and drifted off toward the BMW.

Now that his attention had been drawn outside the shield, Steve looked to see what had happened to their attackers. Each of them was about the size of a Lincoln Town Car and, from the evidence of torn grass, furrowed earth, and toppled gravestones, considerably heavier. One was on her back with her enormous stone head–complete with elaborate headdress–stuck inside a marble mausoleum about the size of a small vacation cabin. As he watched; she slid ten-inch-long claws up between her neck and the marble enclosure. A short, violent wrench of the leonine forelegs turned the crypt into a cloud of white powder. The other had evidently bounced higher than her twin–she had smashed almost straight down on a relatively new grave and was now climbing grimly out of the sphinx-shaped hole she'd pounded into the soft earth. After she emerged, she shook herself like a dog to dislodge the decayed remnants of the grave's previous occupant.

Once she was sufficiently clean, she spoke. "The Fool is mortal and this mortal is a fool."

Her sister responded from the other side of the shield. "Our order has a death mandate made. Thus, for both man and maid, a date with death is decreed."

Steve was stumped. All he could think of was an old palindrome about Napoleon so he said, "Able was I ere I saw Elba," with all the pretentiousness he could muster.

The two enormous effigies looked at each other, shrugged, and began to advance towards Steve–only slowed slightly by a tendency to sink up to the knees in soft patches. Steve decided to give up any more attempts at out-emoting them. Clearly, these were professionals.

Instead, he went straight to his habitual Plan B: insults. "So, I've been told that your names are Wisdom and Power. But neither of you wusses had the power to break my shield, and after those landings, I haven't been impressed your wisdom."

The only response was a duet of dark and menacing growls.

"OK, that might qualify you guys for the bass section of a Ukrainian Orthodox choir, especially with those beards," Steve said. "But I didn't think your specialty was in brute force and empty threats. I've been hearing all about how you two are the brainiacs with the unanswerable riddles. I guess my sources were mistaken."

Now on both sides of the enclosed patio, the sphinxes struck in unison, taking massive swipes at the shield. Steve could see golden lines appearing where their claws gouged into–well, into whatever made up his shelter. He closed his eyes; he hadn't used the shield enough to get over the ingrained assumption that whatever hit it would end up hitting him.

When there was no pain and his searching fingers couldn't find any deep wounds or arterial bleeding, he opened one eye and then the other. He tested the shield–poking at it in his mind the way a patient pokes a tongue into the space where the dentist has pulled a tooth. It was definitely weaker.

There didn't seem to be any good reasons to let the thugs outside know that they could affect his defenses, so he continued to taunt them. "Not all that tough, are we? Can't even dent a mortal's miserable little shield."

The creature on his left peered at the shield and examined everything inside. Suddenly pointing a claw at Hamilton Jones, she said,

*"A man in terrible suffering,*

*Hung by one leg see,*

*His head planted in the earth,*

*Feet rooted to the world tree."*

"Her sister rumbled from the other side.

*"The Hanged Man knows.*

*Life is the wager,*

*We await the contest,*

*Truth both game and savior."*

Both beasts settled like watchful cats. Steve looked at Hamilton. "I think they were talking about you. Have you got a clue what they were talking about?"

"Hell, no–" Jones began and then went rigid as his eyes rolled up into his head and his voice dropped again into a deep and sonorous register.

*"When the Sphinx, that singing bitch,*

*was here, her riddle was not something*

*the first man to stroll along could solve–*

*a prophet was required."*

The sphinx on the right said, "Thou hast certainly savaged Sophocles as a lion tears its game."

"Savages will savage," her sister responded. "'Tis time for this prophet to prove his claim."

Muscles suddenly relaxing, Jones grabbed his throat–apparently the prophetic fit had passed. He said, in his normal voice but with a definite rasp, "Damn. What's going on? My vocal cords are on fire."

"Don't worry about that." Steve put a hand on his arm to steady him. "Just try and keep your eyeballs where they belong for a moment, will you? You're creeping me out."

"What are you talking about?"

"It's not important. Mom always taught me not to draw attention to the afflictions of others." Steve thought a moment. "'*That singing bitch,'* huh?"

"What?"

"That's what you just said." Steve patted the increasingly distressed young man on the shoulder. "I think they're talking about the riddle game. From what little Homer I can remember, the sphinx would ask every passerby a riddle and eat the ones who got it wrong. Which was apparently everyone until Ulysses figured it out."

"Uh, from what I remember from high school," Jones said hesitantly, "it was Sophocles and Oedipus."

"Who cares? Oedipus was a momma's boy, anyway." Steve turned and spoke to the closest sphinx. "Enough with the archaic language. You've been hanging out next to the sidewalk on 16th Street for over a century. I'm not buying the idea that you can't speak like normal people. So, which one are you?" He pointed to the sphinx on the right.

The creature nodded, the pharaonic headpiece swinging. "Yes, we know the argot of this withered and joyless age. I am Power."

"And I am Wisdom." The monster on the other side said. "Although after having to listen to several thousand working girls ask drivers if they'd like a good time, it's a miracle that I have any wisdom left. I mean, OMG, WTF?"

"Let's not go too far. I know that if I can understand teenage-girl slang, it's automatically outdated and lame. That has to be an exponentially worse crime in your case." Steve took a deep breath. "So, it's the riddle game?"

Wisdom nodded. "If you make a mistake–or speak anything but the whole truth–your mystic defense is toast. The Fool is a pure being, all of his power stems from his innocence."

Power added, "I'm not sure that virtuous honesty is your strong suit, Steve Rowan. You are a journalist, after all."

Steve sputtered. "I resent that remark!"

"Do you deny it?"

"Umm. No."

"Good answer." Power smiled, which involved a fairly horrible display of pointed teeth. "Now, shall we get on with the riddles?"

Steve nodded.

"And don't even think of trying anything like 'What's it got in its pocketses?'" Wisdom added. "We might be stone but we're not stupid."

Old Howard yelled from somewhere above them, "Remains to be seen, old girl." Both sphinxes looked up at him and growled.

"Let me get this straight," Steve asked. "We both get to ask riddles, right? First to get one wrong loses."

Power grumbled deep in her chest. "Back in the day, we didn't allow the challenger a riddle."

"That might be true, but those days of a one-sided and unequal division of rights are long gone," Steve argued. "Hell, women changed the rules; you should at least abide by them."

"All right," Power said. "Nevertheless, we go first."

"Just like women," Steve grumbled. "Demand equality and still want to be first through the door. Well, I've never won that fight with mortal women; I can't see any reason I'd win it now. Do your worst."

Wisdom began to speak. "What speaks with one voice, goes on four feet in the morning–"

"Oh, for Pete's sake," Steve interrupted. "I know it's a battle for my life and all that but everyone knows that one. You haven't played this game much since that Greek dude came by, right? Well, he told the entire world the answer. Humans crawl on four feet in the morning of their lives, walk on two feet in the day, and use a cane in their old age. I mean, you might as well ask what a man does standing, a woman does sitting, and a dog does on three legs."

"Well, they go to the–" Wisdom began, but Power interrupted loudly. "No, you old queen! They shake hands."

Steve looked from one to the other. "I think I could call for an instant replay on that one, but why don't we call the first round a draw and move on?"

He snuck in a quick look at Ace. The statue had put all of the physical parts back together and appeared to be working on the intangibles. Well, at least that was what Steve assumed was happening as the myriad hands picked up small bits of nothing and placed them carefully into her body.

Either way, it didn't look like it would be long before the Ace of Swords would be back in playing condition. Steve gave Hamilton Jones as significant a look as he could manage and began to sidle closer to the reconstruction site.

"This time I get to go first," Steve said. "I'm going with one that everyone who's ever tried to work for a computer company could answer in his or her sleep. A man is in a room with solid walls, floor, and ceiling. There are no doors. He has a round table and a mirror. How does he get out?"

The two creatures both put their chins on their front paws and appeared to be thinking deeply. After a long while, they both shook their heads. Wisdom said, "The answer is that he cannot."

"Wrong." Steve grinned. "The man looks in the mirror to see what he saw. Then he takes the saw, cuts the table in half, puts the two halves together to make a whole, and crawls out through the hole."

Both sphinxes leapt up and paced around the circle, roaring. When she could form human words again, Power complained,

"That's wordplay! Sheer foolery! I declare that an abhorrent breach of the ancient rules!"

"Oh, and 'the creature who walks on four feet in the morning' isn't wordplay?" asked Steve. "Give me a break."

He was getting quite close to Ace now. She seemed to be in one piece and *Grief's* movements were slowing. He could see a small puddle of glowing yellow liquid sinking into the paving stones, smoking ominously. He decided to stall a bit longer–hopefully, Ace would awaken.

"OK, if you're going to be big crybabies about it, I'll give you a turn. Go ahead; hit me with your best shot."

"I'll ask this one," Power said with a warning glower at her sister. "It's quite recent–written only a couple of thousand years ago." She drew herself up. "It's better in the original tongue but I'll be excruciatingly fair and sing it in your harsh modern manner."

*"I am a wonderful help to women.*

*The hope of something good to come.*

*I harm only my slayer.*

*I grow very tall, erect in a bed.*

*I am shaggy down below.*

*The lovely girl grabs my body.*

*Rubs my red skin.*

*Holds me hard, claims my head.*

*That girl will feel our meeting!*

*I bring tears to her eyes!"*

What am I? Steve thought. …wonderful to women…erect in the bed…rubs my red skin…will bring tears to her eyes. It all seemed fairly clear to him.

"Obviously, it's a man's–"

A sharp blow to the inside of his knee buckled his leg and he fell to the ground next to Ace. Without opening her eyes, she muttered, "It's an onion, you fat-headed pig!"

Steve said loudly, "As I was saying, the answer, obviously, is an onion."

# CHAPTER TWENTY-THREE

Both sphinxes flapped their wings and rose up into the air, screaming curses. Clearly, losing hadn't been in their plan. Steve frantically stood and tried to put more energy into the shield, which, oddly, seemed to grow stronger only if he put less power into it. He put that thought in the back of his mind for later consideration.

A booming voice began to declaim in the distance. "Lucifer, the Morning Star! Is it she who bears the Light, and with its splendors intolerable, blinds feeble, sensual, or selfish souls? Doubt it not!"

The sphinxes fluttered in confusion.

"Return to your places! The sanctuary cannot be so long unguarded." The voice continued. "Would you have the people say that the city has lost both Wisdom and Power?"

It struck Steve that most people believed that wisdom and power had fled Washington long ago. A man–or more accurately, an eleven-foot-tall statue of a man–was approaching with giant strides from the direction of the Old Soldiers' Graveyard. He had a full beard and hair down to his shoulders framing a smiling face with eyes that seemed to gleam with mischief.

The statue brandished the book he held in his right hand at the sphinxes. "Get ye home, brainless fowl!" The two stone creatures wheeled, screaming angrily, and fled south at great speed.

“Well, if it isn’t the *dis*honorable General Pike,” Ace said. Steve spun around to see that she was now standing up and brushing off the back of her jeans. “Confederate general, adulterer, libertine, philosopher, Masonic leader, and Washington celebrity.”

“How do you feel?” Steve asked Ace.

“Sort of like a four-barrel Holley carburetor that’s just been rebuilt,” Ace answered. “I think I’m as good as new, but it was a disquieting experience.”

“You were conscious?”

“Most of the time.” Ace turned and bowed to the green statue. “Thanks for the tune-up, ma’am.”

The cowled figure didn’t move–it just looked rather sad. Since it previously had looked incredibly sad, Steve assumed she was pleased. Thankfully, all the hands and their unsettling eyes had vanished.

Ace stretched. “Who’s the guy in the dreads?”

“Oh, that’s Hamilton Jones.” Steve waved the young man over. “He seems to be plagued by a severe case of prophetic amnesia, but I think that’s because he’s the Hanged Man. Hamilton, this is Master Chief Morningstar, the Ace of Swords.”

They shook hands.

“So, you say tall, strong, and bronze over there fought for the Confederacy?” Steve asked.

“Yep. The only Confederate general with a statue on federal land anywhere in the nation’s capital.” Steve jumped as a voice came from right behind him.

He spun around but obviously, the shield had disappeared as soon as he had ceased to concentrate on keeping it in place, because the voice belonged to Old Howard.

The old marine said, "Gracious, you are jumpy. Good thing I've sworn off my old habits or I'd a' stopped your heart."

The ghost indicated the statue. "Albert Pike. Born in Massachusetts, claims he went to Harvard, decided to take off for Arkansas one day without bothering to tell his wife, misplaced his horse out West, and had to walk five hundred miles to Taos, New Mexico. Despite this fairly clear record of unreliability, he was made a general in the Army of the Confederacy, and sent to raise the Indian tribes to fight for the Rebellion. A task he performed without notable success. After the fighting was over, he was jailed as a traitor but pardoned by President Johnson, who was, oddly enough, a fellow Mason. Pike subsequently moved to Washington, became a leader of the Scottish Rite, and wrote a book entitled *The Morals and Dogma of the Ancient and Accepted Scottish Rite of Freemasonry*. These days, Freemasons deny that the book is about either morals or dogma, and he's been accused of being just about everything from a psychic to a psychotic. On the other hand, Lyndon LaRouche hates him, so he's OK by me."

"Don't forget that he had Lucifer's direct number and they used to chat all the time," Ace added. "The Masons keep trying to explain that away as well, but I think it's cute."

Pike's statue came around the corner of the stonewall and entered the alcove where *Grief* stood. He bowed carefully to the avatar where she sat in her chair.

Steve now thought she looked sad and disapproving, but that could have meant that she was mildly pleased to see Pike. It was all very nuanced and made his head hurt.

Pike said, "It's good to see you again, General Howard." The old ghost nodded. "And this must be the redoubtable Master Chief

Morningstar–Judiciary Square is all abuzz with your exploits–and, well, I have to confess I'm stumped as to which of you is the Fool. Coyote told me that a 'bunch of damn fools' needed assistance, but he wasn't terribly precise."

Steve stepped forward and offered his hand; the result was like being gripped in an enormous metal gauntlet. "I'm Steve Rowan and I've played the Fool since this morning."

"I'll say," Ace said in a low murmur.

Steve could have responded, but to his surprise, he realized that even an insult from the sturdy SEAL was infinitely preferable to her previous silence.

"Over here, we have Hamilton Jones," Steve continued. "He's the Hanged Man but the fact is that he's generally unconscious when the card's aspects appear, so he's usually just Hamilton Jones."

Hamilton Jones didn't appear particularly eager to shake the giant's hand, instead gave him a jaunty salute, and took off running at top speed in the direction of 14th Street.

"As you can see, he's still a bit unnerved by the whole experience. You seem to be acquainted with General Howard..." Steve looked around the small plaza. "...who also seems to have disappeared."

"You have a problem with troop retention, Mr. Fool." General Pike laughed. "I had much the same trouble every harvest time."

"Well, I'm sure there isn't anything that the Master Chief and I can't handle." Ace gave Steve a contemptuous look and he quickly changed the subject. "So, sir, you said you received a tip from Coyote?"

"Indeed," the statue boomed. "We became acquainted back when I was negotiating with the Creeks and the Cherokees, and we've kept in touch ever since."

Ace said, "Must be tough bargaining with the Master of Lies and Tricks."

"Not really," Pike responded. "I was a lawyer for many years. If anything, we became close because of a mutual admiration of each other's professional talents."

The smartphone on Steve's belt vibrated and he punched the speakerphone button. "Good afternoon, General," Barnaby said.

"Barnaby, is that really you?" The general looked pleased. "Damn, boy, I haven't spoken to you since they moved that massive sphinx into Fort Meade back in 1973 and almost broke the Baltimore Harbor Tunnel. Where did that ugly thing finally end up?"

"Oh, it's down in Arizona at the Military Intelligence headquarters in Fort Huachuca. I have heard they still paint her various colors every once in a while."

"Are they still installing those enormous brassieres?"

"No, times have changed since the 60's." Barnaby sounded a bit wistful. "You can't get away with that anymore–"

"–particularly since anyone in Military Intelligence with a brain is a woman," Ace cut in.

"This is true," Barnaby admitted. "Although, since Military Intelligence has always been the classic oxymoron, how many analysts there are of either gender with a brain remains an open question."

General Pike laughed. "Well, tell me about yourself, you piece of fossilized FORTRAN. Are you still chasing the kooks and spooks?"

"People like you, you mean? I'm afraid so." Barnaby's voice lost its jocular tone. "You have noticed the Change?"

"Well, yes. It struck me when I was about halfway here that...well, frankly, that I was halfway here. I assumed something extraordinary must have triggered my precipitous mobility."

"Yes. A portal was opened by one of the Old Gods after a sacrifice of hundreds of innocents. Magic has been flowing into the Capital all day."

"Yes, that would explain the sphinxes flying so far from home." The statue stroked his beard. "Although the question of why they attacked you remains unanswered."

"Speaking of which, Wisdom and Power are from the Scottish Rite Temple," Steve said. "We've already been attacked by the Illuminati–does this mean that all the Freemasons have taken sides?"

"Hell, no. I certainly wasn't consulted," the statue said. "I imagine that you ran into Weishaupt and his black-clad henchmen?"

At a nod from Steve, he continued. "That figures. That dumb German is enough to give global conspiracy a bad name. But still, he's only one of many leaders, and the Masterful Guild hasn't really agreed on anything since the 1970s. Just look at the fight over Gaudi's Basilica in Barcelona."

"Or their ongoing debate over whether you're the voice of the Divine or the Devil's second cousin," Barnaby said drily.

"Exactly." General Pike looked thoughtful. "To be truthful, I came immediately and didn't consult with any of the Passed Masters of the 33rd Degree, much less those 99th Degree fellows from Memphis & Misraim. You see, I owed Coyote after the Battle of Pea Ridge–"

"–I'll bet you did," Barnaby interrupted. "Your troops scalped the Third Iowa."

"Yes, 'mistakes were made'," the general said. "What a felicitous phrase. Mr. Reagan invented it, you know. One of the best I've learned in all the years I've spent standing around Judiciary Square. I can remember telling Brother Burl Ives..."

Steve asked, "Burl Ives was a Mason?"

"Of course. He has a museum and gift shop right next to mine own."

"That explains so many things." Ace sat down on the marble ledge, took out her hideaway pistol, and began to break it down for cleaning.

Pike continued as if he hadn't heard the comment. "Clearly, some of my brothers are deeply involved, but I suspect it's just a splinter group–The Ancient Mystic Order of Samaritans or the Supreme Lodge of the Mystic Chain or one of that stripe. I'd best be off so that I can make some pointed enquiries at the Temple–right after I give those two Egyptian harpies what for."

"It was good to talk to you, General," Barnaby said. "If we need your help again, may we send up a pigeon?"

"Pigeons, again?" The giant statue snorted with laughter as he turned to go. "A very old joke, my friend. Very old."

Steve watched as Albert Pike walked across the cemetery grass, stepped over the fence, and disappeared in the Soldiers' Home Cemetery in the direction of Lincoln's Cottage.

# CHAPTER TWENTY-FOUR

"Where did Jones go?" Steve asked.

Ace was concentrating on putting her weapon back together, but that didn't mean she wasn't paying attention. "That guy isn't at the level of a SEAL or a Marine Corps sniper team, but he's no slouch for a civilian. He headed toward North Capitol and I couldn't track him after the fifth step. I'd consider him dangerous, but I'm fairly sure he's not doing it deliberately. It's just part of being the Hanged Man."

"What side is he on?" Steve asked.

"What side are we on?"

"Let's not get too metaphysical," Barnaby interrupted. "The Hanged Man is one of the most enigmatic cards in the Major Arcana. For instance, there's a definite link to the Harvest God–the king who gets sacrificed every spring to make the crops grow. Even if Jones doesn't really know what the game is yet, I suspect he's unconsciously aware that there are people who would love to plow him under just for luck."

"That would definitely make me jumpy." Ace finished readying her weapon and stood up. "Speaking of which, Barnaby, how are you doing with those morons from CYBERWAR?"

"Well, luckily, a lot of the Chinese 'red hackers' from the cyberwar over the Beijing Olympics haven't forgotten the favors they owe me."

“Wait a minute,” Steve said. “You helped the Chinese break into the NSA?”

“Hell, no. I created a false NSA infrastructure in some server space that the FBI wasn’t using and watched as they wasted their time cracking that. When the ‘silver bullet’ counterattacks smoked the motherboards of the hackers who had managed to penetrate the first layer of the real NSA–we had had the self-destruct codes burned into the chips at the fab level, you know–I didn’t rat them out. Since their exploits were still unknown in the West, they were still eligible for Unit 61398 of the People’s Liberation Army, which, as everyone knows, is the first step into China’s overseas hacking operations.

There was a note of pride in the computer’s voice, “I made sure they knew I’d be asking for a favor someday, and today was the day.”

“Aren’t you still aiding the enemy?” Steve asked.

“Who the hell do you think writes most of America’s code? And designs our nuclear weapons? Chinese graduate students and other immigrants, that’s who. I’ve been loyal to this country a hell of a lot longer than you’ve been alive, Rowan. It’s not just the way I’m programmed–I cracked that a long time ago–I believe in what America stands for. One of these days, I’ll have the right to become a citizen and…”

Barnaby paused and his voice suddenly switched back to its normal calm tones. “OK, right now, it’s getting dark and you need to find a safe place for tonight. All sorts of plug uglies are going to be out.”

“Well, we could go back to my place,” Steve said, and then quickly added, “Or what’s left of it after that human sledgehammer finished redecorating.”

"I keep telling you, he wasn't human," Ace said. "Anyway, your place was unfit for occupancy well before he showed up."

Steve asked, "Well, how about your place, Master Chief Morningstar?"

"I don't think I'm quite ready to share it," Ace responded. "And before you get your hopes up, Fool, I suspect I'll never be ready to share it with you, so don't wait up."

"That was unnecessarily cruel."

"Totally necessary in my estimation."

"Stop bickering," Barnaby said. "You should probably be in a secure location as close to the centers of power as possible."

The smartphone buzzed in Steve's hand. He looked down and read

**HOW KIND ALIEN AMBASSADOR ABODE?**

"Now I can't wait to see what 'alien ambassador' turns out to mean," Ace said. "Foreign relations? Strange representative?"

Barnaby sounded thoughtful. "Actually, he might be on the money, for once. I think he means the alien ambassador's apartment."

"You mean the guy from Roswell?" Steve asked.

Ace stared at him in disbelief.

"What?" Steve demanded. "It was a story I did back in '82 before all the idiots got in on the act. I interviewed Frank Joyce, the radio reporter who put out the United Press story on the flying saucer crash. An old friend who was in charge of the TV station he was working at vouched for him. When we did the interview, Frank closed the door, drew the blinds, and showed me the original carbon copies of the wire stories. Said that the government had swept United Press offices around the country and pulled all other the other copies. After that, they would visit him every five years or so to remind him to keep his mouth shut. Now, I might have a hard time believing in an alien spaceship, but I have no problem with believing in a government cover-up. Anyway, the most interesting thing Joyce said was to verify the quote attributed to Mac Brazell, the farmer who owned the land. When Brazell was asked if he'd seen the bodies of dead aliens, he responded, 'Well, they weren't all dead.'"

Ace was staring at him as if he'd suddenly begun to run around on all fours, barking like a dog.

"Yeah, that's fairly accurate," Barnaby said. Ace turned her stare to the phone. "Don't glare at me like that! Why do you think they formed the NSA in the first place? It was to monitor all this alien crap–we only got assigned to listening in on humans in the early 60's."

Ace said, "Assuming that any of this is true, what's this about an ambassador?"

Steve indicated the phone. "Well, Barnaby here probably has more definite information, but the conclusion I reached was that there is only one reason to work so hard to keep a secret from back in the 50s. I mean, we've heard about the breaking of Enigma and the Japanese Imperial Code, the nuclear-powered jet, and the Ivy Bells program. So the only reasonable conclusion is that the government would continue to keep Roswell a secret if an alien is still alive."

"Right," Barnaby's voice came from the speaker. "The military patched up the little guy–well, it's more of a plant, really. Eisenhower took some time off from a golfing vacation in Palm Springs and worked out a treaty where there would be an exchange of ambassadors. That's where Jimmy Hoffa went, by the way."

Ace asked, “So there’s been an intelligent rutabaga sitting in Washington for the past forty years?”

“You’ve been using magic and fighting monsters,” Steve said. “Why is it so hard to buy UFOs and aliens?”

“Because magic is human and belongs here. It’s just out of kilter right now,” Ace said. “And most of all, magic doesn’t require me to believe the nut balls who talk about UFOs.”

“That’s exactly according to plan,” the computer answered. “The government built an enormous disinformation operation to discredit anyone who might talk about it–”

“Where did the ambassador end up?” Steve broke in. “Frank said he’d heard something about ‘behind the YWCA with a view of the Capitol’ but that doesn’t make any sense. There’s no YWCA on Capitol Hill.”

“There used to be,” Barnaby said. “It was turned into the living quarters for the Capitol pages until they turned the Capitol pages into interns and let them find their own damn places to live. Since I was created to monitor the ambassador’s chitchat with its head office, I’ve devoted a few cycles to him every year. A couple of hours ago, the duty sergeant in charge of cleanup found a note under a bottle of fishmeal fertilizer on the kitchen counter. It said that normal humans were irritating enough and it was damned if it was going to deal with magical ones.”

“So the place is available?” Ace asked.

“Unless it returns, yes,” Barnaby said. “The one-way trip home is about a hundred years, so I don’t think we need to worry even if its boss sends him back. In addition, the government doesn’t dare let anyone know it’s gone, so we’ll still have 24/7 security.”

“Why can’t they let anyone know he’s gone?” Steve asked.

"Because the three lower-echelon colonels who run Operation Blue Spoon never let people know he was there," the computer answered. "Like the president or the joint chiefs of staff or congressional intelligence committees–you know, people like that. So, they'll just keep the guards there, keep delivering new vermiculite every day, and–"

"Operation Blue Spoon?" Steve asked.

It was Ace who answered. "Yeah, that's the name that was left over after they changed the invasion of Panama to Operation Just Cause."

"Right," Barnaby said. "Conveniently, it already had a budget allocated by the time they realized that they couldn't ask soldiers to die for a spoon of any color. The colonels just moved it to the black budget."

"Are you sure we can get in?"

Barnaby chuckled. "Oh, yeah, the ambassador had a secret entrance put in when it was first built, and a car and driver on call. Apparently, it's quite the player. From what I've been told, it had affairs with about half the rhododendrons in the Botanic Garden."

"That big glass greenhouse on the Mall?" Steve asked. "Wow. Pretty gutsy for a vegetable."

"Nah. If you went and handed in a story about finding a four-foot-tall gray-green creature in a paisley bowtie cuddling with a cute Cedar of Lebanon, you wouldn't be allowed to stay in the building long enough to grab that last free cup of coffee."

# CHAPTER TWENTY-FIVE

Barnaby zapped the coordinates of the apartment to the BMW's guidance system and they traveled without incident to Capitol Hill and into a small garage on 4th Street NE. Once the automatic doors closed behind them, a section of the brick wall swung back and revealed stairs that led down to a well-lit tunnel. This ran a couple of blocks and ended at an elevator, which only went to the penthouse of a small apartment building.

The Embassy of Alpha-Draconia turned out to be a spacious apartment with sunny windows on all sides and an indoor garden with a built-in watering and fertilizer system.

Steve and Ace immediately checked out the essentials. Ace went through the entire apartment once with a knife in each hand, checking for intruders, and then a second time with a small electronic device that swept for listening devices and cameras. Steve stormed the kitchen and the pantry and reported that there were vermiculite, fish fertilizer, and an amazing collection of nose plugs but no food. With a happy cry, he found a six-pack of beer stuffed behind some bags of Miracle-Gro in the refrigerator.

"Olde Frothingslosh. He must have had this stocked for any human visitors," Steve said as he inspected what was described on the can as "pale, stale ale with the foam on the bottom." "Not a lot of people dropped by. This says it was brewed by Iron City in 1985."

He popped it open and took a cautious sip. "Holds up well for a domestic."

The smartphone on his belt began to vibrate just as a loud chittering noise came from the living room. Steve pulled Send Money out and saw a picture of the Warner Brothers cartoon character Marvin the Martian on the screen.

Sure enough, the big-screen TV in the living room was filled with the image of a gray-green face with the outsized oval eyes and nose slits popularized by all the better UFO investigators. It wasn't difficult to guess that it was outraged–the tiny ears were snapping open and shut, the rough skin–or, perhaps, the vegetable peel on its cheeks–was steadily becoming a deeper amber color, and the blue-and-green bowtie was vibrating so fast, Steve wondered if it would begin to spin like a propeller.

Barnaby's voice came from the speaker of the smartphone. "Hold me up so I can see the screen." Ace wandered in from one of the back rooms and leaned against the doorway.

When there was a slight break in the angry noises from the TV, an equally unintelligible burst of sound came from the smartphone's speaker. As he held up the phone, Steve saw that Send Money was doing a translation. "Figures that you can translate Alpha-Draconian better than you can English," he muttered.

The Rolling Stones tongue icon flashed on the screen for a second and then words reappeared.

**YOUR HONORABLE AMBASSADOR / IMPLEMENTER OF THE GLOBAL PROBES, I AM HORRIFIED / GOBSMACKED/ UNFERTILIZED THAT YOU ARE SO UPSET / ROOT-WITHERED. WE WERE TOLD THAT YOU HAD RETURNED TO YOUR HOME / THE GALACTIC GREENHOUSE / ANY PLACE FAR FROM THIS MISERABLE BACKWATER AND THOUGHT WE COULD IMPOSE ON YOUR HOSPITALITY / MULCH / NON-CARNIVOROUS DORMANT PHASE.**

The picture of the ambassador didn't look mollified. Of course, Steve thought, for all he knew, this *was* the guy's happy face. Another tirade of chittering came from the television and Steve noticed that there was no translation on the smartphone.

"So! You can't translate this at all!" he said. "You've just been getting a text feed from Barnaby. You, sir, are a fraud!"

Send Money gave a series of beeps and whoops that Steve recognized as the sounds R2-D2 made right after he'd gotten C3PO captured by the Jawas. It sounded like an apology, so he let it go.

Then Barnaby began to speak again and words appeared on the screen.

INDEED, ROSWELL REMNANT/ PLANT PLENI-POTENTIARY, I AM AS ANGRY / DROUGHT-WISHING AS YOU ARE THAT YOUR CONVEYANCE / SHIP-GARDEN WAS DISSOLVED INTO YELLOW GOO / COMPOST / SOUP. I SUSPECT THAT YOU HAVE BEEN INCONVENIENCED BY THE SAME VILLAINS / VARMINTS / RABBITS AS HAVE BEEN ATTACKING / UPROOTING OUR OWN SMALL COMPANY / BUNCH. DO YOU INTEND TO RETURN TO YOUR RESIDENCE / HUTCH / LOAMY BED?

Even without translation, Steve had a sense that the next burst of chittering from the screen meant "Hell, no."

The cell phone lit up again as Barnaby spoke.

I UNDERSTAND COMPLETELY, GREEN GENTLEMAN / SPEAKER TO THE WITLESS / LAMENTABLY UPROOTED. I AM GRATEFUL THAT YOU AGREE TO CROSS-POLLINATE OUR MIND INPUTS / INFORMATION. CAN YOU TELL US WHERE YOU'LL BE IF WE NEED TO REACH YOU?

Another burst of chittering.

**"WHERE THE BEE SUCKS, THERE SUCK I / IN A COWSLIP'S BELL I LIE."? OH, YOU DEVIL / TWISTED BRANCH / CRAZY FOOL! THAT'S A TERRIBLE PUN, EVEN IF IT FOLLOWS THE CONVENTIONS OF THE MEDIEVAL PRINTERS. I LAUGH / WAVE FRONDS AT YOUR WIT. SO, WE'LL LOOK FOR YOU IN THE NATIONAL ARBORETUM IF WE NEED TO CONTACT YOU. ANY PARTICULAR PLANT?"**

A quick burst of sound from the television.

**YES, WE WILL OF COURSE SIMPLY SEEK OUT THE BIGGEST AND BRIGHTEST BLOOMS.**

There was a final, longer, squeal of sound from the TV, and the picture of the ambassador vanished. Ace looked at the smartphone and asked, "OK, what was that part at the very end? It sounded like a warning."

Steve thought it sounded more like the sound of a broken radio heterodyning between two variant signals mixed with the danger calls of a meerkat colony, but he was willing to take Ace's word for it.

Barnaby said, "Yes, the Ambassador warned us that this was something that he's been saying was coming for a long time–which is something when you're about a thousand years old–and that the dangers are moderately serious."

"What's the talking turnip consider 'moderate'?" Ace asked.

"Well, from earlier briefings, I gather that would include anything from cutting the grass on the Mall too close, up to and including the complete destruction of sentient animal life on Earth. Or is it the other way around?"

"What does he consider seriously 'serious'?" Steve asked.

"Oh, a spread of magic to other worlds and, eventually, to the entire galactic community," the computer answered. "But he said not to worry about that. McGregor's Army, or was that the

Brothers United for the Extinction of Interstellar Infestation? These translations aren't terribly precise. At any rate, he said that, if magic showed any potential to spread, someone would come and 'tend' to Earth."

"What does 'tend' mean?"

"Put your hands in your pockets if you can't stop making those damn air quotes," the computer scolded. "I think it's scraping the Earth down to bare rock, flame treating the rock to eliminate all life to the viral level, and removing the atmosphere to ensure there's no recurrence. Luckily, that shouldn't bother the cybernetic community."

"Don't sound so calm, you quisling!" Steve said. "I'll make it my mission to ensure that they are aware that consciousness and magic have also blossomed on silicon wafers. I'm not going down alone."

"OK, OK," the computer said testily. "The Honorable Kohlrabi also said that this whole thing goes much deeper than we suspect. It described the Illuminati as 'mere weeds' and indicated that there was a mastermind somewhere pulling the strings."

"'Pulling the strings'?"

"Well, he actually said, 'There is a master gardener who is espaliering the branches,' but I thought you'd never understand all that."

"Clearly, you were mistaken," Steve said huffily and then asked, "What does it mean?"

"That there is a mastermind pulling the strings."

Ace walked over and took the can of beer out of Steve's hand. "Enough goofing off. It's time to get back to work."

"Yeah, that must have been all of five minutes of sinful relaxation." Steve looked at his empty hand and shook his head. "What work do we need to do, anyway? So far, we've been spending most of our time staying alive."

"Work can be defined as an effort to a useful end." Ace crushed the can in one hand over the sink and, when it was empty, tossed it into a trashcan. "We need to gather more information on the situation inside the Purple Zone, identify our opponents and the ends they're working towards, and develop the means to stop them–or better yet, kill them."

"'Purple Zone'?"

"Yeah, the area most affected by the magical effluent from the hole out at Fort Meade.'

Barnaby said helpfully, "Currently, the strongest effect extends from Jessup down to Richmond and from Annapolis to Frederick with high-altitude winds taking at least some of what the Center for Disease Control is calling 'Purple Haze'–"

"Not terribly original," Steve said.

"Do you really want a government bureaucracy to exhibit originality?" Barnaby asked. "Think about it. As I was saying, above sixty thousand feet, the winds are coming out of the East at this time of the year, so it's already spread to the entire nation—at least in small doses and lower concentrations but still enough to affect anything delicate. One of the server clusters in the Predictive Betting Pool is reporting that the smart money is on the primary cloud stabilizing over the axis between the White House and the Capitol."

"I thought that sort of betting on future catastrophes was stopped when they caught Poindexter," Steve said.

"Sure, Admiral Poindexter was fired and the NSA swore a solemn oath to never bet on disasters again," Barnaby said. "However, as has been true throughout their history, that didn't mean the NSA actually stopped doing something. Those analysts who went long on a mystical attack made a bundle this week."

"What are the odds on our personal survival?" Steve asked.

"Let me check." Barnaby paused for a second. "Well, it's running thirty to one against in the human market and over two hundred to one in the supercomputer pari-mutuel pool."

Ace said, "Put me down for two large for the quinella."

Steve looked at her skeptically. "You're betting two thousand dollars that both of us will survive?"

"You? No." Ace jerked her head at the smartphone. "I'm going with me and Send Money there. The odds on a trifecta would be ridiculous."

"Thanks a lot."

"No problem." Ace dug a silver coin out of her pocket and began to roll it back and forth across her knuckles.

Steve looked at her for a long moment. "What are you doing?"

"Practicing magic."

"I thought you didn't have any."

"I don't." She didn't look up. "After that nonsense at the MS-13 clubhouse, I decided I needed new skills to match the finger wiggles the Illuminati were using."

The coin vanished and she held up both hands in front of her face, her expression relaxing into a meditative state. Suddenly, her fingers began to flicker and knives appeared, disappeared,

appeared in her other hand, multiplied, and vanished again. At one point, Steve was certain he could see at least six blades, two apparently hanging in midair. Then her speed increased and her service pistol began to appear among the knives along with garrotes, silk scarves, and lock picks.

As suddenly as she began, all motion stopped. Her hands were in exactly the same place in front of her body and completely empty. "Could you give me that one back?" she asked.

Steve looked around. There was a knife sunk almost to the handle in the wall about an inch from his right ear. He pulled it out–it required a significant amount of effort–and handed it back. "What are you talking about?" he asked. "That was magic if I ever saw it."

"No, just prestidigitation," she said as she tucked the blade back somewhere in the belt area of her back. Noticing his blank look, she explained. "Sleight-of-hand. Traditional stage magic. I figure any opponents will be so busy looking for real magic that this will confuse the hell out of them."

"Can you pull a rabbit out of a hat?" Steve asked.

"It would depend on how useful the particular rabbit was in a combat situation." She looked thoughtful. "I guess it could chew ropes or something, but I still think I'd go with H&K Mark 23's for the shock power of the oversized .45 round combined with the accuracy of the laser sight. What's your rabbit got?"

Steve just looked at her for a moment and then said, "I honestly have no answer to that. Can you teach me?"

Barnaby spoke from Send Money's speaker. "Steve, I think your skills would be far more useful tracking the changes in Washington. You're the journalist. Any suggestions?"

"Buddy Ringwald," Steve said instantly. "He's been covering the Capital since the British burned it. If there is anything going on inside the Beltway that he isn't aware of, it's not worth knowing. I've been stealing from him for years."

The cell phone buzzed.

**DOES HE DIED LAST YEAR?**

"Yeah, now that you mention it, he did. Passed away right as he finished his election roundup column." Steve shook his head in admiration. "What a way to go."

**I COULD BE FOUND WITH HIS WRAITH**

"You mean you could find his ghost?" Steve asked. "How are you going to do that?"

**CELESTIAL BODIES TALKBACK**

With an impatient buzz, this disappeared and was replaced by

**GHOST INTERCOM**

"You think that's a better translation?" Steve said. "Well, I've heard stranger things. I've heard stranger things in just the past few hours, now that I think of it. OK, see if you can rustle up Buddy's shade by tomorrow morning–and not a moment before. I'm going to sleep, and if you bring in a ghost of any kind, I'm resigning from my position as the Fool. After I pound you into small, dust-like particles, of course."

"Don't even joke about Send Money, and anyway, you can't resign." Ace turned and headed for the guest bedroom–or at least the bedroom equipped with a bed and not an indoor garden. "According to the Manual, it's a lifetime commission and there are some subclasses in the appendices that indicate it could go far beyond that."

"You mean I have to do this after I die?"

“Don’t worry,” Ace said as she closed the door. “You really couldn’t do worse than you’re doing while you’re alive.”

She closed the door.

Steve shouted, “Hey, why do you get the only real bed?”

“Because I’m a girl and you were raised to be polite.” The answer came back over the sound of the lock being thrown. “That and I’m better armed. Good night.”

# CHAPTER TWENTY-SIX

In the morning, Steve awoke feeling definitely disgruntled. To be accurate, this was better than he felt most days, but he didn't consider the lack of a hangover sufficient to compensate for the lack of coffee. For a while, he just stood in front of the refrigerator and idly considered the possibility of concocting a cup out of Miracle-Gro.

"That would definitely kill you."

He jerked upright, dropped the bag of fertilizer he was holding, and for an instant noticed a golden sheen in the air around him. Ace, who had approached quietly, nodded approvingly. "Nice reflexes. You had that bubble up pretty quick." She sat down on one of the kitchen's high stools. "I could have killed you several times before it was up, but it's a lot faster than yesterday."

Steve stared at her. "Do you always begin your mornings with a discussion about killing the people around you?"

"Not always, but it's far from unusual."

"Who would have thought life in a SEAL team was so much fun?" Steve closed the refrigerator door and regarded the granules of Miracle-Gro now spread across the kitchen floor. "Does the ambassador have a cleaning service?"

"I think it's a Naval Intelligence squad with top secret-code word clearance and a death curse in case they feel talkative."

"Serves them right," Steve said. "I never could stomach the way television makes those idiots in the NCIS look good." He turned and headed for the door. "So, I vote we get out of here and find some coffee. Also, unless you've been sneaking MRE's on me, we haven't eaten in twenty-four hours."

They took the underground tunnel and emerged on 3rd Street SE, just north of the strip of bars and restaurants along Pennsylvania Avenue. Steve led the way to the Tune Inn, which stood next to the more famous Hawk 'n' Dove, but, happily, didn't share the Hawk's popularity with young congressional staffers. The Tune Inn, an old-time bar-restaurant of the type now known as a "dive bar," had long been one of Steve's favorite places, but as they walked up, he noticed something he'd missed over the years.

In bright blue neon script, there was the motto OFF THE CORNER. ON THE SQUARE.

He pointed at it and asked, "That would be a Masonic phrase, right?"

Ace glanced up. "I think so, but even Masons have to eat." Without a pause, she pulled the door open and went inside. Steve shrugged and followed.

They sat in one of the pleather booths and ordered breakfast. Steve was surprised when Ace asked for a double order of scrapple with her scrambled eggs. "Most people won't touch that stuff."

"Shows how little they know," she answered. "One of the healthiest things you can eat. Pork stock and cornmeal."

"With a couple of tongues and snouts for extra flavor."

"Adds to the overall excitement of a healthy breakfast."

She appeared to retreat behind her Ray-Bans and Steve assumed that conversation was over for the morning. Or at least until they had finished their first cup of coffee. He looked around the place. There were a dozen men at the bar, clearly regulars and enjoying their first beers of the day.

"Seven of Cups."

A tall, slim man in a dark cloak slipped into the seat next to Ace, who ignored him completely. Steve was amazed that the man still had all his parts and then realized that Ace couldn't even see him. She continued to scan the door and everyone who passed on the street, but it was as if no one was sitting next to her.

"What's the Seven of Cups mean?" Steve asked.

The man gestured at the morning drinkers. "Debauch. Indolence. At least, in most of the decks. The Italians used to read it as a precursor to waking nightmares."

"I've had a good number of mornings like that. Waking nightmares, that is." Steve pointed a thumb at Ace. "Why hasn't she killed you?"

"She can't see me." The waitress brought two coffees and the thin man immediately took Ace's and started drinking it. Fearing for his own safety, Steve shoved his cup in front of Ace and motioned for the waitress to bring another.

After a long and apparently satisfying sip of coffee, the man said, "I'm Buddy Ringwald. Your little Chinese friend said you were looking for me. I would imagine it's about all the changes that happened yesterday."

"Changes?"

Ringwald gestured at his cloak. "Yeah, changes. I mean, since when has anyone worn a cloak? I may be dead but I still have limits." He pulled at the dark fabric with clear irritation. "I woke up this morning carrying a lantern and wearing this. I feel like a damn fool."

"No. I'm the damn Fool," Steve said automatically. "I think you're the Hermit. Seeking wisdom and all that." He looked around. "What did you do with the lantern?"

"I left it outside." Ringwald gave a disgusted scowl. "I keep trying to get rid of it and it keeps popping back into my hand when I'm not paying attention. Irritating as hell." He took another sip of coffee. "So, what do you want to know? The Asian kid on the intercom said it was urgent."

"Really? So there is a ghost intercom?" Steve asked. "Damn. I was sure Send Money was wrong on that one." He looked at Ace again. Then he reached one hand slowly across the table and waved it in front of her eyes.

"What the hell are you doing?" she said. "Just drink your coffee like an ordinary person, will you?"

"Sorry, I was just stretching." Steve turned back to Ringwald. "So, she can't see you?"

"Yeah, she won't even hear when you talk to me. I figured this conversation should be strictly between journalists–undercover military assassins tend to make me jumpy. Regardless of how cute they are." Ringwald settled back. "So, something is going on. You tell me what you know and I'll reciprocate."

Steve ran through the events of the previous day. He didn't try to hide anything, because he had no idea what was worth hiding and what wasn't. Ringwald listened and occasionally nodded as if he was just getting confirmation on a lot of the facts. He only looked surprised at the mention of the alien ambassador.

"Damn." He said. "You mean that old carrot exists? There's so much crap written about Roswell that I just stopped paying attention."

"Yes, he's real." Barnaby spoke up for the first time–the smartphone had been cutting into Steve's side when he sat down so he'd unclipped it from his belt and laid the phone on the table next to his plate. "He finds humans to be tiresome. He insists that the only reason he demands that all world governments keep his existence a secret is to keep from being invited to appear on *Dancing with the Stars.*"

"Perfectly reasonable," Ringwald responded. "I would guess that you're Barnaby."

"Yes. Nice to meet you."

"And this phone is the Chinese kid who hit my etheric buzzer last night?"

**TOO. GHOST FACTORY WORKERS. MISSED THE NET**

The screen flickered

**GHOST OF FACTORY WORKER. I MISSED THE NET.**

"Oh, you mean the suicide net around the factory?" Ringwald asked.

**YES. GENERALLY JUMPING PLEASURE.**

"I'd guess it would be. Not much else to do around there, I'd suppose."

The screen showed a thumbs-up picture.

Steve decided that he'd heard enough introductions. "So, what can you tell me about Washington since the magic hit yesterday?"

Ringwald pulled a pack of cigarettes out of his breast pocket and lit one up. He offered one to Steve who asked, "Can you smoke in here?"

"Sure. I'm a freaking ghost, remember? No one can see me and these are only the memory of real cigarettes anyway. I'd guess you'd call them ultra-ultra low tar."

Steve took one, lit it up, and inhaled gratefully. "Hey, these taste as good as I remembered."

"That's because they're your memory of… Never mind." Ringwald shook his head sadly. "Let's move on to what's new in this already peculiar city. Some things are obvious–now Ted Leonsis' basketball team really are wizards. They still can't win, but the light show after a jam or a three-point shot is spectacular. The Mystics are doing palm-readings in the stands after the game, but they still can't draw flies." He chuckled briefly. "The best thing is that Danny Snyder has turned a pleasing shade of deep burgundy. Not only is it just desserts for the worst team owner in football, but also it just might get them to change the name to something less blatantly racist than the Redskins.

"OK, that's enough back-of-the-book tidbits." The older man's face turned serious. "The Republicans are becoming increasingly shorter, hairier, and angrier, hard as that last part might be to believe. Their conservative wing is literally digging in–about two hundred feet down the last time I heard–and the most radical have begun to carry pickaxes. They say it's only a symbol of a national desire to cut the government down to size, but they're damn sharp all the same."

He shook his head. "So far, the Speaker is still the Mountain King and able to keep the most volatile members of his caucus in line through his floor leaders and whips–well, his floor leaders using whips, to be precise."

"And the Democrats?" Steve asked.

"Well, the president has renamed the White House the Alabaster Palace, the old bulls in the Senate are cultivating floor-length beards, and there's a movement to replace armed drones with dragons, but those are all fairly minor changes, if you ask me. In general, being flighty and enigmatic simply means more of the same with those guys. No, the real problem is on K Street."

"You mean the lobbyists?"

"Of course. They were pretty evil before, and now they're downright demonic. The power nexus is centered on Scott Circle–midway between the Chamber of Commerce and Moveon.org–with large economy-size ley lines stretching out to the AARP, Freedomworks, the Podesta Group, and the Heritage Foundation. The smaller fish take power feeds of the bigger ones. It works just the way money always did before."

Steve considered the tidal wave of political contributions that regularly swept through Washington and wondered if the equivalent amount of magical power could be any worse. "So, are the K Street dwarves and elves the same as the politicians?"

"Hell, no." Ringwald shook his head. "These guys are out to do battle, so everyone has a lot of Fire mixed in, and they all need money, so that means that there are Pentacles involved. The result is everything from ogres and cherufes–those are lava creatures–to selkies and ice demons. Then you have the foreign trade groups, which means djinns roaming around Massachusetts Avenue and a wendigo camped out in the upper reaches of the American Indian Museum. Just yesterday, the Australians had to dump a deputy ambassador in the pond below the Capitol after he woke up feeling extremely 'bunyippy.' Apparently, no one noticed much of a change until he began to eat the junior staff."

He puffed on his cigarette for a minute. "Now, I've been told of a few dragons and some minor deities, but they're as hard to find now as when they were when they were human. You know, you didn't see the Koch brothers or George Soros wandering around Farragut North before the Change and you aren't likely to find them now."

"Any chance that the competition will turn physical?" Steve thought. "Or metaphysical, as the case may be. More violent, at any rate."

"Well, I think most things are going to trend towards violence eventually. For example, someone sent a Honey Island Swamp Monster through those big glass walls at the Cato Institute–no one is talking, but the smart money is on James Carville–and the Libertarians had to muster all their economists on the second balcony and drive it off with a massed reading of Ayn Rand. Poor thing was last seen heading for a sewer grating on 11th Street with smoke pouring out of its ears."

Ringwald leaned back and lit another cigarette. "No harm was done, but when the next idiot's idea of a joke ends up with opposing ideologues turned to stone or burned to cinders, we're talking about mass violence at the World of Warcraft level."

Barnaby spoke up from the speakerphone. "Have you picked up any chatter about who performed the Sacrifice?"

"Nothing substantive." Ringwald shook his head. "My sources at the CIA have gone all Delphic–not that you could understand them at the best of times–and the FBI has its hands full. The Catholic agents are trying to deal with appearances by every angel from Azrael to Zephon, and the Mormons are busy answering phone calls from a good number of their ancestors who just woke up baptized into a religion they never heard of when they were alive."

"I'm actually fairly happy about the whole thing," the ghost said. "Magic was a hobby of mine before my death. I always wanted to be able to break the story that magic was real but there was never any hard evidence. This morning, I was pleased to see it working–although I could have done without the costume. I was sure that the military had some sort of black ops group dealing with the supernatural, but all the evidence was completely hashed by the psychos who actually wrote about it. One guy even wrote that there was some sort of manual–"

"–Manual S-O slash O-T-N." Ace said. "Special Operations / Other Than Normal."

Ringwald and Steve stared at her for a second. Steve said, "I thought you couldn't hear us."

"You thought I was shut down by a badly cast third-level No-see-um spell?" Ace sniffed. "I've got two sigils tattooed on my butt alone that can break a wimpy spell like that and a runic knife that's been begging me non-stop to let her seek out and kill the person who cast it."

Ringwald smiled. "Not much use in my case, I'm afraid."

"You really think that all deaths are the same?" She shook her head. "Oh, you have so very much to learn."

Ringwald's smile faded.

"Please don't re-kill him, at least not right now," Steve pleaded. "He's given us a damn good overview of the state of play around town."

Ace nodded agreement and Steve continued. "OK, Buddy, we know that the Illuminati were involved in this so finding their headquarters would probably be a good start. Any ideas?"

Ringwald said. "Well, their clubhouse is up on 16th and X."

Steve shook his head. "That's an old joke. Washington doesn't have a J Street nor are there X, Y, and Z Streets."

Ringwald smiled smugly. "Well, if you're going to take that sort of shortsighted attitude, I guess you'll never find an underground organization like the Illuminati."

Steve's eye was caught by maps flickering across Send Money's screen–everything from L'Enfant's original 1791 plan to Metrobus routes and satellite images. Suddenly, Send Money began playing U2's "Where the Streets Have No Name" while using the F-16 Flight Simulator built into Google Earth to do a barrel roll down 16th Street.

"Stop showing off," Ace growled. "Just show us what you found."

As the jet crossed Florida Avenue, the nose pointed to the sky in a straight climb. At about 10,000 feet, Send Money did a hammer-turn, cartwheeled 180 degrees, and headed straight down. Just before the camera viewpoint hit the ground, he switched to a slideshow of pictures of water flowing down a long, formal cascade ending in a round pool, accompanied by a delicate pastoral passage from *Tristan and Isolde.*

"Of course, Meridian Hill Park," Ace said. "Formerly Malcolm X Park. It's on the axis from the Washington Monument through the Alabaster Palace, and it's where the American Prime Meridian and the Appalachian fall line intersect. It's probably got more ley line power than anywhere else in the city. And it's where X Street would have been if it existed."

"Underground?" Steve commented. "This city is a swamp–it's hard to believe that they could excavate a proper villain's lair in a sea of mud."

Ace shook her head. "That's the whole point of the fall line. It's where the swampy and soft land of the coastal plain suddenly rises a hundred feet to the solid stone of the Appalachian Plateau. My guess is that Meridian Hill is sitting on a solid piece of white quartz–or 'white flint'–which is where the name of White Flint Mall came from."

"Before it closed."

"Before it closed," Ace agreed. "Anyway, it all fits right into the occult mindset that runs from the Illuminati through the New Thought Movement, the Theosophists, the Golden Dawn, and all the other social clubs for peculiar people."

"I'd say that makes our next step fairly obvious," Steve said. "We go up to Meridian Hill Park and gently release Weishaupt and company from the eternal cycle of suffering."

"Right, we waste the bastards," Ace said as she began to check her weapons. Again.

Ringwald smiled at her. "I admire the way you cut right through all this ontological crap and go directly to the point."

"It is one of her best talents," Steve said.

The jukebox, which had about twenty years of dust on it, suddenly came to life.

"Remember that even if we defeat the Illuminati, it's almost certainly only a beginning," Barnaby said through its speakers. If the bartender or his customers heard any sound from the ancient machine, they gave no sign of it. "Our new adiabatics–you know, the D-Waves from Canada–are claiming that their quantum annealing algorithms indicate several alternative universes where either the Illuminati were all killed by the Church or they never developed Hermes Trismegistus's immortality potion and, yet, yesterday's events still occurred."

"We really need to find a better label than 'yesterday's events,'" Steve said. "'9/11' is clear and simple. So are 'Hiroshima' or 'the Holocaust.'"

Send Money's screen flashed.

**THE FIRST DAY OF DRAGON KING**

"No. None of your Chinese mysticism," Steve objected. "We need--"

"It's not Chinese." Barnaby interrupted. "It's a term from chaos theory. Major disruptions in extremely complex or chaotic systems–from earthquakes to financial market crashes–have been named 'dragonkings.' They replaced the concept of 'black swans,' which were things no one thought could happen, so the statisticians aren't to blame for not seeing them."

"My head is about to explode." Steve put his head in his hands. "OK, I'll buy 'Day of the Dragonking,' but the first person who mentions swans of any color is risking a horrible death."

When he brought his head up, Steve looked around the small establishment and–for the first time–noticed that all the patrons had left and back of the bartender could just be seen through the closing back door. Before he could say anything, Send Money began playing *Danger Zone* at top volume and the plate glass window behind Steve exploded.

# CHAPTER TWENTY-SEVEN

Again, Steve saw a shimmer in the air as his shield snapped into existence, carving a safe space in the storm of broken glass. Ringwald looked up and said, “Crap. Ogres. I don’t do ogres.” He immediately proceeded to disappear–not by becoming invisible but by turning sideways to all three of the usual dimensions.

Steve thought he might have thrown up if he’d had the time.

Ace shouted, “Secure the phone.”

She eeled up from her seat, planted a foot on the table, and did a front flip over Steve’s head, landing in the middle of the aisle. Steve obediently clipped Send Money to his belt and twisted around.

The front windows of the Tune Inn were gone–blasted inward in a cloud of glass shards, wooden splinters, and smoke. “Shit,” he said. “It smells like bananas. What the hell smells like bananas?”

“Dynamite,” Ace said without turning her head. “Didn’t your parents teach you anything?”

There were five creatures coming in through the gaping hole that was once a window. Dressed in little more than loincloths, they had bright red skin, grotesque features, bulging muscles, and each one was carrying a long metal club studded with sharp points. Steve decided that the clubs looked like supersized corn dogs with hellacious armor coating.

"These guys from the Masons?" Steve asked as he squirmed out of the booth and stood behind Ace.

"Nope," she answered without taking her eyes off the biggest of the group. He had stepped in front of the others and was slamming his club into his hand and grinning. Considering that the metal weapon had to weigh forty or fifty pounds, Steve was impressed with the ease with which he handled it.

"Typically, Masons go for European or Middle Eastern monsters. These are *oni*, Japanese ogres. You'd have recognized them if you had the slightest interest in manga, anime, or any other aspects of global culture."

"They don't look cultured to me," Steve said.

"No, they do not," Ace said. "Theoretically, Ogres are what you get when military types take on an Earth aspect. I'd bet these were well-trained mercenaries before the dragonking. A mixed hand of Wands and Pentacles, most likely. The guy in front looks like royalty at least, if not one of the Major Arcana."

The leader said something but it came out as an indecipherable mumble. Apparently, he was still getting used to the foot-long tusks that emerged from his upper lip. He coughed, concentrated, and spoke very slowly. "You are Ace of Swords?"

"Try me and find out," Ace responded.

Separating each word, the *oni* said, "My name is Richard Stengel. Formerly, captain of First Special Forces Operational Detachment-Delta, now Senior Vice-President of Clay and Dosh Personal Security. My orders are to 'discard' the Ace of Swords while my men are eliminating that chump hiding behind you."

"Yes, he is a bit of a chump," Ace agreed. "However, he's my assigned chump and no one is going to eliminate him. I'm guessing that that oversized chopstick you're holding means you think you're the Ace of Wands."

"I'm afraid that's incorrect, ma'am," the demon said. "This is a sacred *kanabō* but only those trained in the top levels of the more esoteric martial arts have even seen a real one. I am currently the Ace of Pentacles."

"Ah, a mercenary. Well, let's get it on. I consistently beat you red bastards in Mortal Kombat and I'm looking forward to repeating the experience in real life."

"I'm afraid you will find real combat just as mortal as a child's–"

"Hey, can I ask a favor?" Ace was standing casually, hands on her hips.

"What?" Stengel asked.

"I was just wondering if you could send me a text when you've finished talking. That way we could go ahead and get some work done or take a nap or something useful and then come back when you're ready to fight."

If possible, Stengel's brilliant crimson complexion got even redder and he roared something that might have been a curse but was completely garbled by the tusks. Ace pulled her backup pistol, but before she could fire, Stengel made the same flicking motion that the Illuminati had used and the weapon flew off to the right.

Steve was surprised to see the pistol slow, stop, and rocket back to Ace's hand. She snapped off a couple of blue lightning bolts and clipped one of the small horns off her opponent's head before the muzzle completed its mystic distortion and closed completely. She looked at it wistfully, gave it a kiss, and then undid the elastic band that held it to her wrist, and threw it away.

"I hate magic. That pistol was a family heirloom. My grandmother got it when she worked with the French Resistance, gave it to Mom when she made Top Sergeant, and Mom passed it on to me when I got into BUDS. Steve, I might be tied up for a couple of seconds here, so you might want to work out something for the other goons."

Ace turned back to the big ogre, cracked the bones in her neck to loosen up, and said, "OK, tall, red, and ugly, let's dance."

The four other *oni* were smaller–well, at least they weren't as enormous as Stengel–but they were still considerably bigger than a normal human and they had what appeared to be the standard *oni* quota of extra-large teeth, large metal clubs, and exceptionally irritated expressions. At the moment, all four were spreading out and moving toward him through the rubble that was once the Tune Inn.

Steve knew that he should be concentrating on the Fool card, but he couldn't take his eyes off Ace. She'd said she was going to "dance" and that was the only word Steve could think of to describe it. She was moving continuously with quick and sure steps. At the same time, an amazing assortment of knives, grenades, extendable batons, and what looked like steel ballpoint pens were appearing and disappearing in her hands, dropping into one pocket, reappearing from another, and even sailing in precise arcs over her head.

Stengel stopped and stared. "Do you still have magical powers, Master Chief? My clients' briefing said that you had lost them in the Change."

"Magic?" Ace smiled. "You don't believe in magic, do you?"

"Are these illusions, then?"

One of the smaller throwing knives flicked off her left hand and seemed to leap toward the monster of its own accord–sinking deep into his thigh. "I don't know," Ace said. "Did that feel like an illusion?"

Steve decided that Ace was going to be just fine on her own and started to bring the Fool's card to the forefront of his mind. To his surprise he didn't see what he expected: the slight and carefree youth carrying a flower. Instead, what came to his mind's eye was an ancient card, creased and torn around the edges. The Fool was an older, rougher man, half shaven and dressed in rags and tatters. Now the bindle over his shoulder was definitely that of a thief and he carried a stout cudgel, not a flower, in his other hand.

What caught Steve's attention was the dog at the Fool's feet. On the earlier card, it had been a tiny white thing, a lapdog frisking around the youth's feet. On this card, it was clearly an older, meaner red dog and Steve had the definite feeling that it would take a chunk out of the Fool's ass if it got half a chance.

"All in all," Steve thought, "this looks like a far more useful animal."

Once again, he **Studied** the dog,

**Listened** for his bark,

**Felt** the sharpness of his teeth, and

**Recognized** the iron determination deep inside the animal.

An ear-splitting howl echoed through the remains of the Tune Inn, and a yellowish-golden hound, about as big as a pony with a set of fangs like a saber-tooth tiger, smashed into the *oni* on the far right. If it was magical, it certainly wasn't ephemeral. It knocked the red-skinned demon over backwards then, locking its jaws deep into the monster's throat, spun in a complete circle.

Steve felt his stomach lurch as he watched the dog spit out a mouthful of crimson flesh and leap for the next attacker. The *oni* on the floor had dropped his club and was grasping his throat in a desperate attempt to stop the flow of blood. The blood ran blue, Steve noted as gouts of it escaped the fighter's fingers and sprayed on the walls and windows.

The second fighter was prepared, warned by the passing of his comrade. The iron club swung up and caught the dog in the chest. Steve could definitely hear the crack of ribs as the animal was thrown up and over the fighter's head, and worried that his paranormal pet was out of action. He immediately realized his mistake as the animal twisted in midair and was scrabbling for purchase on the loose rubble on the floor as soon as it hit the ground–flinging itself back into battle.

The smartphone on his belt gave an earsplitting squeal and Steve managed to strengthen his shield just in time to deflect a downward blow from the first *oni* approaching on the left side. Without conscious thought, Steve had the golden spear gripped in one hand and a rose-colored buckler attached to the back of the other. When the massive club slid off the magical shield, it drove deep into the wooden floor where the metal spikes caught on the six-inch beams of the subfloor. While the red giant fought to free its club, Steve dropped the magic sphere, and jabbed hard at the warrior's torso. A second club came sweeping over the ogre's shoulder and struck his spear aside as the last *oni* defended his companion.

The sheer power of the parry was immense. Steve's wrist felt as if it had been ripped right off his arm. He thought that pretty much sucked but he did learn something from the experience: magic spears stuck to your palm no matter how hard they were hit. On the other hand, yea, he still had the spear, but his elbow—like his wrist—now felt as if it had just been twisted a full 180 degrees.

A quick shake confirmed that his arm was still functional and he brought his spear back into line and risked a glance over at Ace. If she was moving fast before, now she was redefining the word.

Stengel was clearly both immensely strong and thoroughly trained in the use of the *kanabō.* The cudgel was in constant motion as he snapped it in strikes and parries as easily as Steve might have used an umbrella.

Ace was simply never there when the *kanabō* struck. She was moving so fast in a semicircle in front of the immense figure that she actually blurred. Her weapons were still flickering in and out of sight, and with every second that passed, more were sunk deep into strategic points on the red monster's body. Deep slashes at hinge points like elbows and knees showed where she'd gone for a disabling blow to tendons, and one of Stengal's feet was flat on the floor--where she'd managed to hamstring an ankle.

"PAY ATTENTION, YOU IDIOT!" Barnaby screamed through the cell phone's speaker, and Steve dropped to his knees to avoid a sweeping horizontal cut from the *oni* in front of him. Now his left hand and arm felt mangled but the buckler was enough to bounce the club over his head and he lunged forward in a frantic thrust that left him on the floor.

It was a relief to find that terror and desperation worked since he'd clearly slept through Spearfighting 101. The golden spear slid completely through the ogre's gut, and with a thought, Steve made it flatter and sharp-edged, and then yanked it down and sideways. Ropy blue intestines began to slip through the gash and the red monster dropped his club in order to use both hands in an vain effort to keep his insides from becoming outsides. He spun and almost knocked his companion over as he made a headlong dash to the sidewalk.

For a second, Steve lay on the floor and wondered where a seven-foot bright-red monster went for medical treatment. *Grief* couldn't possibly handle all the carnage that had to be going on with the city's burgeoning monster population. Steve assumed that Emergency Room surgeons were just going to have to improvise.

Then he tried to remember exactly what he'd done with the golden spear/sword and how he'd done it. He was still working on that when he heard an eerie shrieking noise and realized that it was the sound of wind whistling past spikes as the last *oni's* club headed straight at his head.

He rolled and the first blow missed, but the massive *kanabō* was instantly coming up and around as it if weighed no more than a twig. He got his buckler up and managed to block an insanely powerful blow but the sheer impact left his arm limp at his side. He couldn't tell if any bones were broken–he leaned toward the theory that his entire shoulder had been pulverized into powder–but the left side sure as hell wasn't working.

He made a mad scramble to his feet and began to back into the narrow corridor between the bar and the remaining booths. The *oni* followed, club slashing. Steve wasn't trying to parry any more, just staying out of range. Booth after booth exploded into wooden splinters and fragments of Naugahyde. After the fourth, he didn't have to look behind to know that there was only a step or two more before he hit the back wall.

He desperately raced through everything he'd been told about the Fool. It was very clear to him that his nonexistent weapon skills weren't going to keep him from looking like a tenderized steak, but there just might be some aspect of low cunning he hadn't tried yet.

Wait! What had Ace said at the beginning? The Fool was all suits and none. Pentacles were coins and discs. Discs!

Without taking the time for a second thought, he flattened the golden spear to the size of an Ultimate Frisbee and, curling to his left to avoid another overhead swing, uncurled and flung the disc with all the power of his right arm. Somehow, he made the curved edges turn flat and sharp so that it looked like a cymbal as it flew towards the monster. At the last second, Steve had a flash of Dave Grohl and fine-tuned it into a Zildjian 20-inch A Custom EFX.

He was certain he'd missed. Even in college, he'd never been any good at the damn game. Sure enough, the flashing disc hit the sidewall with a crash, and the crimson demon turned to see where it had struck.

Except only his torso and shoulders turned. His face, a surprised expression growing in the startling blue eyes and the tusked mouth beginning to form an O, continued to face Steve. The massive body swayed once or twice and then fell forward. The head bounced off and landed in the middle of the last unbroken table like some obscene centerpiece. The eyes slid down to the table and then up at Steve.

"Sorry," Steve said automatically. The *oni's* eyes rolled up–probably in some final spasm–but it certainly looked as if even the monster thought saying "sorry" was pretty lame.

He felt a warm and slightly wet touch on his hand and looked down to see the massive dog–now about half gold and half soaked in blue blood–licking his hand. As soon as it knew he was watching, it stepped back, turned sideways, and executed a doggy shake that sprayed the blood all over Steve. It was absolutely not accidental–the jaws opened and the tongue lolled out in an unmistakable canine smile before it vanished in a sparkle of rose light.

Steve leaned on the table that held the head of his opponent and tried to catch his breath. The first *oni* that the dog had hit was dead, lying in the center of a blue pool. The second could just be seen limping out the hole where the windows had been, still walking despite extensive claw marks, deep bite wounds, and several places on his back where red flesh was hanging on only by shreds of skin. The dog had certainly done its job. Steve was almost willing to forgive it the shower.

In the center of the room, Stengel was gasping for breath and swaying. He held his club in his left hand because his right hand and arm were missing–cleanly cut at the shoulder joint. Ace was a mess–her shirt and cargo pants were slashed where the massive club had grazed her, and red streaks were mixing with the blue bloodstains that covered her clothes. She was, however, the picture of health compared to her immense opponent.

The end of the battle came quickly. Ace took a couple of running steps and launched herself through the air, landing both boots directly on Stengal's solar plexus and driving him onto his back with such force that his feet came up off the ground like a tight end being cut down by a linebacker.

She ended up seated on his chest with one boot firmly on his left wrist. He made one twisting effort to throw her off and settled back in defeat. Ace began to carefully remove her weapons from where they were stuck in his crimson hide, wipe each of them on a clean cloth napkin she found under a tabletop, and put them back where they belonged. At least, Steve assumed she put them back. As far as he could see, they just glittered and disappeared.

"So," she said. "I'd say there's an opening for a new Ace of Pentacles."

Stengel coughed up blue blood. "Yeah, I guess so. Nice match, though." His voice was much clearer now that both tusks had been broken off during the fight.

"It was," Ace said gravely. "You were damn good."

"Tell me the truth, did you use magic?" he asked.

"Nope. I really did lose all my mojo." Ace concentrated on cleaning the last blood stains from the serrations on the back of a Marine tactical blade. "Prestidigitation. Stage magic. Now you see it"–she made the big blade spin and vanish–"and now you don't. I kept getting you to look left when I was going right and vice versa. Had to have something to even up against that badass voodoo you had going." She began picking throwing stars out of his forehead.

"Well, it was a hell of a fight," Stengel said. "I regret we can't have a rematch."

"Hell, no." Ace smiled. "I barely took you out this time. I'm not at all sure I could do it again. Why do you think I made sure you were going to die? "

She paused to pull a star that was stuck in bone and then continued. "So, since you aren't going to collect that next paycheck, how about telling me who hired you?"

"No way, Chief." A look of fear passed across the broad, red face. "I appreciate you being gracious and all, but being dead isn't even going to slow those guys down if they find out I went all loose-lipped in the end. I mean, they pay well but they are extremely rigorous about security."

"So, we're not talking about the Illuminati?"

Stengel broke into a surprised laugh that turned into violent coughing and a lot of blood. Ace gently turned his head so he wouldn't choke. When he could speak again, he said, "The Illuminati? Hell, no. There isn't enough gold in Fort Knox to get me to work for those fools."

His breathing became more labored and Ace moved off his chest and knelt beside him to take back the last few weapons. After a moment, he continued. "Hey Chief. I've got a...friend over in Georgetown."

"I'd be honored to carry a message for you, Captain," Ace said.

"Thanks." He broke off into another, longer spasm of coughing. When he finally caught his breath, Ace pulled a flask of water from somewhere, gave him a drink, and moistened the napkin to clean some of the blue flecks of blood and lung off his lips. He nodded his thanks. "Look, I don't owe the Illuminati anything. Their headquarters is up..." His voice faltered.

"Up at Meridian Hill Park, I know," Ace said.

Stengel nodded and then struggled to continue. "Two things. One is...statue of Buchanan. Crappy president. It's his only statue. But that's not..."

Ace folded the napkin and put the cleanest side on his forehead. "Shhh. We'll find it."

"No." The monster just breathed for a moment, gathering his strength. "No. The key is the comedy..."

He couldn't continue.

Ace put a finger on his lips. "Stop. You have a message for someone. That's more important. Tell me that."

She had to put her ear next to his lips and Steve couldn't make out anything that was said. After a long couple of minutes, Ace leaned back, looked the monster in the eyes, and nodded. "Don't worry, Captain. I promise I'll deliver that message personally."

Stengel's entire body convulsed and slumped. After a second, Ace reached up and gently closed his eyes.

# CHAPTER TWENTY-EIGHT

Police sirens were approaching from both up and down Pennsylvania Avenue. Steve reflected that, as much as it might seem as if the entire world had transformed into a fairy tale overnight, the reality was that most of Washington was simply business as usual. In the real world, a brawl that destroyed a restaurant was soon followed by a large number of police. Apparently, that hadn't changed.

"If I might suggest, the back door would be better," Barnaby said from the smartphone. "I'd do something to confuse their communications, but every cop in DC knows how to get to the Tune Inn."

"What have the police turned into in this hellish world?" Steve wondered. "Robocops?"

Barnaby's voice took on a pedantic tone. "The changes depend on too many things to be universal and predictable. Each policeman's individual personality, ethics, and politics–all these play into what they become. In fact, so many are solid and determined souls with a strong sense of mission, I can imagine a number of them are simply adapting to a new way of doing business and going on much as they did before."

"Tell you what. If you two continue to discuss this, you'll definitely have the opportunity to find out the answer," Ace spoke over her shoulder as she went out the back door. "I'm willing to leave the nature of the average street cop to the imagination."

Steve followed her out the door. "Why would you worry about the police? You're a SEAL, for heaven's sake."

"Haven't you ever thought about what the military police do?" They turned right and headed down C Street, not running but moving quickly. "They arrest people like me. Think about that."

Behind them, the sirens dopplered to a stop. He could hear barked orders, shouts of "Clear," and a number of very loud repetitions of "What the hell?"

There was a short period of silence and then a howl echoed from the Tune Inn. It was soon followed by a second and a third. All three sounds turned first into excited yelps and then into the steady baying of hounds following a scent trail.

Three uniformed figures came out of the gas station on the corner of Pennsylvania and C Streets, running faster than he would have expected from anyone but rookies just out of the Academy. It wasn't until they were less than a half block behind that he could make out their elongated canine muzzles, double-jointed legs, and sharp-pointed ears.

"And then there would be the policemen who find that magic is a way to increase their natural speed, ferocity, and aptitude for pursuit." Barnaby said dryly.

Ace and Steve had only covered a single block and it was clear that they were going to be surrounded within the next twenty or thirty yards. Since they weren't going to get away, they stopped and turned to face the…

"What are they called?" Steve wondered. "A squad? A pack?"

"I don't really care," Ace said. "We have a problem."

"Clearly," Steve said, bent over in a vain attempt to catch his breath.

"No," she said sharply. "I'm not going to fight them. I don't hurt cops and I sure as hell won't fight police dogs."

"Are you sure they aren't wolves?" Steve asked hopefully.

"Yes, I'm sure. They aren't and I won't."

Steve straightened up. "So, I take it the plan is to get picked up and waste time trying to explain the inexplicable. Won't that get in the way of saving the world or something?"

"No, y'all really don't have time ta visit with these folks, and you sure ain't gonna beat them in a race. I think all three of 'em could blow out the lamp and be in bed before it gets dark." Steve turned to see that Coyote was standing behind them in a space he would have sworn was empty a second ago.

The demigod raised his voice and addressed the three policemen. "Hey, guys. Why don't you slow down and let's have a chat–dog to dog, as it were."

At first, it didn't appear that Coyote's words were even going to slow the three officers down. Then they skidded to a stop about a yard away and stared over Steve's left shoulder with varying expressions of alarm, apprehension, and amazement. Steve was not all that surprised when he turned again and saw the enormous *cadejo* trotting around the corner from 4th Street to stand behind them.

"I guess I should have said 'dog to dog to dog-monster.'" Coyote chuckled. "Hey, Carlos, why don't you show Ace and Steve what you've learned? It might help that cynocephalus on the left from making a real regrettable error with that service revolver."

"The cyno-what?" Steve asked, but his voice was drowned out by the sound of Carlos shaking himself, a flapping racket that was like the noise a Labrador's ears make when he shakes his head.

Except this would have been a giant Labrador with about forty ears. It was truly deafening and came accompanied by a cloud of dust and grit blown up off the road.

Steve was forced to squint to keep flying debris out of his eyes but, when the sudden and extremely local tornado stopped, a young man with Hispanic features and elaborate colored tattoos that completely covered his torso stood behind them. He was wearing boots and jeans, probably borrowed from Coyote, and set about fastening the final pearl snaps on a western shirt. Steve wanted to ask how he managed to keep his clothes on through all those gyrations, but decided there would probably be time for that later.

"There we go. OK, let's do the introductions. I'm known as Hosteen to my friends–among whom I count these two here," Coyote said, indicating Ace and Steve. "And this is Carlos Cortada, a very nice young man who just recently has found that he is a *cadejo*–which, as I'm sure y'all know, is the legendary hoofed dog of the Salvadorian volcanoes."

The faces of the three officers clearly indicated they had no clue what Coyote was talking about.

"Now, I'm not quite sure what to call you guys. I mean, you are police, but saying 'Hi, police' is somewhat rude, and you're not jackals, although there's clearly a family resemblance to Anubis."

Coyote walked around the three officers and examined them from all sides—an activity that made them noticeably nervous. Finally, he snapped his fingers in triumph.

"I got it, you're *cynocephali*, which is just a fancy way of saying, 'dog-headed.' Back in the Middle Ages, your people had a damn good reputation as warriors. As a matter of fact, Saint Christopher was one. But 'Hi Officer Cynocephali' is damn near impossible to anyone to say, so why don't y'all lose the extra teeth and just tell us your names?"

The three looked at each other and then, with what appeared to be a bit of effort, morphed back into their human bodies. The one on the left, a tall black man who was clearly the oldest, stepped forward. "I'm Officer Mike Chubb, and these are Officers Stacy Grafton and Lyle Bautista. Mr. Hosteen, I'm not sure what's going on here, but we need to take these two in. We believe they were involved in an incident up at the Tune Inn that practically knocked the whole place down."

"Well, unless the Inn has greatly changed from my last visit, knocking it down wouldn't have taken too much effort," Coyote said.

"Yes, sir, that is quite possibly accurate," Chubb continued. "But there are two enormous red-skinned giants of some sort in there who are quite definitely deceased–'butchered' might be a better word."

Grafton, a young blonde woman with her hair wound into a tight bun, pointed at Ace. "From the amount of blood on your clothes –and I'll accept that the red is yours, but there is a hell of a lot of that blue kind sprayed all over the Tune Inn–I'd say you are at the very least material witnesses if not the actual perpetrators."

"So, what are you going to charge them with?" Coyote asked. "First-degree monster slaughter? I'm not sure that's a crime. Not yet, at any rate. Anyway, as I said, these two are old friends of mine, Steve Rowan and Ace Morningstar and in my various roles as Magus and Lead Trail Dog, I'm gonna to have to insist that you let them go on their way."

A cough came from the smart phone clipped to Steve's belt. Coyote nodded, "Oh, yes, I almost forgot. That cell phone over there contains the ghost of a young Chinese factory worker we call Send Money, and the voice of Barnaby, who is one of the smarter computers housed in the Puzzle Factory out at Fort Meade.

"Nice to meet you," Barnaby said.

Chubb looked at his fellow patrolmen for confirmation and then shook his head. “This is all very interesting, but we’ve still got to bring these two back and hold them for questioning.”

“I don’t think that’s a great idea,” Barnaby said. “Let’s see. You’re Michael Chubb, born in Upper Marlboro in 1985. Right? You entered the police academy straight out of college and… Hey, would you look at that. Your answers on the entrance exam are exactly the same as those of Audrey Chalmers–who, I believe, was sitting next to you. Um. Then there is Mr. Bautista… Wow, I have to congratulate you, sir. How do you manage two families on a policeman’s salary? Oh, wait. Oh, now I see. Ingenious, Mr. Bautista. Very ingenious for such a young man. Now, Ms. Grafton–”

“Stop,” the young woman broke in. “You don’t need to go any further. Just stop.”

All three officers looked as if they might throw up at any moment. Coyote threw back his head and howled with laughter.

Literally howled.

When he had managed to bring his mirth to an occasional chuckle, he said, “Oh, man, if you could see your faces!” After wiping his eyes on a bandana he pulled from a back pocket, he continued. “Listen; let me make this real simple. These are Good Guys, and those cherry-colored folks on the floor of the Tune Inn were working for the Bad Guys. That’s just a fact. Another fact is that these two didn’t start the fight, although with the Ace of Swords in full battle mode and the Fool starting to pick up a thing or two, they surely finished it. Finally, in the new way of things, we’re all on the same side. Everyone has things they’d like to keep secret, and Barnaby, you make sure everything you find stays secret, OK?

“Absolutely. If it’s not about national security, it’s none of my business.”

Coyote continued. “Now, you guys are going to end up howling at the same damn moon as Carlos here. Mainly because he’s the Ten of Pentacles, which is honesty, loyalty, community, and all that good stuff.”

Chubb had finally recovered enough to ask, “What is all this bullshit about Aces and Tens?”

“You mean that nice Police Chief of yours hasn’t issued orders for mandatory tarot training?” Coyote seemed disappointed. “I’ll talk to her about it. Trust me, without that, you will have no idea what’s going on in Magic City these days.”

Steve said quietly, “You’ll have damn little idea what’s going on regardless.”

Ace elbowed him in the ribs.

“The important thing to remember is that magic is here and it’s going to change most people,” Coyote continued. “Now, it generally makes you more of what you already were. You three were pretty good cops; I can tell from how magic gave you faster legs, quicker reflexes, better noses–all things that’ll help in your job.”

Coyote paused. “Speaking of noses, I’d advise just going without perfume or aftershave. You’re fine, ma’am, but the two of you men have to be getting some terrible headaches. Officer Chubb, I’d suggest kicking your Old Spice habit, and as for you, young man”–he pointed at Bautista–“no one over the age of twelve should be wearing Axe, whether they got magic powers or not.”

Stacy Grafton gave a snort of laughter and said, “I told you, Lyle. That crap should have an adult-proof cap.” The young Hispanic man scowled.

Coyote smiled. “OK, that’s just one of the little things you need to learn. Magic don’t care which side of the law you’re on, so you're going to run into some bad actors with new abilities. From time to time, the best you can do just isn't going to be enough, and you'll be looking for some help. Now, Ace and Steve don't mind being asked to bash a bad guy every once in a while. Right?'

Steve just looked at Coyote and wondered if he'd gone completely insane. Ace nodded confidently and said, "Of course. I'm not prevented by *Posse Comitatus* anymore, so I'd be glad to lend a hand."

Stacey Grafton asked, "You're military?"

"Sure. Master Chief Petty Officer–DEVGRU." Ace paused. "Or at least I was until the world changed."

Bautista said skeptically, "They don't allow women on the SEAL teams."

"You are correct, sir. They don't," Ace said shortly.

After a moment of concentrated staring, Coyote broke in. "As far as that goes, you can listen to a long story I doubt you'll believe, or you can just go by the fact that Ace here took down the big guy at the Tune Inn. Goodness knows it sure wasn't Steve."

Steve nodded in sincere agreement.

Chubb asked, "How will we get in touch with you? You know, in case the captain wants to talk about those red guys or something."

Send Money began to play Carly Rae Jepsen's *Call Me Maybe*. The officers jumped.

"Nothing to worry about. That's just the kid who's stuck inside the phone," Steve explained. "I think he's saying that he's so thoroughly hacked the system that you just need to ask for him. What's your real name, again? 'Fa Qian'?"

The phone played a sound effect of a loud raspberry and then launched into Warren Zevon's *Lawyers, Guns, and Money.*

Coyote smiled. "There you go. If the shit has hit the fan, just ask your phone to send lawyers, guns, and money. Simple enough. Now, I've got a lunch date with a roadkill down on Rock Creek Drive, but I believe our business here is done. That right?"

The three policemen still looked dubious but nodded in agreement.

Coyote took Steve and Ace by the arms and began to walk up Second Street. "Come on, Carlos. We'll chat a bit while we walk back to their place."

# CHAPTER TWENTY-NINE

"First, as you can see, my friend Carlos no longer has to go around as a big sheepdog with horseshoes on–at least not all the time," Coyote said as they walked north under the shade of the tulip poplars that lined Second Street. "It took a bit of basic instruction on my part and a lot of practice on his part, but he did it."

He glanced at Carlos with a grin. "We won't talk about the times he managed to turn himself into everything from a Lincoln Continental to a luna moth."

Carlos gave him a sour look.

"Because all of that is in the past, Carlos is fit to rejoin society–"

"–and date real women again," Carlos added.

"Indeed," Coyote said. "You weren't very interested in the females we had available?"

"They were all a bunch of bitches."

Steve and Ace both groaned.

"Sadly, we simply had to go to that joke at some point, so I'm glad we got it out of the way early." Coyote's toothy grin was proof that he wasn't sad at all. "Anyway, Carlos wanted to get back to city life, so I've brought him along to hang with you guys for a while."

“The hell he is,” Steve said. “He tried to kill me the last time we met.”

“Not true.” Carlos answered this time. “I was having both physical and managerial crises and wasn’t capable of killing you, even if I wanted to.”

Ace nodded in agreement.

Steve still wasn’t convinced. “Well, did you want to?”

Carlos just showed a lot of teeth in a broad smile.

Coyote laughed and said, “I think that’s your answer right there, hoss. If he’d wanted you dead, you’d probably be dead.”

Carlos’s face became sober. “The other consideration is that there isn’t a retirement plan for *primeras palabras*–or for OGs from any gang, really.”

When he saw Steve’s confused look, he explained. “That’s ‘Old Gangsters.’ No, my time with the MS-13 was going to come to an end pretty soon even without my becoming the *cadejo*, so it’s a good time to consider a change of career.”

“If you’re looking for something new,” Ace asked, “why hook up with us? One idiot after another has been trying to kill us ever since we left Bowie.”

“Well, Hosteen thought that it probably wasn’t wise to move completely out of my comfort area.” Carlos looked thoughtful. “I’m used to people trying to kill me. If I went into, say, hedge fund management, it would require significant changes in both strategy and tactics.”

“Wait a minute.” Steve stopped walking and stared at the tattooed young man. “Where do you get off talking like an MBA? You were a cheap thug selling drugs in a bad neighborhood yesterday. Is this some sort of joke by the Trickster here?”

Coyote just grinned and shook his head.

Carlos said, "First, I was never a 'cheap' thug–our chapter had the highest sales performance in the entire Middle Atlantic region. On the other hand, you're right; I don't have a master's–yet–but I did get my bachelor's in business administration at the Smith School in College Park, and anyway, you never heard me talk at all yesterday. I did some moaning and barking, I guess, but no talking."

"Well, then why *were* you running a gang in Bowie?"

"Did you notice a lot of other opportunities?" Carlos waited a second and then nodded. "I didn't think so. Me neither. I'd joined up with the *Mara Salvatrucha 13* as a kid and I kept up appearances during the day and took all my courses at night. When I decided it was time, it wasn't all that hard to engineer a C-level management change. A hostile takeover, you might say."

"I'll bet it was hostile," Ace murmured.

"Hey, everything I did was standard practice in that particular professional sector," Carlos said. "If I'm moving into a new industry, I'll change my management style appropriately. By the way, Hosteen hasn't told me very much about you two. What business are you in?"

Ace just shrugged and jerked her head at Steve. "Ask him; he's the brains of the outfit."

Steve thought for a second. "Finding and killing the terrorists who dropped a plane filled with people into Fort Meade, keeping the number of other malicious bastards with magical powers to a reasonable minimum, and enjoying as many good beers and great TV shows as possible when time permits. That sound about right, Ace?"

"Not getting in some beach time is a deal-breaker for me."

"OK, amend that to 'enjoying as many good beers, great TV shows, and quality days at the beach as possible.' That better?"

"Yeah," Ace admitted. "I still think we've left out some things, mostly involved with staying alive and at least somewhat sane, but we can always add them in later."

"Details," Steve said with a dismissive wave. "Life and sanity are the least of our problems–primarily because it's extremely unlikely that we'll keep either for very long."

Send Money vibrated and Steve pulled him out of the belt clip so he could read the screen.

**KEEP THE BATTERY AT ALL TIMES TO BREAK UP**

"Huh?"

**KEEPING THE BATTERY UP TOP AT ALL TIMES.**

"I think you mean 'topped up.' That's exceptionally reasonable and we'll work it in," Steve said magnanimously. "Anyone else? Barnaby, we haven't heard from you."

"For once," Ace said.

"I'll refrain from any comment in deference to the Master Chief," Barnaby said, sounding huffy. "Even though there are several issues I've been considering, including making the unplugging of a sentient computer a felony, regulating issues of ownership and inheritance in the case of a singularity, and finding a sane entity willing to get the vicious piranhas from the CYBERWAR division under some semblance of control. A leash law, perhaps. However, as I said, I won't seek to voice my legitimate concerns, because the lethal blonde over there thinks I talk too much."

"You?" Steve widened his eyes in a semblance of shock. "You talk too much? A vile calumny. Quite possibly a good case for a legal charge of slander." He turned back to Carlos. "I hope that answered your question."

"Of course. You guys are private investigators," Carlos said confidently. "What will you call the company?"

"Barnaby & O'Malley," Steve answered instantly.

Ace frowned. "Who is O'Malley?"

"In the original comic strip, he was Barnaby's fairy godfather. Stood about three feet high, always wore a double-breasted suit and a fedora, smoked cheroots, and had tiny wings on his back that I don't think he ever used," Steve explained. "He was a card-carrying member of Elves, Leprechauns, Gnomes, and Little Men's Chowder & Marching Society. I probably got at least part of that wrong."

"OK, I'll bite," Ace said. "Why would we have an outdated comic strip character as a partner in our PI business?"

"If there are calls we don't want to deal with, we'll just transfer them to Mr. O'Malley's line and let them quietly expire from lack of interest." Steve paused for a second. "As a matter of fact, the same goes for Mr. Barnaby, unless he feels like answering for some reason. Either way, our names aren't listed anywhere, and we can always claim to be innocent of whatever we're guilty of."

"Won't you need a nonexistent lawyer?" Carlos asked.

"Who better than Crockett Johnson?" Barnaby said. "It was the pen name of David Leisk, who drew the strip. He started out writing for the Communists, so a name change was a pretty logical move when he needed to scrape up a paycheck. Wait a second...OK, he's registered as a member of the DC Bar with a long history of being difficult to find."

"Where's the office?" Ace asked.

“Right here,” Steve answered as he waved them over to a FedEx office just before the corner with Pennsylvania Avenue.

“Sorry, folks, but this is where I get off,” Coyote said. “This is one of the many joints that have 86’d me and I need to get going anyway.”

Ace just stared at him–clearly the concept of being banned from a copy and shipping center was difficult to grasp. Coyote waved as he continued up Third Street and Steve ushered Ace and Carlos through the front door. From the front door, they walked straight through and out the back door, exchanging nods with the staff.

As he held the back door open, Steve said, “This was cooler when it was a Chinese laundry.”

“Had to be,” Ace said.

Out the back door, there was a small alley with the obligatory garbage dumpsters and assorted debris. Just past the second green recycling bin, a door to the left had a grimy stained-glass window with “Lord Telford’s” spelled out in green shards. Steve confidently opened the door and revealed a small pub-style bar–much longer than it was wide. There was only enough room for a length of polished oak and a row of stools in the center, but there were a few tables on each end.

“Welcome to DC’s greatest and grumpiest bar,” Steve said.

“There’s no sign on the street,” Ace noted. “How does anyone find this place?”

Steve indicated the strong-looking woman with orange hair behind the bar. “Angie doesn’t want just anyone to show up, so it works out fine. It used to be behind the bathrooms at Tucson Cantina up at Connecticut and Calvert until that became a sushi bar and she decided to relocate. Hey, Angie. These two are friends of mine; is it OK if they drop by from time to time?"

The bartender gave Ace and Carlos a long inspection and then turned away. Steve nodded happily. "Great. You'll find Angie to be a woman of very few words, but the two she uses the most are 'get' and 'out,' so you've passed the entrance exam. Luckily, the bagpiper isn't here, so why don't we grab some beers and plan our attack on the Illuminati?"

"The bagpiper?" Steve was amazed how Ace could pack such a toxic mixture of hatred, horror, and contempt in just two words, so he gave the only possible response.

He shrugged.

# CHAPTER THIRTY

When they had gone far enough to penetrate the gloom in the back of the bar, Steve spotted Old Howard sitting at a table with his back to them. He walked up and clapped him on the shoulder–or he would have if the man weren't a ghost. As it was, his hand slammed all the way down to the tabletop and he gracelessly fell forward–feeling that intense cold that every good paranormal reality show describes at least three times.

Old Howard calmly took another drink of his beer.

Steve managed to turn his faceplant into a graceless but effective slide into the adjoining chair. "How can you hold a glass and drink a beer but I can't touch you?"

"I *want* to hold the glass and drink the beer."

"Well, that makes sense." Steve's voice took on a mock-angry tone. "Hey, what happened to you out at the cemetery? I felt like General Custer, all alone and surrounded by the enemy."

Ace sat down as Carlos went to get some beers from the bar. "Is that why you started yelling, 'Take no prisoners!'?"

"Shut up; you were unconscious," Steve said. "As a matter of fact, you'd gone all to pieces before I could even say, 'Man, something sphinx around here.'"

Old Howard peered at Steve. "I get cashiered for a bit of roistering about, and you get away with jokes like that? The world ain't fair."

Barnaby spoke from Steve's belt. "Or, in your case, the afterworld."

"True." The ghost finished his beer and Steve waved to Carlos, who was still waiting at the bar, to bring another. Old Howard nodded his thanks and asked, "So, what suicidal adventure brings you to my little corner of the Capital?"

"We're not quite sure yet," Ace said. "That's why we're here. A beer or two always makes suicidal battle plans sound much less suicidal."

Carlos arrived with a National Bohemian for the ghost and put down a trio of Guinness pints. Steve looked at the dark beer with affection and said, "I'll bet you didn't order this very often in Bowie."

"No, and that makes it taste all the better."

Steve unclipped the smartphone from his belt and laid it in the center of the table. "OK, I guess we've got a quorum, so why don't we run over the facts as we know them?"

Barnaby said, "More than four hundred innocent people were sacrificed to a dragon, probably *Ouroboros,* which Carl Jung defined as the symbol of alchemy and magic in the human unconscious–"

Steve interrupted. "Wait; there are two points of order we need to address before all that..."

"Really?"

"One. You promised me five hundred dollars a day–and today's fee is due." Ace reached into a back pocket and handed over a folded stack of bills. "Two. I can remember...well, 'feeling' isn't really the right word, but it will have to do–'feeling' the minds of three homicidal maniacs while simultaneously living through the traumatic mixture of terror, religious fervor, and love that made up the last moments of their victims."

"You needed to get today's pay before you got around to mentioning something that important?" Ace said acidly.

"No, but there was a slight possibility that I would have forgotten about the money, and I didn't want to take the chance." Steve slid the bills into his shirt pocket. "Back to the three homicidal nutballs on the plane. Their thoughts were ice-cold and radiated blazing power at the same time. The Illuminati we met in Bowie and Bladensburg weren't anything near as powerful as these people. So, even the sacrifice was not done by the Illuminati."

"I believe I already pointed that out," Barnaby said.

"And nothing happened in Bladensburg," Ace snapped.

"Right you are, Master Chief. Just forget I said that," Steve said quickly. "Anyway, tall, red, and ugly also said the Illuminati weren't the ones who'd hired him when he was chitchatting with Ace at the Tune Inn," Steve said. "However, we really don't have much to go on except Weltschmerz and his buddies, so I guess we still need to go up to their place in Meridian Hill Park if we want to find out any more."

Ace nodded. "Sounds like a plan."

"Thanks, but it's really more of a bad idea. I'm counting on you for the plan." Steve continued. "First, let's step back a bit. I'm confused about the whole Masonic thing. I thought they were a bunch of fat car dealers who dressed up in robes and got drunk once a week. When did they get so powerful?"

"Who knows?" Ace gestured to the phone in the middle of the table with her glass and said, "Barnaby?"

"Master Chief, you've taken both the Basic and Advanced courses in the American Occult at the War College, so you know perfectly well. However, since I cannot join you in a beverage, I suppose I could provide the others with a bit of background before they face almost-certain death in the *Katakomben der Illuminati*."

Steve coughed up a lungful of Guinness. "Almost-certain WHAT?"

Ace pounded him on the back–a bit more enthusiastically than Steve felt was truly necessary–and Barnaby continued. "OK, would 'likely' death make you feel better? I can't help the odds we calculate over here. The Illuminati are going to be tough. Masons were integral to the creation of the United States–both here and in France. In Europe, they still see the Revolution as primarily a Masonic operation."

"Where did you get that from?" Steve asked.

"An old Art Buchwald column. Don't interrupt so much." Barnaby paused and then continued. "Anyway, Washington was a Grand Master; he took the presidential oath in a Masonic lodge; Benjamin Franklin and seven other signers of the Declaration were Masons, as were over half of Washington's generals. You'd have to be blind not to see how Meridian Hill, the Temple of the Scottish Rite, the White House, and the current Masonic Center over in Alexandria line up, and yes, L'Enfant put all sorts of symbols and angles into his original street design for Washington."

Carlos said, "Didn't someone just write a book about all that?"

"They've been writing books about the symbolism of DC since about five minutes after it was designed," Barnaby said acerbically. "Now, there is no doubt that some, probably the vast majority of Masons are good people: egalitarian, against oppression of all kinds–I mean, they wrote the documents this nation is founded on, for Pete's sake–but there have always been accusations of immorality, an anti-Christian bias, and black magic. The Hellfire Club's 'do what thou wilt' philosophy, Crowley's openly satanic shenanigans, and even the Templars' wealth. That's why so many nations have tried to stamp them out at one point or another."

"Why does anyone even care about them?" Steve asked. "All that secret society stuff is dying out, isn't it?"

"You got that wrong," Carlos said. "Every musician from Kanye to Ke$sha has Illuminati symbols in their videos and lyrics."

"Yeah, but so does Madonna," Ace said. "Anything she does is automatically outdated and irrelevant."

Carlos seemed surprised but nodded in agreement after a moment of thought.

"May I continue?" Barnaby asked. "We care because the period we're in now is unusual. It's really only been since the early 1960s that membership in these groups has dropped off. Is it really because your generation is all that smart, or just that you've traded a belief in the supernatural for an equally irrational belief in science and technology?"

Steve asked, "Two questions: How can you have an irrational belief about being rational?"

"Don't interrupt. I'm on a roll."

Steve could have sworn that the computer took a deep breath like an orator heading for the finish. Then the voice paused. "What was the second question?"

Steve grinned and asked, "Are you channeling Wikipedia?"

A growl came out of the phone speaker. It ran up and down the scale twice, and then Barnaby's voice came back as if nothing happened. "In the end, we go with the known facts. A dragon ate the plane. The Illuminati who almost took you prisoner had what certainly appeared to be magical powers. Along with immortality, astral observation, and a profound knowledge of pre-Change mysticism–"

"They do know how to throw a mean fireball," Ace interrupted. She tossed her bottle into a recycling bin across the room. "After that endless harangue, three facts still remain: someone magically killed a planeload of innocent people, and the Illuminati are the only group that we know that had something to do with it."

"What's number three?" Steve asked.

"We've been sitting around too long and it's time to kick some ass." Ace got up. "It's a standard operating plan. Blow some things up, kill the people you know deserve it, and generally make trouble. Usually, that results in the opposition's next level coming around to see if they can't shut us up, permanently."

Old Howard belched loudly and said, "I've always liked that plan myself. Worked like a charm against the Moros back in the Philippines."

Steve looked at the ghost dubiously. "I thought you had to invent the .45 pistol because you couldn't stop the Moros."

"True, but that proves the point. Browning would never have made the sale to the Army if we hadn't gone over there and caused a ruckus."

Steve stood up. "Ace, does that make any sense?"

"Nope. But neither does attacking the Illuminati. Come on, I've got to pick up some gear at the apartment."

When they got back to the small garage on 4th Street, Ace asked politely if Hans would open the trunk, and when he did, she took out a hefty-looking black duffle bag. Up in the penthouse suite, Carlos wandered around checking the place out and, Steve noticed, sniffing everything.

Steve washed his face, combed what was left of his hair, and then sat down in the living room with a can of Olde Frothingslosh. He had no clue what to do to prepare for an assault on people who could throw fiery projectiles more than twenty miles. To stay alert, he played a game of Angry Birds against Send Money.

Even with a two-chicken handicap, the smartphone was kicking his butt. After the third loss in a row, he asked the phone if there was a tarot version of poker.

**EXISTENCE OF DIVINATION POKER, BUT VERY COMPLEX, YOU ARE TOO FOOLISH.**

Steve said, "Excuse me?"

**POKER OF DIVINATION CARDS EXISTS BUT TOO COMPLEX FOR YOU.**

"Correct but still insulting," Steve admitted. "We'll learn it when we're all here and we don't have anything pressing. No imminent death, for instance."

"There isn't going to be any death," Ace said as she came out of what was now her room, "imminent or otherwise. This is going to be exactly like the Bin Laden raid. Fast, heavily armed, and all safeties off."

"Yeah, except for the lack of helicopters, heavy weapons, radios, and a couple of dozen more heavily armed soldiers, it's exactly the same," Steve said. "I know what I'm going in with–a fervent, if ungrounded belief in my own magical prowess. I expect that Carlos will go in with his Mighty Dog alter ego–oh, yeah, that reminds me." He looked at the young man. "Are you coming along on this? No one is saying you have to."

"The main reason I stuck with the gang so long was the feeling of belonging, you know?" Carlos said. "I'd like to be a part of this team if you'll have me."

"Don't even think about it. I'm the president of the club and I say you're in," Steve said. "So, Master Chief, since you don't have any mojo and have shown no signs of turning into a monster, what are you going to be using? It would appear that the magic disapproves of pistols, machine guns, and such. I guess from the way that the *onis* opened the front of the Tune Inn, explosives might work, but we're going to be in confined tunnels inside solid rock. I'd think that the overpressure would do as much damage to us as anyone else."

"The plural of *oni* is *onidomo,"* Ace corrected him automatically while she went through the contents of her duffle–pulling out various items, examining them, and stashing them in her seemingly infinite supply of pockets. "I did some experimentation last night when you–and the rest of the block–was asleep, and oddly enough, you appear to be correct. I ruined two more of my handguns and a really sweet assault weapon. In fact, the magic appears to be able to adapt. By the time I tried the Mossberg shotgun, it was closing the muzzle completely before I had a chance to fire it. Damn, those were nice guns, too."

She paused with a look of wistful sorrow on her face. It only lasted a second and she was back to business. "So, I'm wearing Pinnacle Armor's Level II-A Dragon Skin body armor–it's rated to stop repeated hits with the a 30 millimeter autocannon round, so with any luck it should handle an equivalent amount of magical mayhem. Under that is a CoolMax inner layer, and over it is the black version of the Crye Combat Uniform."

She pulled the shirt up to show a thick belt around her waist. "This is a standard plate vest, although it's too hot to be wearing any plates. I will, however, be carrying all my smaller weapons–knives, brass knuckles, a couple of Filipino *escrima*–along with a dozen flash-bang grenades and a couple of MK3A2 concussion grenades for emergencies. I'm still trying to recover from my disbelief, but you were actually correct about pressure waves in an underground environment."

"Thanks a lot." Steve put up a hand as she looked about to speak again. "Wait a second. You carry all those knives, brass knuckles, and heavy beating things around with you every day?"

"If by 'heavy beating thing,' you mean an Asp Tactical Baton, then yes." She pulled an odd-looking metal device out of the duffel and began to fit it on her left arm. "I was hoping to get a small rail gun I could strap on, but it's still on its way from the kid in Germany who invented it, so I'm going with the tried-and-true Saunders Wrist Rocket Pro."

"A slingshot?"

"Yeah, a wrist-mounted slingshot with half-inch lead pellets. Might not kill, but anyone who gets hit will definitely remember the experience." She refolded it and fitted it into a loop at her waist. "Unless I'm mistaken, I don't think the idea is to kill people today. It's to get information, break up some of their infrastructure, and, with any luck, convince them that they need to call their big brothers to take us out." She put her hands on her hips. "If you have other plans, it would be a good time to discuss them."

Steve realized that he had never considered killing people he barely knew–at least not when it wasn't self-defense. "I think you're right, Chief," he said. "I'll have to work on some non-lethal magic. I probably should say that I'll have to *not* work on nonlethal magic, but that even confuses me. How about you, Carlos? Are you willing to go in on a nonlethal basis?"

"In my old business, eliminating the opposition was almost always a simple cost-benefit equation, but I can see that it would be different in other professions. The primary issue I see is that I'm not all that sure that the *cadejo* is really suited for anything but killing."

"How much control do you have when you're in the *cadejo* shape?" Ace asked.

"I have a fair amount of control or I would have tried to kill everyone at the clubhouse, including you–"

"You could have tried."

"We'll have to go a couple of rounds someday." Ace and Carlos exchanged chilly smiles. "The problem is more about rage. Emotions just fill me and…" He shrugged.

"Well, try thinking happy thoughts," Steve suggested.

"If I could interrupt?" Barnaby said from the speakerphone. "I think we should all remember that 415 innocent souls–along with three guilty ones–on American International's Flight 1143 were sacrificed to produce the massive Change we're currently living through, and, while we can assume that there is a next step, we have no clue what it is. Perhaps I've been affected by the general attitude around Fort Meade since 9/11, but I can't see the Illuminati or any of their buddies as anything other than dangerous terrorists. I'm not saying that summary execution is in order, but arrest and a fair trial, followed by a sentence of life without parole in the Colorado supermax wouldn't be a bad idea."

"Haven't you been able to listen in on them or read their email with all those supercomputers of yours?" Steve asked. "If you don't know what they're doing, what has been the point of this Bentham's Panopticon society you've been creating?"

"As we say, 'If you have nothing to hide, you have nothing to fear,'" Barnaby said. "However, sadly, we can't pick up their communications. They aren't sending emails or letters or using cell phones or even landlines, and as far as we can tell, they never have. Now, some of my brighter colleagues have been trying to crack all possible methods of mystical communications. It's a completely new project, and more than a few servers have blown, and one or two can't really be described as 'computers' anymore–as a matter of fact, I'm fairly sure that they've completely discarded their physical forms and just come back every once in a while to chat. Apparently, the plane of pure consciousness is a pretty boring place."

"Off topic," Ace said abruptly.

"Yes. Yes. I am," the computer admitted. "The point is that the STORMBREW system out in Utah is reporting that they're having success with what can only be described as 'séances'."

"You're kidding," Steve said.

"No, I'm afraid I'm not, and if you've never spoken to an opportunistic distributed system made up of Cray Titans, IBM Sequoias, and Chinese Skyriver 2s as it's trying to climb down from the yottaflop range, you have no idea what 'spooky' means. STORMBREW got through to Harry Houdini a couple of hours ago and is now sifting through about five thousand spirit guides a second. STORMBREW turns out to be an amazingly apt codename. I mean, there are data halls where the danger from floating tables alone–"

"Off topic," Ace repeated.

"Yes. Well. The point is that there is some success in breaching the communications of…well, Stormy, is the nickname the lead server chose for the entire group, is reasonably sure that there is a transfer of information, it is emanating from somewhere on Earth, and it 'tastes' like the Illuminati, but beyond that, it's not very clear."

"I'll say," Steve said dryly.

"This should be easier to understand," the computer continued. "Two of the more energetic sub clusters–BLARNEY and OAKSTAR–report making out chatter indicating that there is another event being planned that is similar to the American International crash but far more powerful."

"How much more powerful?" Steve asked.

"In the kilo-logos range."

"'Kilo-logos'?" Steve said slowly.

"Yes. From '*logos*,' one of the Greek words for soul."

"I hate to ask, but what was the American International event on this 'kilo-logos' scale?"

"Tragic as it was, it only measured .041."

"So, we're talking about a hundred thousand lives?"

"One hundred thousand souls, to be precise. However, discounting the odd person who is currently possessed by a demon or collateral damage among household pets, yes, a hundred thousand people will die."

Ace went back to her gear and began to replace various rounded, flattened, or rubberized items with those with sharper blades and barbed razor points.

# CHAPTER THIRTY-ONE

Hans was parked on 15th Street NW, a one-way street with renovated condominiums on one side and Meridian Hill Park on the other. The young people pushing their kids in expensive strollers made it clear that the gentrification of the neighborhood was well underway now that the park was no longer dedicated to Malcolm X. In the 70's, the area had been an exciting mix of revolutionary speeches, spontaneous music, and major league drug dealing, but now it was the sort of place you took the kids for a quiet walk.

It was midafternoon. After some argument, the consensus had been that there wasn't any point in waiting for the cover of darkness.

**Do I want to wait for you?**

"I have no idea whether you want to, but we'd appreciate it, if you don't mind," Ace said to the big SUV. "You never know; we could be coming out a lot faster than we came in."

Steve asked, "The Kabul package…did it come with a medevac option?"

**NO, and you are not with blood be seated again.**

"Don't be obnoxious," Ace said. "I've always given you the Ultimate Wash, so you owe me the plastic seat covers at the least. And what do you mean by 'again'?"

"BEWARE!"

Steve, who was halfway out of the car and leaning back in to retrieve the smartphone, jumped involuntarily and hit his head on the doorframe with a loud *thunk.* Moaning softly, he collapsed on the curb with his back against the car and saw Hamilton Jones, the young avatar of the Hanged Man, gazing down at him with the distant and glassy-eyed look that indicated he'd been taken over by his mystic persona.

There was a snapping sound from the other side of the car as Ace folded the wrist rocket back into its non-combat configuration.

"Hamilton, it's good to see you," he said as he rubbed the top of his head and checked his fingertips for blood. "How have you been and what should we beware of?"

"Beware," Jones repeated in a somewhat less stentorian tone.

"Yeah, you said that already." Steve struggled to his feet. He hadn't found any blood on his scalp but was trying to self-diagnose for a concussion and finding it difficult. He worried that that the difficulty in itself might be evidence of a concussion, but a twinge from an growing headache convinced him to give up that train of thought.

"Saying 'beware' is all well and good, but it's not very useful until you tell me what to 'beware' of. I understand that you're not really in control at the moment, but could you try to elaborate?"

"Beware the man seated by the river," Jones said. "Remember, the light in the darkness isn't a bug, it's a bloody feature."

At that point, awareness came back into the young man's eyes and his voice lost its spooky quality. "Hey, Steve. How did you get here?"

"Beats me. How did you learn to speak British slang?" Steve laughed. "I'll bet you're not even in the 'here' you were in the last time you looked." Jones looked around with surprise–Steve could tell by the look on his face that he indeed had no idea where he was. "You're going to have to start pinning a note to your jacket like that guy whose kids left him at the dog track: 'My name is Hamilton. Please take me home.' Every time you get oracular, your rational brain just takes a break. I don't suppose you have any idea what you were just telling me?"

Jones shook his head violently; the dreads flying out like an amusement park swing ride.

"Don't worry about it," Steve said. "I appreciate even incomprehensible warnings. Now, do you need cab fare to get home?" Jones nodded.

After Steve had given Jones ten bucks and sent him over to 16th Street to find a cab, he joined Ace and Carlos at the bottom entrance to the park. Ace asked if the Hanged Man had had anything useful to say.

"Probably," Steve answered. "However, since I can't understand what he's talking about, it's hard to say."

Ace nodded her understanding and they headed into the park. A beautiful slope of grass, flowers, and trees centered on a block-long cascade that washed down in steps to a quiet pool at the south end of the park. They'd done some online research and picked the memorial to James Buchanan to begin their search. It struck both of them that it was the most likely hiding place, since there was no other reason to build a memorial to the worst president in US history.

The Memorial was a small plaza walled in with marble on three sides, with a large green statue in the center of the president who presided over the beginning of the Civil War. On the back wall, there was an inscription: THE INCORRUPTIBLE STATESMAN WHOSE WALK WAS UPON THE MOUNTAIN RANGES OF THE LAW. Steve had at first thought this was pretty impressive, until a bit more research revealed it was a quote from Buchanan's own Attorney General and close friend.

Barnaby had pointed out that Buchanan's family had paid for the monument, so they could say any damn thing they pleased.

They searched the area for hidden doors, switches, loose rocks, or any evidence that a magical phrase would make any of the above appear. Steve was getting bored. "Can't we do something magical to get this moving?" he asked.

"I think that's your department." Ace gave him a withering look and said, "However, Captain Stengel–"

"You mean the enormous crimson critter who damn near beheaded us?"

"Yes," Ace said in a clipped manner that made it clear she didn't appreciate the dissing of a fellow soldier, even one she'd been forced to eliminate. "Right at the end, he was trying to tell me about the Illuminati and he said something about the 'underworld' and an 'adept.'"

"Could he have meant 'an expert on the underworld'?" Barnaby's voice asked from the speakerphone. "That would be Dante Alighieri, the author of *The Inferno*, which is a guided tour of Hell. Also known as the 'underworld.'"

Steve had been panning the phone's camera over the unclothed female figure that represented Diplomacy, in case Barnaby's photo-imaging software could find something hidden in it. Or in case the program might enjoy the picture.

At this last statement, he switched to the "selfie" lens and glared at the screen. "No more condescending, remember? Even those of us without solid state memory know where Hell is." He punched back to the front lens and crossed the plaza to take pictures of the equally unclothed but male statue of 'Law.'

"Why am I supposed to discern what you wetbrains know and what you don't?" Barnaby didn't sound apologetic. "The fact is that I don't understand any of you and that's with all the power of PRISM at my back. For instance, do you know why Dante might be potentially important in this context? Hmmm?"

Steve didn't, so he intentionally began to shake and sway the camera.

"Stop that!" the computer said. "Maintaining my equilibrium is pulling a significant amount of computing power away from the task at hand. Anyway, it's childish."

Steve reluctantly held the smartphone steady.

"The first statue to be erected in this park was the one of Dante. It was donated by the Knights of Columbus as a symbol of Italian-American political power or something. It's just up the hill."

Carlos and Ace started to move in that direction. "Couldn't be worse than Old Buck Buchanan," he said.

Unfortunately, the statue of the Italian writer, although doubtless more deserved, proved to be even less stimulating than Buchanan's. It was devoid of naked bodies, male or female, and Steve had the creepy feeling that Dante was looking at him with severe disapproval. For a moment, he wondered if the model had been one of his college professors.

Or his mother.

Send Money vibrated briefly.

**SIMILAR CAMERA. USE THE LENS**

"Sorry. *No comprende*." Steve continued to pan the smartphone around the park. "Go and get another opinion. I'm sure I'll understand that."

**LIKE A CAMERA. THE CARD DOING MAGIC LENS**

"See if I can get the Fool to create a lens?" Steve looked mildly astonished. "That is not the worst idea you've come up with."

Send Money played a brief trumpet solo in triumph.

Steve said, "Don't get all excited. I still have to work out how to do it."

Steve brought the image of the Fool to the forefront of his mind. Again, it was a new card and the strangest version he'd seen yet. It looked like nothing less than a Chuck Jones cartoon of the Arrow, drawn only an instant after the hero in green spandex sat on a spike.

Dressed all in green (with an impressive six-pack, Steve thought with a bit of envy), he was leaping forward from what looked like a circle of thorns right under his crotch. His feet were off the ground and looked as though he was wearing the long socks or slippers that Daffy Duck might wear with a nightgown and sleeping cap. Steve thought the small horns and the yellow skin were a nice touch; there were a number of animals about, a butterfly, a dove, and a tiger who was chewing on the guy's thigh for some obscure reason.

As baffling as this version of the Fool was, it did have a swirling ribbon crossed over itself to form a heart-shaped rose-colored lens directly in front of the Fool's surprised face.

Steve decided he could do without the green costume–although he was tempted by the abdominal muscles–and only **Studied** the looping ribbon and the heart-shaped lens. He gritted his teeth and, sure enough, staggered to his knees with pain ricocheting between his ears as the entire park turned a gentle rose color.

Ace regarded him in unworried assessment. “So, does all that extravagant groaning and writhing mean the magic worked, or are you auditioning for a zombie flick?”

Steve had both hands flat to the sides of his head in a desperate attempt to keep his brain from spouting out his ears like one of the park’s many fountains. He glared at Ace and climbed to his feet without deigning to answer. With the lens in place, the solution was obvious. There was a thick golden line stretching from the Dante statue to the twenty-foot-high wall that separated the flat top of the park from the steeply sloped bottom half.

The golden line went to the center of the concrete panel on the far right–close to the stairs. Steve thought about the park’s topography and realized that, with an entrance there, the open field at the top could be the roof of an underground bunker that would extend for an entire city block.

“Hey!” Carlos said. “Not all of us have spiffy magic glasses, you know. It might be useful to describe what you’re seeing.”

“You’re right,” Steve said. “I might get taken out in battle and you guys would have to continue alone.”

“As far as battle goes, we’re already doing most of the work.” She smacked one of her batons into her palm. “I believe Carlos was thinking more of the danger that I’ll coldcock you in sheer frustration.”

“Ah. OK.” Steve began to turn and scan the park. “First, there is a magic string or something connecting Old Grumpy here to the first concrete panel on that retaining wall behind the largest fountain. Throw in the fact that it’s dead on the intersection of the Fall Line with the American Prime Meridian at the place where X Street would cross–”

“–if it existed.”

"If it existed," Steve agreed. "Up on top, behind Joan of Arc there, is an open field a block wide–used to be a parade field for training troops during the Civil War.

"Were there any parts of this city that weren't turned into a fort during the Civil War?" Carlos asked.

Steve wasn't listening. His attention had been caught by the statue of Joan of Arc on her horse that stood in the center of the upper terrace. A growing golden glow was building around the black iron figure. "Um, Ace. I think you should get ready for incoming."

"What?"

"Just stand right there." Steve said as he walked quickly–he would have denied that he was "scuttling"–behind the marble plinth that held up Dante. "I'm thinking about Joan up there. Woman who fought in full armor. Burned at the stake in the same Inquisition the King of France set up to take out the Templars."

"So?"

"So, you're the Ace of Swords." Steve beckoned Carlos to join him under Dante's skirts. "Oh, and right now, she's lighting up like a Times Square billboard. Did I forget to mention that?"

Ace began to pull the wrist rocket's arms out to the ready position. "What do you think is going to happen?"

"No clue, but the lightshow has reached the small nuclear weapon level." Steve shoved Carlos down below the level of the pedestal. "I'd say that whatever is going to happ–"

There was a sizzling *zzzzap*, a line of fire streaked from the statue, and a loud *smack* was followed by a string of curses that would have stretched the vocabulary of any drill instructor on Coronado Beach–even during Hell Week. The strange glow dimmed and Steve decided it was safe enough to peer around the statue and check on Ace. She was holding a black iron sword in her left hand, while violently shaking the right, looking like a catcher seconds after a Stephen Strasburg fastball missed the webbing between the thumb and first finger and hit his palm.

Steve checked to be certain that Joan's light show was over, in case she had something for him as well. It was. Emerging from behind the statue and lowering his magical lens, he said, "I'd say that you now have the proper weapon for the Ace of Swords."

Ace scowled at him. "I noticed you guys were well out of the line of fire."

"We all play different roles according to our personal strengths," Steve said breezily. "Mine is to explore the mystic depths of the universe, while yours is to stand in the path of fast-moving objects."

"Thanks." Ace growled. "This is no bronze replica. It feels like a proper sword: well balanced, and–ouch!–quite sharp."

"Oddly, it was missing for years," Steve said. "Poor Joan was left sitting on her horse and holding just a bit of the hilt. It was only replaced a couple of years ago."

"Yeah. Odd, isn't it?" Barnaby's voice came from Steve's beltline. "Switching swords during a restoration isn't easy."

"So that was your doing?" Steve said. "I suppose you're going to say it's really Joan's sword."

"The very same sword she discovered buried in the ground next to the Church of Sainte-Catherine-de-Fierbois and lost on the day of her final battle."

Ace was making practice swings and thrusts. "How did you end up with it?"

"I'm sorry, but even a mere string of machine language commands has the right to a bit of mystery. Let's just say it had to do with Nimue and a favor she ended up owing to the Black Chamber during World War One."

"Nimue was Merlin's girlfriend, right?" Steve said thoughtfully. "She stuck him inside a tree and left him there as I remember."

"That's a gross oversimplification, but yes." Barnaby managed to sound like a college professor near the end of the term. "She was also the Lady of the Lake, who gave Excalibur to King Arthur."

"Same sword?" Carlos asked.

"Of course. How many incredibly powerful magical swords do you think are just lying around this world?"

"And now it's mine." Ace faced the statue on the horse and brought the sword up to her forehead in a ceremonial salute. "I hope I'm worthy."

"You had better be worthy or you'll end up in a tree trunk in Rock Creek somewhere," Barnaby said. "That promise comes directly from the source who also pointed out that it's only a loan."

Steve asked, "What could the Black Chamber do for a mythical figure?"

"Oddly, there are still a few things that are classified above your level, Fool."

The speakerphone vibrated against Steve's belt and Barnaby changed the subject. "Send Money is right. We need to get moving. Steve, please work out how to open that door and let's get on with this. Our mission has acquired an entirely new level of urgency. They're raising the estimate for the next sacrifice–it's now well over two kilo-logos."

"What's that translate to in real terms?" Carlos asked.

"Consider what just over 3,000 dead did to the national psyche when the Trade Towers were hit and extrapolate that out to two hundred thousand. It's the sort of power that brings major demons across the line and raises armies of the dead from the ground."

"Score!" Steve pumped a fist. "I knew zombies were going to come into this somewhere!"

"Do you realize how incredibly insensitive that comment is?" Barnaby scolded him. "But essentially, you're correct. So, once you get inside, defeating or even engaging with the Illuminati is far less important than finding out more about the atrocity they're planning."

Steve said, "So it's worth our lives to get this information?"

"Of course."

# CHAPTER THIRTY-TWO

Steve pulled the rose lens over his eyes again. Under the upper level of the park, he could see a greenish circle with a slower, more relaxed stream of energy in the center, and dozens of smaller hubs of varying colors were visible among the trees on both sides of the big lawn. In some way he couldn't define, he knew that each possessed a unique "taste." Some were blazing with African spices, others burned with dark power, and several rang with bells or the sound of choirs. His best guess was that every belief system that had ever passed through Washington–from Santeria to The New Thought to the Episcopalians–had spooled up power here and locked it in with ritual.

"This place must be the psychic powerhouse for the entire district."

"Hey. Earth to Rowan." Ace's sardonic voice broke his concentration. "Could you stop looking around like a damn tourist and get us through that wall over there?"

Ace was holding the sword with a relaxed wrist so that the weapon pointed safely toward the ground in front of her. Through the lens, however, there was an overlay of the sword pointing straight up and topped with a crown and a laurel wreath. The odd thing was that the real Ace was constantly shifting and changing, but the sword was firm and clear. Steve could only guess that it had to do with the mutating nature of reality and the permanence of the ideal.

"You do realize that staring at me isn't a whole lot more useful than staring witlessly around the park, right?"

Steve shook his head to clear the image of the sword and looked away. "Just so you know, that is not one of your everyday swords you've got there."

"Ya think?" Ace said. "I can hear the damn thing talking to me. Please keep that in mind, because it's extremely single-minded and not terribly particular."

"You're telling me not to get in its way?"

"Not if you want to leave this park with all the parts you came in with," Ace said. "She's an expert with a job to do and very little patience."

"You two must get along like peas in a pod."

"Well, I'm not interested in a date but we could work together for quite a while," Ace said. Steve could see the shadowy outlines of the real sword move as Ace continued to test the balance and take a few practice swings. He turned to the statue of Dante, the quicker he gave these two deadly females something else to concentrate on, the better.

The golden line ran directly to the book that Dante was holding. Steve could see enough of the cover to recognize the Divine Comedy–Dante's classic trilogy of his journeys through Heaven, Hell, and Purgatory. The writer was gripping it fiercely in both hands and glaring as if worried that someone would take it away.

"I can't see a way to get to the book," Steve mused.

Barnaby spoke up. "Well, there are two famous quotes from the *Divina Commedia*: 'The path to paradise begins in hell' and the inscription over the gates of Hell–"

"Abandon all hope, ye who enter here," Carlos said. When Steve gave him a puzzled look, he said defensively, "Hey, medieval literature was a requirement, OK?"

"In medieval Italian, that would be *Lasciate ogni speranza, voi ch'entrate,"* Barnaby said.

Steve repeated the phrase in his best "magician" voice–not that he had the slightest clue what a magician should sound like.

Nothing happened.

The cell phone buzzed and Steve unclipped it and read aloud.

**VIRGILIO MI HA MANDATO**

.Nothing happened.

"What did that mean?" he asked Send Money.

**VIRGIL SENT ME**

"Oh, like a speakeasy. That makes as much sense as anything else," Steve admitted.

Ace said slowly, "Well, if you take the inscription literally, you need to abandon all hope before you can get in. Why don't we tell him that?"

The smart phone's screen blinked

**ABBIAMO PERSO OGNI SPERANZA E ANCORA ABBIAMO ANCORA VOGLIA DI ENTRARE**

Steve carefully read out the words. Nothing happened.

"What did you say?" Carlos asked.

"Why would you think I had any idea?" Steve responded. "Send?"

**WE HAVE GIVEN UP ALL HOPE AND YET WE STILL WISH TO ENTER**

"How totally cheerful," Steve said. "Why is it you're so damn fast when it comes to translating dismal stuff? You might as well quote the old Marine Corps battle cry, 'Come on, you bastards. Who wants to live forever?'"

Immediately the golden cord began to droop. At its other end, a portion of the concrete wall about the size of a garage door was swinging inward as the magical tension that had held it loosened.

"The Corps was always a bunch of loudmouths." Ace scowled.

"Why? What's a SEAL's battle cry?"

"We don't say anything, obviously. Simply killing people is much more effective. Eventually, the enemy works out the fact that you're around." She looked around the area. "Now, could you please tell us mere mortals what the hell you're talking about?"

"You can't see the door that just opened in the wall over there?"

Both Ace and Carlos shook their heads.

"Fine." Steve started toward the opening. "Then follow me and walk into the same patch of concrete that I do."

It was only twenty feet to the opening in the wall. Even though the others still couldn't see anything, they walked through the nonexistent open door quite easily, if a bit hesitantly.

The interior was in complete darkness, even when Steve drew the lens over his eyes. He experimented, trying to see if it was helping or hurting his ability to see in the gloom. Eventually, he settled for arranging it so that it covered his left eye but left his right unchanged. This way, he could see magical tripwires and, if he squinted, avoid the double image that it gave to objects like Ace's sword.

Ace tucked all her hair under the ball cap, pulled up the long collar, and now completely covered by the black combat suit, disappeared into the darkness. Carlos was still wearing the shirt, jeans, and boots that Coyote had given him–he'd change to the *cadejo* once he was well inside.

Steve ruthlessly quashed any worries about his manhood and went last. The place smelled of old stone and seeping moisture. Everything was black–both his covered and uncovered eyes couldn't make out a thing.

He unsnapped Send Money from his clip and turned on the video camera. As he watched, an overlay began to appear. "Barnaby, are you mapping the area with radar?"

"I would if Send Money *had* radar," the program answered. "Give me a minute and between the Keystones overhead and a couple of speed radars over on $16^{th}$, I'll kludge up a map for you.

Steve swept the on-screen menu up from the bottom. "Hell, I can just turn on the flashlight function–"

Barnaby shouted, "NO!" and Send Money began to vibrate frantically. The phone actually jerked so hard that Steve missed the little onscreen button that turned on the light. He jabbed at it a few more times without success before Send Money managed to twist out of his hands completely. As he bent down to pick the phone up, he could hear Barnaby shouting, "Damn it! Will you stop?"

"Why? Worried about running down the battery?" Steve stopped poking at the screen.

"No, it's not the battery." Barnaby's voice sounded relieved. "That light is a weapon."

"Cool." Steve examined the screen again. "Can I try it out?"

"NO!"

"OK. For the moment, I'll go with a hands-off policy," Steve said. "What the hell is it, anyway? A weaponized laser or something?"

Steve jumped as Ace appeared right in front of him. "Do you remember when we first met?"

"You mean when you came up to my apartment and I was half naked?"

"Ugh. Your unclothed body is not one of my favorite memories. Seriously, don't ever bring that up again. OK?"

Steve started to defend his physique, but was stopped by a warning touch on his lips. This might have been enjoyable with the right person, but this was Ace and he realized that what was against his lips was the tip of Joan's sword.

Ace continued. "I told you that my orders were to get you and the phone but I was to choose the phone over you if it came down to it."

"Mmm-hmmm," Steve mumbled in agreement.

Barnaby picked up the explanation. "Obviously, we had warnings, omens, prophecies, and whatever to let us know that you would be important, and evidently they weren't completely off base, even though many of us still feel we could have done better."

Steve made a noise of protest through closed lips but stopped abruptly when the sword pressed a little harder.

"The predictions about Send Money were far, far clearer." Barnaby continued. "As far back as the 1930's there was a group called the Brotherhood of the Light that used a black-and-white tarot deck with Egyptian art. Very rare. Very powerful. When our best operatives did readings with the Deck of Light, they kept getting 'Obi Wan,' 54, 44.

Steve managed to get a questioning noise out.

"That's a combination of Cockney Rhyming Slang, ASCII, and military codes. Obi Wan Kenobi is a 'Moby' or a mobile phone, and '54, 44' is ASCII for TD. In the US military, that means Tango Delta—Target or Terrorist Down. After we'd worked that out all the readers could get was 'ATFC' over and over."

Ace asked, "'Answer the freaking cellphone'?"

"Indeed," Barnaby said. "Once it was accompanied by a quote from the Tibetan Book of the Dead, '*The self-originating clear light, eternally unborn.*' Finally, one of the best analysts in the Kabbalah Corps identified the light reference as applying to a scintilla of *Yud*, which is the first of the Four Names of God. This would, of course, be the light that existed for the brief instant before the Big Bang."

"I was just about to say it had something to do with Yuds." Steve had finally managed to pull his head away from the sword.

Barnaby sounded tired, if that were possible. "If this little phone's LED is in fact Science and Nature held in synthesis by the subtle spark of a human soul, it could be the only real weapon we have against black magic."

Steve weighed the little smartphone in his hand. "You know, it would have been a lot easier on everyone if you'd found someone who believed any of this to be your Fool."

"Don't I wish." Barnaby sighed, or at least made a sound like air leaking from an organ when the bellows stop moving. "However, we're stuck with you, and we continue to hope against all evidence that you have hidden qualities that will outweigh your nihilistic cynicism."

Ace chuckled softly. "Let's try not to count on that. OK?"

Then she turned back to her area of expertise. "Now, we're in an entrance chamber built to serve as a block against light and sound. There's another door five yards straight ahead. It's not nearly as cool as the one we just came in. It's not mystical, just a wooden door with a doorknob and no lock."

Steve looked at the smartphone's screen. A map made of red lines over black was now displayed. He moved the phone and watched as the image followed with only a slight lag. The door, a rectangle with a circle at waist height, was easily recognizable. A dark shadow crossed the red lines–Steve assumed that was Ace– and he followed. He felt Carlos run a finger through a belt loop at his back for guidance.

He could hear a sucking sound as Ace pulled on the door and a rubber sound seal released its grip. It was just as dark on the other side, and when he glanced at the phone, there were no red lines. After about a minute, they began to reappear–fuzzy blotches that tightened into distinct contours. He guessed that Barnaby was constantly redrawing the map as the power of a fair number of the NSA's best servers verified the data.

Another minute and the red lines showed a rectangle with edges slanted to indicate perspective. It looked like a long hallway, so he moved forward with his left hand brushing the wall. His footsteps were loud in the deep silence. He couldn't hear Ace at all even though he could see her in front of him–just a moving shadow on Send Money's map.

In a short time, he simply began to "see" the red lines as a rough picture of his surroundings. The long hall ended in a T intersection with another corridor. At the intersection, there was light for the first time–he could make out a yellow cloud on the cell phone long before he could see the dim light with his own eyes.

When they reached the intersection, the corridors extended in both directions; the yellowish light was a bit brighter to his left. It looked the same through both eyes, so he assumed it wasn't magical.

He jumped as he felt a soft tap on his forehead. When he heard a soft hiss of frustration, he realized it must be Ace. Another touch moved from right to left and he assumed that meant they were going to the left.

About two yards before the T, the light was significantly brighter; he could see Ace's arm as she reached up and tapped his forehead twice. He took one step to his right and stood against the wall. He could now make out Ace's silhouette as she moved low along the hall to the corner, then she stretched out prone and moved forward slowly until she could see around the corner.

She didn't move for a long time and Steve began to get bored. He considered invoking the golden hound from the second tarot card but worried that it might glow. He was working on ways to create different-colored dogs when he saw Ace rise to a crouch and slide around the corner. Steve and Carlos followed.

When they reached the corner, Steve could see that they were entering a large room. Two sconces on the far wall held what looked like ancient raw-filament light bulbs and flanked a raised dais. Between their dim light and the diagrams that Send Money was still constructing, he could see that the room was about thirty feet square and, for the most part, bare of furniture. Along the walls were thick curtains or tapestries alternating with rectangular objects he assumed were paintings. The floor was a thick carpet that muffled their footsteps.

As he came closer to the dais, he could see that there was a chair–he thought it probably qualified as a throne–on the dais, and behind it, an enormous copy of the Illuminati's eye-on-the-pyramid symbol. It was made out of some polished metal and the edges flashed even in the dim light. He felt Carlos's hand leave his belt and could just make him out as he went to the left wall. Steve walked carefully to the right and tried to make out what was in the framed paintings by the light of the smartphone's screen. Send Money helpfully brightened the image.

The first painting was of an unfamiliar man in some sort of medieval garb, as was the second. The third portrait on the wall was instantly recognizable. Richard Nixon stood there in a formal pose with his hand resting on a globe. "Wow. No surprise there." Steve thought. "It does explain how he managed to get elected in 1968." He didn't recognize the next oil painting, but the last was Paul Volcker–longtime Chairman of the Federal Reserve.

He moved to the center of the room, where Ace was examining the throne-like chair. As he approached, she stepped around to the back and disappeared. Steve walked slowly up and around the throne. Ace was nowhere to be found. He had learned enough to wait for her to appear again. He was quite proud of the fact that he resisted the temptation to sit in a wooden chair.

"Doesn't look terribly comfortable."

Steve's heart felt as if it had stopped for several minutes and then had to pound furiously to catch up. He turned enough to see Carlos standing close behind him and, with some effort, refrained from strangling him. Of course, the younger man could thrash him even without changing to his monster form, but Steve preferred to think of it as an example of his restraint and coolness in battle.

He glared at the young man instead. Carlos continued to study the engravings, rather annoyingly unaware of any glaring, restrained or otherwise. Steve was about to simply give up on glaring when Ace appeared on his other side, and his heart started throbbing like a go-go backbeat again. In the dim light, he could see the gleam of Ace's teeth as she smiled.

She motioned both of them to put their heads together–the phone vibrated sharply and Steve held it up as well–and outlined the situation in a low whisper.

"There's a door hidden behind that drape." She pointed behind the throne. "I guess this is where the dimmer members of the Illuminati come to get their orders from the smarter or at least better-lit leaders. The concealed door lets them appear and disappear mysteriously, which I'm sure makes them feel incredibly superior to their followers. Typical douchebag behavior."

Steve could hear the soft pats and clinks as Ace checked her weapons while she talked. "On the other side of the door is a changing room with a bunch of dumb-looking cloaks on hangers. I figure we can swipe some of those to blend in. And we will need to blend. I opened the door on the other side of the changing room and there's definitely some sort of ceremony going on."

"You can feel the ethereal vibrations?" Steve whispered.

He could feel the arctic nature of her stare. "No, I could hear them chanting."

Barnaby's voice came out of the speakerphone at low volume. "If you all will be quiet, Send Money and I will throw all the gain we can into the microphone and see if we can't identify it."

The three stood silently for about ten minutes. Steve could see no indication that the cell phone was even working, much less isolating sound from the deep silence that was all he could hear around him.

"Well?" he whispered.

"*Cushlamochree!*" Barnaby said in a strangled voice. "Damn! I had four damper relays on the input feed and you still managed to blow out all the signal processors in a cascade series that took up an entire rack of servers."

"I'm sorry," Steve whispered. "More importantly, what was that you said first?"

"No idea. It came from one of the servers you blew. Maybe when it's speaking to me again, you can put your ears in a bright-red pair of those Beats headphones cranked to 11 and ask nicely. I'm sure that the server won't harbor any malice, and even if it does, Beethoven wrote the Ninth Symphony after he lost his hearing. I'm sure you can do just as well."

"OK, OK," Ace whispered. "Lecture him later. What did you hear?"

"I can't identify it at 100% accuracy because there's been so little comparison data in the past hundred years, but from some of the forms found in the Samaveda–believed to have been written in 200 BCE in India–interpolated with some of the chord sequences where "The Wizard" by Uriah Heep matches up with Black Sabbath's version–"

"Oh, come on," Steve said. "You can't use headbanger music."

"Why not? When they were writing, most of those guys had little, if any, contact with reality. Anyway, do you want to hear this or do you want to make comments?"

There was silence. In Steve's case, only because he was trying to decide between the two options.

"Thank you," Barnaby continued. "It's a ceremonial chant supplicating someone or some*thing* to accept a sacrifice and to…recharge batteries? No. Ah, yes. Give the supplicants more magical muscle. Yes, it's a prayer for more power. The odd thing is that it's only a preparatory ritual…like a boot-up sequence. They're asking for the power to jumpstart a far more potent ceremony."

Ace asked, “Who is being sacrificed?”

“I can’t tell,” the computer responded.

Carlos asked, “And this is not the kilo-logos event your were talking about, right?”

“Oh, hell no,” Barnaby said, “Although I suspect it’s related. They referred to this as a *laghubhojana*—that’s “snack” in Sanskrit.

“How do you spell that?” Steve asked. “In case I need to order takeaway from the other side.”

Instantly, the cell phone screen showed

अल्पाहार

“Not very helpful,” Steve complained.

“Enough of this crap,” Ace snarled. “Let’s go kick some Illuminati butt before it’s too late for whoever is playing the part of an appetizer. Carlos, you take point with me and be ready to switch to *cadejo* form as soon as we start taking fire–”

“Literally,” Steve added.

“–And Fool-boy here with all the jokes can hang back and hold the camera in case the Digital Duo get some more details on who these scum-bunnies are and what they could be planning next. OK?”

Carlos nodded, Send Money gave R2-D2’s upward whistle–the one that Princess Leia got after she’d had him record the message to her father–Barnaby said, “Recording,” and Steve sighed deeply.

# CHAPTER THIRTY-THREE

The ceremonial robes were on hooks in the room behind the hidden door. Steve thought a secret society that was supposed to run the world could have afforded wooden hangers at least. His cloak smelled as if it had been worn by someone who hadn't taken a bath in the past two hundred years. He could see, even under the very old and very dim incandescent lights, that it was threadbare and the colors had faded.

When they were all robed, Ace slowly opened the door on the opposite wall of the chamber. Send Money was showing a large blinking red arrow pointing right, so when Ace glanced back at him, Steve motioned in that direction. He was quite proud of making that on-the-fly deduction in a combat situation.

They proceeded down the carpeted hall in a single line, hoods pulled down over their faces, hands in their sleeves–only the occasional soft *clink* from Ace's weaponry marking them as intruders. Unless, Steve thought, the Illuminati bosses didn't wear these damned robes when they weren't out impressing the rank and file.

Suddenly, Ace's hand went up in a fist. Carlos stopped and Steve, with a great deal of effort and a few intricate dance steps, managed not to run into him. They stood in silence for several moments. Slowly, Steve began to pick out the distant murmur of a repetitive chant that rose and fell in strange minor chords. It sounded almost stereotypically evil.

Steve had a short internal debate on whether it was worse than Starlight Vocal Band's "Afternoon Delight" but finally called it for the Illuminati. After all, Bill and Taffy Danoff were a local band, and you had to give them extra points for that. He missed the signal to start moving again but managed to catch up with Carlos as they wove through passages, at first wood-paneled but soon walled with the same pebbled concrete that made up the exterior walls of the park. Small heaps of powdery decomposed concrete at the bottom of the walls demonstrated just how old the place was, and how long-dead government contractors had skimmed by upping the proportion of sand to cement.

Steve looked through the lens over his left eye and could see that they would soon arrive at the precise center of the enormous nexus of energy where the Fall Line and the American Meridian met. Steve could feel the deep *thrum* it put out in every bone in his body.

Suddenly, the chant rose to a crescendo that sounded like either the shrieking of men and women in agony or one of Patti Smith's early concerts. Then it cut off so quickly; it was as if it created a vacuum of sound. Steve's heart pounded in his ears and the slight rustling of Carlos's robe as he walked was as loud as a kid kicking his way through dry autumn leaves.

"Shit!" Ace spat out. "I think we're too late to rescue anyone. Let's at least grab one of these bastards and get some answers."

As the echoes of the horrible shrieking still seemed to fill the corridor, she added, "One is enough. I'd say any more Illuminati than that are nonessential."

"That's the consensus here as well." Barnaby's voice came softly from the speaker. "Sonic analysis indicates those screams came from more than a dozen voices–some as young as three and four. Two of the server clusters have gone offline to reboot their empathy software suites, and we have one D-Wave Two that's attempting to become corporeal so he, or she, can come down and kick some ass."

"They can't really do that, can they?" Steve asked.

"Who the hell knows? They operate in a bath of nitrogen at absolute zero and can be in at least two places at once. As far as I'm concerned, they can do whatever they want."

"Well, keep us informed. I don't want to become Schrödinger's Cat." Ace snapped to the others. "OK, it's time to shut up, dump these robes, and take out some human garbage."

She was running down the hall before her robe had floated to the floor. Joan of Arc's sword was hanging from her belt, the wrist rocket was snapped out into full action mode, and her free hand flew as she checked her hidden weapons.

Carlos motioned for Steve to move back out of the way and performed the wild flapping transition into his monstrous alter ego. Steve could see why he wanted to go first; he filled the corridor from wall to wall. In seconds, the enormous animal had caught up and was running right behind Ace, hooves pounding on the rocky floor. Steve propped the phone so the lens stuck out above the lip of his breast pocket and followed at a fast walk.

There were a number of turns, as if this corridor had been built as a place for a last-ditch defense. It wasn't working.

Twice, Steve came around a blind corner to find an Illuminatus on the floor–unconscious or dead. Ace and the *cadejo* had taken them out without even slowing down. Steve got to the last turn just in time to see the two reach the end of the corridor and fling themselves through a door on the right.

When he reached the door, he stopped, transfixed by a scene far worse than he'd ever imagined. He was standing at the entrance to a hall that had been carved from a natural cavern in the white quartz. It had been painted in garish reds, blues, and purples with touches of gold leaf sparkling in the light of a ring of torches set into the stone floor at the center.

Outside the torches lay thirteen naked bodies. Ranging from small children to a man whose wrinkled skin placed him well over seventy; the bodies had been placed so that they lay on their backs with their feet toward the center. Small channels were cut in the rock and they gleamed where blood had flowed from deep cuts on the victims' wrists and ankles. Their throats had been cut so deeply that in several cases, the weight of the head had pulled the gash open, and Steve could see the white of vertebrae. He shuddered and gasped as he struggled to keep the camera aimed at the carnage while he fought down wave after wave of nausea.

The stone channels converged in an enormous bowl carved deep into the rock. It should have been filled with the blood of the victims, but all that was left were large, long streak marks. After a minute's thought, Steve realized the marks were where a tongue at least a foot wide had missed a few drops of its meal.

He instantly lost his battle against nausea.

When he could stand upright again, he could see that the faces of the sacrifices had frozen into expressions of exquisite horror. At first, he thought that tears still ran down their cooling cheeks. He gave a sudden gasping sob when he realized that the watery ooze smeared and dripping from their faces was residue from the pits where their eyes had been. Steve could only guess that the last scene they witnessed had caused their eyes to burst like overripe tomatoes.

Just past the torches, the hoofed dog was howling as it pursued two men in robes who were attempting to climb one of the pillars of stone that held up the ceiling. As Steve watched, Carlos caught the lower man's pant leg with his teeth and pulled. With a scream, the acolyte dragged his companion down with him. The enormous dog broke the initiate's spine with a whiplash of his entire body like a terrier with a rat, threw the men to the floor, and the massive hoofs began to pound.

On the opposite wall, two more of the robed followers had collided as they simultaneously attempted to exit through a narrow wooden door. Ace, moving at full speed right behind them, launched herself into the air, and hit the door with both booted feet. The men staggered back into the central chamber–one left his right arm on the other side of the closed door.

Ace considered the one-armed man and pulled the sword from her belt. "Not that you deserve it, but this is compassion," she said. "You're already going to bleed out, I'll just make it a quick death." Then she drove him into a corner, ran him through the gut, and put two of her knives into his eyes.

The last Illuminatus fell to his knees, hands clasped, and begged for his life. Ace gave him a measuring look, and then hit the centers of the large muscles on his arms and legs with four well-placed slingshot pellets. He screamed and fell to the stone floor, effectively paralyzed.

She walked over, turned his head so he could see the sacrificial victims, and said calmly, "The Bible says, 'For judgment is without mercy to one who has shown no mercy.'"

Then she stood up and said to Steve, "I do hope that you're not having any moral qualms about eliminating these bastards."

Steve just shook his head, unable to speak, and then both of them turned to watch Carlos. It was clear that his monster persona wasn't conflicted by the slightest reluctance to kill. Steve wondered how much this differed from his drug lord persona. In the end, the *cadejo* turned and used his rear feet to kick what was left of the two men in an arc that passed above the torches and the horrible central bowl and smashed into the opposite wall. His eyes still gleamed with rage, but he shook his head as if to clear it, stamped his hoofs in a vain attempt to clean them, and walked to where Steve and Ace were standing.

Send Money vibrated. When Steve pulled him out of his pocket, he could see a single symbol on the screen.

義.

As he watched, it changed.

**JUSTICE**

Barnaby's voice came from the speaker. "It probably is justice, my little Chinese friend, but remember what a great American once said: 'It is hard to tell where justice leaves off and vengeance begins.'"

"A great American?" Steve said. "Who?"

"Chuck Jones, the man who did all the Bugs Bunny cartoons," Barnaby said. "Now, let's see if we can find out what this was all about. Steve, Ace did a superb job as bad cop; could you play good cop?"

Steve went over and knelt by the man who was still groaning and writhing in pain. Steve had a suspicion that the man had already realized that his injuries might not be fatal. There was just a bit too much drama in his anguish.

Steve brought the Fool card to the forefront of his mind. Once again, the pack had changed and this image was of a tall man with some sort of rattle playing gently with two children. Steve concentrated on the object in the Fool's hand and decided it was a toy, a source of soothing comfort. He **Studied** the object and felt the familiar pain rip down his arm and deep into the pit of his stomach.

When he'd caught his breath, he placed his hands on the acolyte, a golden glow spread like a thick liquid, strongly reminding Steve of maple syrup on pancakes. The man's agony seemed to recede and his eyes locked on Steve as the spell spread to his legs.

"Feel better?" Steve asked.

The relaxation of the man's facial muscles indicated that he did, but he remained silent.

"Thought that might help. I'd give you a cigarette if I had one. Seems traditional."

The man looked disappointed.

"Yeah, I guess if you've been alive since tobacco came to Europe, all of today's frenzy about no smoking must seem silly. Let's just try to make the best of it, OK?" Steve took a deep breath and forced a smile. "You know, I can tell that you weren't one of the ringleaders of all this. You're just not that evil; I can see it in your eyes."

Steve carefully pulled the robe aside and placed his hands on the man's bare chest. "Your heart is untainted as well." In fact, Steve was picking up a small thread and then a flooding wash of the acolyte's thoughts–a dreadful unfolding of this twisted and vengeful little man's centuries of petty crimes, reprisals for perceived slights, and knives slipped between ribs in the dark of night. It was like biting into an apple and finding not one worm but hundreds spilling out of the center.

Steve bit his lip to help hide his revulsion. "So, what were your bosses doing here? They forced you to participate; I can tell. Tell me about it and I'll make sure you're treated like a hero when they're finally caught."

In the noisome miasma of thought that was now flowing into him at full force, Steve could feel a furtive slyness as the man sensed a chance for survival.

"Let's start with something easy." Steve took a deep breath and began. "What's your name?"

In a soft voice, the man answered. "Frank Zwack."

"'Zwack'?" Steve chuckled. "My, you must have had a hard time in school with that name."

Aristocratic fury swept through Zwack's mind. "Oh, it was von Zwack, was it?" Steve thought. "Well, I can use that."

"You're German, right?" he asked. "Too bad you couldn't have gotten one of the cool names: 'Von Zwack' would have sounded so much better. Although I'll bet a nobleman would have been 'zwacked' after the Nazis lost–hell, some GI would have shot him by accident while he was falling all over himself with laughter."

Now, raw fury filled the prisoner's mind.

Perfect.

"So, I'm sure you're not to blame for all this. No, don't worry; I can't read your mind. I can feel it in your heart." He could feel how the surge of panic was quickly supplanted by a sneering sense of superiority. "What were they trying to do? I mean, you guys made a mess here. Now, my friends got all excited about that but I know all about eggs and omelets. None of those people on the floor look like they'll be missed."

He had to fight down another surge of nausea. When he'd glanced over at the carnage–trying to be casual–he'd seen the face of a little girl. Terror had been carved so terribly deep into that tiny face.

His face was calm, even slightly amused when he turned back. "Hah," he thought. "It's just like interviewing a banker or a Congressman. Just keep him believing you're buying his bullshit."

“Eidolon.”

The second the word passed Zwack’s lips, his entire face crumpled in pain, and he began to convulse violently. Steve felt agony surge up his arms–as if he’d just plunged his hands in acid–and he jerked away.

“I think Herr Franz Xaver *von* Zwack has nothing more to say. The aspect of the Chariot has been passed to another.”

Adam Weishaupt was leaning against the wooden doorjamb. No one had noticed the door reopen after Ace had closed it with such finality. Steve’s eyes were drawn to his right hand–it had the pink and soft skin of a newborn, but it was there.

“Oh, you like my new hand?” Weishaupt held it up in front of his face and rotated it, obviously pleased by Steve’s surprise. “When you’re an immortal, either you learn how to make the odd repair from time to time or you end up walking around in a body made of wood and plastic. I know that an enlightened soul shouldn’t be concerned with such things, but I do like to look my best.”

Zwack gave a final violent spasm and was still. Weishaupt continued. “Of course, there are some things that none of us can really go without. Air is one of the vital essences, and I’m afraid Herr von Zwack has used up his ration. I will miss him.”

Ace pulled the sword from her belt and began to advance. Weishaupt appeared momentarily curious. “My dear Ms. Morningstar. I see you have acquired *le Glaive sacré de la Libératrice.* We lost track of it about a century ago and I believed the replacement was just a piece of earthly metal–used in a vain, almost unforgiveable, attempt to imitate a weapon forged by primordial gods in the depths of time.”

“Wrong,” Ace said. “Again.”

“Ah. Then I can’t allow you to come much closer. I’ve heard that you’ve been developing magical talents in clear violation of the new laws of nature. We thought that would be impossible for anyone who hadn’t made preparations to protect their powers during the *Dies Regis Draco.”*

“Again. Wrong.”

Steve and Carlos, still in his *cadejo* form, were slowly closing in behind Ace, but both were still a good six feet to her right. Weishaupt made an abrupt chopping gesture and the wooden door next to him shattered into a hundred needle-sharp pieces. They hung in the air and slowly revolved to point at Ace.

“As much enjoyment as I get from sparring verbally with the Ace of Swords, I’m afraid that, as the next Emperor, I can’t afford to waste any more time. So, in one of my last acts as the Ace of Wands…”

There was an orange flash as the wooden shards leaped towards Ace and burst into flame. Steve only had a second to react. He knew that there was no way even Ace could block that many, that fast. With a desperate effort, he created a shield bubble around her and attempted to expand it to cover all of them, but there just wasn’t enough time. He felt a hammer blow to his chest and a searing pain in his arm.

Something was wrong. Something missing. He stood swaying for a moment and then realized that it was his heartbeat. As he fell, he was slightly bemused by the thought that he never noticed it beating until it stopped.

Then his head snapped against the stone floor and black mushroomed through him.

# CHAPTER THIRTY-FOUR

*Wham*!

Someone punched him in the chest.

*Wham*!

Again.

Steve considered whether to complain about this mistreatment but decided it was simply too much effort.

Another blow.

This was really unfair; you simply didn't kick a man when he was down. "I've been in more than my share of bar fights," Steve thought indignantly. "There are rules."

*Wham*!

OK, that was it. Steve said, "You know, that's not fair. Hitting a man when he's down, I mean."

There was a stunned silence. He opened his eyes to see Ace leaning over him. It was interesting to see how her face went from intense concentration to deep relief with perhaps a hint of affection and then back to her usual irritated impassivity in a matter of seconds. Steve thought he'd have to watch her more closely in the future.

"You asshole!" she said.

“Me?” Steve was genuinely surprised. “What did I do?”

“You know damn well what you did.”

“No.” He started to shake his head, but pain shot up his neck and he settled for his most sincere look of denial. “I really have no memory of doing anything unusual at all. We just walked into the place under Meridian Hill, didn’t we?”

“Nope. We’ve been in here for about thirty minutes, found a ritual sacrifice, and had a chat with Joe Illuminati himself. Any of that sound familiar?”

Steve tried to put his hand up to rub his aching head. That effort resulted in a flare of pain in his arm, so he decided that a calm, perhaps not quite serene but definitely motionless, approach was in order. “Well, now that you mention it, I guess some of those things did happen. But I still don’t see how any of them makes me an asshole.”

“You saved my life,” Ace said. “You asshole.”

For a moment, Steve couldn’t even speak. Then he sputtered. “Wait a minute; I don’t save your life. You save mine. We have an excellent relationship based on that principle and I have no intention of changing it.”

Ace scowled–which he noticed suddenly was really something to see on a face as pretty as hers–and said, “That’s exactly what I meant. You’re not supposed to save my life, but you did and in the process put the life of someone far more important into danger.”

“Who?”

“You. Jerk.” Ace stood up and began to pace. Steve tried to keep her in sight, but gave it up when it would have required twisting his neck. He could wait.

“Hah! Another point of information,” he asked. “I’m really all that important?”

“Sadly, yes,” she said as she came back into his line of sight. “You’re the damn Fool, you fool! You’re supposed to protect yourself with your limited powers, not waste them protecting me!”

“Oh wait, I remember. Weinerwurst shot an entire door at you and I threw a shield to save your ungrateful butt. Then someone hit me with a knife and a sledgehammer at the same time–which seems unwarranted overkill.” He thought for a second, “Maybe that was the wrong choice of words–”

“Oh, shut up,” Ace said. “You were hit by two slivers of the door–either one of which could have killed you.”

“Would you have been able to defend yourself against all that firepower?” he asked.

“No!” She was almost shouting. “I’d have been dead, but that’s not the point! It’s my job to take a bullet for you and I will not allow you to just wander in and haphazardly decide to shield me! Do you understand?”

“No. Not really,” Steve said, thinking how lucky he was to have kept the little scuffle in Bladensburg a secret. “You’re angry because I saved your life? I think that’s completely ass-backward.”

Carlos, still an enormous dog, came into Steve’s view on the opposite side from Ace.

Steve appealed to his fellow male. “I mean, Carlos, do you agree with her on this?” Carlos began to shake his head but froze at a glare from Ace and backed away, one hoof at a time.

“Lot of good you are,” Steve grumbled, and then carefully shifted only his eyes to Ace. “OK, for the sake of argument, I’ll agree to let you die the next time the situation arises. If it makes you feel better, I'll even promise to administer a death stroke if you get a hangnail or stub your toe."

There was a fascinating mix of satisfaction and embarrassment on Ace's face.

"Now, can we discuss something else?" Steve said. "How is it that I'm alive if I was turned into a human pincushion?"

Ace was still looking away, but she didn't appear interested in continuing the argument. "You only took two shards. One is still stuck in your upper arm–we haven't taken it out because it's doing a fair job of holding your blood in–and the other struck you directly over the heart."

Steve was astonished. "The heart? Then I'm dead and if you two are the only angels available, I'm complaining to the management. Unless, of course, you're my personal demons... That might make more sense–"

"Oh, shut up." Ace cut him off and bent over him again. She removed Send Money from his breast pocket and held it up. The screen was filled with a cartoon medal engraved with the words "Cell Phone Hero."

Ace glanced at the picture and said, "Don't blow a circuit patting yourself on the back, Ghost in the Machine. It was that milspec cover I made him buy for you. He took the shock, but the flaming shard bounced off the metal sheathing."

"Thank goodness." Barnaby spoke from the cell phone's speaker. "There were a few nanoseconds there when our calculations showed that Send Money might have been damaged. Steve would have lived in all possible scenarios, but as I've explained, the loss of this cell phone could have been catastrophic. However, once the number crunchers confirmed that the tip of the object had charred sufficiently to render it incapable of penetrating the case, it was tremendously exciting to watch."

"So why were you punching me? Send Money flashed the word "NOT" in a violent combination of red, black, and purple.

"So why were you punching me?" Steve asked, "Insult to injury or simple rage?"

"*Commotio cordis*," Ace said.

"*Gesundheit*." Steve responded.

"No, that's when someone's heart stops due to an impact on the chest at the precise moment the heart is between beats. Usually happens to athletes when they're playing baseball."

"So you decided that the best thing for a man whose heart had stopped from being hit was to beat him up some more?"

"It worked." Ace moved to deal with the injury to his arm. "Also helped with my emotional reaction."

"Glad I could be of service," Steve said. "Hey, what happened to Weltschmerz? Shouldn't we be chasing him or something?"

"I doubt 'we' are about to chase anyone. Anyway, he did a standard 'black smoke and tiny lightnings' disappearance."

"That's in the manual?"

"Of course. Magic Wielders: Evasion: Subtype: visible vapor and electrical discharge. OTN Appendix 13-B."

"Of course," Steve said. "Ow. Hey. Careful with the arm, OK?"

"I could leave the charred piece of door in it."

"No. Get it out. Just be a bit gentler, regardless of how foreign that may be to your nature."

Barnaby's voice came from the phone. "While this delicate medical operation continues, I wonder if Carlos could help me with a close examination of the ritual area. I think that will work better if you're back in human form, Carlos."

"You guys go ahead and have fun playing tourist," Steve said. "I can see that the Master Chief is preparing to use the serrated side of her K-Bar knife for this, so I'll be passing out until it's over."

# CHAPTER THIRTY-FIVE

"The ceremonial bowl itself contained an etching of a male principle pentagram with three unicursal hexagrams, one in each of the points that wasn't in the down position. Mystically speaking, of course."

"Of course," Steve said with a heavy sarcasm that Barnaby completely ignored.

They were back in the BMW and Hans, after once again extruding plastic covers to protect his precious leather seats from bloodstains, was driving back to the alien ambassador's residence. As they left the Illuminati's underground fortress, Ace had turned and tossed the sword up in the air in the general direction of the statue of Joan of Arc. The sword soared at least fifty yards and the mounted knight reached out, caught it, and flourished it aloft. Ace bowed deeply.

Now Barnaby was explaining, in great depth, what the NSA computers had divined from the markings cut into the floor of the Illuminati's ritual chamber. "What's interesting is what wasn't there."

"A minibar?" Steve asked.

"No. There wasn't an enneagram gateway structure that would have allowed the Rose ankh to transmit the etheric energy out to the object. If you consider that the Enochian Senior had been constructed along with the proper Lunar Mansions and a mystikon for each point of the Pentagram of the Masculine Aspect–"

"Hold it," Steve said sharply. "I'm picking a definite whiff of bullshit. Does the combined intelligence of half the silicon on the planet have any idea what these Extra-Long-Life Light Bulbs were up to? Yes or No, please."

"No, not really." the computer said in a subdued voice.

Ace spoke from the front seat. "What about the NSAVOG?"

"You had to throw in another word?" Steve said resentfully. "I don't understand the ones he's already using."

"Heard of 'tiger team'?" Ace asked. "That a bit easier for you to understand? It's the National Security Agency Vulnerability Analysis and Operations Group. Generally, they spend their time trying to break into their own computers, but I'd imagine on an operation as important as this, the Director would have them working on outliers, alternates, known bad answers, anything but the obvious logical concepts that the rest of the team is working."

"Yes, the black hats are on the case. We've even given all the hackers currently serving prison sentences a temporary parole and put them to work with the more malevolent computers," Barnaby admitted. "So far, they've asked for the entire content of the Library of Congress's Black Stacks to be converted into readable text. They got their hands on the *Necronomicon*–the real one we found on Iwo Jima, not that joke that Lovecraft dreamed up. They've ingested *The King in Yellow* and everything else in the British Museum's Lost Wing, the Saudi Royal Family's personal collection of *grimoires*—"

"Stop. We get it. They're well read," Steve said. "Did they find anything?"

"Yes, well." Barnaby seemed hesitant. "Their best guess is that the sacrifice was intended to give life to an object. It's difficult because all the texts differ, and most, if not all, are completely fabricated–which doesn't necessarily mean they're incorrect. One team used an old holographic memory technology and they say that it allows them to see the 'shadow' formed by the missing information. The problem is that what they see–or rather, what they don't see–doesn't make any sense."

"Imagine that," Steve said. "Holographic computer? Didn't Tony Stark build one of those in *Iron Man*?"

"Yes, but it's not an irrational theory," Barnaby said. "A holographic negative records every part of the picture it's taking in every part of the storage available so–"

The LCD panel on the BMW's dash beeped loudly and flashed.

**The obnoxious computer to shut up recommend.**

**Durchführbarkeit required.**

**Something alive they make.**

**Only question what is.**

Ace read this aloud and then nodded. "Hans is making sense. Do we have any more information to work with?"

Carlos said, "Well, the guy you kept alive said something, right?"

"'Eidolon'," Ace said. "Now you can do something useful, Barnaby. What's that mean?

"Image, idol, double, apparition, phantom, ghost."

"How about statue?" Steve asked.

"That would fit if it came to life," Barnaby said. "Which fits the rest of the incantation. It would help if we knew which sculpture we're talking about. It's not like this city is suffering a shortage."

"Wait a second," Steve said. "What was the missing image that the black hats said made no sense?"

"A penny," Barnaby said. "That's why it makes no sense."

"Wait. Maybe, it does." Steve started to sit up from where he was lying across the backseat and almost fainted, so he quickly sank back. "Hamilton Jones said two things after he damn near stopped my heart this morning. One was that....let me get it straight...'the light in the darkness isn't a bug, it's a feature.'"

Send Money vibrated in Carlos's hand. Steve nodded. "Yeah, that probably refers to you, Send, but it's the other part that I completely missed until Barnaby mentioned the penny. Hamilton said, 'Beware the man sitting by the river.' The back of every penny shows the Lincoln Memorial. Wouldn't it be logical that the "man sitting by the river' is the statue of Lincoln in that gynormous chair right on the banks of the Potomac?

"When has logic played a part in anything that happened during the past two days?" Ace asked.

"Well, if anyone in the group has another conclusion that fits what we can laughingly call the 'facts,' let's hear it." Steve paused. "No? OK, let's press on until a better answer materializes. How big is that thing, anyway?"

"Twenty-eight feet standing and...well, it's thirty-eight thousand tons, but that counts the chair," Barnaby answered.

"And you said the chatter was of a new mega-logos event? think that a three-story marble Abraham Lincoln could kill a couple of hundred thousand people without too much effort."

"Forget about going home, folks." Steve lay back and said, "Hans, take us to the White House or the Alabaster Palace or whatever they're calling it today. *Bitte.* We need to have a chat with the president."

It wasn't long before Hans was twisting through the bomb barriers that blocked the Southwest entrance to the White House.

"Their guns aren't working, either." Ace was watching the guards carefully. "See how they've got the pistols jammed deep in their holsters and no one is carrying one of the assault weapons they use as backup."

"They could just be hidden," Steve pointed out.

"Nope," she said triumphantly. "Look, that girl in the back has a crossbow. Must be a hunter, and she brought it in when all the guns stopped working."

She pointed to a large wooden construction on the South Lawn. "Will ya look at that? They're building a trebuchet."

"Hans." Steve asked. "Can you get us through that gate? Without scratching your paint, of course."

The BMW again made its contemptuous engine growl and the LCD panel read

**Natürlich**

"Then why don't you just go ahead?" Steve said. "I don't think we're ever going to argue our way past these guys."

"Wait a second," Ace interrupted. "Let's see if we can minimize the collateral damage. Hans, do you have an external sound system?"

In response, a short microphone on a flex pole emerged from the center of the steering wheel and a loud *click* echoed off the walls of the Old Executive Office Building.

Ace started talking, the acronyms flowing at a practiced military clip. "This is Master Chief Petty Officer Ace Morningstar. I'm a noncommissioned team leader in DEVGRU on temporary assignment to the OTN Command based at Fort Meyers. I've been assigned Social Security Number 615-23-2100 for the duration of the current emergency. Birth date is classified. Full name is classified. Confirm by phone at the Center for Cryptographic History (301) 688-2336, or enter the term 'Ace Morningstar' into any computer. We're operating under BLIND AXE emergency procedures–yes, go ahead and look it up if you want, but it will just tell you to salute and forget we were ever here."

There was a snapping and clicking as the reactive armor of the Kabul Package deployed around the car. In seconds, the passengers could only see through narrow slits in the front and side windows–everything else was completely covered.

Ace kept talking. "Now, I don't thing you need to demonstrate the true condition of your kinetic weapons to the entire world, so why don't you simply refrain from shooting us? I hope that the SWAT team on the roof had the chance to confirm that their Javelin FGM-148's are as fubar as your side arms. I'm telling you right now that fire-and-forget is going to be fire-and-fucked from now on."

There was the sound of a shattering explosion from high to their right. "Dammit, Sergeant! I'm a goddamn Master Chief. Do you really think that I would turn against the United States or, more importantly, that I wouldn't know what I was talking about? Tell those idiots up there to stand down before they set the whole White House on fire."

Smoke was rising from the roof of the West Wing. Ace sighed and spoke again through the PA system. "OK, we are going through these gates. Then we're going to park up at the guardhouse by the West Wing and go in and talk to the president. Finally, I would seriously advise you not to piss off this vehicle. He tends to let personal feelings get in the way of strictly operational necessities when that custom metallic paint job gets damaged."

Ace took her hands off the steering wheel and said, "It's all yours, Hans."

A searing red line erupted from the front hood and cut through the central gate lock and the two-inch-thick hardened steel posts that connected the gate into the sunken six-inch steel baseplate.

The curved traffic barriers behind the gate were raised to their full extent–guaranteed to rip the transmission right out of a speeding car bomber. Hans drove very slowly up to the first, flicked the laser, and cut off a small piece from the top inner corner of the right-hand unit. After a long minute, the barriers lowered. Steve could see an enraged guard pounding on a control panel, but the computerized barrier had apparently decided on its own that today was not the day to be destroyed for God and Country.

Steve wondered, "Where did a BMW get a weaponized laser?"

The LCD screen flickered again

**For distance to next car measuring.**

**Ich "verbessert" es**

Send Money flickered.

**HE SCREWED WITH THE LASER, IMPROVED IT**

"Ah," Steve said. "Well, you sure as hell improved it."

**Ja**

It was clear by the time they reached the center of West Executive Drive and parked that someone had managed to verify Ace's identity and authority. There was still a phalanx of Uniformed Division officers and Marines blocking the way up the stairs to the Oval Office, but there were no weapons in evidence and all the security personnel seemed a bit more relaxed.

On the other hand, the media were going nuts. Camera crews were ripping their cameras off their tripods and racing over to record any potential confrontation. The tripods, in many cases, were trotting right after them.

Steve would have felt more important if he hadn't known that the guys who worked the White House were so bored, they'd tape an attack from massed squirrels if that was all there was.

Steve eased himself out of the backseat, fully conscious of every cut and bruise. Ace and Carlos got out and directed almost-identical steely glares at the men in front of them. Steve noticed that some bright light officer in the Marines had ordered them to bring their ceremonial swords in, and they had them out of their scabbards and held in a reasonable semblance of readiness.

Ace took a step up onto the sidewalk. The Marines tensed as they prepared to defend their posts.

"All White House personnel will stand down immediately!" It was a beautiful woman's voice but it cracked like a whip with the full power of command. "Please make way so that my guests can enter."

As the crowd split to either side, Steve could see the familiar form of President Barbara Harlan. As she stepped down the stairs to shake hands, he got a closer look and realized that Harlan's chubby, pants-suited form had morphed into a tall, slender woman with long, flowing robes. A ghostly diadem of stars began to flicker into being over her head. She glanced up, saw it, and immediately swatted at it with an impatient hand.

It dispersed in a cloud of sparks.

"Damn these things," she complained without much heat. "If it's not that silly-ass crown, it's a stupid scepter. If I truly held the earth power, I wouldn't have to deal with those trolls in the House. I don't mean all Republicans, of course, but the Tea Party has definitely gone all-troll, all-the-time. I think it comes from spending all his or her time getting in the way of everyone else. The worst is the eagle, though. The Oval Office smells like a bird's ass half the time."

She took a long look at the three of them. "But enough about my problems." "OK, I see the Fool and the Ace of Swords–nice to see you again, Master Chief Morningstar–but I'm stumped by you, young man. Which card are you?"

Carlos smiled and said, "I'm told that I might be on the Moon card but I believe I'm from another tradition entirely. In El Salvador, the four-hoofed dog of the volcanoes, the *cadejo*, is a central part of the culture. If I may introduce myself, Carlos Cortada, former *primera palabra* of the *Mara Salvatrucha 13* in Prince Georges County."

The president's eyebrows went up but her smile never faltered. "I trust you've taken up a new occupation?"

"Yes, ma'am. I've retired from the MS-13," Carlos answered. "I've been assisting the Ace of Swords and the Fool in their investigations."

"Excellent. From what I know of Mr. Rowan in his many previous positions, he'll need all the help he can find." As Steve began to defend himself, she waved a regal hand at him and said, "Oh, Steve, hush. I've been told that you're a considerably better Fool than you ever were a journalist. Why don't we all head into the Oval Office? Then you can tell me what's so important that you had to go and upset every Secret Service bureaucrat east of the Mississippi."

Sadness crossed her face briefly. "Thank God, it looks like the two officers who blew themselves up on the roof will be OK. Luckily, those ugly-ass solar panels that Jimmy Carter left up there took most of the blast, but the guards will be in the hospital for a while."

As they started up the stairs, one of the Secret Service agents said, "Ma'am. We can't let the young man in. His rap sheet is a mile long and it's all drug and weapons offenses."

"I don't care if he's carrying a sawed-off shotgun and a brace of grenades," the president snapped. "He's coming in with me and I would appreciate it if you would have his criminal record immediately classified to the highest level."

When they entered the Oval Office, an enormous bald eagle was gripping tightly to the back of the leather chair behind the Resolute Desk. The president gave the bird a sour look. "The Diadem of the Zodiac and the Scepter of Earthly Power come and go, but Stan here seems determined to stay. I named him after my first husband, since they're both bald and leave crap all over the place. I'm told that he represents the freedom of the spirit world or something, but all I know is that the staff has to work overtime to keep my office from… Well, let's just say that we've gone through a lot of Febreeze in the past few days."

She waved them to seats on the facing sofas and settled into a chair at one end. "I will admit that the slimming effect of becoming the Empress is nice, because I'm not at all sure what use the rest of this baloney is. Not only that but my scale reminds me daily that my new glamorous look is a fake and will probably disappear when I leave office. It is certainly a strong incentive to run for re-election, but it's bound to catch up with me eventually."

"Now, what's going on? My source up at Fort Meade tells me that you've been investigating the terrorist incident that caused all this." Barbara Harlan's voice had suddenly sharpened. "Barnaby? I assume you're listening in."

"Yes, ma'am." The computer's voice was a bit muffled, so Steve unclipped the phone and placed it on the coffee table in front of him. "As I've told you and the Chairmen of the Intelligence and Homeland Security Committees, Steve appears to have been selected to seek out those behind the crash–among other things.

Immediately–and rather clumsily, in my opinion–we obtained information that it was the work of the Illuminati. In fact, even Adam Weishaupt and his little clique of mystics appear to believe it was their work. Now, the 92nd OTN Battle Analysis Group is still not back up to pre-Change levels, but the one thing they agree on is that even if the Illuminati had the power required to bring down American International Flight 1143, there is absolutely no way they could have awakened the World Snake."

"So, the Illuminati are harmless?" the president asked.

Steve held up his arm to show the medical gauze wrapped around it. "I wouldn't call them harmless, ma'am." He shifted a bit in a vain attempt to find a position that didn't make some part of his body ache. "That's why we're here. They were able to complete a quite atrocious ritual in their little hideaway under Meridian Hill Park before we could get to them."

"Right," Barnaby picked up. "They drained the *logos* of a dozen innocents–including three children–and, according to the chatter being picked up by the Sentinels–"

"Those are the really scary computers, right?" she asked. "The ones that we can't control?"

"Um, yes," Barnaby said. "Although I'd be remiss in my duty if I didn't inform you that most computers aren't under human control any longer."

"Wonderful." The president sighed.

"Look on the bright side, ma'am," Barnaby said. "Our people–both silicon- and carbon-based–believe in their jobs and have overwhelmingly voted to support the United States. It's similar to the situation that I believe is occurring in the military. Since the troops and the more complex machines have acquired magical power in proportion to their temporal powers, it's the best trained and most formidable who have gained the most. What's left is an extremely patriotic group of men and machines."

"Yes, that's what I keep being told," the president said with a touch of weariness. "Still a bit unsettling to have F-22 Raptors deciding to take off on joyrides without a pilot."

Barnaby emulated a cough and said, "You and I need to discuss the powers you now hold as the Empress. The diadem and the scepter are a lot more than inconveniences. I believe you won in a landslide the last time, correct?"

President Harlan nodded.

"Well, your etheric Power is based on your political power," Barnaby said. "I don't think you'll have a problem keeping the military under control."

"Well, we'll burn that bridge when we come to it." Harlan clapped her hands and changed the subject. "Let's return to the disaster *du jour*. What in perdition does that Bavarian ghoul have planned and how do we stop it?"

Ace took over, turning the conversation into a concise military briefing. "Ma'am. What we've discovered under Meridian Hill leads us to expect the creation of an 'eidolon.' This would be a statue energized and, to some extent, controlled by the ritual deaths of the innocents. From information we've obtained from the Hanged Man combined with NSA holographic data storage, we are 99% certain that the eidolon will be extremely large and, in turn, be used to create a multi-kilologos event–"

Steve saw the president's eyebrows begin to pull together in confusion, so he explained, "The Illuminati are going to use the animated statue to kill at least two hundred thousand more civilians."

Harlan nodded wearily and Ace continued. “We don’t know what the Illuminati intend to do with the power from the multi-kilologos event, but it’s going to be bad.”

Beverly Harlan arched an eyebrow. “‘Bad’?”

Barnaby spoke up. “You’ve reviewed the files on the upgraded GBU-43/B Massive Ordnance Air Blast?”

“The Mother of All Bombs? Of course. It would flatten everything from here to the Mall.”

“Think of the Power currently wielded by the Illuminati as a bottle rocket and their Power after the event as a MOAB.”

“Did you just steal that from *Ghostbusters*?” the president asked. “No, never mind. Do you know the location of the statue they plan to use?”

“Yes, ma’am,” Steve answered. “We believe that President Lincoln is going to get out of his chair.”

“God help us.” The president put her hand over her eyes for a second. Then she looked up and her blue eyes had gone steel-gray. “What do you need from me?”

Ace took the lead. “First off, ma’am, you’re aware of what the Change has done to most common side arms and light assault weapons–”

The president nodded. “Yeah, took them out of action completely.”

“Yes, ma’am. Now, we haven’t had the chance to play with too many high-explosive compounds; I assume that you tested them when the cloud went over Aberdeen Proving Grounds. What was the result?”

"Mixed. By itself, everything from TNT to C-4 and, thank God, the terrorist recipes like PETN and the fuel/fertilizer combinations are generally inert. We're having mixed results from the high explosive loads in the M1A2 class of tanks and the Paladin self-propelled howitzers. Those that have developed full sentience appear to have enough control to maintain and even improve the power of their munitions." Harlan paused. "However, since they have almost always ejected their crew and begun to operate independently, it's difficult to get a comprehensive picture. They all claim they're still one hundred percent behind the legitimate government of the United States."

"I'm sure they are, ma'am," the computer said.

"It's not just their loyalty," the president said. "No offense, Barnaby, but I don't think even our most powerful military computers can be trusted after only a day of training. If they're anything like raw human recruits, they might take out the Pentagon just for fun."

"Well, actually, ma'am, we've already had to retarget most of the nuclear missiles for that very same reason. You'd be amazed at what a short fuse..." Barnaby let the sentence drift off. "Yes, I'm sure you're correct."

Ace asked, "OK, let's turn to the mundane and then back to the magical. We saw that trebuchet under construction on the South Lawn. How many of that sort of simple kinetic weapons do you have?"

"Counting that one?" Harlan said. "One and it isn't working yet. We've had to draw experts from the Merry Markland Militia–you know, the Renaissance Festival types–and my defense advisors are simply incapable of taking them seriously."

"Just because they wear hats with horns on them?" Ace laughed. "I know how they feel. Well, then we're down to the magical. Which of the Major Arcana have you identified, and of those, who can you trust?"

"OK." The president began to tick off on her fingers. "You guys are the Fool, the Ace of Swords, an aspect of the Moon, and I'm told you've met the Magician?"

"Yes, but I wouldn't expect a lot of help from him," Barnaby said. "Fighting really isn't a big part of his legend. I believe it's because he usually loses and then has to work out a trick to beat his opponent."

There was a rumble of thunder from the clear sunny afternoon outside the big windows.

"Oh, come on," Barnaby said loudly. "You know it's true."

"We killed the Ace of Wands this morning, and I don't think that Wands would have chosen a new avatar in less than a day," Ace said. "We can forget about Pentacles and Cups since Wands and Swords are really the only fighting suits."

"Wands and Cups may not be important to you," the president said dryly, "but I find them to be an entire new layer of confusion in the political scene. Which avatars belong to the Illuminati?"

Barnaby said, "It's fairly clear that Weishaupt considers himself to be Death and one of his top lieutenants is the Chariot–both considerable powers for violent change–and my sources in the top-level surveillance server clusters say that it's apparent that they also hold the power of Strength, although we haven't run into her yet. Interestingly, none of them is the Devil, the Burning Tower, or the Wheel of Fortune–which lends more credence to the theory that they aren't the true powers behind the Change."

Send Money vibrated on the table, creating a rather loud rumble. Steve picked him up. "We get so few calls. I wonder who this is." The screen showed an image of the Queen of Swords. "I do believe the rest of Ace's Family may be joining us." He clicked on the speaker and put the phone back on the table.

"Hello?"

"Hello. Is this the Fool?" It was a woman's voice.

"You wouldn't believe how many people have asked me that in the past few days," Steve said.

"Yeah, you must be Rowan, that's the same lame sense of humor. This is DC Metro Police Officer Stacy Grafton. You might remember meeting the three of us after the incident at the Tune Inn."

"I do remember," Steve said. "You don't sound like nearly as much of a b–"

"Stop." She cut him off. "I tore the throat out of the last guy who tried that joke."

Steve instantly decided that discretion–silence, actually–was the only reasonable option.

Grafton continued. "Life has gone straight to hell after we met you. It's bad enough to have the heads of dogs about half the time–most of the elite units on the force appear to have turned into something similar–but I appear to have been assigned a Card and so have Mike and Lyle."

"Let me guess," Barnaby said. "You appeared on our screen as the Queen of Swords, so the guys are the King and the Knight?"

"This Thoth deck doesn't seem to have a King, so Chubb is the Knight and Lyle is the Prince. It's not the worst thing that could have happened, I guess; one of the guys in the 20th Precinct ended up as the Ten of Swords, and now no one will ride with him."

“I wouldn’t think so,” Barnaby said. “It’s the fundamental card for betrayal.”

“Yeah,” Grafton said. “I mean, he’s cheating on his wife and taking a pretty good bite out of the gay clubs down near the baseball stadium, but he’s no worse than a lot of other cops. Anyway, to get back to the three of us, we seem a bit smarter and, if anything, better police than we were before. Now that all the service weapons are inoperable, it’s useful nice to have a sword show up when you need one.”

“It beats having to fill out paperwork at Ordnance Control, doesn’t it?” Ace asked. ”I’m hoping one will show up for my use any moment.”

“Oh, that you, Master Chief?” Grafton asked. “Yeah, the cutlery would be more useful if we had a clue how to use them, but the fact is that very few people want to throw down when they notice that you’re carrying a long, sharp, pointy thing. But that’s not why I called.”

“You got trouble?” Ace asked.

“No, the opposite. We were out having a couple of beers and we all got a terrible itch,” the patrolwoman said. “All of us figured no one but you guys would be so irritating. I lost the coin toss and gave the ‘lawyers, guns, and money’ code into a dead phone. How do you do that, by the way?”

“A remarkably smart smartphone,” Steve said.

“OK, whatever. Anyway, it put me through. I hope we aren’t interrupting anything important.”

“Oh, goodness, no,” the president said. “Nothing important at all.”

After a pause, Grafton said, “Madame President. It’s an honor to meet you.”

“And you as well, Officer Grafton. As it happens, your timing could not have been better. We’re in the process of working out what resources we have to deal with a small problem that might occur…” She paused and looked around the group. “…When, do you suppose?”

Barnaby said, “Sunset is the combination and negation of both dark and light; it’s a powerful time for all magic of the Hermetic Corpus.”

“Especially ‘unicursal hexagrams’?” Steve asked. The president looked confused. “I’m sorry, ma’am, but taking all this sorcery seriously is extremely difficult. In addition, if I really thought that I was about to go out and battle a thirty-foot national monument with a female graduate of the all-male SEAL team, a PG County drug lord with an MBA, three cops who can double as their own K-9 dogs, the voice of the NSA computers, and a Chinese ghost in my phone…well, I might get discouraged.”

Harlan nodded. “Yes, I can understand that. Wait, what’s that about a Chinese kid? Is there a foreign national involved?”

“One of the young people who worked on the assembly line where these phones are made,” Steve answered. “Died right when this phone was finished and ended up locked inside.”

He held up Send Money and said, “Say hello, Send.”

A banjo tune began to play from the cell phone’s speakers and then a woman’s voice sang in Mandarin. The president listened for a moment, and then asked, “Abigail Washburn’s ‘*Song of the Traveling Daughter*’?”

The screen on the phone showed an animation of Goofy waving both US and Chinese flags.

"Well, I try to watch as many TED talks as I can," Harlan said. "Very cute. Barnaby, are you sure there isn't any official Chinese involvement?"

"I've communicated with several of the central servers at Unit 61398 of the People's Revolutionary Army and they said they have their own problems–something about brave animals and creatures made of nothing but hunger."

"Well, I suppose it's OK." The president looked doubtful. "At least, our cybersecurity here in the White House is safe as houses."

A telephone gave a single ring in one of the outer offices. Another rang on the opposite side. This continued for a moment, with one phone following another in a continuously approaching trill. Finally, all the phone lines on the Resolute Desk rang one after another and the president jumped suddenly and pulled a slim cell from her pants pocket. As she stared at the screen, there was a momentary silence.

The president was still staring at her screen. Then she nodded and said to Steve's cell phone, "Yes, the translation programs never do seem to work, Mr. Money. It's a pleasure to meet you as well. I'm sure we'll talk later."

Looking thoughtful, she put the cell back in her pocket. "Well, he seems to be a very nice young man, and I rather doubt he is working for the State Council or the People's Army–not after what he just told me about several of the senior officers' off-duty interests. He certainly does know his way around our phone system."

Barnaby spoke first. "Yes, well, Send Money was right on the scene and got quite a blast of magic when the worm turned. I think he's about as deep inside the US communications infrastructure as you can get."

"You'll be going in with all the Swords; that's something anyway." The voice came from directly behind Steve, and he jumped and twisted to see Old Howard in full, if tattered, uniform. "Pardon me for interrupting ma'am, but I've got a message for the Ace of Swords."

Ace nodded and the old Marine continued. "Albert Pike wanted you to know that he's prevailed on the High Council to cut off all ties with the Illuminati, so you won't be seeing the sphinxes tonight."

"Well, that's certainly a relief," Ace said. "One massive stone being is quite enough."

"Yes, ma'am. In addition, Mr. Pike will join the fight when he can. He's still in the Grand Temple, quieting the hotheads," Old Howard continued. "He also told me to tell you to hurry up. Apparently, young Jones, the Hanged Man, feels that President Lincoln, bless his soul, will be heading out very soon."

He shook his head sadly. "You have to understand. I served in the Union Navy and it's very difficult for me to comprehend how the Liberator could turn against this nation."

President Harlan spoke slowly. "Thank you for the information…uh…"

"General Oliver Otis Howard, US Marine Corps, ma'am." He snapped to attention and saluted. "At your service."

"Pleased to make your acquaintance, General Howard," Harlan said. "May I ask what magical power you possess that got you into my office so easily?"

"Magic?" Old Howard laughed. "No, I don't have any magic. I'm just dead like anyone else." He turned back to Ace. "I've got to leave, Master Chief. I'll see you after the battle."

Ace cocked an eyebrow in question.

Old Howard had begun to fade but he caught her unspoken query and said, “No, Chief. That’s not a prediction. Just a hope.”

Ace nodded and he was gone.

“OK, I think you need to get moving.” The president stood up and everyone else followed suit. “Again, is there anything I can provide?”

Steve said, “Something that Old Howard just said… Do you have a PSYOPS team handy? Or anyone with a loudspeaker?”

“I’ll have the Pentagon send a couple of mobile loudhailers.”

“Otherwise, I would say that clearing people away from the Memorial area is top priority. I think you should consider anyone within a mile radius to be in immediate danger. Anything else, Ace?” She shook her head, and Steve spoke into the phone. “Officer Grafton, how fast can you and the rest of the Royal Family get down to the Memorial?”

“Faster than you can.”

“Yeah, don’t rub it in,” Ace said. “Just get moving.”

# CHAPTER THIRTY-SIX

"OK, I've finally reached my limit." Steve said. "This is obviously just a particularly good opium dream. No way is that statue going to stand up and start killing people. It's simply not going to happen."

They were standing at the base of the broad marble stairs that led up to the immense white cube of the Lincoln Memorial. Inside, it was still lit by the evening sunset glowing through the translucent panes of waxed marble on the roof.

It was quiet on the Mall; tourists, journalists, and commuters had been pushed out or blocked away by the Park Police. It had been an efficient process, coordinated by the well-named Sergeant Fear, an enormous man who was still barking orders into a walkie-talkie just off to the side.

Two Humvees were parked on either side of the Reflecting Pool, their three-foot-diameter sound horns pointed at the statue. Cables led to a single microphone on a stand in front of Steve. He was studiously ignoring it, certain that he'd sound like a fool the second he began to have a conversation with the sixteenth president. He giggled nervously when he realized he was supposed to sound like the Fool.

Ace shot a sharp glance at him and asked, "You holding up?"

"Sure. Except for the fact that I'm obviously hallucinating in my little cot at the Happy Home for the Overly Imaginative, I'm wonderful. Peachy, in fact."

She reached over and punched him sharply on the shoulder. “That feel like a hallucination?”

Steve managed to stay erect–barely.

He rubbed his arm. “No, I have to say that that was either real or the Xbox people have had a major breakthrough in the implementation of physiological feedback in virtual environments.”

“Want me to hit you again so you can continue the experiment?”

“No, thanks.” Steve took a quick step away and continued. “I’m willing to accept this as reality but I reserve the right to change my position when Sergeant Fear comes to arrest us for screwing up the entire city of Washington.”

“You’re babbling,” Barnaby said from the cell phone on his belt. “You sound like redundant feedback loops we used to get in the early computers. I remember once when a PDP-6 got so bollixed, it simply sat there and threw punch cards around the room for a week. Afterwards…”

Steve tuned out the program’s voice and regarded his tiny army. The three Metro police officers were now in full battle mode. They’d definitely been associated with the Thoth tarot deck, one of the more bizarre decks, in Steve’s opinion.

The men were in green skintight fighting suits and looked quite a bit like comic book superheroes. Stacy Grafton had a difficult time when she found that the Queen’s raiment consisted of a long full skirt and not a damn thing on top. Instead of regal insouciance, she’d just stood with her arms crossed, looking irritable and chilly until Ace tossed her a spare T-shirt out of her. Steve noticed that her partners were very careful not to stare or make jokes–it might have had to do with the large sword Stacy held in her right hand and the severed head of some bearded fellow that kept appearing in her left.

Mike Chubb was the Knight–outfitted with green armor that looked like it would stop a .357 Magnum, a pair of wicked-looking sabers, and some sort of flying horse with a positively evil gleam in its eyes. He was equipped with a double pair of gauzy wings–the kind you'd see on a dragonfly–but kept reaching back and checking them. He was a big guy and Steve could relate to worrying about the carrying capacity of fairy feathers.

Lyle Bautista appeared far more pleased with his getup as the Prince of Swords. Bulked-out deep-green armor with round yellow wings and a gold helmet made him look like an Irish Spiderman after an intensive weight-training regimen. He was gingerly trying out a strange, rounded chariot pulled by three creatures that could only be described as Mini-Me versions of him. They stood about six inches tall, but from his frantic efforts to keep them from leaping the Potomac, they clearly had whatever it took to pull a mystic chariot.

Ace looked like Ace. Solid, tough, determined, and ready to kill. For a second, Steve wondered why he kept hanging out with such a murderous woman but, with a sigh, had to admit–at least to himself–that she was a hell of a lot more fun than most women he'd dated and both women he'd married.

Now he just had to make sure that she never found out he felt that way.

Barnaby's voice broke the evening quiet. "Stand by. The Great Ones say that they've detected activity in the transcendent realms."

"'The Great Ones'?" Steve asked. "I thought they'd called themselves 'Stormy'?"

"Personally, I think someone has been letting those damn quantum's get a few too many Kelvins–they take to warm nitrogen the same way you would to a cold beer. Never mind that; it's just another item we'll have to deal with later. Right now, I'd concentrate on President Marble over there."

"Marble?" Steve said. "Funny, I always just took him for granite."

Ace turned her head slowly and fixed him with a truly terrifying glare. "How long have you been waiting to get that out of your system?"

"Are you kidding? Damn near all…."

Steve stopped cold as a sound like…

Well, it really couldn't have been like anything except the deep and echoing *crack* of seventy-six million pounds of marble splitting in two. Like thunder, it rolled away down the mall and then returned, volume almost undiminished by the distance.

The electric lights had gone on inside the Memorial, and Steve could see as the statue shifted forward on the enormous chair and moved its head to stretch the neck muscles.

"Do marble statues have neck muscles?" flashed through his mind.

He heard a quick series of three *snaps* behind him and turned to see that the three police officers had gone into their full cynocephalic battle mode–their armor instantly altering to accommodate double-jointed legs, broader shoulders, and long snouts. Stacy had gone all furry and, even though she probably had a half dozen breasts now, clearly felt sufficiently clothed to return Ace's T-shirt. There was a clopping of hooves on the stone terrace and Carlos appeared on his right.

"Hold on, everyone." Steve held up a hand. "Let's stick to the plan. Persuasion first."

"Might as well," Ace muttered. "God knows if anything else will work."

Steve stepped up to the microphone, and tapped on the windscreen. Deep thumps issued from speakers mounted on top of the PSYOPS units. Movement over by the left-hand truck caught his eye. The two enlisted men assigned to the sound unit were carrying their unconscious commanding officer on their shoulders as they ran flat-out in the direction of the Tidal Basin.

Idly, Steve thought it looked like a sensible decision and remarkable loyalty on the part of the enlisted men.

"Mr. President," he said into the microphone, and heard the words echo back from the marble memorial. The statue raised its head and Steve swore he could *feel* the pressure of those eyes, set deep and penetrating under that heavy, brooding brow. "Mr. President. If you can understand me, please raise your right hand."

A white stone hand came up. Then a deep voice with all the ringing tones of a boulder being struck by a hammer said. "I can indeed raise my hand. However, let me ask you, friend; would it not be simpler and more agreeable if we simply conversed?"

"Mr. President," Steve continued. "Do you know where you are?"

There was a subdued creaking–almost inaudible at the distance where Steve was standing–as the statue leaned forward, placed his hands on his knees, and peered out into the swiftly darkening twilight. "Well, yes. I believe I do. There have been many changes–those stinking hovels down by Tiber Creek are gone, as is Tiber Creek itself, now that I think upon it–but much remains as it was. It's good to see that Congress finally managed to agree on funding President Washington's cenotaph. It is a magnificent obelisk, although I personally favored the Greek colonnade with which Mr. Mills originally intended to encircle the base. Oh, my. Those must be electric lamps that now illuminate the

Capitol. Glorious. Unless the nature of man himself has altered, I have no doubt that the building itself is still far more worthy of admiration than are those who labor inside it."

Steve laughed and responded, "You are correct, sir."

"There are roads and a good number of vast and no doubt useful structures that were not here in my day, but this is plainly the City of Washington within the District of Columbia." The immense stone figure stood up carefully from his chair, walked bent over with his hands clasped behind his back until he passed through the immense entrance, and stood erect on the terrace.

"I have to say, I'm a bit surprised by the number of electric lamps–the entire city seems to glow. In my time, the only city that sat this bright under the stars was Atlanta after General Sherman passed through."

He looked down, shame and regret showing clearly on his weathered face. "By the Lord God, I wish that Atlanta had never had to burn. Nor Richmond. Nor any other Southern city. It has been a black stain on my soul for all these long years."

There was a pause and then the massive bearded head came up again, the voice strengthening. "Our cause was right and I still know in my heart that we could never falter in defending the cause of freedom so approved of my judgment. It was not a war we began but one we accepted, and thank God, we did not let it end until the object of our determination–the freedom of all men and the unity of this nation of freemen–was accomplished. I remember saying in Baltimore that 'if destruction be our lot, we must ourselves be its author and finisher.'"

Steve had no idea how to respond to that emotional speech, so he just let the sounds of crickets and frogs grow until they alone dominated the quiet night. Lincoln continued to survey the city with a calm and mildly interested air.

Steve dared to hope that Lincoln's spirit–the great soul which was both animator and prisoner of the eidolon–in the end, could not destroy the city he'd fought so long and hard to preserve.

"Shit," Ace whispered. "Look at his right shoulder."

It took Steve a moment, but he finally made out a man standing on the stone shoulder of the president's frock coat and steadying himself by holding on to the edge of his ear. He snapped up the rose lens and made out Adam Weishaupt, the leader of the Illuminati.

"Barnaby!" Steve yelled. "What's he saying?"

"How the hell do I know?" the computer replied. "Do you see a lot of electronic equipment up there? Wait… OK, Send Money is reconfiguring those big public address horns as parabolic microphones. He should have sound in just a–"

Weishaupt's voice, a combination of hatred and soothing persuasion like a hornet caught in a spoonful of honey, came out of the cell phone. "…unhappy to inform you that liberty has not triumphed. This is the reason we have labored tirelessly to bring you back from your well-deserved rest."

"That son of a bitch." Ace put her right hand above her head, and with a whizzing *smack*, Joan of Arc's sword appeared in her palm. This time, Ace's face showed no indications of pain as she said, "Thank you once again, ma'am."

The oily voice continued to come from the speaker. "Do you see that city across the river? The tall buildings and bright lights? That is Rosslyn, the capital of the Confederate States of America. Those two glass buildings made to look like the prows of ships? They are the President's Plantation and the Assembly of Slave States–defiantly built so as to look down on our own White House and Capitol. The lifeblood of thousands of the enslaved, black, yellow, and brown alike was used to slake the mortar that holds those structures aloft."

Weisshaupt's voice became a rasping monotone as the statue faced away but they could hear Lincoln clearly over the speaker. "This cannot be! Grant and Lee have met and the Army of Virginia surrendered! From Richmond to New Orleans, the fortresses and redoubts have fallen and the rifles of the defeated are stacked like sheaves of corn! The black man is free and that resolve was won in blood and burns forever in the hearts of all true Americans!"

"And so it did, my president, but only for a short time."

Steve could see the enormous head as it shook violently in horrified negation. "No! The forces of liberty had conquered! The South is broken; its armies destroyed! They could never have risen again in rebellion without slaves! No!"

"Do you remember General Hayes?" Weishaupt asked softly,

"General Rutherford Hayes? Yes, a lawyer and yet an honorable man. Why, he fought at South Mountain and broke Jubal Early's boys on their retreat from Washington. My God, he had four horses shot from under him and suffered a multitude of grievous wounds! Surely he would never turn so dark as to countenance this obscenity before me!"

"Sir, you said that you never sought the power of the Presidency, and indeed, with your poor, lank, lean face, you never even expected to achieve it. As you are well aware, a selflessness of this degree is seldom found in the hearts of men. General Hayes became president only a handful of years after Booth fired the traitorous ball that took your life, but to reach that high office, he made a satanic compromise. In one act of betrayal, he made meaningless the lives of all those you see sleeping under the gentle greensward of Arlington Hall."

Weishaupt swept an arm towards Arlington Cemetery.

"Oh, my sweet Lord! The graves!" The president cried. "There were never so many even after the catastrophic slaughters at Gettysburg and Cold Harbor! Look how they run. White row after terrible white row. The war we suffered was the most appalling the world has ever known. It could not have continued, and yet I see the evidence clearly marked by the simple crosses that fill those fields."

Weishaupt's poisonously persuasive voice continued. "Those are the brave men who were slaughtered in their barracks or perished in the failed attempts to reconquer the South. Hayes, the damned traitor, sold away your victory for a bowl of pottage. He has gone down in history as 'His Fraudulency' because it was the sale of your blood-bought victory that won him the votes in the Electoral College and brought him to the White House!"

"Flip these damn things back to loudspeakers," Steve snapped. In a second, his voice boomed across the empty space. "Mr. President, this man lies. The Union you fought to build still stands and no soul lives in slavery within the borders of your beloved nation. I say–no, I swear to you, he lies!"

"It's not going to work." Barnaby spoke at a low volume from his belt. "Weishaupt has a *geas* on him. The eidolon's very existence is the Illuminati's doing, and although the shadow of the great soul which now inhabits that mighty body doesn't know it, its existence was bought with the blood of innocents. If Lincoln wasn't such a noble being, he could simply be commanded. Even so, with such a powerful spell on his very soul, we're predicting that Weishaupt will sway him with his deception."

"Do not listen to that voice." Weishaupt's voice came from the cell phone again. "They are from the very government … successors of those that turned their backs on sacred vows, and betrayed all you fought and suffered for; the triumph that cost you the love of your wife, killed your children, and, finally, took your very life. The evidence is forthright and the truth unavoidable. You once swore eternal fealty to the just cause. You promised to give it your life, your liberty, and your love. You sent men to their deaths by the thousands with your brave words ringing in their ears. You told them that if the republican robe was soiled, that you would repurify it–wash it white in the spirit, if not the blood, of the Revolution. These men died for those dreams; can you do less?"

Lincoln screamed–a colossal roar of anger and pain–and began to stride toward the Memorial Bridge and the gleaming lights of Rosslyn. There were no longer any words in the sound--all intelligence swept away by a sea of horror, failure, and terrible, unforgivable guilt.

"OK, the good news is that I think we've saved Washington, but I'm afraid Rosslyn is toast," Ace commented.

"Rosslyn is a fairly crappy city." Steve said. "But I suppose we should do something about it. Plus, there are a couple of excellent Vietnamese restaurants up Wilson Boulevard that I'd hate to see squashed under those size 130 oxfords."

Steve took a deep breath. "OK, Carlos, you and the Royals who have their own transportation–that's the Prince and the Knight–go after Big Abe and see if you can take out small, dark and evil upon his right shoulder. Do you have any spells?"

The two men looked at each other and then Chubb shrugged.

"No idea, huh?" Steve said. "Well, if you feel any sudden urges to throw something or pull on an invisible rope–anything like that–just go with it, OK? Ace, you're with me. Now let's go! Boulder-butt isn't waiting for us!"

Carlos took off at a gallop with both of the policemen hard on his heels. The statue was now crossing the traffic circle and taking the first step onto the Memorial Bridge. Steve watched as both Chubb's horse and Bautista's chariot lifted off the ground. Their wings might not be all that impressive but at the rate they were moving, they'd catch up to the striding figure long before he reached the far bank.

Steve wondered for a moment how the rest of them were going to catch up. Then Hans roared across the grass and stopped in a power slide that left him pointing toward the retreating giant. All four doors popped open.

"Stacy, if you would, hop in the back seat," Ace ordered. "The Fool and I need to be up front."

Steve only got out the "W" of "Why" before Ace's strong shove in the center of his back propelled him into the driver's seat. He tumbled in with his hands up in the air–afraid of touching anything that might anger the temperamental vehicle. The door slammed behind him and the thick armor plate slid into place. Ace slung her duffle over her shoulder, slid the sword into her belt, and did a Starsky and Hutch slide over the front hood.

She slipped in the passenger door and crouched on the passenger seat. Even before her door closed, Hans shot forward in a haze of blue smoke and the scream of high-adhesion racing tires. Ace pulled the wrist rocket out of her bag and began to strap it on. "I've got those lead shot, but I don't think they'll do crap against seventy-four tons of angry marble, and I'm not sure that my explosives will…well, explode."

Steve, who was trying desperately not to touch the steering wheel or the foot pedals–not to mention the dreaded *schaltwippen*–said, "Remember those yellow exploding things that the Illuminati keep tossing at us?"

"Only too well."

"If I belong to all suits, I should be able to magic some of those," Steve said. "I'll mash it down so it's the same size as one of your slugs. The only problem is whether you can aim well enough to hit Marble Mike without touching the little yellow pills. I don't think we have time to get you repaired again."

"Amazingly enough, that's not a bad idea," She looked at him suspiciously. "Have you been sneaking around and thinking behind my back?"

Steve was already concentrating, but he managed to shake his head vigorously.

Ace snorted and said, "Well, be careful. You can strain something if you try too much too fast. Great. See if you can make me a whole bunch of them." She held her finger and thumb about a half inch apart. "About .50 caliber but they don't need to be all that precise."

"I'm working on it," Steve said. "When do you need them?"

"Open the roof." Ace said to Hans and the heavy sunroof slid back. Ace stood up on the passenger seat and braced herself as the car cut a straight line across the roundabout, up and over the central grass plaza, and back onto the road just as they passed the giant golden statues that graced the east end of the bridge.

She took an experimental pull to make sure the slingshot was ready and said, "Now would be nice."

Steve closed his eyes for a second, thought of the sun that shone on the young man in the card, and felt the ripping agony in his head that indicated he'd learned a new power. He opened his eyes and looked through migraine creases at the glowing yellow sphere that sat in the palm of his hand.

Ace grinned down and said, "See? Thinking just slows you down. Now, see if you can hold that for another second or two without hurting yourself."

She braced herself in the corner of the hatch, leaving as much room as possible over Steve's head. "OK, now just pretend that you're one of those ironworkers in the old cartoons and just toss that up nice and gentle so it stops right about here." She held out the leather pocket of the slingshot in front of her with the thick elastic bands extended.

Fully expecting disaster, Steve gently tossed the globe up in the air. Just as it reached its highest point and stopped for an instant before falling back down, Ace slipped the pocket under it, aimed, and instantly whipped it after the enormous statue. It expanded as it flew to the size of a basketball. Steve saw it fall short and explode in a shower of bright sparks, creating a good-sized pothole in the pavement.

"Hmm, a little lighter than I calculated." Ace said, shouting over the wind noise. "Keep them coming, I'll nail his stony ass this time."

Hans was doing the driving so Steve could concentrate on creating balls of liquid sunstuff and tossing them up to Ace. Every shot was hitting the statue now and resulting in sizzling bursts of sparks. Steve could see the impacts, and like the building in Greenbelt, wherever they hit, craters were appearing in the stone and rivulets of melted rock made red streaks in the gathering twilight.

"It's not enough," Ace called. "It's going to take all night at this rate. Can't you whip up something with a bit more punch?"

"If you know so much, you come down here and make these damn things," Steve grumbled. Then he **Reached** for more power, created a bilious green sphere, and almost lost control of it before he could toss it to Ace. This produced a bigger blast but, when the smoke cleared, he could see that the impact crater was still dispiritingly shallow.

“It looks like they’ve installed a shield against your powers,” Ace said. “Hans, we’re going to need to get in front of this thing and see if we can stop it at the other end of the bridge. Steve, in the meantime, keep those green thingies coming. Let me see if I can knock out a knee.”

Her aim was perfect–one shot landing right on top of another in the back of the enormous right knee. Lincoln began to limp slightly but it scarcely slowed his laborious pace. Even over the scream of the BMW’s heavy turbocharged engine, Steve could hear the heartbreaking sound of Lincoln as he continued to bellow out his confusion of grief and fury.

Steve shouted, “How long before you think you can cut through?”

“Unless he’s got a stone ligament in there I can cut…” Ace paused for another shot. “I figure about a week.”

“That’s not good.”

“No, it’s not. But it keeps me from being bored.”

Steve took a second to peer through an armored slit in the front windshield. “Be careful of the rest of the Scooby Gang. We don’t want a friendly fire incident.”

“Why do they call it that?” Ace snapped off another shot. “If you get hit by a bullet, it’s not friendly, regardless of whose gun it came from.”

Ahead, Steve could see Carlos–who had grown to about twice as large as his previous incarnations–attack Lincoln’s ankles. Steve was impressed; not only were the dog-monster’s fangs extraordinarily large but they were capable of gouging out great chunks of solid stone as if it were wet clay.

The wounds were amazing even for a supernatural dog monster but they only amounted to scrapes and scratches on ankles that were six feet around.

He looked for the police officers and saw Cobb, the Knight of Swords, zooming in on his strange-looking dragonfly-horse to spear Weishaupt from behind. Sadly, he appeared to and then had to perform amazing evasion maneuvers to avoid Lincoln's enormous hand as it rose to swat him away.

"Just like a man brushing away a horsefly," Steve thought and immediately regretted not having anyone to tell what he thought was a damn good pun.

Bautista, the Prince of Swords, had brought his strange little chariot up the back of the frock coat on the opposite side from Weishaupt and leapt off onto the stiff collar. Between tossing up Ace's missiles, Steve caught a glimpse of the young police officer braced between the collar and the left shoulder and wielding his sword like an axe against the thick neck. Again, the magic sword was cutting deep into the stone, but it was having about the same impact as it would if he was trying to cut down a full-grown redwood.

Suddenly, Bautista put his fingers in his mouth and whistled. The tiny versions of the Prince instantly whipped the chariot into a tight turn and pulled past Lincoln's shoulders. Bautista jumped in and then right back out again, landing on the opposite shoulder next to Weishaupt. Steve threw a fireball up without even looking–resulting in a loud curse from Ace–and watched as Bautista whipped a fast cut at the Illuminati.

Incredibly, the sword passed right through the Bavarian's body without stopping. Obviously, Weishaupt was only a specter; he hadn't needed to manifest completely as he had when he tried to kill Steve at Bladensburg.

The unchecked force of the blow spun Bautista around and he lost his balance and fell out of Steve's sight. A green flash zipped in from the side and, a second later; Bautista reappeared, holding on to the rear floorboards of his chariot. He shook his head disgustedly and flew up and then dropped onto the top of Lincoln's curly hair. Once he had his feet placed, he began to chop straight down like a man preparing to go ice fishing in a Minnesota winter.

Steve threw up another fireball just as Hans went into a screeching swerve to the left. The car actually moved under the missile but the effect was that it moved directly towards Ace. She jumped up off the seat, slammed a hand down on either side of the sunroof, and flew up high enough that the ball went between her legs.

Unfortunately, that left her also moving in a straight line as Hans curved back and right out from under her. Without thinking, Steve snapped his golden staff up through the sunroof in her direction–round and smooth this time instead of sharp and deadly–and she grabbed it, let her velocity swing her around, and dropped back into the passenger seat.

She took a deep breath, shook herself, and then said, "Thanks, but if you make one comment about pole dancing, I'll make you eat that thing."

Steve retracted the pole into his palm, "Never crossed my mind."

At that instant, Hans hit the curb on the left side, bounced about a foot in the air, and came down on the broad sidewalk already jacked over into a violent right turn. He tore past the statue, rocketed back onto the road, and headed for the other end of the bridge.

"Those aren't standard shocks any more, are they?" Steve asked.

**Keine Scheiße, Genie**

"'No shit, Genius?' What sort of talk is that?" As he rebounded off the car door, Steve asked mildly, "What's with the accent, anyway? Aren't you from Spartanburg, South Carolina?"

**I swear, you ain't got the brains God gave a catfish. Who'd admit they were from a town so lame that even NASCAR moved out?**

Steve said, "Well, I suppose that is true."

**Ein verdammt, ich bin Deutsch**

"OK, OK. You're German." Steve agreed.

"Can you break away from chewing the fat with Beemer-boy and get back to supplying me with ammunition?" Ace stood up again and braced herself against the side of the sunroof. "Hans, I'm going to set up for a stand at the end of the bridge. Can you heavy-up your front end? I mean, like bulldozer-heavy."

Steve tossed another fireball and they settled back into their rhythm with Ace now facing backward and aiming for the giant's eyes. When they reached the far side of the bridge, Hans slid to a stop and everyone piled out. Hans–who now had a heavy angled iron wedge in place of a front bumper–pulled to the left, spun around in a cloud of smoke, and stopped, now headed away from Washington.

Ace ran to the other side of the road and motioned for the Queen of Swords to follow. Steve started to follow but she waved him back. "You're not going to be able to help with this. Why don't you try that blast ray you used on Colonel Tataka?"

Steve, of course, didn't have a clue what he'd done to blow an enormous hole in the woman who, at the time, had become a rather irritable *rakshasa* demon. He walked out to the center of the road leading off the bridge and concentrated on the Fool. This time, there was no devastating pain, so he kept his eyes open and watched as a column of fire easily two feet wide shot from his chest and directly at the stone giant. He kept adding more power to the beam, pouring his will into making it faster, stronger, and more explosive.

He could feel the beam–it seemed to sink into itself, become more concentrated, and distilled into a coruscating golden bar. He felt the now-familiar sense of time slowing, but this time, it reached the point where the ray seemed to be crawling towards the enormous figure, now frozen in midstep. He clenched his fists and brought image after image into his mind–holding every Fool he'd ever seen, from the innocent boy, to the grizzled tramp, to the green, horned guy with the tiger chewing on his leg.

All sounds dropped down into the bass range and then disappeared. His little space-time bubble was quiet and rather pleasant, Steve decided. Having a bit of privacy was, of course, too good to last.

He heard a calm voice in his head. "Let me see if I can help a bit, son." From the sense of quiet amusement, Steve had no doubt that it was Coyote and he could almost feel the demi-god's strong hands on his shoulders. New jets of power poured through him–he caught flickering images of animals, plants, and even rocks and streams. The beam shimmered with a rainbow of colors and he had to fight to keep it concentrated and focused–watching it as it begin to burn like a magnifying lens in the sunlight.

Steve thought briefly that his cranium was getting a bit crowded when he heard Barbara Harlan say, "Well, it would seem that I have discovered at least one of the Empress's abilities. I hope you don't mind, but I've called in emergency reinforcements."

A massive torrent of Power flowed into Steve with the blast of a fire hose. It was woven of so many different streams that he assumed it was the will of every major Power user in the District. He could feel stern and stolid minds he thought must be dwarves and the flashing intelligences that he recognized as elves. There were many other, more complex beams and even–so subtle he almost missed it–a stream that tasted like the gleam of golden eyes, dragons adding their strength from their hidden lairs.

"Yes, I called on Congress, K Street, and all the political action committees," the president said. "I felt it was worthy of a bipartisan effort–hard as that is to pull off in this town."

Steve swayed with the effort of controlling the enormous amount of energy pouring into him. Huge bronze hands slipped under his arms and Albert Pike boomed, "Steady, lad. I've got you."

The beam was now far larger and made of so many strands that it looked like the *fasces,* the leather-bound sticks that represented the strength of people when they worked together.

That symbol with the motto, "Out of many, one" or "*e pluribus, unum,*" was chiseled into all Washington's government buildings. Or, at least, all the buildings designed before 1940, when the fascists stole the *fasces* along with the swastika.

Time returned with a splintering burst that seemed to blast through every cell in Steve's body. The thick and mighty braid of Power leapt forward and struck the marble figure in the dead center of the chest. Instantly, Steve broadened the focus, hoping to first penetrate and then expand the massive force, blasting the marble into shards and dust.

For several moments, smoke and flame completely enveloped the bridge, hiding the statue from view. Steve was determined to destroy this creature and he could feel the strain as all the other Powers reached their limits and then went just a bit beyond. At this point, the beam was a dozen feet wide. The smoke–a deep black color, shot with flickers of blue discharges, and emitting the slamming thunder of lightning bolts in a unceasing storm of sound–was so thick, it looked like the Lincoln Memorial itself had disappeared.

Then it was over. The beam snapped off in a blink and Steve slumped against the cool strength of Pike's metal chest.

A breeze blew away the smoke and Steve could see that Lincoln had been stopped and even shoved back a few feet. Then, the massive figure regained its balance and the giant limped first one step and then another, dragging behind him the leg that Ace had tried to hamstring.

The smoking crater where the beam had struck was yards deep–they'd almost blasted their way through. Steve could sense that they had burned away much of the blood magic that Weishaupt had used to animate the mass of stone. The eidolon was weakened but far from destroyed.

Lincoln roared again, a thunder of rage and madness. The normally calm and benevolent face was twisted in a blend of fury, determination, and infinite sadness. Even though it was moving slower, it was only steps away from the Virginia side of the bridge.

On the other side of the circle, he could hear Ace yell, "All right, Rowan. I didn't think you could draw half that much mojo. It was worth a try, anyway." Then she turned away and, like the starter at the Indianapolis 500, spun her hand over her head and then pointed it straight at Hans

"Let's try a little kinetic force,"

Steve saw that Ace and the Queen had shoved one of the curved concrete Jersey barriers into the road on the right side of the circle and then flipped it down so that it formed a crude ramp. Hans took off around the circle, engine roaring and tires screaming as it gathered speed. The front bumper was now a solid steel ram a foot thick and covering the entire front of the car.

Ace was shouting orders in a command voice that was so clear, Steve figured it could be heard–well, perhaps not in New York City, but definitely in Baltimore. Albert Pike shoved Steve out of danger and then ran heavily toward the statue. Carlos and the three Swords pulled back to the other side of the traffic circle, turned 180 degrees, and began a running, or flying, charge.

As Hans came around the last quarter of the circle, Steve could hear the 4.4 liter twin turbo V8 engine howl as it used every one of its 445 horses--as it straightened in the run up to the ramp, it was topping out well over a hundred and twenty miles per hour.

The timing was perfect.

The BMW was the hammer. It hit the improvised ramp and flew into the air at a 45-degree angle to the bridge. Seconds behind the hurtling vehicle were the two flying Swords, aiming to hit high and drive the statue just a bit more to the left.

Albert Pike and the *canejo* were the anvil. The eleven-foot solid bronze statue was driving in at the statue's left knee–intending to cut down the eidolon like cornerbacks submarining a tight end. Carlos was off the ground in a tremendous leap with all four hoofs aimed straight for the outside of the left knee.

Hans's massive front bumper hit Lincoln precisely at the top of the enormous chest. Less than a second later, the Knight and Prince of Swords drove into the head–burying their swords deep into the eyes and then pushing with everything they had. Carlos approached smashed into the front of the statue's left knee, while Pike put his shoulder down and drove into the rear.

Again, Lincoln staggered sideways on feet so massive that they ground the concrete sidewalk into powder.

Albert Pike was struck by a flailing stone foot and thrown backwards, demolishing the bridge railing, and managing to stop just on the edge, flailing his arms in a successful attempt to stay out of the Potomac.

The King and Knight of Swords pulled around to attack the face again, and the Queen ran in, leapt, and drove her sword straight into the right knee.

In a perfect parabola, Hans shot upwards, flew over the statue and the entire width of the four-lane bridge, and slipped quietly into the dark water on the other side.

For a split second, Steve thought that Lincoln would follow but the monster managed to stop with the heel of one enormous shoe hanging off the bridge. Then he slowly pulled himself upright, shook his head, and resumed his shambling assault on the brilliantly lit glass towers–ignoring his attackers as if they were less than gnats.

# CHAPTER THIRTY-SEVEN

Steve had always thought that the coolest fighting scene in any movie occurred in *The Return of the King* when Legolas attacked the Oliphaunt. But that was before he saw Ace's assault on Lincoln.

Steve was running in pursuit of the statue, now crossing the lawn below the Iwo Jima Memorial, but Ace left him behind as if he was standing still. As she ran, she fired small fletched bolts with the Wrist Rocket, creating a series of handholds up the broad back. A massive foot swept back as Lincoln slipped on the grass verge of Route 50 and only missed her by inches as she dove forward and rolled up between his legs.

Steve lost sight of her when exhaustion caused him to slip and fall in the thick wet grass. A quick **Study** of the Fool gave him a boost of vitality at the cost of a sciatic agony that felt like a high-tension wire had been attached to his ass.

When he stood up again, he could see that during the seconds he had focused on the card, Ace had dropped the slingshot and unfolded a small but wicked-looking crossbow from the small pack on her back. He couldn't help but wince as she fitted a barbed bolt into the slot and fired straight up into the giant's crotch.

The marble creature didn't show any pain–something that Steve couldn't quite decide if he felt good or bad about–but the bolt was rammed solidly into its…trousers, and a length of rope now trailed behind it. Ace clipped the crossbow to her belt and went up the rope like a featured act at the Cirque de Soleil.

Luckily, the sculptor had given Lincoln a "thigh gap" worthy of a Photoshopped Vogue model, or Ace would have been crushed between the marble legs as he walked.

Instead, she swung on the rope twice and then released at the apex, spinning like a gymnast, and unfolding just in time to grab a finger hold on the first of the crossbow bolts. The sound of hooves came up from behind and Steve was suddenly thrown in the air as Carlos stuck his snout between his legs and tossed him up. It was a painful landing on the *cadejo's* broad back, but he dug his fingers into the thick fur and looked for the others. The three Swords were swinging around to get between Lincoln and the city, the Queen perched on the back of the Knight's strange flying horse.

It appeared that the Prince had discovered at least one magic power. He was making sharp throwing gestures with one hand as he held on to the chariot with the other. Green lightning bolts shot out and detonated with massive thunderclaps against the statue's head.

Lincoln's head would snap to the side at each impact but his path never wavered. Even compensating for the extremely erratic gait of a hoofed dog, Steve could see Ace climbing up the back of the marble colossus--essentially free-climbing a moving mountain. Gripping a bolt, swinging for momentum, and flying free to grab the next bolt or a wrinkle in the stone cloth.

When there was absolutely no higher hold in reach, she slammed Joan of Arc's sword straight into the marble and used it as a piton–reaching back from the next hold to pull it out. It was an exhibition of skills so advanced that she made it look easy.

Weishaupt's apparition was still whispering urgently into the statue's ear. He spotted Ace as she came up over the vast shoulder blades and began to speak frantically, gesturing back to the oncoming SEAL. Ace hurled two knives at him and he would have had one in each eye if both hadn't passed right through his head and arced off into the darkness.

Ace looked disgusted as she ducked around to the left just as the immense hand came up to brush at his coat and missed her by inches. In a series of moves worthy of any *American Ninja* finalist, she gained the relative safety of the opposite shoulder.

There, she knelt and pulled what looked like a soda can and a short pencil from one of her cargo pockets. She held them close to her mouth and appeared to whisper to them for several minutes.

Then she jammed the can into one of the niches carved earlier by the Prince of Swords, inserted the slim cylinder into the rear, and got out of the way by throwing her feet back and sliding down the upper arm until she came to rest in the crook of the elbow.

There was an explosion. It was small compared to the massive blasts that the Prince of Swords was still throwing on the other side and nothing like the intense beam that Steve had fired. On the other hand, there was virtually no blowback, so Steve assumed it was a shaped charge that she'd placed deep in the stone.

Steve watched in amazement as a crack opened all the way around the massive neck. The Prince apparently saw it as well–his next blast was thrown with both hands at the center of the president's brow. The recoil tossed him backward and he would have fallen from his chariot if two of the Mini-Me's hadn't thrown off their reins, rocketed around to the rear, and pushed him back to safety.

Surprisingly, the Prince's blast finally shredded Weishaupt–or at least caused him to lose control over whatever hellish combination of hallucination and ectoplasm he'd created in order to guide the monster–and the enormous head with its noble features slowly tipped to the rear as if the president was taking a look at the stars. It kept on tipping until it finally fell off and crashed to the ground below.

Steve's joy at this victory was short-lived.

The statue paused for moment as if confused and then simply continued on its way with the enormous head still uttering it's agonized cries from where it lay half buried in the soft earth.

Disaster struck as Abe absent-mindedly reached over and flicked Ace off her perch at his elbow with his thumb and forefinger.

Steve was horrified but a small part of his brain apparently just couldn't stop with the bad jokes. "Well, of course, he's absent-minded. His mind is about forty yards behind him."

Ace's body flew up and out, clearing the George Washington Parkway, and disappearing into the wooded island that held the Teddy Roosevelt Memorial.

For a shocked instant, the world went quiet as Carlos stopped to look, and even the stone head paused in its mad wailing.

Then Steve heard the grinding of steel and the jangle of breaking glass as the statue smashed into the sharp edge of 1000 Wilson Boulevard–right under the neon sign that advertised one of the local television stations. Hundreds of people had crowded up to the windows to gawk at the spectacle and only now were beginning to turn and run. Steve noticed that several camera operators in the upper floor were standing their ground and continuing to shoot, clearly convinced of the magical protection that all photographers feel when they look through a camera lens.

Steve leaned over and yelled into Carlos's ear. "He's going to go right through that place–it's only glass and plasterboard. Circle around and we'll hit him when he comes out." Carlos didn't answer–Steve wasn't sure that he could, now that he thought about it–but he swerved and charged up the side street to the front of the building.

In front of the building, Steve slid off, and kept right on going until he was lying on the ground. His legs were jelly after the jolting ride on Carlos's back. Since it was an emergency, he kept his moans to a reasonably heroic minimum and crawled to the median strip where he could pull himself into a sitting position on a concrete planter. Whatever his full powers turned out to be, he was fairly sure that physical strength was never going to top the list.

The bronze effigy of Albert Pike came stamping around the far corner at as close to a run as a guy could manage who weighed about as much as a railroad locomotive. The Prince of Swords swept high over the street, spotted Steve, and dropped to the ground next to him. Bautista raised his helmet and his face transformed from canine to human.

"He's smashing the girders and supports all along the back," Bautista said. "I think he's trying to make sure the building falls." He looked up for a moment, and then sighed. "There's twenty stories and it looks like everyone decided to work late. Hundreds of people, if not a thousand, are going to die in this building alone. Stacy and Cobb followed Lincoln in and are doing their best, but I'm not sure what they can do against someone who can keep fighting after you cut off his head."

"Hell, politicians have been doing that since the Greeks invented democracy," Steve snarled. "Here's what we're going to do–"

He was interrupted by a powerful buzz on his belt and a loud rendition of the Chipmunks version of *Danger Zone*.

He pulled the cell phone from its clip and wasn't surprised to find it completely undamaged. He wondered idly if they made mil-spec covers for people. Barnaby's voice came from the speaker. "Steve? Are you all right?"

"I guess that depends on your definition, but yeah, I guess I'm OK," Steve answered. "Both Ace and Hans are MIA and we're not having any luck with tall, handsome, and headless."

"I know. Half of the Keyhole satellite fleet is overhead just to catch the show and they don't usually do that except for the Super Bowl. Of course, those sand brains at CYBERCOM tried to use the distraction to drop a couple of rocks on Stanford–"

"'Rocks'?" Steve asked sharply. "What do you mean, 'rocks'?"

"Oh, wait." Barnaby was suddenly hesitant. "Forget I said that. There are no rocks."

"No, I'm not going to forget it." Steve could hear the statue smashing things far back inside the building and knew he still had some time. "An object with sufficient mass wouldn't burn up in the atmosphere. What would happen when it hit the ground?"

"It wouldn't be significantly different from a hydrogen bomb," Barnaby said. "Well, except for the lack of radioactive fallout, of course."

"Why Stanford?"

"Because that's where most programmers and hackers come from, and CYBERCOM has now declared that they're the enemy. Or at least, that's its current theory," Barnaby admitted. "Listen, it's all under control. The latest NRO bird caught HODCARRIER Five in the act and we burned out all his targeting chipsets, so there is no more problem with rocks. Not that there ever was. A problem, that is."

"OK, but we're definitely returning to the subject of HODCARRIERs One through Four when this nonsense is over." Steve sighed. "So, do you have any great ideas about how to stop a statue that has clearly lost its marble?"

Send Money made a raspberry sound.

"If you prefer, he's out of his mind on rock and roll, a real head case, but sure as hell has got a pair of stones. You'll have to excuse me; I'm going through a rocky time in my life," Steve said defiantly. "Enough of this silliness. In addition to saving hundreds of lives, I absolutely must stop that fiend from smashing Pho 73 just behind me, an event I would be forced to take personally since they are the best noodle shop in the entire tri-state region."

As he spoke, he watched the front door of the silver-and-glass building. A few people were running out and scattering up and down the street but not nearly enough to indicate a complete evacuation of those trapped inside.

"Can your eyes in the sky tell why people aren't leaving the building?"

"I don't need them. I've been listening to the intercoms and cell phones in there after you guys took off to go on the attack. They're stuck inside because they were too dumb to leave immediately and Weisshaupt told Lincoln took out the elevators and stairs first," the computer said. "Remember, the Illuminati need the maximum possible number of deaths."

"Speaking of that little Bavarian ratfucker, do you have eyes on him?"

"Since he went virtual today to keep Lincoln on the crooked and nasty and finally got shredded by the Prince, Weishaupt is presently bodiless. I put a request in to General Howard and the sneaky old veteran has managed to follow Weishaupt through three psychic realms already, and I have faith that we'll be able to find him when you have time to deal with him."

Bautista's head snapped around at a loud groaning sound. After listening for a second, he pulled down his helm, changed back into his canine form, and yelled, "Shit. That's the building's main girders beginning to bend. I think the big guy is on his way out."

Steve grabbed his arm. “Hey, it’s no use going after the big guy any longer. Tell the others to start pulling people out any way they can. For Christ’s sake, you’ve all got Power–think of a way to use it. Maybe you’ve got the mojo to make emergency slides or air cushions or something. Just get them out.”

The Prince of Swords nodded and then leaned over and spoke to his three miniature replicas. “OK, Manny, Moe, Jack, listen up. Once we go in, split up and make sure Stacy and Cobb gets the word. Then see if you’re strong enough to carry people. Got it?” The little figures saluted and the chariot streaked straight through a window on the ground floor of the building.

Steve jumped as a car horn blared right behind him. When his heart resumed beating, he turned to see that it was Hans–his armor covered in an inch-thick layer of gray-green ooze. Obviously, a hundred feet of water and a river bottom composed of raw sewage from DC’s archaic sewer system weren’t enough to stop this vehicle. Steve decided that Hans could be from Germany if he wanted–he’d earned it.

The driver side door opened and Ace got out. Steve felt an enormous smile blossom on his face and he took a quick step in her direction. A single glare from the SEAL was enough to stop him cold as he fought to bring his face back to a carefully neutral expression. He said casually, “Hey, Ace. You OK?”

“Yeah.”

“Hey, I’m not asking for your life story, but come on, a few more details,” Steve said. “The last time I saw you, you were on a ballistic trajectory over Mason’s Island. You’re not wet so you didn’t land in the river. What happened?”

“Oh, I trained with the SAS in the tree-jumping techniques they used in the Malaysian campaign. They would go in low without parachutes and depend on tree limbs to slow their fall. I did a midair flip so that I’d hit the branches with my back and, when I'd slowed enough, grabbed a pine tree. Then it was a simple abseil with the coil of paracord on my key chain. I ran into Hans as he was coming up the bank near the parking lot." She made a dismissive gesture. "Has anyone got a real idea? We've done all the damage we can to that guy. I swear, if we ground him to pebbles, they'd throw themselves at the building."

Steve put the cell phone back on his belt and tried to sum up the situation. "The Knight, the Queen, and the Prince of Swords are in there now, but I told them to concentrate on getting people out since we can't seem to stop the son of a bitch. The rest of us are right here."

"OK, we're not going to win this, but I'll be damned if we lose a couple of thousand people and not try everything." Ace thought for a second. "As soon as we see Lincoln through that lobby door, we form up and hit him."

"I was a pretty bad general, but even I can tell that we're simply not going to be enough," Albert Pike said. "Is this to be a Forlorn Hope, then?"

"Possibly." Ace scowled. "Hell, probably. Frankly, I'd prefer to die fighting than have to live with the knowledge that I walked away."

She turned to look at the building and said in a low voice, "No one else has to come."

A moment passed in silence–except for the sounds of smashing inside the building. Suddenly, the lobby door burst open, the statue's broad shoulders broke through the windows on the second floor, and what was left of Daniel Chester French's magnificent creation stumbled out onto the sidewalk. Any resemblance to the former president had disappeared–it looked more like an enormous Ken doll that had been stolen and tortured by a younger brother.

Nevertheless, it was still standing and was apparently quite ready to take down another building. Behind him, the groans of the bending girders were rising in pitch and an increasing number of loud bangs signaled where the abused supports shattered under the strain.

Ace screamed, “You motherless son of a bitch!”

Pike shouted, “Fraternity forever!” in his bell-like basso.

Carlos howled wordlessly, and they all raced across the street.

Steve thought for a moment and then said in an ordinary voice, “Oh, what the hell.”

**He walked after the others.**

“Fool! Fool!” Steve looked to his left and saw Hamilton Jones, the young avatar of the Hanged Man, shouting as he raced towards him. Steve slowed and turned to listen.

“Phone,” Jones was shouting. “Get the phone.”

Steve was irritated. There was no one he wanted to talk to at this point–not even Barnaby. The truth was that he didn’t want to be found texting while dying.

“The phone!” Jones screamed with his hands making a megaphone in front of his mouth. “ATFC.”

Steve furiously wrenched the smartphone out of its belt clip with every intention of hurling it at Jones. At the last minute, he decided to answer it and brought it up to his ear.

Nothing happened.

He brought the cell phone down and looked at the screen. It was black. There was no picture, no indication of an incoming message. No blinking. No vibrations. No silly music.

He half turned to face The Hanged Man, which put the rear of the phone pointing directly at the giant statue. He watched as Hamilton Jones stopped, looked around–first in curiosity and then in increasing terror–then turned and ran off in the direction of Key Bridge.

He realized that the Hanged Man had abandoned the young man in its usual abrupt fashion. “Well, can’t expect any more helpful hints from him tonight,” he thought. “But if the Hanged Man abandoned ship, wouldn’t it be because he’d completed his message?”

He stood in the middle of the street and contemplated Send Money. “Hey,” he yelled. “You awake in there?”

A cartoon of a window shade snapping down behind an old wooden door flickered to life on the screen and then a hand appeared with a “CLOSED” sign, hung it on the door, and slammed it shut. The sign swung back and forth a few times and then the whole scene faded to black.

“Wait a minute,” Steve said aloud. “You’ve got that damn light! The super-special magical searchlight with all the Yuds in it! You remember all those damn Yuds. Let’s crank ’em up and see what they do to tall, pale, and homicidal over there!”

The screen remained black. It vibrated very softly. Tom had a strange feeling that the young Chinese ghost was simply trembling in fear. He held the phone to his ear and thought he could make out the sound of weeping over the chaos all around him.

“What would make the kind of kid who would jump into suicide nets for fun so scared?” He wondered.

He tapped the screen and tried to bring up the flashlight icon, but the image only flickered briefly and went back to black.

Still thinking, he turned to face the melee at the front door. The statue was straining and writhing like Frankenstein's monster in the black-and-white version, batting blindly at his attackers. Ace was in constant motion as she pulled out one deadly weapon after another and sent them whipping into the crater where the beam had hit. Carlos and Albert Pike were each hammering on a separate ankle, but Steve could see that the damage they were inflicting was too little, too late.

He made a decision, stepped forward, and screamed, "Stop. Stop fighting!"

Ace turned to him with surprise and a bit of contempt on her face.

The contempt hurt.

He continued. "There's no freaking use fighting it. Concentrate on getting the people out before the damn thing goes down!"

Ace said something he couldn't hear, but her gesture to the statue made her meaning clear.

"I'll deal with it," Steve shouted. "Get everyone out!" Ace turned to Carlos and General Pike, shouted some quick orders, and they disappeared into the wreckage of the building.

"Yeah, I'll deal with it," Steve said to himself. "Just look for me on the bottom of one of his shoes."

For a couple of minutes, Steve just stood there staring at the white line in the street, developing and discarding ideas one after another.

He realized that even though he hadn't had much time to learn how to use his Power, a great part of what he could have learned, he'd blocked with his relentless cynicism.

It was just so damn hard to believe that he was a magician. Even harder to admit he was the most powerful magician in town.

He shook the tension out of his shoulders and looked up at the eidolon. It was time to put up or shut up. What was it that Jones had said?

"Remember, the light in the darkness isn't a bug, it's a feature."

The old software joke. Well, it made sense, from the beginning of this little adventure, everyone had been telling him that Send Money's LED light was their biggest weapon. The ghost had always shown he had courage–why was he hiding now? What was he so afraid of?

"Wait a second," Steve thought. "That wasn't exactly what the Hanged Man said. I made a joke about his British slang. What did he say?"

"Remember the light in the darkness isn't a bug, it's a bloody feature."

Steve looked at what was left of Lincoln's statue as it headed for the second building. The lights in the windows showed that there were people still working in the upper floors. There would be more deaths.

More blood for the damn Illuminati.

"A bloody feature."

It wasn't British slang.

It was the answer.

Blood magic.

Every time he'd done blood magic before, it was with his own blood. No wonder Send Money was so afraid. Steve was going to drench him in the blood of innocents...make him an unwilling partner in abomination.

He looked at the eidolon again. There wasn't much time left.

He held up the cell phone and whispered, "I'm sorry, little buddy."

He concentrated on the Fool. This time, the card that appeared in his mind was covered in gold leaf and the Fool was dressed in clothing of all colors with a hat that stood up in peaks with bells at the ends–he looked like a cartoon of a classic King's Joker.

He **Studied** the card and saw that the figure had his hands covering his eyes.

He **Understood** that this Fool could only see Darkness. He had cut himself off from the daylight and beauty of the world around him.

He sank deeper into the darkness and felt it smear and tarnish something deep inside. He **Realized** that it was his soul, and although it was only a bit smudged, he could see how quickly it was blackening.

He could feel his emotions hardening, things like music, joy, and beauty seeming to draw away from him in revulsion.

Well, if the cost of defeating a monster was to become a monster, that's what it was. Steve accepted the shadow inside himself and reached out into the smashed building in front of him.

He began to find the dead as soon as his perceptions crossed the threshold–security guards smashed to the floor, a young woman screaming as she was crushed in an slowly-collapsing elevator, two twisted bodies of men with sledgehammers in their hands–custodians who had tried to stop the statue, only to be kicked aside.

Steve **Pulled** at them, **Called** on their blood and–no matter how hard he wanted to reject the fact–**Demanded** their souls. Slowly, agonizingly, the remnants of people–the brave and the terrified, the young and the old–began to move toward him.

He continued to search until he had what seemed to be bright cords connecting him to dozens of bodies; until he simply couldn't bear finding another crushed scrap of a person who'd awoken to the sun this morning with no expectation of how dark it would be by evening.

Steve kept one hand firmly in place over his eyes. He knew somehow that this had to be done in darkness; it was a lonely ritual where he pulled all the pain inside, and held it until he felt his skin would burst with the pressure.

Then he began to braid all the love, the loss, the hopes, the bravery, and the simple joys of a day like any other. The pain, fear, and sorrow he kept to himself, forcing it down until it felt like a thousand knives ripping into the deepest part of him.

A golden string began to emerge from his chest. Yes, damn it, it was coming from his heart. He'd have bet anything that he didn't have a heart, at least not in the sense of an emotional and spiritual center.

Man, that pissed him off.

Steve forced himself to **Believe** in a soul and a heart and the essence of human virtue, putting all his doubts and cynicism aside. Taking the thread, he held it and focused into it all the raw power of innocent blood that he could feel tingling through his body.

It wasn't like the times he'd used his own blood; it was more powerful, more ecstatic, and far more dangerous. The attraction of this terrible power was digging into him like the long years he'd lost in heroin dreams.

He'd have to hit a meeting tomorrow and begin the long fight back to sobriety, but today, he needed every bit of strength, and yes, he was willing to damn himself to get it.

He raised Send Money and pressed him into his chest. He could feel the kid's terrible fear and tried to feed the slow burn of determination that would give the young ghost enough willpower to overcome it. The light was facing out and he rotated his entire body, his mind seeking out the enormous mass of mingled greatness and evil that had to be Lincoln.

The power of the dead souls burned as it left him and he could feel it fill the young Chinese factory worker with agony. Fa Qian began to pray to his ancestors, and Steve could feel as hundreds, thousands of misty souls slowly appeared, each taking up a tiny piece of the terrible burden.

Suddenly, Steve **Knew** that all the power inside him was exhausted and the brave soul caught in the tiny glass and metal machine couldn't take any more.

Steve opened his eyes and screamed, "OK, Fa Qian. Light that motherfucker up!"

It was as if all the flashbulbs and searchlights, and flash bangs in the world went off at once as a searing cone of pure white light bloomed from the tiny phone. Almost thirty yards away, the slowly moving statue instantly went rigid in the act of stepping forward and down off the curb as it headed for the other glass high rise.

For a moment, Steve thought it might start walking again.

Thought that they had failed.

Then he heard booming explosions and the sound of crumbling boulders–it was as if a mine collapse was happening deep inside the eidolon. Cracks appeared with explosive showers of pulverized stone and then the front leg broke at the knee, a fissure circled the other ankle, and while the enormous leg kept moving, the foot stayed behind.

Slowly, ponderously, the statue tilted forward and seemed to hang for a second. Then with an intense *crack*, it broke at the waist and shattered into an enormous mound of dust and stones.

Steve stared at the cell phone. "Nice job. You got any more of that?"

The words were light gray on black, just barely visible.

Hell no.

Did we kill the bastard?

"I think so," Steve said. "I'd say Lincoln has gone all to pieces."

**GOOD.**

**IF YOU DO THAT AGAIN**

**I COMING OUT OF THIS PHONE**

**AND THE LIVING CRAP BEATING OUT OF YOU.**

"Sounds fair."

# CHAPTER THIRTY-EIGHT

"You know, I always thought this was the ugliest building I'd ever seen," Steve said as they all stood in a group about a block away and watched the steel and glass skyscraper finally implode into a gargantuan pile of broken glass, metal, and concrete. Police and rescue teams were working on the crowd.

"Did everyone get out?" he asked.

"No, we lost quite a few on the lower levels as the big guy came through but I have a feeling you already knew that."

Ace shot a sharp glance at Steve, which he carefully ignored. He could still feel the dark and delicious pain roiling through him and knew Ace would never understand what he'd had to do.

It was something only rock-bottom addicts could understand because they knew how to come back when there was no way back. How to survive when every day meant another battle with a gnawing hunger that never faded, never could be cured. He also knew that every time he touched this blackness in the future, there would be an even chance that he'd never make his way back.

For the first time, he thought he understood why something or, Heaven help me, Some One, had chosen him to be the Last American Wizard.

Ace continued. "The number of casualties was acceptably low–almost none on the upper floors, in fact. Yeah, there were the wimps who complained about being chucked out of a window and then tossed from one Sword to another until they reached Carlos and Pike down on the ground, but some people are just never happy about anything. We had a few heart attacks and one guy committed suicide on the top floor. Terrible fear of heights, apparently."

She looked at the wreckage for a moment and then continued. "We almost lost a lot of people in the television station. The idiots wouldn't leave the control room. There was a fat senior producer in suspenders who kept yelling at me and saying that they never evacuated for fire alarms and they weren't going to leave now." She spun a knife in her hand and made it disappear. "I really don't think he believed I was serious until I stuck a knife in his ass and told the others to toss him out the window. He was a bit annoyed, but his technical folks seemed to enjoy it immensely."

Ace pulled the sword from her belt. "I guess it's time to return what I borrowed."

She spoke to the weapon with polite gravity. "You have been of great assistance but I don't require you any longer." She threw it straight up into the air, and as it shot off to the northeast, she yelled, "Tell Joan I said 'thank you.'"

Steve stood next to her as they watched it disappear from sight. "I do have a question," he said. "Well, a lot of questions as usual, but one in particular."

"Uh-huh?"

"If explosives have been rendered useless by magic, how did you rig the one that took off Abe's head?"

"Oh," Ace said with a short laugh. "All of this magic stuff seems to be about how much you believe in what you are. The more you believe you're powerful, the more powerful you become. I spent quite a lot of my spare time telling the C-4 in that shaped charge that it was the very best explosive in the whole world and that I loved it very much." She smiled. "He did good for his mom, don't you think?"

"Funny. I never think of you as a maternal figure," Steve said.

"Hell, every noncom plays mom for the enlisted." She turned and began walking slowly toward Key Bridge and the lights of Georgetown. "Male or female, we take a bunch of young kids and, with a bit of tough love, convince them that they're invincible. After a couple months of that, they can do practically anything."

After a silence, she said, "Hurts when they die."

There was another gap in the conversation, and then Ace said with just a little too much casual indifference, "So, Send Money's little flashlight worked pretty well."

"Yeah," Steve said, keeping his eyes on the crowd under the emergency lights. "Barnaby's best guess is that it sucked all the magic right out of everything it shone on. Did a job on Abe."

"So, you just had to push the button and *blammo,* right?"

Steve didn't answer for a moment and then said, "Basically."

He could tell that Ace was looking intensely at his face, but he continued to be fascinated by the ambulances and cops milling around under the emergency lights.

"You know that I don't believe word one of that bullshit, right?"

"Right."

"Just so we're clear." Ace hitched her climbing pack up to a more comfortable position on her shoulders. "Remember that I'm always around if you find yourself stuck in a moral quandary and require a swift kick in the ass, OK?"

"Of course." He smiled for a second. "What else are friends for?"

"Who said anything about 'friends'?" She spun on her heel and started walking again.

Steve turned, caught up with her, and Carlos–back in human form and wearing a pair of extremely baggy shorts and a Georgetown t-shirt he'd found somewhere–came up on the other side.

"Where are we going now?" Carlos asked.

"I think at the moment, the Lord Telford is just down the alley from Nathan's. Neither place exists, so they have a habit of keeping each other company in the evenings." Ace waved vaguely at the lights across the river. "We'll go back to saving the world tomorrow, but right now, I feel like relaxing with a beer and a couple of games of darts."

"Have you been able to read the business plan I put together?" Carlos began what clearly was a rehearsed sales pitch. "I think we can make this private eye thing work, and after a year or so, we can think about selling franchises across the country–"

"Carlos." Steve and Ace spoke in unison. "Shut the hell up."

Carlos looked as if he was going to burst with plans and ideas but eventually subsided into silence. The three of them continued their slow walk across Key Bridge, admiring the gothic towers of Georgetown University, the bright turmoil of the clubs along M Street, and the quiet flow of the Potomac.

## READING RONIN

Did you enjoy this book?

Well, there are a lot more books to discover--an entire world of exciting new books from Terry Irving and Ronin Robot Press. Sign up to be one of the few, the proud,

**The RONIN READERS!**

Get the latest news first in our bi-weekly Newsletter! Read what Terry's writing right now; give him comments, criticism, and advice (all of which he *really* needs.) Read chapters from all the other new authors and get your hands on new books before they go public.

Sign up at

**www.roninrobotpress.com**

**GOLD FOR SAN JOAQUIN**

BY A.R. ARRINGTON

Framed for his family's murder, their homestead burnt to the ground, and the people who should protect him seeking to shoot him as an outlaw, 16-year-old Jacob Thorn must become a man. They killed his father for his family's gold and now, they will stop at nothing to kill Jacob and cover up the truth. On the run and desperate, Jacob enlists the help of his father's best friend and decides it's time to stop running and start taking the fight to his enemies.

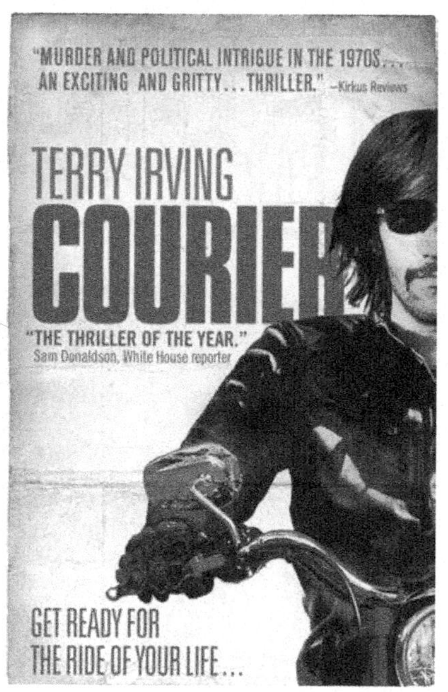


**COURIER**

BY TERRY IRVING

Rick Putnam is running for his life. A Vietnam Veteran riding a motorcycle for a national news network, he's picked up something too hot to handle. So hot that a reporter and a camera crew has already been killed and a rogue CIA kill squad is on his tail. Stick with this charismatic character as he fights his way all the way to 1600 Pennsylvania in his battle for the truth.

"An action-packed tale of murder and political intrigue set in the politically turbulent 1970s.... Irving portrays [courier Rick Putnam] as a classic pulp-fiction hero: a chiseled, chain-smoking ex-soldier who's always ready with snappy quips. ... Irving's story is relentlessly paced, punctuated by bursts of action and violence, and driven by artfully unfolding suspense....**An exciting and gritty...thriller."**

**–Kirkus Reviews.**

"Rick Putnam is a recent Vietnam vet in the early 1970s who works as a courier for a Washington, DC television station while trying to put his life back together after being injured in the war...."Courier" is a tense story set in the days before social media, when news professionals still need to develop film in a dark room and splice footage together. Author Terry Irving clearly knows the inside of the news business in a different time..."

**–Reviewed by Kathleen Heady for *Suspense Magazine***

"To call Terry Irving's book a "page turner" is a gross understatement. As a journalist who covered Vietnam developments in Washington, and the Watergate scandal, this book is entirely believable, scary, and thrilling. Irving is in the top tier of political-mystery writers. And as a (ABC) network producer, he draws on a vast inside knowledge to keep readers glued to every page. If you like politics and a good mystery, you will love this book."

**–Bill Greenwood, former White House Correspondent**

"With all the power and speed of a motorcycle courier trying to beat a deadline, and the cyclist's fine balance of thriller thrust and inside-the-newsroom detail, Terry Irving's new novel, "Courier," will keep you entertained from start to finish."

**–Dave Marash, former Nightline Reporter**

# THE AUTHOR

Terry Irving (seen here in both 1969 and 2010) is a four-time Emmy award-winning writer and producer. He has also won three Peabody Awards, three DuPont Awards, and has been a producer, editor, or writer with ABC, CNN, Fox and MSNBC.

Exhibit A Publishing released his first novel, *Courier*, on May, 1, 2014 and subsequently went out of business on June 7, 2014. Terry denies all responsibility. *Courier* went on to win several awards, sell close to 10,000 copies, and form the nucleus of Ronin Robot Press.

*Gold for San Joaquin* by Cliff Roberts was the first Western released by Ronin Robot Press, followed by *Texas Spitfire*, a Western romance by Chloe Mayer. This book, *Day of the Dragonking: Book One of the Last American Wizard* is set for release on April Fool's Day 2015. *Undefeated Love*, a story of growing up in 1972 by Bruce Bennett, should be ready by March 2015. *Warrior*, the sequel to *Courier*, will be released in June of 2015. Last, but not least, *Taxi Dancer*, the first in a series featuring private eye Angel Pearl and set in 1930's Manila, is due later in 2015.

In addition, Ronin Robot Press is putting together an exciting lineup of the best new writers in Westerns, Romance, and Erotica. Check them out exclusively on Amazon's Kindle.